"Mongo is a character born of our times . . . using the sounds of pain and violence and the elusive music of morality, Chesbro writes songs that few of us want to sing but that all of us need to hear."

—*The Washington Post Book World*

Mongo, the dauntless detective, is caught between being his brother's keeper and getting him killed as an assassin's bullets and a KGB plot make this his most pulse-pounding adventure yet!

THE COLD SMELL OF SACRED STONE

"Good entertainment. Mongo becomes plausible as a gutsy little intellectual with violent tendencies."

—John D. MacDonald

"This new detective hero is one of the more engaging sleuths to come by in a long time . . . circus freak and acrobat, as well as an outstanding lecturer on criminology, [Mongo] houses his giant intellect in the body of a dwarf."

—*Business Week*

"Not-quite science-fiction and suspense make a thrilling combination, and nobody does it better than Chesbro."

—*Playboy*

Books by George C. Chesbro

The Cold Smell of Sacred Stone 1988
Jungle of Steel and Stone 1988
The Golden Child 1986
Two Songs This Archangel Sings 1986
Veil 1986
The Beasts of Valhalla 1985
Turn Loose the Dragon 1982
An Affair of Sorcerers 1979
City of Whispering Stone 1978
Shadow of a Broken Man 1977
King's Gambit 1976

THE COLD SMELL OF SACRED STONE

George C. Chesbro

A DELL BOOK

Published by
Dell Publishing
a division of
Bantam Doubleday Dell Publishing Group, Inc.
666 Fifth Avenue
New York, New York 10103

ISBN: 0-440-20394-5

Reprinted by arrangement with Atheneum

Printed in the United States of America

Published simultaneously in Canada

September 1989

10 9 8 7 6 5 4 3 2 1

KRI

The Cold Smell of Sacred Stone

PROLOGUE

GARTH'S Credo, as it came to be called after it was codified by others, grew out of a body of offhand remarks, many delivered half in jest, that Garth made to reporters and other individuals after the "miracles" in an attempt to explain just what it was he thought he was up to. The Credo was simple, and he stuck to it consistently to the end, despite the fact that all during his long illness he was whacked to the gills on nitrophenylpentadienal. Spy dust.

His deeds and his motivation, Garth patiently explained, had nothing to do with altruism; his behavior was rooted in selfishness, for he had discovered that the only help for his own affliction was to attempt to alleviate the suffering of others, in whatever way he could. He was never quite certain what others meant when they talked about salvation, and he was certainly not seeking it for himself. He simply needed to nurse the fever of the world so that he could be at peace and sleep without the night terrors of his own fever dreams.

Personally, he no longer believed in God, a concept he now viewed as a dark fantasy, an ineradicable cave painting from the prehistoric nether world of racial memory, a kind of ambiguous and menacingly capricious Santa Claus for grownups, a superghost who in one hand carried a bagful of superpresents, like eternal life, for those who somehow managed to obey His remarkably confusing and often contradictory dictates, and a bagful of burning coal, superagony, in the other hand for those who didn't.

Once Garth had believed in God, but thinking back he realized that the God he had believed in had been a kind of ultimate secular humanist, with a gentle and abiding love for all people, patience with their folly, pride in humankind's accomplishments, and sorrow at their suffering. The God my brother had believed in had been a Creator, not an administrator or auditor, and had had no need to be noticed, much less worshiped; He certainly had no need to witness ritual posturing, and to demand it of the creatures of His creation would smack of pettiness and insecurity.

This being the case, the vast multitude of supernatural belief systems that had sprung, and continued to spring, from the fertile soil of the human imagination were at best irrelevant and a waste of time. At worst, they became licensed franchises of stupidity and fear where the product manufactured and delivered was a decidedly intoxicating but poisonous mush of intolerance, bigotry, hatred, stunting of the intellect, dehumanization of others outside the franchise, torture, and murder. Clearly, what these people thought was good for God was not good for people, an irony that must have sorely tested God's considerable sense of humor when He saw the first totem being erected, the first goat or child sacrificed before it. The God Garth had once believed in would not have been pleased.

In what eventually became known as the Dime and a Little Time Parable, Garth had idly wondered out loud what would happen if humankind decided to declare a kind of moratorium on its collective obsession with occult power for a decade or more, say until the year 2000. During this time, each day, every man, woman, and child on the face of the planet would donate ten minutes or the equivalent of ten cents in a personal attempt to better the lot of somebody, anybody, else who might need a hand to hold, or a slice of bread to eat.

Always, Garth prefaced these random thoughts by pointing out that he was no longer a member of any religious franchise and did not presume to speak to or for anyone. He did what he did simply to make himself feel better. Others could interpret his words as they saw fit; he had no preachments to make to anyone, no prescriptions for living for anyone but himself, no tickets to heaven—which he considered a myth anyway.

With that kind of crazy talk, it was probably no wonder that a lot of people would take into their heads the notion that my poisoned brother was the Messiah.

PART I

Imprinting and Rebirth

1.

I was on an errand to help an injured friend who scoffed at my insistence that he was in great danger from a pale-eyed, monstrous *ninja* who could do just about everything but walk on water, and who was working for a dead man. I hoped I wasn't too late.

It was dark by the time I reached the East Village, and the streets were crowded with people of all ages, types, colors, and dress strolling about and enjoying an unusually balmy early spring evening in New York City.

The crowds gradually thinned out, and the streets were deserted by the time I reached the deteriorating, desolate block where Veil Kendry lived. I parked my Volkswagen in front of the otherwise gutted factory building housing his loft, smiled when I looked up and saw the bone-white mercury vapor light spilling out of all the windows; despite the fact that he had his right arm in a sling, Veil was back to work, painting. I wondered what changes, if any, would now show up in his work after months of subtly hunting, and being hunted by, Orville Madison, Veil's ex-C.I.A. controller and United States secretary of state, recently appointed and confirmed, and even more recently deceased when my brother had blown his brains out.

The feud between Veil and Orville Madison had extended over two decades, its poisonous seeds having been planted during the war in Southeast Asia. Madison, who had always hated anyone whose spirit he could not crush, had particularly hated Veil, who—on a good day, in the best of moods— had been unpredictable, supremely contemptuous of authority, and prone to unexpected violence. Destroying Veil became an obsession to Madison, and he had finally struck at the man whose code name was Archangel with a plan marked by stunning deviousness, subtlety, and cruelty. Veil, when he realized just what it was Madison intended to do, had struck back with stunning directness and brutality.

My friend had prevailed, inasmuch as he had thwarted Madison's plans for him and the Hmong people he had fought with for years, but there had been a heavy price to pay. In the course of his duel with Madison, Veil had been forced to betray his countrymen in order to save a Hmong village from destruction. Veil had been stripped of all his honors, and his service records altered to erase most traces of his military career and make it appear that he had been discharged from the army because he was a psychotic. Madison, convinced that Veil would self-destruct in civilian life, had nonetheless added an unusual, and secret, punishment of his own: an indeterminate sentence of death. The day Archangel ever experienced true happiness or peace, Madison told Veil, would be the day Archangel died.

But Veil had not self-destructed. He had found sanctuary from his private, savage demons in art. And Orville Madison had gone on to bigger and better things in government.

Which was the way things would have remained, except that the poisonous boil inside Veil's enemy had come to a head a few months before when a thoroughly mad Orville Madison had decided to celebrate his nomination to the post of secretary of state in President Kevin Shannon's newly elected administration by having a loyal employee put a bullet through Veil's skull. The C.I.A. assassin had missed, setting in motion a bizarre and complex chain of events that had caused the deaths of many innocent people and spawned a manhunt across the breadth, and deep into the soul, of this land called the United States of America. The manhunt had ended three days before, in a vast, dusty hearing room in an unused section of the Old Senate Office Building, when Garth had splattered Orville Madison's brains against a wall that had already been pockmarked by bullets from Veil's submachine gun. In line with a decision that it was in everyone's best interests to keep the people of the country innocent of the fact that their charismatic new president had had the bad judgment to choose as his secretary of state a maniac who was a mass murderer, and thanks to the fact that every elected representative and civil servant who had witnessed the killing had his or her own very good reasons for joining a conspiracy of silence, arrangements had been made successfully to make the death look like the result of an unfortunate hunting accident. Sure enough, the morning papers had carried the news that Orville Madison, vacationing in Maine, had died in a tragic hunting accident when he had tripped over a log and his rifle had discharged, firing a bullet into his head.

Madison had tripped, all right—over his obsessive hatred for a man who'd become a legend as the mysterious and deadly "Archangel" during the war in Southeast Asia.

So Orville Madison had met his match and his end—but it was not the end of the matter, at least not for me. Garth, his own brains apparently fried by doses of a rare and little-understood drug he'd been fed during the course of an investigation he'd been conducting before being abruptly reassigned by the NYPD to help me search for Veil, had fallen into a rigid catatonic state immediately after he'd blown away Madison's head and put a bullet into Veil's right shoulder. Mr. Lippitt, our seemingly ageless friend who was the Director of the Defense Intelligence Agency, was of the opinion that being forced to become involved in my search for Veil had actually saved Garth's life. Even if that was true, it was little comfort to me; fifty minutes before, I had left Garth, slack-jawed and glassy-eyed, staring vacantly at the beige-colored stucco ceiling of his room from his bed in a secret D.I.A. clinic at the Rockland Psychiatric Center, a few miles upstate.

Nor did I think the matter was finished for Veil, despite his contrary opinion. During the course of my search for Archangel, Veil, I had crossed paths with one of the most terrifying men I had ever met—Henry Kitten. Kitten was not terrifying because he was mindless, or because he was big—which he most certainly was—or because he was capable of great savagery; indeed, Veil Kendry, when he chose to be, was probably as merciless as Kitten, if not more so. No; Henry Kitten was terrifying for the same reason I would find Veil terrifying if Veil were my enemy instead of my friend. Like Veil, Henry Kitten was a man who gave the impression—a correct one—that he was a human weapon against which there was virtually no defense, an inexorable killing machine which, if loosed on you, was an occasion for a quick trip to your lawyer's office to update your will, if you had time. Like Veil, Kitten was a master of the martial arts, a man who'd literally dodged my bullets and, with a single blow, left me paralyzed on a snow-covered field in a park in New Jersey while he'd dumped two men who hadn't dodged my bullets into the Hudson River. Veil and Kitten were two awesome warriors.

Although the white *ninja* with the triangular face and pale, khaki-colored eyes could have killed me on that day, he hadn't. Yet Henry Kitten hadn't spared my life out of kindness or mercy, but simply because he found me useful in his own hunt for Veil. I had been left alive to play the dual roles of stalking horse and Judas goat. Unlike Veil, who made his living as an artist and used his martial skills only when necessary, Kitten was a free-lance assassin, reputedly the global underworld's best and highest paid. He'd been hired by Orville Madison, who'd used him in the past, to finish the job Madison's assassin had botched. Veil, who claimed never to have heard of Kitten, had dismissed my suggestion that the sudden death of Kitten's employer would make no difference at all to the assassin. But Kitten was a consummate professional who had made it clear to me that he took great pride in his work, played for an international audience of potential future employers, and always finished an assignment. I half suspected that Veil's attitude of casual disregard of my warnings was intended to protect me by keeping me out of harm's way. Under other circumstances I wouldn't have been concerned, since I'd put my money on Veil in a *mano-a-mano* fight with any man, using any weapons, in any kind of test, from a duel with machine guns to a spitting contest. The problem now was that Veil's right collarbone had been cracked by the bullet my brother, as he plummeted into the mindless void where he was now lost, had fired into him, and it seemed to me that Veil's damaged arm tipped the odds a bit too much in Kitten's favor. Veil Kendry was a friend who'd saved my life and Garth's on more than one occasion in the preceding months. If Henry Kitten was still coming at Veil, and there was no doubt in my mind that he was, I wanted to be at Veil's side when the *ninja* arrived.

Which was why I was now sitting in my car outside a gutted factory building in the East Village trying to think of new arguments I could use to convince Veil that he should at

least let me sit down with him and help him plan offensive
and defensive strategies against a deadly shadow who, as
matters now stood, seemed to control all the options.

Suddenly the lights in the loft, and all along the block,
winked out. The rest of the neighborhood appeared to be
unaffected; I could see lights in the adjoining blocks and in
the skyscrapers in midtown continuing to glow, but I was left
sitting in a car in the middle of a rectangle of unrelieved
night. I quickly ducked down behind the dashboard and drew
my Beretta from its shoulder holster.

Henry Kitten, I felt almost certain, had come to call.

I crawled over the gear shift and hand brake, then pushed
open the door on the passenger's side. I sucked in a deep
breath, rolled out of the car and, keeping low, sprinted across
the sidewalk to the steel door cut into the side of the building. Although I did not know why, I strongly sensed that the
door would be unlocked—just as it had been months before
when I had passed through that portal to investigate a loft
flooded with light but empty, and found a cryptic oil painting
and an envelope containing ten thousand dollars in cash
addressed to me.

I was right. The steel door banged open on its well-oiled
hinges when I hit it with my shoulder, and I sprawled on my
belly on the floor in the small foyer at the foot of the elevator
shaft, gun held out in front of me with both hands.

My somewhat melodramatic entrance was greeted with
nothing but silence. Wherever the assassin with the triangular
face and khaki-colored eyes was, assuming my fears were
well founded, he was not in the foyer. And he was not
outside on the street, watching and waiting; the open door
told me that. This time the door was open not because Veil
had left it unlocked for me, but because Henry Kitten had
shunted the alarm system, picked the lock, and passed through
before me. He was somewhere in the building, perhaps already up in the loft itself, stalking . . .

I did not dwell on the question of how Henry Kitten had managed to short out all the lights in a single block, although I suspected it could be done with detailed maps of the city's sewer system and power grid, and a delayed-time charge placed on one of the main power lines beneath the street. Nor did I dwell on how he had managed to get into the building, and perhaps up into the loft, without encountering an extremely warm greeting from Veil, who would have immediately recognized his stalker from my description. The *ninja* assassin had performed an almost equally remarkable feat a few weeks before when he'd bypassed a state-of-the-art alarm system, gone unnoticed by a cadre of bodyguards, then scaled the wall of a four-story mansion like a 220-pound fly to crush the skull of a Vietnamese, an ex-ARVN colonel, with a single blow of his fist. Henry Kitten was no slouch in the stealth department; however he had done it, I felt deep in my guts that Henry Kitten was here, probably wearing infrared night-vision goggles and armed with—whatever. If I was wrong, if I found Veil upstairs stretched out on his bed and reading by candlelight, I would certainly feel very foolish; I would apologize for disturbing him, and he could remind me that it was precisely this kind of bizarre behavior that led some people to think me eccentric. Then we could have a drink and laugh about it. But I wasn't worried about feeling or looking foolish; I was worried about finding Veil dead, and maybe joining him.

I got to my feet, looked around. The only illumination in the foyer came from a faint band of moonlight spilling in through the open steel door, but it was sufficient for me to see that the freight elevator Veil used to get to and from his loft was not at ground level. I imagined I could manage to reach the fire escape running up the side of the building, but that would only get me outside a locked, wire mesh–covered window on the fourth floor, where I would be silhouetted against the moonlit sky. Not a good idea. Although I could not see it in the darkness, I knew there was a second steel door to my right, and beyond it fire stairs that could also get me up to the fourth floor. I knew where the key to the door was hidden, but the problem was that anyone on that stairway would make a ridiculously easy target for anyone with night-vision goggles waiting above. That didn't seem like such a good idea either.

Out of curiosity, I groped my way along the wall until I came to the door, then pushed on it. It swung open. Kitten must have picked this lock, too, and was either lurking on the stairs or already in the loft.

I waited a few beats, put my Beretta back in its shoulder holster, then pulled the door shut with what I hoped was just enough force to allow the sound of steel clicking against steel to be heard by two *ninjas* listening in the silent darkness four floors above me; it would tell Veil that help—if that was an appropriate word to describe me and my rather untenable position—was on the way, and could serve to distract Kitten. At the least, I hoped it would have the *ninja* assassin looking in the wrong direction if and when I joined the party.

After slipping out of my light jacket and dropping it to the floor, I jumped out into the elevator shaft and grabbed hold of the thick guy cable that ran up the center of the shaft and was attached to the bottom of the elevator. Then I began hauling myself hand over hand up into the pitch blackness.

It had been a long time since my days as a headliner with the circus; I was a lot older than when I'd made a living climbing, swinging, flipping, and soaring, but I made it a point to stay in peak physical condition, and I found the going up the steel cable probably easier than I had any right to expect. By stopping occasionally, wrapping my legs around the cable and allowing my arms to hang free for a few moments, I was only slightly winded, with a mild case of palm burn, when I finally reached up and felt my knuckles graze the rough, splintered surface of the elevator floor.

Trying not to think of the chasm that yawned below me, I groped to both my left and right, found a warped slat to my right, wrapped my fingers around the edge and swung away from the cable. I dangled for a few of the most exquisitely exciting seconds of my life, twisting back and forth, then found a second warped slat farther to my right. A second swing got me to the steel and wood frame of the chute, and within seconds I was up and over the side, in the box of the elevator. I again drew my Beretta, got down on my belly, and crawled forward toward the open end of the box. The fingers of my left hand touched the steel lip at the four-foot-wide entrance to the loft; the gate was up. The elevator was eight feet wide, which left me a two-foot "safety zone" on either side of the opening. I slithered to my right, sat up in a corner to ponder just what it was I planned to do next.

I had been up in the loft enough times for me to be able to picture its layout clearly in my mind. The freight elevator entrance to the loft was about three-quarters of the way down its length. Just inside the entrance, to the right, a plywood partition separated Veil's austere living quarters from the vast work area. The entire wall at the opposite end was comprised of a bank of windows; normally, Veil pulled a heavy drape over the windows at night, but when I had approached the entrance I had glimpsed to my left a large, cross-hatched patch of pale moonlight—which only served to make the rest of the loft seem darker. In the far corner, to the left of the windows, there were thick mats, punching and kicking bags suspended from the ceiling, and a large wooden box filled with martial arts weapons. There were three support columns marching down the center of the loft. The entire floor would be covered with stained tarpaulins, paint pots, palettes, mauled tubes of oil paint, brushes soaking in jars of turpentine— all of the paraphernalia for a different kind of battle, one of the mind, that Veil waged constantly in order to produce the kind of eerie, multipaneled mural that covered most of the wall directly opposite me.

Once inside the loft, I could scramble for cover to one of the support columns, or try to make it around the partition into the living quarters. But either route I chose, there was no guarantee that I wouldn't run right into the deadly embrace of Henry Kitten. Then again, if he was indeed wearing night-vision goggles, he could simply put a bullet in my head the moment I showed myself. On reflection, it seemed a good idea to stay right where I was.

"Yo," I called softly into the darkness. "Anybody home?"

There was no answer, which didn't surprise me. Both men would be crouched inside somewhere in the darkness, poised, waiting for the other to make some kind of mistake and show himself, or betray his position. The difference was that Kitten had use of both his arms, and could undoubtedly see.

"Yo, Kitten," I continued in a conversational tone as, taking care to keep pressed against the side of the elevator with my gun at the ready, I sidled closer to the entrance. "This is the cavalry speaking. You could have killed me up in Fort Lee, but you didn't; I figure I owe you one. I won't kill you unless you force me to. I say it's better to light one little candle than to die in the darkness. Drop whatever it is you're carrying, then walk on over and stand in front of the windows with your hands in the air. Then the three of us can chat about what we're going to do with you. If we wait around here long enough, the lights are eventually going to come back on, anyway. Then you're finished; if Veil doesn't nail you, I will."

I paused, listening intently, but there was still no answer or sound of movement from inside the cavernous loft. Despite my conviction that sudden death crouched somewhere beyond the entrance, I had to admit the possibility that I'd rolled and bounced into Veil's building, hauled myself up four floors on a steel cable, to end up sitting in a freight elevator and talking to myself.

I had no way of knowing how long it would be before Consolidated Edison recognized the problem and restored power to the block, especially if Kitten had blown up an entire circuit. In the meantime, at that very moment Kitten could be on the move in the darkness—heading toward me. He would not want to fire a gun, because the muzzle flash, if not the deafening blast, would give away his position to Veil, who could see pretty well in the dark even without night-vision goggles. But Henry Kitten had a few dozen other ways to kill, and the thought of him skulking in my direction and suddenly popping up beside me in the elevator sent a chill through me and caused the small hairs on the back of my neck to sit up and take notice. Sitting in the darkness and talking to myself was decidedly too passive a strategy to use against the *ninja* assassin, and so I decided it was time to up the ante in our silent poker game.

I transferred my gun to my left hand, arched my back, and stretched my right arm around into the entrance. I groped around on the floor until I felt the paint-stiffened edge of a tarpaulin. I wrapped my fingers around the canvas, began pulling the tarp into the elevator. I heard something tip over, and then there was the sharp, eye-watering smell of turpentine. Perfect.

"We're going to play a little game of chicken, Kitten," I said as I continued to haul the tarpaulin into the elevator. Finally my fingers touched what I had been hoping to find—a turpentine-soaked paint rag. "I presume to speak for my friend when I say I believe he'd rather lose his loft than his life. If you're not silhouetted in front of those windows in ten seconds, I'm going to set this place on fire. With all the wood, canvas, turpentine, and oil paint in there, it'll go up fast. But you're the only one who's not going to get out of here. The first glimpse I get of you, I'm going to put a bullet thr—"

I ducked away just as something whistled through the air, sliced through the front of my shirt, and planted itself in the

wood siding of the elevator with a solid *thunk*. *Shuriken*. So
much for the pleasant fantasy that I might be talking only to
myself. Wherever Kitten was, he now had an angle on me. I
crabbed sideways back into the corner of the elevator, grop-
ing in my pocket for the book of matches I always carried,
since a cold day in Wisconsin years before when Garth's life
and mine had depended on a single match I'd found in a
grimy book at the back of the glove department of a car.
Lying on my side in an attempt to make myself as small as
possible, hoping I wasn't going to catch the next star-shaped
blade in the throat, I put a match to the corner of the paint
rag. Instantly, it burst into flames. I sucked in a deep breath,
got to my feet, and dove for the opposite side of the elevator,
hurling the flaming paint rag into the interior of the loft as I
sailed past the opening. I landed on my shoulder and rolled
over on my belly, crawled back to the entrance and cau-
tiously peered around the corner.

The rag was burning brightly a few feet away from a
support column, and from its epicenter tongues of flickering,
blue-white flame were licking along in all directions on the
surface of the tarpaulin, sending up plumes of black, foul-
smelling smoke and stabbing fingers of light into the surrounding darkness. I estimated that in less than two minutes
the interior of the loft would be a raging holocaust.

Chicken, indeed.

Assuming that the flickering light from the flames would
be playing havoc with Kitten's night-vision goggles, I heaved
the upper half of my body into the loft and used both hands to
sweep my Beretta back and forth in front of me, ready to fire
a fusillade of bullets into anything that moved that didn't
have shoulder-length, gray-streaked yellow hair.

"All right, Frederickson!" It was the familiar, rich baritone
of Henry Kitten, somewhere off to my left. I immediately
swung my gun in that direction. He coughed, and then there
was a thud as something heavy hit the floor. "That was my
gun! Now I'm going over by the window!"

"No! Step out into the firelight where I can see you! I want to see your hands flat on top of your head, fingers laced together!"

A few moments later the looming figure of Henry Kitten, thick smoke swirling around his waist, appeared at the edge of the spreading circle of light from the flames. A pair of bulky night-vision goggles hung from a strap around his neck, and his hands were dutifully clasped on top of his head. Coughing, squinting against the acrid smoke, he slowly turned toward me.

"May I suggest you put out the fire, Frederickson?" the big man with the pale eyes said laconically. "It's getting a little close in here."

"I've got it, Mongo," Veil said easily as he suddenly appeared behind and to the right of Kitten, walking quickly through the firelight and smoke.

Whatever had happened before I'd arrived on the scene, Veil had obviously managed to get to his equipment box; *nunchaku* were draped around his neck, and he had two throwing knives stuck in the waistband of his jeans. His clothes, his face, and his hair were speckled with paint, which meant he'd done some rolling around on the floor, probably an instant or two after the lights had gone out. He disappeared behind the partition, emerged a few seconds later with a fire extinguisher braced under his right arm in its paint-stained sling. He pushed a lever on the extinguisher, aimed the nozzle with his free hand, and began pumping foam over the spreading flames. In less than a minute the flames were out, the swirling smoke caught in drafts and mercifully being sucked out of the loft through three open panels in the bank of windows. Throughout, I remained flat on my belly, gun aimed at the center of Kitten's barrel chest.

"Now back up to the window," I said as I got to my feet. "Take slow, easy steps. If I see anything but your feet moving, I'll put a bullet in your heart."

"Like I said up in Fort Lee, you can be a real pain in the

ass, Frederickson.'' There was just the slightest trace of a
smile on Henry Kitten's face as he slowly backed toward the
ceiling-high bank of windows. ''How the hell could you
know I'd be here tonight?''

''I didn't; I just knew you'd show up eventually, despite
what happened to your employer. You made that clear to me,
remember?''

''Obviously I talked too much.''

''I was coming down to talk to Veil about you. We seem
to have arrived at about the same time.''

''You showed up at a most inopportune time.''

''I couldn't disagree more,'' Veil said dryly from somewhere behind me and off to my left. There was a faint *click*,
and the beam of a powerful flashlight cut through the smoky
air and moonlight, spotlighting the assassin's broad torso and
head. Eddies of smoke still whirled around Kitten as he stood
in front of the window, feet braced slightly apart. I might
have been in hell, talking to the devil himself, and when I
had to cough I made certain my right hand remained steady
and I didn't blink. Kitten's moves, like Veil's, could be
measured in milliseconds.

Veil propped the flashlight on a stiff fold of tarpaulin, then
came over to stand beside me. ''Thanks, Mongo,'' Veil
continued as he studied the man caught in the beam of the
flashlight. ''I was in a bit of a spot there.''

''You're welcome.''

''Obviously, this is the guy you kept trying to warn me
about.''

''That's him,'' I replied tersely, backing away slowly
while I kept my eyes on Kitten's face, which seemed remarkably impassive in the bright light. When I bumped up against
a wall, I slid down it until I was sitting on the floor. I
brought my knees up and rested my forearms on them so as
to be able to keep a steady aim on Kitten's chest while
making myself as small a target as possible. Even with my
gun trained on him while he stood with his hands clasped on

his head, I didn't intend to lose my concentration for a second.

Veil moved a few steps to his left, then leaned casually against a support column as he continued to study Henry Kitten. "Why did you come up here?" he asked easily as he hooked his left thumb into a pocket of his jeans. "You certainly don't look stupid, and Mongo tells me you're actually quite clever. It must have occurred to you that there were easier ways to try to kill me. Why didn't you just blow up the place, or pick me off out in the street?"

Henry Kitten's response was a shrug of his broad shoulders —a slight movement that almost cost him his life, since I was ready to pull the trigger at the least provocation. I'd seen the *ninja* assassin in action, and wasn't taking any chances; in my opinion, Veil still wasn't treating the other man with sufficient respect and seriousness.

"I'm afraid I underestimated you, Kendry, not to mention the prescience of your friend over there. I thought this *was* the easy way."

"Are all the lights in the neighborhood out?" Veil asked as he glanced over in my direction.

"Just this block."

Veil grunted. "A time-delayed charge, in just the right spot. Interesting. In addition to his other talents, Mr. Kitten here appears to be a master electrician."

"Yeah. How'd he get in?"

"Up the fire stairs. He managed to pick the locks on both doors downstairs without my being aware of it, but I'd already seen the needle on the security system monitor fall, indicating that the entire system, including the battery-powered emergency backup, was out. I was just getting ready to check out my batteries when the lights went out. It seemed a bit too much of a coincidence for my alarm system to go out at the same time as the power failed, and I hit the floor about a second before Jumbo here came crashing through the upstairs door. I managed to get over to the equipment box and take out some weapons without getting shot, and I just stayed there. He couldn't move over these stiff tarpaulins without my hearing him, and he obviously didn't want to test my skills with a throwing knife. It was a standoff until you showed up.''

Henry Kitten, who had been following our conversation with mild interest, now smiled, his lips parting to reveal even, white teeth. ''I saw in the morning papers that the man who hired me is dead. Somehow, I strongly doubt that he shot himself in a hunting accident; Orville Madison never took vacations, and people were the only prey he was ever interested in hunting. Somehow, you managed to find out who he was and get to him, didn't you, Frederickson? The profile I gave you in the park led you to him. That was a nice piece of work. You did a hell of a lot better job of flushing out Madison than I did with Kendry here.''

''Which just goes to show that you have to pay attention to quality in choosing your clients,'' I said.

''I'll remember that in the future.''

''You don't have a future,'' I replied curtly. I was in no mood for—and had no intention of being lulled into—light chitchat with Henry Kitten.

''So, Mongo,'' Veil said easily, ''what are we going to do with our visitor?''

It seemed an excellent question, one for which I didn't have a ready answer. Perfunctorily gunning down in cold blood a man who had spared my life—albeit for his own good reasons—didn't really appeal to me, and turning him over to the police would pose any number of serious dilemmas, any one of which could tear apart a carefully constructed and necessary tissue of lies. An enormous amount of political power had very recently been brought to bear to conceal the fact that the dead secretary of state had been a murderous psychopath responsible for the brutal murders of a lot of innocent people, and that it had been my brother who'd killed him. The way things had worked out seemed best for all. But with the world's most wanted assassin sitting in jail awaiting trial, the whole thing could start to unravel virtually overnight. Captured, with what I presumed were death sentences hanging over him in two dozen different countries, Henry Kitten would have no reason whatsoever to keep quiet about his own long association with Orville Madison, and the events of the past few months. People would start asking questions, and reporters would begin comparing notes. Neither Garth, Veil, Mr. Lippitt, President Kevin Shannon, nor I needed the attention Henry Kitten's tales would bring us.

"Do I detect a note of indecision?" Henry Kitten asked in a mild tone. "Why not just turn me over to the police? They can book me for breaking and entering."

I said, "They'll book you for a whole hell of a lot more than that, Kitten."

"Will they? Somehow, I get the impression that you're keeping things from me. Exactly what did you and your brother discuss with President Shannon, Frederickson?"

"You know about that?" Kitten only had it half right; I was the only one who'd actually talked to Shannon. But Kitten's intelligence was still impressive.

"I guessed. I tracked the two of you to Washington, and I saw you heading into the park toward the Viet Nam War Memorial. Considering the large numbers of police and Secret Service agents hanging about, I figured it had to be the president you were going to see. At that point, I decided that it was a waste of time to keep tracking the two of you in an attempt to find Kendry, because Madison was finished—*how* finished he was I didn't fully appreciate until I saw the papers this morning. Anyway, with Madison destroyed, I naturally assumed that it wouldn't be long before Mr. Kendry would come out of hiding and be . . . available to me."

"You should have gone home yourself, Kitten."

"That's not my real name, you know."

"You say."

"I'm impressed that you came up with a name at all, but that's not the right one."

"Who cares? They can bury you under 'John Doe.' ''

"Oh?"

"What is your real name?"

"Did the president personally issue the order for Madison to be killed, Frederickson? Is that why you can't quite decide what to do with me?"

"Veil?" I said. "What do you think?"

"Kitten," Veil said to the huge figure standing before the window, "I know you spared Mongo's life. Would you consider getting out of here and forgetting about killing me?"

"You'd accept my word?"

"I would. I believe you act on your own strong code of honor, which is the real reason you chose to attack me the way you did. Even if you're forced to take a sizable cut in future earnings, it's still better to lose some of your reputation and fees than all of your life. Remember that I don't owe you anything, and I might just break your neck now and be done with it if I think you're going to be a headache in the future."

"Do you really think you could do that, Kendry?" Henry Kitten asked in a low, even voice. "Do you think you could do it even with the use of both your arms?"

"With the friend that you mentioned and his gun over there, Kitten, I'm not obliged to give you lessons. As I said, I take you to be a man of honor and great pride. Will you promise that I won't see or hear of you again if Mongo and I let you walk out of here?"

"It's certainly a tempting offer," Henry Kitten said, and shrugged his shoulders again.

That was one *ninja* shrug too many, and I pulled the trigger on the Beretta. As the gun roared, his left arm—which had shot out from the top of his head with the speed of a striking snake—jerked back. He spun around and grabbed for his left shoulder at the same time as what felt like a white hot branding iron sliced across my forehead, just above my eyes. I pulled the trigger three times in rapid succession, firing blindly now as a thick, warm curtain of blood flowed into my eyes. I heard glass shatter.

Stunned, I fell over on my side and frantically swiped at my blood-filled eyes with my free hand as I heard the *thud-thud-thud* of bodies colliding and blows landing. I felt nauseated and light-headed, and knew that I was close to fainting.

My left hand found a paint rag. I used it to wipe away the blood from my eyes, then pressed it tightly against the *shuriken*-split flesh of my forehead. I struggled to my feet, swaying, then leaned back against the wall and squinted at the blurred tableau in a pool of moonlight almost perfectly bisected by the powerful beam of the flashlight.

What I saw was two *ninjas* doing battle, dancing on the balls of their feet as they spun and charged, firing side and high kicks at one another's body. I noted with some satisfaction that I'd managed to even the odds a little, since Henry Kitten's left arm flopped uselessly at his side, and blood seeped from the bullet hole I'd put in his shoulder. Like Veil, the assassin was now forced to rely primarily on kicks, while taking care to protect his injury.

Incredibly, at least to me, Veil had chosen to toss aside his deadly *nunchaku* sticks, along with the two knives he'd had in his waistband; it seemed he intended to give Henry Kitten a few lessons after all.

Veil was nothing if not creative in his practice of the martial arts. He had mastered the *kata* of a dozen different systems, but used no system exclusively; indeed, he had devised what he laughingly called a no-system, which was all his own and which he considered superior to any of the many systems that were traditionally taught. Strict and sterile adherence to any one school's *kata* could be a deadly trap, he had warned me on more than one occasion, inasmuch as it could telegraph your next moves to a knowledgeable opponent and provide him with a killing *suki*, or opportunity.

Consequently, much of my training with Veil had consisted of my trying to unlearn the formal system of karate *kata* I had dutifully mastered in order to earn my black belt. Therefore, it was with some surprise that I watched Veil initially set up and move in a *taijutsu* mode, *kata* emphasizing distorted body angles, as if to protect his injured arm. Even Kitten, his triangular face briefly illuminated by a shaft of moonlight, seemed startled by what he must have assumed was his good fortune; and then the white *ninja* proceeded to execute a series of *koppojutsu* moves designed to penetrate Veil's defensive maneuvers, to smash bone. His mistake. At the last moment, a microsecond, Veil spun out and away from a side kick, wheeled back in, and delivered an elbow strike to Kitten's jaw that shattered teeth as it whipped the assassin's head back.

First round, first blood, to Veil. Not too trashy, I thought. In the future, which was looking brighter all the time, I vowed to pay even closer attention to the things my teacher had to say.

But Kitten had his own ideas about the future. Seemingly oblivious to shock and what had to be considerable pain, he leaped high in the air, twisted, fired a high kick that would have broken Veil's neck if it had landed. Veil leaned back, letting the foot fly past his head, then drove his left fist into the inside of Kitten's heavily muscled thigh, just above the knee. Kitten grunted with pain and surprise. He landed on his other leg—awkwardly—and just managed to duck under one of Veil's kicks that would have crushed his temple.

I raised my gun with a badly trembling hand, trying to track Kitten, but did not pull the trigger. Both men were constantly spinning and circling, darting in and out of the smoky light, and I would have had a hard time telling which was which even if my vision hadn't been constantly slipping in and out of focus. Also, blood had soaked through the rag I held over my forehead and was once again seeping into my eyes. I wiped away blood with the back of my gun hand, then sidled along the wall, angling closer to the two figures, looking for one clean shot.

Limping slightly, Henry Kitten stepped back and began slowly to circle Veil, who had stopped moving and was now standing calmly in the center of the patch of moonlight, the flashlight beam highlighting his head and shoulders. Suddenly Kitten attacked with what was to me blinding speed, faking a side kick with his left leg, then spinning counterclockwise and launching a flying high kick at Veil's damaged right arm. Veil spun the other way, inside the kick, and drove the point of his left elbow deep into Kitten's momentarily unprotected groin. Kitten cried out and doubled over while he was still in the air. He landed on his side, immediately sensed the danger and managed to scramble to his feet, although he was still clutching at his groin, inhaling and exhaling with great whooping sounds. He tried to back away, but he wasn't fast enough. Veil's fist shot out and landed squarely on the other man's bullet-damaged shoulder. Kitten screamed, took one hand from his groin to clutch at his shoulder. For a moment I thought he would go down, but he managed to keep his balance while he spun around and began to stagger toward one side of the loft. Veil facilitated Henry Kitten's attempt at walking by stepping up behind the man and grabbing his belt, lifting him up on his toes. In what seemed to me an astonishingly brief time, Veil had achieved *zanshin*—total physical and mental domination of his opponent. He steered the other man around and marched him toward the end of the loft. When they were a few feet from the bank of windows, Veil flexed his knees, and with a mighty pull and shove hurled Kitten through the air. The *ninja* assassin disappeared into the night in an explosion of glass. Henry Kitten didn't scream; amid the tinkling of glass came the sound of his body landing in the mounds of jagged junk and mushy, rotting garbage in the narrow alleyway four stories below. When Veil turned away from

the window and came toward me, he didn't even seem to be
breathing hard.

"Not bad for a painter," I managed to say before the gun
slipped from my fingers and I slumped unconscious to the floor.

2.

I awoke to find myself lying on Veil's bed, with Veil
bending over me applying the finishing touches to taping a
thick bandage in place on my forehead. The smell of turpentine was strong in my nostrils, and I suspected it was coming
off me. The lights were back on, and I could hear the
thrumming of the two giant exhaust fans in the work area as
they carried away the last traces of the acrid smoke from the
fire I had started. A teakettle was whistling in the kitchen
behind the thin partition beside the bed. I started to sit up,
but Veil put his hand on my chest and gently but firmly
pushed me back down on the bed.

"Easy, Mongo. You've lost a lot of blood. Start moving
around too quickly, and you'll pass out again."

"How long have I been out?"

"A little more than an hour; you had a nice nap, but
considering the shock to your system and the blood you've
lost, it probably wasn't long enough. The lights came back
on about ten minutes after you fainted. I cleaned you up a
little, and managed to stitch the wound."

"Jesus. With one hand, no less."

Veil shrugged, then wiggled the fingers of his right hand.
"The arm may be in a cast, but I can still use the hand.
Suturing is a little skill I picked up out of necessity during the
war, when I had to tend to my own knitting, so to speak. I

think I managed to clean out the wound pretty good with peroxide, and the sutures will keep it closed until we can get you to a plastic surgeon to have it done properly.''

"I'm sure the sewing job you did is as good as I'm going to get anywhere.''

"Wrong. You could end up with a nasty scar, and I can't be sure there won't be an infection. I poured a bottle of peroxide in there, but the rag you used to stanch the bleeding was covered with green paint; you looked like a Christmas decoration. As soon as I get some herbal tea down you, I'm going to drive you to a hospital emergency room.''

"The wound bled a lot, right?''

"Indeed.''

"And the stitches you put in will hold until it heals?''

"As long as you don't do a lot of walking on your hands or opening doors with your head, they should.''

"Good. I'll pass on the trip to a hospital. I'm too old to worry about my looks, and a scar on my face is probably just what I need to put a good scare into my enemies.''

"Mongo—''

"I don't want to have to answer a lot of questions, Veil,'' I said seriously, "and that's what will happen if I go to a hospital emergency room. I can't very well claim I cut myself shaving. I can always claim I was slashed by a mugger, but then somebody's going to want to get the police involved. Considering our somewhat complicated situation, I don't think that's a good idea.''

"You could have a point.'' Veil paused, grinned. "All those cute little co-eds who already think you're so sexy will really go crazy with lust if you show up in class with a huge scar on your forehead. Then again, you may be asked to head up the school's German dueling society.''

"I'm not teaching any longer,'' I said, trying and failing to keep the bitterness I felt out of my voice.

Veil raised his eyebrows slightly. "No?''

"You don't know about it, but the university lined up with

everyone else who tried to squash Garth and me while we were looking for you. Madison's people got to both the police and the school. The NYPD suspended Garth, without pay, for supposedly aiding and abetting a criminal—me; Christ, they assigned him to tag along with me and then busted his ass for doing precisely that. The university took all my classes away from me and started making noises about taking away my tenure on the grounds of moral turpitude. Then they offered me a raise and the chairmanship of the department after it was all over. I told them to shove it, and I submitted my letter of resignation yesterday. I wanted nothing more to do with those people."

Veil studied me for a few moments, then slowly nodded his head, perhaps sensing that my aborted teaching career wasn't something I felt like talking about. "I'm going to make you some of my super-duper herbal tea," he said at last. "It will perk you right up."

"I'd rather have Scotch."

"Somehow, that doesn't surprise me at all," Veil said, walking away toward the entrance to the kitchen. "First, the tea."

"I feel like a Goddamn old lady," I called out, slowly sitting up on the edge of the bed, then bracing myself with my hands and closing my eyes when the room started to tilt.

"Why?" Veil called from the other side of the partition.

"I don't usually pass out so easily."

"Hey, my friend, when somebody bounces a *shuriken* off your forehead and you lose as much blood as you did, the only reasonable thing to do is pass out. Ask anybody. You're lucky you have a thick skull. Incidentally, I'm sorry I wasn't able to stop him from doing that. I should have kept a closer eye on him."

"You're sorry *you* weren't able to stop him?! I was the one with the gun, remember? By the way, that was some number you did on him. But why the hell didn't you just bop

him on the head with your *nunchaku,* or stick a knife between his ribs?''

''You'd already put a bullet in his shoulder,'' Veil replied
dryly. ''It didn't seem quite sporting for me to use weapons.''

''Sporting?!''

Veil came back into the bedroom carrying a huge ceramic
mug filled to the brim with a steaming, perfectly foul-smelling
liquid. ''Well, you'd been telling me what a bad-ass this guy
was, and he obviously thought he was a bad-ass, along with
his various employers. I was curious as to how he'd fight; I
thought I might learn something.''

At first I thought he had to be joking, but when I looked
into his face I could see that he was serious. I shook my head
in amazement. ''Jesus Christ. I knew you were damn good,
and I never doubted that you could beat Kitten, but I never
imagined that anyone could have done it so *easily.* I think I'll
start calling you sir.''

''Drink this,'' Veil said, handing me the mug. ''Watch it;
it's hot.''

I sipped at the disgusting brown liquid, almost gagged.
''What the hell *is* this stuff?!''

''I told you; super-duper herbal tea. Mother Kendry's magic
healing potion.''

''It tastes like you washed your socks and jock in it after
our last workout.''

''Drink it; *all* of it. It will make you feel better.''

He was right about that. With Veil occasionally prodding
me by raising my elbow, I drained off the mug. The throb-
bing in my forehead eased dramatically, the room no longer
threatened to turn upside down on me, and I felt decidedly
stronger, less groggy.

''So,'' I said as I set the empty mug down on the bed's
side table, ''now we have to figure out what to do with our
departed assassin.''

Veil nodded as he sat down next to me on the bed and

absently adjusted his sling, which he had changed. "If we call the police, they're going to be all over the two of us; Kitten just doesn't look like your average burglar, especially in this neighborhood."

"You got that right. If they identify him—or if they *can't* identify him, which seems more likely—the cops are going to be leaning very heavily on us for explanations, which we can't give. Shannon's done his part, and we're all home free at the moment; but it's all over if anyone manages to make a link between that dead assassin and Orville Madison. If the cops check with Interpol, they'll find out that Garth filed a request for information on a guy that turned out to be Henry Kitten. A lot of worms will come crawling out of a lot of cans."

"Worms," Veil said, and smiled thinly. "You feel up to helping me with a little spring planting? I'll reward you with a Scotch from your special reserve I keep under the kitchen counter."

We gained access to the alley, which was blocked off from the street at both ends by rusting chain-link fences, through a triple-bolted steel door in the basement of the gutted building. Clambering through a treacherous jungle of rubber tires, twisted shards of rusting metal, various unrecognizable objects, garbage, and a host of scurrying, dog-sized rats, we finally made our way to the mound of junk on which the broken body of Henry Kitten lay askew, leaking blood from all its orifices. Along the way I'd picked up half of a broken steel pole, with one jagged, splayed end. Veil kicked aside some soggy cardboard, and I began digging with my makeshift shovel in the soft, rotting earth which had been exposed.

"Easy does it, Mongo," Veil said as he leaned back against a tangled pile of lumber and steel. If he was the least bit concerned about having a corpse buried beneath the windows of a loft where he lived and worked, he certainly didn't show it. He'd assured me that it would be at least a hundred years before anyone found the remains of Henry Kitten,

and—considering the neighborhood—nobody in the next century would give them a second thought. Our conversation-
spiced spring planting expedition might have seemed a tad
macabre to me if I hadn't been so happy to be rid of Henry
Kitten. "You don't want to start that wound bleeding."

"Listen, pal, with that tea you gave me I feel like I could
staff an entire gravediggers' union by myself. What the hell
is in that stuff? Cocaine?"

"Just herbs. It's a recipe I picked up in Laos, from the
Hmong. Very good for whatever ails you. I'll give you the
recipe, if you'd like."

"No, thanks. I'm not sure I could handle it."

Veil selected a jagged wood stick from the pile he was
leaning against, gripped it tightly in his left hand and began
helping me dig. "How's Garth?" he asked quietly.

I paused in my digging, leaned on my pole, sighed, and
shook my head. "No change from the way you saw him
three days ago at Langley. He's just . . . gone away. His
eyes are open, but there's no life in them; they look like dull
marbles. He blinks, breathes, pisses down a tube into a bag,
shits through another tube into another bag, gets fed through
tubes in his nose, and doesn't object to being massaged and
rolled into another position four times in every twenty-four
hours."

"EEG?"

"Damn near normal, which is what's so frustrating. Maybe
I could accept the fact that my brother's become a zombie if
there were some sign of brain damage, but there isn't. All of
his organs seem to be functioning quite normally, considering
the fact that he's totally sedentary, but there's nothing *going
on* with him. He reminds me of the way I found your loft that
night; all the lights are on, but there's nobody home."

"Are you satisfied with his care?"

"Lippitt says it's the best, and I have no reason not to
believe him. You know, the clinic is at Rockland Psychiatric
Center, but it's a secret Defense Intelligence Agency facility,

staffed by their people and under their control. I don't know
enough about what's required in Garth's case to be in a
position to evaluate the care, but all of the equipment looks
like state-of-the-art, there are plenty of nurses who really
seem to care running about most of the time, the food is
good, and the rooms comfortable. There's a shrink for every
three patients. The place is run by a shrink named Charles
Slycke, who doesn't seem to care for me very much."

"What's his problem?"

"Beats me. I only met him this afternoon, before I headed
down here, but I sensed a lot of hostility. Actually, I don't
give a shit what he thinks of me just as long as he sees that
Garth gets the best care."

"I'm sorry, Mongo."

"Yeah; me too. It's a bitch."

"Maybe if I'd handled things a little differently at the end,
if I hadn't put that gun down where he could reach it, he
wouldn't have snapped the way he did."

"Hell, you were surrendering to him," I said, feeling
bitterness well up in me. "How could you have known what
was going on in his head? If anyone should have picked up
on what was about to happen, it was me."

"Come on, Mongo. It's not your fault."

"You say."

"Lippitt says. If you can't trust the head of the Defense
Intelligence Agency, who can you trust? He says Garth would
have died if he hadn't been taken off the case he was
working on and assigned to tag along with you."

"He may have been trying to make me feel better."

"No. Lippitt wouldn't do that, Mongo. That old man loves
the two of you like sons; he loves you enough, and knows
you well enough, not to lie to you."

"There's more to it, Veil," I said distantly as I suddenly
heard ghosts from the past whispering, laughing, in my ear.
"Something . . . very bad happened to Garth and me a few
years ago."

"During the time when you disappeared for more than a year?"

I swallowed hard, nodded. "It was a bad thing, Veil; body breaking, mind bending."

"So I gathered from some snippets of conversation between you and Lippitt I picked up," Veil said carefully. "I take it Lippitt was involved."

"I can't talk about it."

"Okay," Veil said easily.

And then, naturally, I began to talk about it. It was time. "It was an act of utter madness called Project Valhalla," I murmured.

Under the vacant, unseeing eyes of a dead *ninja*, I proceeded to tell Veil about Siegmund Loge, a Nobel-winning scientist, and his plan to save the human race, essentially by destroying it and turning our species into . . . something else. This quintessentially mad genius had constructed a mathematical model, the Triage Parabola, which had convinced him that humankind's self-destruction, within a time parameter of twenty to three hundred years, was inevitable. We were doomed, because of a propensity to murderous tribalism and religious nonsense that Loge believed was embedded in our genes, to join the thousands of other species that had become extinct over the aeons since life had emerged on earth. Humankind was just one more evolutionary dead end.

Loge's solution, his plan to hoodwink Mother Nature, was to loose an epidemic that would affect every man, woman, and child on the face of the earth, playing havoc with the genetic code in human DNA and causing every member of our species to rapidly devolve to something resembling the primitive creatures our prehistoric forebears had been, in the hope—Loge's word—that we could, over a few hundred thousand years, once again evolve into humans, but without the crippling psychological, intellectual, and moral cracks in the human psyche he considered fatal. There would certainly be no more large-scale wars, holy or unholy, since all the guns, tanks, and planes strewn over the planet would be nothing more than objects of curiosity to the creatures we would become, and it would be all we could do to learn once again, through the glacial crawl of millennia, how to manipulate sticks and stones.

The Valhalla Project.

He was a clever one, that Siegmund Loge, with a most curious fantasy. The problem was that he had the intellectual and technological capacity to make the nightmare a reality—if only he could find a way to iron out a few minor kinks that had developed along the way in his chemical formulations.

Alas, the Frederickson brothers, with their decidedly mixed bag of genes, would turn out to be just what the doctor ordered, as it were.

To lay the groundwork for this ultimate experiment in social engineering, Loge had masterfully exploited precisely those pockets of infection in the human spirit he deemed to be the genetically based time bombs that would eventually kill us all if not scraped out. Incredibly, there were individuals and groups all over the world who were helping him, in the remarkably naive—but predictable—belief that whatever it was he was up to would serve to make *their* particular group or religious faith supreme on earth. Loge had been not only a scientific genius, but a genius at collecting the unquestioning loyalty and aid of true believers all over the world. And it made no difference at all that each group of true believers believed something different about him. Indeed, the seemingly infinite capacity for individuals and groups to be religiously and politically manipulated was a point Loge went to great pains—both literally and figuratively, for both him and us—to make to Garth and me. Loge controlled the fanatical loyalty of dozens of religious communes circling the planet. Each commune was insulated from the others, and each had a radically different theology. The one belief they shared in common was that Siegmund Loge, whom they called Father, was the Messiah, or God incarnate.

What they didn't know was that they were to form the human seedbeds he would use initially to grow and then to spread the genetic holocaust he'd planned.

But the persistent kinks remained, and he could not infect his commune members, his Children of Father, until he had worked out a proper formulation for the serum that was to be the principal agent of the epidemic.

Garth and I had ended up with our systems filled with the stuff as the result of an attempt to kill us. Normally, an organism—animal or human—injected with the imperfect serum died a quick and horrible death as its cells, their genetic code hopelessly short-circuited and confused, almost literally "exploded," resulting in a mass of melted flesh, feathers, scales, claws, fangs . . .

But, for some reason, the serum "took" in Garth and me, and a slow, controlled process of devolution began taking place in our bodies. It was just what Loge had been looking to achieve, and thus we became human Petrie dishes, the "keys to Valhalla" Loge could use to solve his problems and launch his holocaust—if we could be caught, dissected, examined. We weren't too eager to be dissected, but neither were we too enthusiastic about completing the transformation into whatever beasts we were slowly but inexorably changing into. He needed us to destroy the world, and we needed the knowledge in his head—or thought we did—to keep from being destroyed. For almost a year, until it came to a cataclysmic end in fire and ice in the Arctic, the Valhalla affair had threatened forever to alter not only the Fredericksons, but our entire species.

It had been a real bummer—not least because the basic premise Loge had gleaned from his Triage Parabola and acted upon, that we were inevitably doomed to extinction within a relatively brief time, remained unrefuted. I was convinced that Garth, who had suffered the most, had never fully recovered from the horrors of Valhalla, and the thought persisted that Valhalla—perhaps residual effects from the serum combined with the poison he had ingested—could very well have something to do with his present condition.

"Jesus Christ," Veil said in a hollow voice when I finished.

"Aside from the people who were involved, you're the first person who knows anything about this. Lippitt feels there are serious national security considerations, and I agree with him. It's hard to know how people would react."

"It won't go beyond me."

"You see my point? Garth remained under a great deal of stress, and the signs that he was ready to come apart were there all the time we were tracking you. I should have seen them, and then done something about it."

"Like what? Take time off? Madison and his men, not to mention this Henry Kitten, were breathing as hard on your ass as they were on mine—harder, since they usually knew where to find you. Kitten had threatened to kill Garth if you stopped looking for me, remember?"

My response was to shrug, and then resume poling away dirt in the deepening trench in which I stood.

"Run the present situation by me again, Mongo," Veil said quietly. "That is, if it doesn't bother you to talk about it. What was Garth poisoned with?"

"A chemical called nitrophenylpentadienal, also known as NPPD or 'spy dust,' " I replied in a flat voice. "Because it bonds very strongly to flesh and clothing, and can be seen under ultraviolet light, it's used by a lot of intelligence services to track people. Most information on the stuff is classified, and they're not even sure what the long-term effects may be for people whose flesh has been exposed to it. It sure as hell isn't meant to be eaten.

"Garth was working undercover on an industrial espionage case in a place called Prolix Pharmaceuticals; it's one of a handful of plants in the United States authorized by the government to manufacture NPPD and conduct classified research projects. The D.I.A. suspected a security leak at Prolix, and Lippitt arranged with the NYPD for Garth to be put on the case. There must have been a leak at the NYPD, or Garth made a mistake, because the spy or spies at Prolix got on to him. They began poisoning him with NPPD.''

''How?''

''Lippitt thinks it was done slowly, over an extended period of time. Maybe they dosed his coffee a few times, or sprinkled small amounts on his food.''

''Do you suppose whoever did it to him knew what the final effects would be?''

''There's no way of knowing that until they catch the guys. Garth may strongly suspect who did it to him, but we won't know unless—until—he comes around.

''Anyway, I'd just begun pondering the problem of where you'd disappeared to. As you know, Madison sent his men to find out what you might have told me over the years, and then burn me to death. When they succeeded in burning out a whole floor of my apartment and killing five people, that made it a case of arson and murder, and Garth was assigned to tag along with me to try to find you, since you were considered a material witness. The transfer put a stop to the slow poisoning, but he'd already absorbed a lot of shit into his system—his brain. You saw him snap; he killed Madison, and tried to kill you, and then sank into the catatonic trance he's in now.''

''What's the prognosis?''

''There is no prognosis—not yet. Nobody's ever been poisoned with NPPD before, so Garth's the test case. Since there is no standard treatment, everything now is a wait-and-see show.''

Veil shook his head, then reached down, gripped my shoulder, and pulled me out of the trench. ''That's deep enough, Mongo. Let's put him under.''

Veil grabbed hold of one of the corpse's splayed arms. I took hold of the other, and we dragged Henry Kitten down off the mound of junk, into the shallow grave. Together, we poled and kicked dirt over the body, then piled up refuse over the site.

''I'm ready for my Scotch,'' I said when we had finished.

*   *   *

Our clothes and bodies reeked of death and garbage. Fortunately, because Veil and I often worked out together in his
loft, I kept a spare set of sweats there. I stripped off my
clothes and threw them away; then, while Veil showered, I
soaked in a hot bath, taking care to keep my bandage dry.
Afterward, I toweled off, dressed in my clean sweats, and
joined Veil at the kitchen table, where he had a tumbler of
Scotch over ice waiting for me.

Veil said, "Since you've quit teaching, I assume you'll be
spending as much time with Garth as possible?"

I sipped at my drink, nodded. "Yeah. The hospital's a
little more than an hour's drive from lower Manhattan, depending on the traffic."

"Oh, I know where it is, all right," Veil said softly. "I
spent time there, as a kid. Didn't you find that out?"

"I wasn't sure it was a subject you'd appreciate me bringing up."

"Thanks, but it doesn't bother me to talk about it. The
staff in the children's division saved my life and mind in a
dozen different ways."

"I could commute from Garth's apartment, but I don't
want to. Lippitt arranged for me to get a small apartment in a
staff dorm they've got there, and he gave me keys and a pass
that will get me into the clinic any time I want; I intend to
take full advantage of the privileges. I want to be at Garth's
side until this thing is resolved . . . one way or another. Until
they tell me Garth is going to stay a vegetable, I want to stick
close in case he needs me."

Veil nodded, then studied me as he sipped the tea he had
brewed for himself. "Any other plans at all?" he asked.
"Will you do any work? What about your P.I. practice?"

"Shut down, at least for now. I don't have any cases
pending, and anything that comes along I'll refer to some of
my colleagues. I've got enough money put away so that I
don't have to do anything if I don't want to, at least for a

while. I've been giving some thought to working at the Children's Hospital there. There's a whole separate facility, which they didn't have when you were there.''

''Teaching?''

''Yeah. The school's right there in the hospital. I'm not certified for teaching emotionally disturbed children, but you don't need certification to substitute, and I've been told they have a hell of a time getting substitutes. If they want me, they've got me.''

''You'd be great teaching those kids, Mongo,'' Veil said, his voice low and serious. ''Forget certification; with disturbed kids, it's the singer, not the song. You've got a great voice.''

''Thanks. We'll see.''

Veil smiled thinly. ''Then again, teaching at Rockland Children's Psychiatric Center won't exactly be like teaching at the university, Mongo.''

''You don't say?''

''You don't get admitted into RCPC unless you're either homicidal or suicidal—sometimes both, which was my case. It's bottom-line work. You'll be dealing with some very sick puppies there—and not a few of them will be dangerous.''

''So I've been told.''

''I think it's a great idea for you to teach there while you're looking after Garth—but I want you to know what you're getting into.''

''Thanks. I appreciate it.''

''What about Prolix, Mongo?''

''What about it?''

''Who's continuing that investigation—the D.I.A. or the police?''

''I really don't know. I didn't think to ask Lippitt, and I'm not sure the NYPD would welcome inquiries from me.''

''I thought your problems with the city cops had all been smoothed over.''

''Maybe,'' I said with a shrug. ''Maybe not.''

Veil was silent for some time, sipping his tea. Finally he leaned back in his chair, ran both hands back through his long, yellow hair, fixed me with his blue eyes. "My relationship with the NYPD is about the same as it's always been—a lot of cops dislike me intensely, but not all. I may be able to find out a few things, if you want me to. I can do it, and still keep a low profile. It's up to you."

"Veil, right now I'm not thinking about anything but seeing that Garth gets better. Sure, I'd appreciate any information you can give me—but not if it's going to get you into any trouble."

Veil nodded slightly.

"I've got to go," I continued, draining off the Scotch and getting to my feet.

"Stay the night, Mongo. You came close to getting killed earlier, and you've got a hell of a nasty cut on your forehead. It's not a good idea for you to drive all the way up to Rockland, which is where I assume you're going."

"Yeah. This is Garth's first night in the clinic, and I want to be with him when he wakes up in the morning. Thanks for the invitation."

"From what you tell me, Mongo, he won't know whether you're there or not."

"Nobody seems to be certain what Garth knows or doesn't know, what he sees or doesn't see. Remember; his EEG is almost normal. I want to be there, Veil."

Veil nodded again. "I understand. I still think you should have a plastic surgeon look at that cut as soon as possible."

"I'll stick with what I've got. Thanks for the sewing job."

"Thanks for the rescue job."

I wrote down my new address and phone number for Veil, and left. As I drove off, I glanced off to my right, into the dark alley where the Archangel affair had ended at last. For everyone but Garth.

3.

THE Rockland Psychiatric Center complex covered hundreds of acres, and was virtually a city unto itself, with its own locksmith shop, fire and police departments; there was a summer camp in the woods beside a large reservoir, cornfields—now leased to local farmers—where patients had once been encouraged to tend crops, an outdoor swimming pool, small parks nestled among a myriad of tall, ivy-covered stone buildings which were, for the most part, designated by numbers. In many ways, RPC reminded me of an Ivy League college campus.

Many of the buildings were now unused; years before, with the best of intentions, the state had decided that many of its mentally ill but otherwise harmless patients would be better served by so-called community support services, and these patients had been released by the thousands from state hospitals. The problem was that there had been no adequate community support services, and the results of this decision could be seen in the surge of numbers of homeless, helpless men and women living on the streets of New York, and many other cities. In addition, many of the criminally insane at RPC had been transferred to various other institutions throughout the state. Consequently, a number of the buildings with bars on the windows were empty, although a few had been converted to staff residences and recreational facilities.

The Defense Intelligence Agency clinic was housed on the upper floors of Building 26, and that was where I headed at seven o'clock the next morning, walking the short distance

from Building 18, where I had been assigned an apartment.
An armed guard who had not been on duty the previous
afternoon sat in a kiosk discreetly set back behind a row of
trees, near the entrance to Building 26. The guard, who had a
harelip only partially hidden beneath a bushy handlebar
mustache, frowned when I handed him the plastic-shrouded,
beige-colored identity card with my picture on it. He turned it
over a few times in his fingers, as though he could not
believe it wasn't counterfeit, then telephoned somebody. He
recited my badge number, said something behind his hand
which I couldn't hear, then listened for a few moments.
Finally he hung up, handed me back the pass, and waved me
on. I used the same pass card to open the magnetic lock on
the entrance door, then clipped the card to my shirt pocket
and took the key-operated elevator to the fourteenth floor.
Two orderlies pushing a racked cart loaded with insulated
food trays gave me a strange look as I stepped out of the
elevator into a corridor, but they passed by and I was not
challenged.

Garth's room was the fourth on the left in the corridor to
the right of the elevator, and I went directly there. My
brother was lying in the same position as when I had left
him, on his back, with a pale blue sheet pulled up under his
chin; his eyes were open, staring vacantly at the ceiling.

"Garth?" I said quietly as I stared down into his eyes and
rubbed the back of my hand against his stubbled cheek.
There was no response, and his flesh felt cold.

I started slightly at the sound of a cart rolling into the
room, behind me. I turned to find myself looking at a tall,
solidly built man dressed in a starched white hospital coat,
pushing a cart on which were arrayed a variety of toilet
articles—a stainless steel bowl filled with steaming soapy
water, a second bowl of clear water, rubbing lotion, wash-
cloths and towels, a cup with toothbrush and toothpaste,
shaving equipment. The man had large, bright hazel eyes and
long brown hair, which he wore in a ponytail secured by a

tooled leather band. In his left earlobe he wore a tiny gold earring. Despite the fact that it was early spring, the man was deeply tanned—which probably meant he was an avid skier. He looked very fit.

"Dr. Frederickson," the man said easily, coming around from behind his cart and extending a large, heavily muscled hand. His voice was high-pitched and carried just the trace of a lisp. His grip was firm. "It's a real pleasure to make your acquaintance; I've heard a lot about you. I'm Tommy Carling—one of Garth's nurses."

"I'm pleased to meet you, Mr. Carling."

"Please; call me Tommy."

"My friends, and people who take care of my brother, call me Mongo."

Carling smiled, revealing even, white teeth that looked as if they might have been capped, then pushed the cart next to Garth's bed. "Then I'd better start taking care of your brother, hadn't I, Mongo?"

I watched as Carling checked Garth's pulse, then examined the levels of the fluids in the bottles attached to the tube city that had grown up around Garth's bed. Next, he carefully removed the tubes from Garth's nose and the needles from the implants in his veins. This done, he pulled the sheet down to Garth's waist. He lathered my brother's face with shaving cream, then proceeded to shave him expertly with an old-fashioned bone-handled straight razor, occasionally rinsing the blade in the bowl of soapy water, drying it on a towel he wore draped over his shoulder. Tommy Carling, I thought, had a light, gentle touch, and he seemed fastidious and sincerely caring as he went about the business of tending to Garth. Garth, of course, wasn't about to lodge any complaints, and it was possible that the male nurse was putting on a good show for a relative and visitor—but I didn't think so.

I asked, "Are you permanently assigned to Garth?"

"When I'm on duty," Carling replied, carefully lifting

Garth's nose with his left thumb and forefinger in order to shave his upper lip.

"Good. I like your style."

Carling laughed easily. "My style? I haven't even finished shaving him."

"Still, I like what I see."

"Thank you."

"I hope I'm not in your way."

"Certainly not."

"I wanted to be here early, just in case Garth was . . . awake. I guess I was being silly and overoptimistic. I guess you could say Garth is always awake—or always asleep, depending on how you look at it."

"A little optimism never hurt anybody, patient or relative," Carling said as he finished shaving Garth, wiped his face clean with a towel, then splashed on some English Leather cologne. Next, he proceeded to brush Garth's teeth, carefully massaging the gums with the rubber tip of the toothbrush. As he did so, he nodded toward the pass I had clipped to my shirt pocket. "Incidentally," he continued matter-of-factly, "with that ID, it's irrelevant whether or not you get in anybody's way. That particular piece of plastic entitles you to go anywhere you like, any time you like, and do whatever you want, just as long as it doesn't interfere with any patient's treatment. It's heavy."

"This badge is different from the usual visitor's badge?"

Carling laughed as he finished brushing Garth's teeth, then rubbed some astringent on the gums with the tip of his finger. "A regular visitor's pass is green, with a broad yellow stripe across it. It will get you as far as the Day Room downstairs—or into a patient's room only if the patient is absolutely immobile. You'd have an escort from the time you entered the building until you left. That badge you're wearing is a Z-13; God knows why it's designated that, but it is. We call it a brown bomber. It gives you unlimited access to this facility, and also gives you the authority to ask questions of anyone, and get answers. Except for clinical matters, that badge gives you equal authority with the doctors here. That badge makes me, and the other nurses and attendants, your subordinates.''

"I didn't know.''

"I've only seen a brown bomber three other times in the five years I've been here, and those were worn by an official from D.I.A. headquarters in Washington and two congressmen from a select oversight committee. As far as I know, you're the first relative of a patient ever to be issued one of those. It means you have either a very high security clearance or very powerful friends in very high places. Don't be surprised if it raises a few eyebrows.''

So Mr. Lippitt had really taken care of me; perhaps too much so, unwittingly creating enmity and suspicion toward me among the clinic's staff. It could explain Dr. Slycke's attitude.

Tommy Carling was obviously curious as to how I'd secured my brown bomber—but I didn't feel any great urge to tell him, and he didn't press. Quickly and efficiently, Carling stripped off the top sheet and then removed Garth's pajamas, leaving my brother lying naked on another sheet stretched over a rubber mat. He detached Garth's colostomy bag, dumped it into the toilet, and attached a fresh one to the rubber tube extending out from the gash in Garth's side. He did the same with the urine bag, then proceeded to wash Garth. I smoothed down Garth's thinning, wheat-colored hair, then joined in with the washup, using a second washcloth from the cart, and starting with Garth's feet. There was one striking change in my brother's condition: he had been absolutely rigid when he had collapsed in the Washington hearing room, but his muscles were now completely slack, and his limbs flopped wherever they were placed. Now that the sheet was off, I could see that his head was propped in a face-forward position by two foam rubber supports which had been placed on either side of his jaw. I suddenly felt an overwhelming sense of sadness, futility, and loss; I blinked back tears.

"I don't want any authority over anybody," I said quietly as I worked my way with the soapy washcloth up Garth's legs. "I'd appreciate being kept informed of my brother's treatment and progress, but most of all I just want to be able to be with him."

"You've got it. But, as I said, don't be surprised if you get some strange reactions. It's not only your brown bomber, but the fact that your brother is here in the first place; neither of you works for the D.I.A.—unless we've been lied to, which is what *some* people around here whose names I won't mention may think."

"Wasn't Dr. Slycke briefed?"

"Of course; all of us were briefed. The fact that Garth was poisoned with NPPD makes him a very special case. Remember, I said *some* people may be suspicious, but there are always people whose noses get out of joint over changes in routine. Let me tell you, just about everyone is watching Garth with a hell of a lot of curiosity about what happens when—" Carling abruptly stopped speaking and glanced down at me with genuine alarm in his eyes. "I'm sorry, Mongo. I didn't mean to sound insensitive."

"It's all right. I know all about the curiosity, and it's why Garth is here—obviously. Why should anyone think differently?"

"What I'm saying is that not even psychiatrists—maybe especially not psychiatrists—are immune to a touch of paranoia from time to time, so don't be too surprised if you run into it around here."

"I still don't understand. If everyone's been briefed, why should anyone be paranoid about Garth and me?"

"Not so much Garth as you and your brown bomber. The question is how and why *you* rate such a high security clearance in order to be with him."

For the first time it occurred to me that Mr. Lippitt not only might be open to charges of nepotism, but might actually get into serious difficulties because of his understanding and kindness toward me. I decided it was time to change the subject. "Exactly what are they doing with Garth now, Tommy?"

Carling cleared his throat. "Officially, you're supposed to direct all of your medical questions to Dr. Slycke," he said in a low voice. "Unofficially, I'll tell you that Slycke hasn't designed a therapy program yet."

"Garth isn't getting any medication?"

"Not yet. For now, all they're doing is conducting blood and chemical tests, and observing."

"I understand that I signed a blanket consent form for any and all treatment, including experimental drugs, but I'd like to be kept informed of what's happening; and I'd like to know what they're going to do *before* they do it."

"You'll have to take that up with Dr. Slycke."

"What about the other psychiatrists on the staff?"

"Slycke has taken personal charge of Garth, so the other doctors will refer you to him."

"Fair enough. Thanks for the information." I strongly suspected that if Tommy Carling hadn't told me about the privileges I enjoyed with my brown bomber, nobody else would have.

We finished washing Garth, and toweled him off. I combed his hair, then stepped back while the male nurse applied rubbing lotion to my brother's body and massaged him, kneading the muscles and flexing the joints. He dressed him in clean pajamas, made the bed around and under him, then rolled him over on his right side and pulled the clean sheet up to his chin. The whole operation had taken less than a half hour.

"We'll leave him with a little music," Carling said, turning on a small table radio and tuning it to a classical station.

"Why? He can't hear it."

"Why not? Who knows what he can or can't hear?"

"You're right," I replied, and touched the bandage on my forehead. My wound had begun to throb. "Tommy, you wouldn't have a couple of aspirin around this place, would you?''

"Of course," Carling said, and frowned sympathetically. "Obviously, you've been hurt. You're in pain?"

"I've got a headache."

"May I ask what happened?"

"It was just a stupid accident; I bumped into something sharp."

"I'll be right back," Carling said, and walked quickly from the room.

He was back in less than a minute, carrying a bottle of aspirin, a glass of water, and a small medical kit.

"Tommy," I said, "I don't want a fuss; just a couple of aspirin."

"You look a little pale. When did you hurt yourself?"

"Yesterday."

"Did you get a tetanus shot?"

"Yes," I lied.

"Well, it won't hurt to have a look at it to make sure it isn't oozing, and put on a fresh bandage. Just sit down in the chair there."

Tommy Carling was a persistent healer who obviously didn't like to take no for an answer. I sighed, sat down in the chair next to Garth's bed. Carling loosened the strips of adhesive tape over the thick gauze Veil had applied, then carefully peeled back the bandage.

"Man," Carling said, and grimaced. "That is a *nasty* cut. You did that by *bumping* your head?"

"Yeah."

"It looks like someone slashed you with a razor."

"I bumped it hard."

Carling shrugged. "It looks clean," he said, and opened the medical kit. He took out a bottle of peroxide and a gauze pad. "I'll just touch it up a little and put on a fresh bandage."

Carling handed me the bottle of aspirin. I shook out three tablets into my palm, washed them down with the water he had brought. Then I sat still while Carling expertly and gently daubed the wound with peroxide.

"That's an interesting stitching job."

"Mmm."

"Whoever did it did a good job. I don't think you'll have much of a scar. It's an unusual style."

"The scar?" I asked, and allowed myself a small smile.

"The stitches."

"I didn't know there was such a thing as a 'style' in stitching up wounds."

"Oh, yes. Doctors are taught to tie off sutures in a particular way. These sutures are perfectly adequate, but I've never seen knots like these."

"My doctor must fancy himself an individualist."

Carling grunted as he finished washing the wound. Then he quickly applied a fresh, much smaller, bandage.

"Nice job," I said when I examined Carling's handiwork in a small mirror in the bathroom. "Now I don't look like a mummy. Thank you."

"You're welcome," Carling said, closing up the medical kit and putting it on the cart. "I've got to do a meds round now. Want to tag along and see the rest of the clinic?"

"I don't want to raise the paranoia index around here."

"With that Z-13 clipped to your shirt, you can raise anything you like. I thought you might be interested."

"I am."

"Then let's go."

I kissed Garth on the cheek and told him I'd be back in a few minutes, then followed after Tommy Carling. We went to a large, glass-enclosed office near what I assumed was the center of the clinic, where Carling traded in his personal hygiene cart for another, larger cart on which was arrayed a host of tiny paper cups that contained pills of various sizes, shapes, and colors, as well as slightly larger cups with liquid medicine. Each cup was stapled to a file card listing the name of the patient and the medication, along with spaces for the signature of the staff member administering the medication, and the time. There was also a large, frosted pitcher of orange juice.

"As I'm sure you know," Carling said as he rolled the cart out of the office, "this is both a research and care facility. However, for all intents and purposes, we're much more oriented toward care than research—with the notable exception, of course, of your brother. You understand; we know what happened to him, but the fact that he was poisoned with NPPD is descriptive information, not prescriptive. The doctors have to make a determination as to exactly what's wrong with him before they can embark on a treatment program. With most of the other patients, the treatment is rather standard and straightforward—conservative and a bit too Freud-oriented, in my unqualified opinion, but that's the way it is around here. Freudians tend to flock together." He paused, shrugged. "But then, so do psychiatrists of various other persuasions. Don't mind my gossip."

"If the treatment of most of the other patients is so straight-forward, why couldn't they be put into any good mental hospital, anywhere in the country? Why here, and why all the secrecy?"

"Secrecy about what we do isn't the point so much as the security of the men we're doing it to. All of the patients here were either field operatives or occupied equally sensitive positions. Their mental illness may or may not—usually not—have any connection with the work they did, but they simply carry too many secrets around in their heads to allow them to enter just any hospital and talk to therapists or other staff who don't have the required security clearance."

"Got it."

"Which is not to say that the care here isn't the best; it is. Dr. Slycke and the other psychiatrists are topflight. All of the attendants are R.N.s, well paid, and we like to think we're pretty good. Everyone, psychiatrists and nurses, has been specially trained to deal with the special psychological problems you might expect D.I.A. field operatives to suffer from.''

''Garth doesn't fit into that category.''

''Your brother doesn't fit into any category; he's a unique case. Here, at last, the doctors don't have to worry about gaining classified information about NPPD.''

''Do you have any . . . permanent patients? People who never recover?''

''A few,'' Carling replied quietly. ''It's much too early to worry about Garth becoming one of them, Mongo.''

We went from room to room, with Carling dispensing the appropriate pills or potions to the various patients. I saw no women, either among the patient population or on the staff. Most of the men were up and about, eating the breakfasts that had been brought to them by the two attendants I had passed on the way in. Some were in bed, others dressed and sitting. Most seemed interested in my presence. Carling always introduced me, and we usually stayed a few minutes in each room to chat.

The tour continued, by way of the elevator, to the floor below us, where there was a fully equipped gym, mini-theater, and a huge game room with everything from chess sets to video arcade games. We went back up, down a corridor which was painted orange and blocked a quarter of the way down by a locked door of thick, wire-reinforced glass. Carling took a set of keys out of his pocket, but made no move to open the door.

''The secure unit,'' Carling said, turning to me. ''We have five men in there now, two of them long-termers. All these men are considered potentially extremely violent, and unpredictable. The unit is completely self-contained; they have their own cafeteria, gym, and game room. The most interesting—and probably most dangerous—man in here is a patient by the name of Marl Braxton. He'll probably want to talk to you.''

''Why is he so interesting, and why should he want to talk to me?''

"He's particularly interesting to me because he's the only patient in here whose file is classified above my level; I have no idea what his background is. Around here, you usually pick up all sorts of personal shit, whether you want to or not, from the patients themselves—but never from Braxton. I suspect even Slycke doesn't know the background information on Braxton, because Braxton's therapist—a Chinese by the name of Dr. Wong—comes in from the outside, three times a week, and he's the only therapist who's not part of the regular staff. All we get is specific treatment information. I know Braxton's a loony because he's here, but you'd never know it to talk to him; Wong's got him stabilized pretty well on a chemotherapy program."

"If he's stabilized on medication, why keep him in the secure unit?"

Carling raised his eyebrows slightly. "Because he kills people."

"Oh."

"By which I mean he's killed a few people in the past. *That* much I know, because it's essential clinical information. Wherever he was and whatever he was doing, he began suffering severe psychotic breakdowns—and you didn't want to be around when that happened. There was never any warning, which is why I suppose they don't want to take any chances with him. Braxton's a pretty spooky guy."

"How long has he been here?"

Carling shrugged. "I don't know, and I don't have any way of finding out unless Braxton or somebody else tells me. He was here when I was hired. Anyway, he's got a near-genius IQ, and he's extremely well read. If I knew who you were, he will too. He'll be curious—he's curious about everything. He's been through every book in our library, as well as that of the main hospital, and he keeps the people in the interlibrary system working overtime. He's extremely articulate, and about the only time you'll even get a hint that he's not wrapped too tightly is when he starts talking about his 'maid of constant sorrows.' "

"Who's she?"

"Maybe Wong knows. I don't—and as far as I know, nobody else around here does either. She's just somebody he occasionally refers to."

"What about the others?"

"The same—crazy and dangerous; but more obviously crazy and dangerous. They're all under heavy medication, so there shouldn't be anything to worry about. Still, it *can* get hairy in the secure unit, and you can pass if you feel uncomfortable."

"What? Not complete the tour? I'll stick with you."

Carling turned a key on his ring in the lock, and I held the door open while he wheeled the cart through. When I released the door, it sighed shut, locked with an audible click.

It appeared that this section of the fourteenth floor had been extensively remodeled to meet the needs of the secure unit; there was lots of open space, making the sections of the clinic I had already seen seem relatively cramped. Individual rooms, without doors, radiated off a huge, circular commons area which contained a large projection TV, game tables, a music system with half a dozen sets of earphones, a mini-library stocked with a few hundred books, current newspapers and magazines, and a work-study area complete with word processing equipment.

"Depending on tension levels, the other patients are allowed in here a few at a time to socialize or use the equipment," Carling said as we headed across the commons area toward three men who sat in armchairs beside the barred windows. "But these men don't come out."

"I'm impressed," I said, and I was.

"Meds time, gentlemen," Carling said cheerfully as he brought the cart to a stop a few feet away from the men.

"Remember, we don't call this place Club Med for nothing; a pill a day keeps the nasties away."

Two of the men took their pills without comment, washing them down with orange juice, then walked away. Carling signed the cards, then held out a cup filled with a purple liquid. "Down the hatch, Mama," the nurse continued easily.

The third patient, a rangy man wearing rubber thongs, cut-off jeans, and a tank top with camouflage design, made no move to take the cup, and I hoped nothing in my face or manner betrayed the revulsion I felt when I looked at him. Suddenly I found myself taking comfort in the fact that there were five other white-coated male nurses, all reassuringly big and burly, standing or sitting around the area.

The marks on the man's face and shaved head hadn't been applied in any tattoo parlor; the dye-stained, ragged scars were obviously self-inflicted, probably with a razor blade. Circling his head was a crown of thorns, complete with scar-puckered drops of blood extending down over his shoulders, chest, and back. JESUS, in red-stained capital letters, was carved into his left cheek, SAVES into the right. The man was looking directly at me with bright, slightly unfocused green eyes, and it had been a long time since I'd seen as much naked hatred in a face.

"Mama?" Carling continued in a low, hard voice which had lost all traces of its lisp. "What's up, Mama? Talk to me."

"I'm not sure I want to take my medication today," the man called Mama said in a low, guttural voice that was close to a snarl. Rage mingled with the hatred in his eyes as he glared at me, and the muscles in his jaw clenched and unclenched.

Something about me was seriously upsetting the man, and I wasn't sure whether walking away would pacify him or enrage him even more. Consequently I remained very still, dropped my gaze, and stared at the floor in what I hoped the man would take as a gesture of passivity; but I made sure I kept him well within my range of peripheral vision. If he got tired of talking and nasty faces and made a move for me, I was prepared to drop him with a kick to the groin or the side of the knee.

"You suit yourself, Mama," Tommy Carling said in the same low, hard voice. "Nobody's going to force you to take your meds, and you know it. But you also know what's going to happen if you *don't* take it. By noontime, you'll be hopping around inside your skin. Then you'll want to calm down, but you won't be able to; you'll ask for your stuff, but by then it will be too late for oral medication, pill or liquid. You'll get belligerent and want to fight. You'll throw some furniture around. You'll be confused, and you'll get very threatening. That's when we'll have to take you down, put you in a camisole, and stick a needle in your ass. You'll end up in the Critical Care room for a minimum of twenty-four hours, trussed up in that camisole and lying on a mat. You know it's going to happen, Mama, so why don't you just take your meds now and save us all a lot of grief?"

"Why the hell did you bring a dwarf in here?!" the man shouted, half rising from the chair and clenching his bony fists. "God hates dwarfs! Dwarfs are evil, and God wants them all dead! I wouldn't be here if it weren't for dwarfs! You bring one in here, it's bad luck for all of us!"

Ah, yes. It just didn't seem like a good time to try to point out all the sterling qualities of dwarfs, and so I remained still and silent—but ready, balanced on the balls of my feet.

"Mama, I'm sorry," Carling said in a voice that had suddenly become soothing. The other nurses, who had hurried over as soon as the man had begun shouting, now stood shoulder to shoulder in a semicircle behind his chair. "This is something new, a view of yours I wasn't aware of. I didn't mean to do anything to upset you, and I'm going to make it right. I'm going to take this man out of here right now. When I come back, you're going to be calmed down, and you're going to take your meds. Okay?" Carling paused, inclined his head toward me, continued evenly: "Walk to the door; I'll be right behind you."

I certainly didn't need any prompting—but as I turned to leave I found my way blocked by someone with a slim waist connected to a pair of massive thighs, very close. I hadn't heard anyone come up behind me, and I was thoroughly startled.

"Take your medication, Baker, and stop this bullshit," a voice above me said curtly.

I stepped back, looked up at the man who had spoken. The owner of the thighs and the deep, commanding voice was about the same size as my brother, six feet two or three. He obviously spent a lot of time in the gym, for his chest and heavily muscled arms bulged inside a short-sleeved knit jersey. He had a rugged but not unhandsome face, with a straight nose, pronounced cheekbones, and an ocher tinge to his flesh that made me think he might have more than a little American Indian in him. His eyes were black—bright, piercing. He had a full head of hair only slightly tinged with gray around the temples. The sharp widow's peak that extended low on his forehead gave him an elfin—or devilish—look. I put his age at around forty-five.

"This is none of your business, Braxton!" Mama Baker shouted. His eyes had grown very wide, and both JESUS and SAVES were outlined in pink as he flushed. He continued to tremble with rage, but something else—respect, and perhaps fear—moved in his green eyes, and he eased himself back down into his chair.

"It's the business of everybody in this unit, Baker, when your bullshit involves our privileges," the tall man with the piercing eyes said evenly. "The *last* time you refused to take your medication, it was less than three hours before you went apeshit. You busted up the place, and it took two months to get the television and stereo repaired."

Marl Braxton paused, glanced at Tommy Carling, and held out his right hand. Carling handed a paper cup to the big man, who swallowed the two tiny pink pills in it without juice or water. "See?" Braxton said quietly to the man with the scar-shrouded head. "Nothing to it. This man you've been insulting is Dr. Robert Frederickson. I have no idea what he's doing here, but he should be treated as an honored guest. I mean, we wouldn't want Dr. Frederickson to think we're *too* crazy, would we, Mama? In any case, I wish to think of him as *my* honored guest. He's a most accomplished and interesting man, and I'd like to speak with him about many subjects. If he leaves prematurely because of you, Baker, I'll take personal offense. Now, calm down and take your medication."

Mama Baker swallowed hard, and his knuckles were white where they gripped the armrests of his chair. "Are you threatening me, Braxton?!"

"No," the big man replied mildly. "I'm asking you to do what you should be doing anyway. The rest of us don't care to suffer because of your stupidity."

"What are you going to do if I don't?"

"I'll do nothing. But there's always the chance that my maid of constant sorrows may visit you one night."

"Fuck you and your creepy maid of constant sorrows."

"My maid of constant sorrows will most assuredly fuck you, Mama." Marl Braxton's voice, calm and quiet to begin with, had become softer—which only made it more chilling. "She'll really stick it to you. You won't like it."

There was a prolonged silence during which Mama Baker glared at Marl Braxton, who calmly gazed back at him.

"Give me the fucking stuff," Baker said at last.

There was a barely audible, communal sigh of relief around the room as Mama Baker took a cup from Tommy Carling's outstretched hand, swallowed the purple liquid. He crumpled the cup and hurled it to the floor, then jumped out of his chair and stalked away.

"Ah, yes, just another boring day at the office," Tommy Carling said as he picked up the crumpled cup and dropped it into a slot in the side of the cart. He nodded to the other male nurses, who then walked away to various sections of the commons area. "Mongo, meet Marl Braxton."

"Mr. Braxton," I said, extending my hand.

Marl Braxton stared down into my face, but made no move to take my outstretched hand. He continued to stare, and then he frowned slightly. "You're afraid of me," he said at last.

I dropped my hand back to my side, said nothing.

"No," the other man continued thoughtfully, after a pause. "Not afraid; but I make you nervous."

"I'm a little strung out at the moment, Mr. Braxton."

The man with the widow's peak and bright black eyes nodded toward Tommy Carling. "Our ponytailed friend here has been talking to you about me, hasn't he? Tommy really loves to gossip; I'll never understand how he got a security clearance. They must tape his mouth shut every day when he leaves here."

"What would you like to discuss with me, Mr. Braxton?"

"Please don't patronize me, Frederickson," Marl Braxton said evenly, and then sighed. "I'm just crazy; I'm not simple. I've read many of your monographs on the so-called criminally insane, and I found them most impressive. You're a professor, with a doctorate in criminology; you're an ex–circus headliner, a noted private investigator; you have a black belt in karate. I just wanted to talk."

"Then let's talk. Maybe we can get some coffee, and—"

"No," Braxton said curtly. "Not today; not when the air has been poisoned the way it has. Perhaps some other time."

Marl Braxton turned on his heel and walked quickly away, disappearing into one of the rooms that radiated off the commons area. When I looked back at Tommy Carling, the male nurse's expression was thoughtful.

"Well, now you've met Marl Braxton," he said dryly.

"This Mama Baker was afraid of him."

"Oh, yes. Baker's real name is Marion, incidentally, in case you're interested. *He* insists everyone call him Mama, and we oblige. Anyway, there's a pecking order here, just like there is in all groups."

"And here, Marl Braxton is at the top of the pecking order."

"You've got it."

Suddenly, I heard the door to the unit bang open. I turned, saw the director of the clinic, his face flushed with anger, hurrying toward us. Dr. Charles Slycke was a man in his late fifties or early sixties, and most of the time acted like an extremely stressed individual in need of a good psychiatrist—at least that's how he seemed to me. He was a couple of inches under six feet, overweight but not obese, with thinning gray hair that stuck out at odd angles from his head and watery gray eyes with dark pouches under them. At the moment, those eyes were flashing with anger—and, I thought, perhaps just a touch of insecurity.

"What is this man doing here?!" Slycke snapped at the male nurse.

"Sir, he has a Z-13 identity badge, and I just thought—"

"I'm well aware of what kind of badge he's wearing, and I don't care what you thought! Sometimes you go too far, mister! Do you think this is some kind of a game?!"

Carling shook his head. "I don't know what you mean, sir," he said evenly.

Slycke sucked in a deep breath, took a step backward, shoved his hands deep into the pockets of his checked sports jacket. "Did he ask you to bring him into the secure unit?"

"No, sir, but—"

"Excuse me, Doctor," I said to the psychiatrist in what I hoped was a properly soothing and thoroughly deferential tone. "There seems to have been a misunderstanding, and it's my fault."

Slycke continued to ignore me as he glared at Tommy Carling. "Why wasn't I even informed that this man was in the building?!"

"Sir, with his Z-13, I didn't think—"

"That is correct! You didn't think!"

"*Excuse* me, Doctor," I said a bit more forcefully. "I apologize for any inconvenience or trouble I've caused, and I'll try to make certain it won't happen again. I'll be more than happy to follow any procedure you want to lay out. Mr. Carling was just trying to be—"

"Come with me, Frederickson," Slycke snapped, abruptly wheeling around and heading back toward the door, which was being held open by two nurses. "We have to talk."

4.

FEELING like nothing so much as an unruly student in tow behind a stern principal, I dutifully followed Charles Slycke out of the secure unit and back to his dimly lit office, which was off a small foyer leading to the fire stairs. I sat down in a chair without being asked as the portly man went behind his scarred wooden desk, nervously ran both hands through his unruly hair, then sank down in a leather swivel chair and opened a thin, pale green folder. He seemed highly agitated, and I strongly suspected that his distress sprang from a lot more than his having found me in the secure unit.

"Frederickson," the director of the clinic mumbled without looking up, "this is your brother's file I have here. I'd like to ask you a few questions about his medical history."

"I'll be happy to answer your questions, Dr. Slycke, but I filled out an extensive set of medical questionnaires on Garth yesterday. Don't you have them in the file?"

Now the other man looked up, fixed me with his pouched, rheumy eyes. "Are you certain there's nothing you've left out?"

Nothing that Slycke would believe, and nothing that would

be of any use to him; the formula for, and all samples of, the serum that had twisted everything in us but our minds horribly out of shape during the Valhalla affair had been destroyed in a volcanic explosion in Greenland. If and when Garth regained consciousness, he might well feel the need to talk about our experiences; until then, there was nothing I could say about Valhalla that could serve as anything other than an unnecessary distraction.

"No," I replied. "He had the usual childhood diseases, tonsils and appendix out, and a few broken bones. You've got it all in the forms I filled out."

Slycke closed the file and pushed it to one side, then folded his hands on top of the desk and studied me. For the moment, at least, he seemed to be holding his hostility toward me in abeyance. "We've found a curious anomaly in your brother's blood chemistry, Dr. Frederickson, and I was hoping you might be able to shed some light on the matter."

"What's the anomaly?"

"He has some very strange antibodies which aren't listed in any reference book; their chemical makeup is quite unlike anything the medical profession has ever seen. Are you sure your brother never suffered from some peculiar affliction? Perhaps he picked up a tropical disease while he was traveling, or in the service?"

"Not that I'm aware of. You can always check his service medical records, but I'm sure he would have told me about anything like that. Does it make a difference? We know he suffered his breakdown after he was poisoned with NPPD."

"Frederickson, your brother seems to possess antibodies in his blood for a disease that doesn't exist."

A disease called the Valhalla Project, I thought, now mercifully banished from the face of the earth—except, obviously, for antibodies left in Garth's blood. And mine. "Could the existence of those antibodies—or whatever caused the antibodies—have something to do with Garth's present condition?"

"That's impossible to say until we know what it is we're

looking at. It's somewhat perplexing to discover, in your brother's case, that we're dealing with not one, but two unknowns; the effect of nitrophenylpentadienal ingestion, combined with what may be long-term, lingering effects from whatever disease caused those antibodies.''

"I can't explain it," I said. "Maybe the antibodies are a reaction to the NPPD in his system.''

Slycke shook his head impatiently. "There are many things about nitrophenylpentadienal we don't know—it may or may not have a long-range toxic effect on internal organs, and it may or may not be able to penetrate the blood-brain barrier. However, since it is an inorganic chemical, it cannot possibly create antibodies. Your brother was definitely exposed to some kind of exotic disease at some time in the past.''

"I'm sorry I can't help you, sir.''

"Your brother is in a profound catatonic state, Frederickson, and it's not going to be at all helpful to him if you play games with me.''

I stiffened in my chair. "Games?''

"I require your full cooperation, and it would be most troubling to me if I thought . . . you were keeping something from me I should know.''

"Look, Dr. Slycke," I said carefully, "I've sensed your suspicion and hostility toward me from the moment we met, and I don't understand it. I don't want to interfere with clinic procedures, and I certainly don't want to upset anybody. All I want is to be with my brother, regardless of whether or not he knows I'm there. Is that so difficult to understand? What's the problem?''

"Your brother isn't in the secure unit. What were you doing there?''

"I was just looking around," I said with a shrug. "As a matter of fact, I'm very impressed with your operation. You should be commended.''

"Why were you looking around the clinic?''

"No particular *reason*," I said, seeing that flattery was going to get me nowhere with Charles Slycke. "I was just curious.''

"Did you ask Mr. Carling to take you there?"

"Look, Doctor," I said after a moment's hesitation, "I don't want Mr. Carling to get into trouble because you're peeved with me. I've watched him working with Garth, and I've very pleased. He seems to me an excellent nurse. When he invited me to accompany him on his rounds, he was just trying to be friendly and courteous. Where's the harm in that?"

Slycke frowned slightly. "Then it was Mr. Carling who suggested you look around?"

"Yes. As I said, he was just trying—"

"And you didn't demand to be shown the secure unit?"

"Demand? I didn't even ask; I didn't even know you *had* a secure unit. I keep telling you; my only real interest is in being near my brother while he's sick."

Slycke studied me with his watery eyes, apparently pondering my answer, then seemed to relax slightly. "Mr. Carling was a fool to take you into the secure unit. Marion Baker hears voices that tell him to kill dwarfs."

"Obviously, Mr. Carling wasn't aware of that."

"Ignorance of the danger is no excuse for foolishly exposing you to it. Can you imagine the explaining I'd have to do if Baker had harmed you?"

"I can take care of myself, Dr. Slycke, thank you very much," I said evenly. "Besides, what difference does it make? My being there was my responsibility, not yours. No regulations were broken; it's my understanding that the ID badge I'm wearing gives me unlimited access to all areas of the clinic."

It had been the wrong thing to say; Slycke straightened up in his chair, and his round face grew dark. "Are you going to tell me what your rights are in this facility?"

"It's the furthest thing from my mind, Doctor," I replied quietly.

"*I* run this clinic!"

"Most assuredly, Doctor. I didn't mean to offend you. I

just want to look after my brother and mind my own business."

"Is that what you thought you were doing when you accepted an invitation from a *nurse* to wander around a secret facility? Did you think you were minding your own business?"

Charles Slycke was beginning to try my patience, which could be in short supply even under the best of circumstances. I was perfectly willing to offer obeisance to him just so that he wouldn't be distracted from thinking about my brother, but it was becoming increasingly obvious that nothing I could say to him was going to make any difference—and I couldn't help but wonder why.

"Why don't you tell me what's really on your mind, Dr. Slycke? You've been on my case since the moment I walked in here. Do you have a thing about dwarfs, too?"

The psychiatrist leaned back in his swivel chair, narrowed his eyes, crossed his arms over his chest, and raised his chin slightly. "Were you sent here to spy on me?"

I shook my head slightly. "Come again?"

"Our previous conversation leads me to believe that your hearing is perfectly all right."

"Who the hell would send me to spy on you?"

"That senile old man in the Pentagon that the president sees fit to keep on as Director of the Defense Intelligence Agency," Slycke said in a tight voice that trembled slightly.

"You're referring to Mr. Lippitt?"

"Of course I'm referring to Mr. Lippitt!" Slycke snapped. "Did he send you here to spy on me?!"

"You have got to be kidding."

"Answer me!"

Anger welled in me, and I struggled to control it. I looked down at the backs of my hands and took a series of deep breaths before again looking up at the florid-faced man sitting behind the desk. "I'm not a spy for anybody, Slycke," I said quietly. "If you and Mr. Lippitt have some kind of personal feud going on, that's your business. I want no part of it."

"The man is incompetent! He's too *old* for that job!"

"In your opinion."

"What did he say about me?!"

"He didn't say anything about you; in fact, he never even mentioned your name. He had Garth transferred here because—and he said this—he considers this the best facility of its kind. It seems to me that the obvious ill will is all on your part."

"Oh? And is that why he sent a man who isn't even a D.I.A. employee to a secret D.I.A. facility?!"

"Now you're being disingenuous, Doctor. You know perfectly well why Garth is here—to care for him, yes, but also to keep whatever is learned from his experience with NPPD safely under wraps within the intelligence community."

"Yes, but that doesn't explain why you come as part of the package. What are *you* doing here?"

"Garth is my brother, for Christ's sake."

"Being a relative of a patient doesn't entitle you to a Z-13 identity badge. This procedure is absolutely unprecedented, and it's an unacceptable breach of security."

"Whoa. There's been no *breach* of security, and there won't be—at least not on my part. Now, you may consider me a security *risk,* but Mr. Lippitt obviously doesn't think I am. He personally signed this badge, which makes me *his* responsibility, not yours. So maybe you should just get on with your business, which is healing, and let Mr. Lippitt worry about whether or not I'm a security risk."

"But why should he give you such privileges and . . . authority?"

"Are you suggesting that either Mr. Lippitt or I would take advantage of my brother's condition just to spy on you?" I snapped, no longer even making an effort to contain my anger. "Maybe you think we poisoned him in order to sneak me in here? If Mr. Lippitt wanted to spy on you, don't you think—as senile and incompetent as you may believe him to be—he could have thought of a subtler way of doing it than sending me here? If you'll pardon a momentary lapse in good manners and taste, I'm telling you that's insane.''

Surprisingly, my angry outburst seemed to have a calming effect on the other man. Slycke blinked slowly, then seemed to slump slightly in his chair. ''I'm saying you have no business carrying a Z-13 pass, because you have no official business here. Is it any wonder I'm suspicious?''

''Garth is my official business, Doctor.''

''You're a college professor. How can you spend all this time away from your classes?''

''I resigned.''

''What are you living on while you spend all your time hanging around here?''

''That's none of your business, Slycke,'' I replied curtly. ''This is how I choose to spend my time until my brother gets well.''

''Your brother may never get well.''

''Thanks a lot, Doctor; you've got a great bedside manner.''

''I've heard rumors that you and your brother have a close personal relationship with Mr. Lippitt.''

''That's also none of your business.''

''You're a licensed private investigator!'' Slycke was getting himself worked up again.

''So what?''

''A licensed private investigator, carrying a Z-13 badge, here under the auspices of a man who may well bear a personal grudge against me!''

''If Mr. Lippitt bore a personal grudge against you, Dr. Slycke, he wouldn't have sent me to tell you about it.''

But Slycke wasn't listening to anything but the voices of his own paranoia. ''I *expressly* advised against appointing that man Director, and I was overruled. Imagine; the man is demoted to no more than a security guard position in some godforsaken place in Nebraska. The facility *he's* responsible for gets blown up, he disappears for a year, and when he surfaces he's appointed *Director* of the agency. It's inconceivable!''

Valhalla again. Siegmund Loge and his minions were continuing to haunt me, his legacy hanging like a poisonous mist even over this mental hospital in Rockland County. It would be interesting to see what Slycke's reaction would be if he knew what Lippitt had been up to during that year—but I wasn't about to tell him. "I don't know anything about that, Doctor," I said tightly, "and my guess is that Mr. Lippitt couldn't care less about your opinion of him; Garth is here because Mr. Lippitt thinks highly of you and your facility. You're looking for enemies where there aren't any; they must have a term for that in psychiatry."

"*I* run this clinic, Frederickson, not Mr. Lippitt! This is a *medical* facility, and I have the final say here!"

"I've tried to be polite to you, Slycke," I said evenly, getting to my feet. "Obviously, simple professional courtesy and good manners aren't high on your list of priorities. I don't owe you explanations about anything, and I resent having to expend physical and emotional energy defending myself to you when my brother lies sick in bed here. I repeat; you have nothing to worry about from me, I'm not spying on you or anybody else, and my only concern is in seeing that my brother gets the best possible medical care. It's definitely not in Garth's or my interests to have you, or any other member of the staff here, distracted and looking over your shoulders because of me. So please stop doing it."

Slycke sprang to his feet, and his hands began to tremble. "Are you suggesting that personal considerations could cause me to provide anything less than the best possible care for a patient?!"

"I'm suggesting that you stop losing sleep over me and my ID badge, and I'm suggesting that you get off my back and get on with your business. Mr. Lippitt seems to think you're a pretty good psychiatrist, and I'll go along with his judgment. For now."

"For now?"

"Your hearing is no worse than mine."

"There really is no alternative care for your brother, Frederickson, considering the circumstances and cause of his condition."

"You say. If that's true, then we're stuck with each other, aren't we? I'm not about to stop visiting my brother just because you've got a problem with me."

Slycke dropped his gaze, absently patted his hair, sat back down again. "Look, Frederickson—"

"*You* look, Slycke. What you think of Mr. Lippitt and me is your business, but I take it as a serious personal insult for you to imply that I might use a desperately sick brother as an excuse to spy on you. Now, as far as the facility here is concerned, you *do* run it. I'm sorry I wandered somewhere you preferred I didn't go. From now on I will personally make it a point to notify you when I enter the building, and again when I leave; if you're not around, I'll leave a note taped to your door. In the meantime, I intend to proceed as if this conversation had never taken place. I will certainly try to stay out of your way, but I will also expect to be kept fully informed of any treatment prescribed for my brother, as well as his progress—or lack of it. That's my right as a close relative, not someone with a Z-13 badge. Good day."

Slycke started to say something, but I was in no mood to listen to any more of his nonsense; I wheeled and stalked out of the office, slamming the door behind me. I was definitely not pleased with the man in charge of Garth's medical treatment. I wanted to call Mr. Lippitt to complain, or at least ask him to try to assuage Slycke's anxieties, but knew I wouldn't. Slycke, I thought, was probably right; he and the D.I.A. clinic were probably the only game in town, and getting our ancient friend to intervene personally in this unexpected conflict might not only be construed as inappropriate, but could well prove counterproductive—after a phone call from Lippitt, Slycke's paranoia index would end up topping the charts. Charles Slycke was my problem. I would try solving it by doing as I had promised; I would stay out of his way, and hope that he focused his attention where it belonged, on finding wherever it was Garth's mind had gone, and returning it to him.

5.

I was highly agitated when I left Building 26, but on reflection I decided that Charles Slycke was probably no more paranoid than a lot of other high-ranking civil service bureaucrats, jealous of—and constantly feeling compelled to defend—their turf. In retrospect, I could see that Mr. Lippitt had probably used poor judgment in issuing me a high-powered Z-13 ID badge, but he had erred out of compassion, total trust, and friendship. There was just no way to describe to the overexcited head psychiatrist the nature of the strong bonds that existed between Lippitt, Garth, and me, a relationship that had begun many years before, in New York City, in connection with a bizarre case I was working on, and which had culminated in the horror and death of the Valhalla Project. In any case, I believed I had made my point with Slycke that I was going to be close by at all times, and expected to be consulted at all stages of Garth's treatment, whatever that treatment might be. Now I thought it might be a good idea to lie low for a while.

That meant I was going to have to find a way to keep myself occupied, off the streets and out of trouble, when I wasn't visiting Garth. To that end, I walked four blocks, turned left, walked down a hill and crossed a large field next to the reservoir to the locked entrance of the Rockland Children's Psychiatric Center, rang the bell.

If at first glance I seemed an unlikely candidate to work as a substitute teacher—a pesky and most trying endeavor in the best of schools with the mellowest of student bodies—in a psychiatric hospital where half the population was unpredictable and dangerous, the educational director, a pleasant and attractive but obviously tough woman by the name of Gladys Jacubowicz, didn't show it; she was simply delighted to find somebody—anybody—who was willing to work as a substitute in her school. I didn't mention my Z-13 badge, which I had put in my pocket; I did tell her I had a Ph.D. and had done a good deal of college teaching. I was hurriedly signed on. She personally took me on an orientation tour, and as she was unlocking the door to let me out asked somewhat tentatively if I could possibly come in the next day to substitute for a social studies teacher who was taking a day of personal leave. I said I would be delighted to come in.

"My name's Frederickson," I said to the seven high-school age students and one huge, black, stony-faced cottage worker who sat in wooden desks, staring at me.

"Who let you in here, shorty?"

I had arrived at the school ninety minutes early in order to familiarize myself with the teacher's class lists and lesson plans, check out the appropriate patient files, and read the "cottage sheet"—a record of disturbances and other incidents that had taken place in the cottages during the night which the teachers should be aware of. If information is a weapon, which it most decidedly is, I was loaded for bear.

The heavyset boy with the pockmarked face and hooded eyes who had spoken would be Dane Potter.

Dane Potter, now a few months shy of eighteen years of age, had, with his parents' consent, enlisted in the Marines at the age of sixteen as an alternative to being sent away to reform school. In the Marines he had gotten into drugs, finally fried his brains with angel dust, then gone over the edge—and the hill; he'd deserted, taking his semiautomatic rifle along with him. He'd paused in his travels long enough to hold up a service station, then tried to call his girl friend in order to tell her he was on the way home. He hadn't much liked it when he found out she was on a date with another boy, and he'd proceeded to shoot up the station. He'd been put into a Detention for Youth facility—"kiddie jail"—and then transferred to RCPC when, as his file phrased it, he had begun to display "bizarre behavior"; he'd tried to rape his social worker. He'd been diagnosed schizophrenic with a personality disorder—one of the most dangerous kinds of psychotics. For the past week he had been extremely prone to violence, in school and down in his cottage, and was now heavily medicated, with enough Thorazine in him to give a rhinoceros the staggers; his muddy brown eyes were glassy, saucer-wide beneath their heavy lids. Also, he had been placed on a "level one," which meant that he had to be accompanied at all times by a male staff member who could never be more than an arm's length away from him. The big man nestled in the desk next to the boy wasn't there to give me moral support, help me maintain class decorum, or help me with anything else; he was there for the sole purpose of pouncing on Dane Potter if the boy went berserk, to prevent him from hurting himself or others. As far as teaching was concerned, I was on my own.

It seemed it was time to try earning my spurs.

"I like to be called *Mr.* Shorty, Potter," I said evenly, thrusting my hands into my pockets and smiling at him. "Always be polite; courtesy costs nothing, and you never know when it will pay off."

"How the hell do you know who I am?"

"I'm psychic; that's why they let me in here."

"What did you do to your head? Somebody mistake you for a football?"

"My clipper slipped while I was cutting my toenails."

"Fuck you, shorty."

"Thank you very much, Dane. Fuck you, too."

That got a laugh out of the others in the class, which I was beginning to sense was on my side. However, the way I figured it, I was being paid to try to reach and teach all the kids who came into my classroom, not just the ones who didn't give me any trouble. Dane Potter had lobbed a few verbal darts at me, and found that I wasn't that easy a target to hit. Now he was really cranky. I knew hospital procedure, and knew that nobody was likely to play patty-cake with Dane Potter—least of all the burly cottage worker assigned to accompany him throughout the school day. If Potter exploded, which he now seemed very close to doing, he'd be perfunctorily taken down and dragged off to the crisis room—a small, windowless room not much bigger than a closet, where Potter would be restrained until he either calmed down or had to be given a shot and sent back to his cottage to sleep it off. All I had to do was goad him a bit more and he would be gone and out of my hair; but that wouldn't solve my long-range problem with him, assuming I was invited back, and it wouldn't make me feel very good to know I had taken the easy way out of a situation by manipulating a very sick kid. Something else was called for.

"Why the hell do they send us a dwarf teacher?!" a now very distraught Dane Potter shouted.

"Hey, Dane," I said quietly, casually moving across the room to lean against a radiator running beneath a bank of thick, Plexiglas windows, "maybe it's because I'm a crazy dwarf. I actually *want* to be here teaching you crazy kids. That must make me crazy, right?"

That got another round of appreciative laughter from the other six kids—and just the trace of a smile from the cottage worker.

"Right on, Frederickson," a pretty girl with ugly, puckered scars on her wrists called from the back of the room. "Come on, Dane, give the guy a break. He seems okay."

"Shut up, bitch, or I'll give *you* a break!" Dane Potter shouted at the girl who had spoken. His fists clenched and unclenched on top of his desk. "And I'll break this fucking dwarf if I ever get the chance!"

It was time to get Dane Potter's attention—and the attention of all the other Dane Potters I was certain to meet at the children's hospital. If I couldn't do that, I thought, I might as well quit; the somewhat less than refined teaching technique I planned to employ might well get me fired, but I didn't intend to quit.

"Dane, my good man," I said with a sigh, "let me tell you a little about myself—if you'll pardon the pun. I used to be a star performer—a tumbler of sorts—with the circus. I also happen to hold a black belt in karate. Not bad for a dwarf, huh?"

"You're full of shit, shorty."

I'd never been much into breaking bricks or boards, since the force I could generate was limited by my stature; the skills I'd parlayed into a black belt were based on quickness of movement and surprise; my moves were designed for self-defense, not showboating. Still, I understood the mechanics of force breaking, and what I wanted to do seemed worth a try.

"Let me show you some of my shit, Dane," I said, then abruptly turned around and did a back handspring in the narrow aisle between the desks and the blackboard. My second back handspring gave me additional height and momentum, and on the third I did a half twist in the air and came down with both feet precisely in the center of the top of the desk at which Dane Potter was sitting.

I was perfectly happy with my performance, which I hoped would impress Potter and calm him down, but as luck would have it I landed perfectly, with maximum force at a critical point; there was a sharp crack, and the desk split very nicely down the center, with me landing on my feet between the halves, inches away from the boy's ashen, open-mouthed face.

"Damn, I missed that last flip," I said as I stepped back to the blackboard. "Sorry about your desk, Dane. I must be out of practice."

Dane Potter's eyes went even wider, and he jumped sideways, virtually into the arms of the big cottage worker. The other students stared at me in shock for a few moments, then began to whoop and applaud. Even the cottage worker began to laugh as he slapped—none too gently—his charge on the back.

"What do you say, Dane?" I continued, stepping up to him and holding out my hand. "How about letting me try to teach you guys something in the twenty minutes we've got left?"

Potter didn't shake my hand—but he remained silent and still, which was fine with me. I spent the rest of the period talking about my years with the Statler Brothers Circus, and the time I had talked a hairy friend of mine—a three-hundred-pound Bengal tiger—back into his cage after he'd escaped.

Word that there was indeed a crazy dwarf in the building who could do super back handsprings and break desks spread almost instantly through the small student population, and my next class—suicidal elementary age children—entered the room, accompanied by a teacher aide, very tentatively, eyes wide. By special request, I did one back handspring, performed a few simple coin tricks I'd picked up from a stockbroker friend of mine whose hobby was performing as a mime in Washington Square Park on weekends, then settled the four children down to what I thought was a pretty fair lesson on American Indians of the northeast. I rewarded them for their good behavior and attentiveness with another back handspring, this one with a half twist. Afterward, the teacher aide told me she'd never seen them quieter or more attentive.

Veil was right, I thought; teaching at RCPC certainly wasn't like lecturing or giving seminars at the university. In many ways, this was more rewarding. A reasonably bright, motivated university student will learn what he or she has to learn, and most good students will learn *despite* what bad teachers may do to them. Not these kids. Working with emotionally disturbed kids—or any handicapped kids, for that matter—an individual teacher could have an enormous impact. The singer, not the song; that was what I was learning on my first day at RCPC. I was having a good time, and it helped to keep my mind off Garth and my troubles with Slycke.

Four more classes, eight back handsprings, one lunch and one work period later I was finished for the day. By that time I figured I had met—or at least glimpsed—just about every one of the sixty-five students in the school; those who weren't in any of my classes had popped their heads in the doorway to check me out. As I walked through the halls at the end of the day, kids on their way back to their cottages in the opposite end of the building called out to me, and a couple of the little ones jumped into my arms.

It seemed I wasn't to be fired because of my rather unorthodox teaching technique, or even billed for the desk I had broken. A number of the teachers insisted I stick around for coffee and talk, and on the way out Gladys Jacubowicz asked if I would come back the next day to substitute for the science teacher, who wasn't feeling well and would undoubtedly be out. I said I'd be there.

From the children's hospital I went back across the field and up the hill to the main complex, and Building 26. I went directly to Slycke's office to let him know I was there, then went to Garth's room.

Garth was the same—except that he had been rolled onto his other side, and the smell of lotion told me that Tommy Carling had been in recently to rub him down and massage his muscles again. Garth's eyes were still open, but glassy and unseeing. I'd asked Slycke if any decision had been made about medicating Garth, and the man had replied curtly that they were still in the process of observation and evaluation. I'd bitten off a sharp retort, realizing that I was being impatient.

I spent the next two hours pacing around Garth's bed and talking to him, chatting about anything and everything that came into my head. I told my brother all about my first day teaching at the children's hospital, and how exhilarating it had been for me.

Through it all, Garth, with the tubes up his nose and the needles in his arms, lay as still as a corpse, totally unresponsive. When I had talked myself out, I simply sat on the side of the bed and held his hand.

Tommy Carling came in around six o'clock, bringing me a tray of food and a small thermos filled with hot coffee. He was off duty and on his way home, but Slycke had authorized him to tell me that in two or three days Garth might be put on small doses of Halidol, an antipsychotic drug of choice for catatonics, along with other drugs he would be given to counteract some of the nastier side effects of Halidol. The chemotherapy was fine with me; as far as I was concerned, nothing could be worse than Garth's present vegetative state.

Thoroughly depressed by now, the exhilaration I had experienced during the day completely drained from me, I sat with Garth until a little after ten, then went back to my apartment in Building 18. I downed two stiff drinks, then went to bed and slept fitfully.

6.

I got up early to clean my wound, which was healing nicely, and put on a fresh bandage. Once again I arrived at the children's hospital ninety minutes early in order to check my class lists against patient records, and review the teacher's lesson plans.

The cottage sheets were interesting. Two older adolescent boys had been up most of the night arguing—and finally exchanging blows—over the question of which one was really Jesus. A cottage worker had found a young girl sitting on the edge of her bed and talking in the darkness to Satan and two lesser demons. The worker reported that the girl had gone back to bed and slept peacefully after being given some crackers and a glass of milk; the report didn't say whether the girl had shared.

The files indicated that one of the older adolescent girls in my third period class, Kim Trainor, was extremely bright and gregarious, but suicidal. As a baby, Kim had been in her grandmother's arms when the lady died; three years later, both Kim's parents had died; four years later, her aunt and uncle, who had taken Kim in, had been killed in an automobile accident. Kim had grown up with the people she loved all dying around her, dropping like flies, and she blamed herself. On an intellectual level, Kim claimed to understand that the deaths were not her fault, but on a much deeper emotional level she considered herself a pariah, a bringer of death, who did not deserve to live. The staff psychiatrists considered her prognosis good.

During the day I had a talk with Chris Yardley, a schizophrenic whose prognosis was not so good, one of the boys who'd been arguing over who was Jesus. I suggested to Chris that it was all right to *think* he was Jesus, and positively commendable to *behave* like Jesus, but that he had to learn to function on the outside, to work at a steady job and support himself; I suggested to Chris that if he wanted to get out of the mental hospital he had to stop *telling* people he was Jesus. Then he would be left alone, and he could go about normal business. Chris indicated that he could see my point, but that God had commanded him to tell people he was Jesus.

So much for the sly intellectual approach with psychotics.

* * *

My classes all went well. I'd apparently made a lasting impression the day before, and the kids were eager to come to my class. I kept them entertained with jokes, and I was presumptuous enough to think I might even have taught something to a few of them.

Dane Potter wasn't in any of my classes, but I saw him in the hall and he waved. He was walking alone, which meant he had been taken off his level. I was pleased.

I got through to the end of my second day in the school at the children's hospital without having to do a single back handspring.

After school I took a bus to a large shopping mall in the nearby town of Nanuet, where there was a Music World outlet which I hoped would have what I wanted. They did. I purchased the boxed set of tapes, a hefty supply of AA batteries, and a Sony Walkman. I also picked up a roomy shoulder bag from a leather goods store, then headed back to the hospital.

In a day or two, Garth would be put on psychotropic drugs; before that happened, before whatever perceptions he might still enjoy in his silent world were altered, there was something I wanted to try. I had a few therapeutic notions of my own.

Toward the end of the insane nightmare that had been the Valhalla Project, Garth and I had been captured by Siegmund Loge and imprisoned in a vast underground complex in Greenland. There, for his own twisted reasons, Loge had attempted to explain and justify to us why he'd done what he had done—acts that had caused the deaths of many innocent people, the murders of my teenage nephew and a friend of his. The vehicle for this "explanation" had been a kind of bizarre sound and light show which he had spent most of his life putting together, an epic, sixteen-hour-long film comprised of cascading images—photographs, paintings, movie stills, sketches—depicting humankind's apparently intractable stupidity and cruelty unto itself, from prehistoric times to the present. These horrifying images, hundreds of thousands of them, had been masterfully edited to correspond to the rhythms and melodies of Richard Wagner's titanic master-piece, *Der Ring des Nibelungen: Das Rheingold, Die Walküre, Siegfried,* and *Götterdämmerung.* The images had been car-ried to the depths of our souls and branded there by the music; it was an experience neither of us would ever forget, as much as we might want to.

It was hard for me to imagine how Garth's mind could be damaged more than it already was, and Tommy Carling had said there was no way of knowing what Garth heard or didn't hear. If there was a sound he would respond to, anything at all that could reach into the dark silence in his mind and touch some part of him that was undamaged and could fight back, it was *Der Ring des Nibelungen.*

The four operas making up Wagner's *Ring* cycle comprised a pretty bulky package of tapes, which was why I had pur-chased the shoulder bag; I didn't care to get into explanations of my idea of music therapy. I put the tapes, the Walkman, and the batteries into the bag, covered them with books and magazines in case anyone was inquisitive, then went over to the D.I.A. clinic. Slycke was off duty, but I reported my presence to the indifferent psychiatrist in charge before going to Garth's room. Tommy Carling was there, checking Garth's pulse and other vital signs. I chatted with the ponytailed male nurse until he had finished.

Five minutes after Carling had left I glanced out into the corridor, saw no one. I took the Walkman out of the bag, put the player next to Garth's shoulder, under the sheet. I placed the earphones on his head, the connecting metal band behind his neck so that only the tiny earplugs showed. I snapped Act I of *Das Rheingold* into the cassette player, reached over to turn it on—and hesitated as I felt a chill, a distinct sense of foreboding, run through me. I took the phones out of his ears and took a few minutes to talk at his vacant face, explaining what it was I was going to do, and why. Then I replaced the earplugs, took a deep breath, and turned on the player. Very faintly, I could hear the long, E-flat passage that opened the epic cycle flowing through the plugs into Garth's ears, perhaps his mind and soul.

"He looks different."

I had been so intent on peering into Garth's face, looking for some response, that I hadn't heard Tommy Carling come into the room. Startled, I jumped, then turned to my left to find the male nurse standing at the foot of the bed. I wondered how long he had been there.

"Uh . . . hi, Tommy."

"Hi, Mongo," Carling replied somewhat absently. He had crossed his arms over his chest and seemed to be studying Garth intently.

"What did you say?"

"I said that Garth looks a bit different to me. I actually think there's more expressiveness in his face."

Garth didn't look any different to me, and I said so.

The male nurse absently tugged at his earring, said: "Maybe it's my imagination, but his eyes don't seem quite so vacant." He paused, shrugged his broad shoulders. "Then again, maybe I'm just seeing what I want to see. Well, it's time to change his colostomy and urine bag."

"Tommy . . . ?"

Carling paused on his way to the other side of the bed, looked at me quizzically. "What is it, Mongo?"

"Nothing," I said, and shook my head.

Carling pulled back the sheet, immediately saw the Walkman and the earphones on Garth's head. He looked at me again, raised his eyebrows slightly. "What are you playing for him?"

"I've got *Das Rheingold* in now. You might say Garth has a thing for the *Ring*."

"Really?" Carling said, and pursed his lips slightly. "Pretty heavy stuff."

"Oh, yeah. I remembered that you turned the radio on for him, and I figured . . . well, I thought it couldn't hurt to play something for him that I know he, uh . . . likes. The music has a lot of personal associations for him."

"Does it really?" Carling said in a curiously flat, distant voice. He studied me for a few moments, then looked back into Garth's face. The man seemed momentarily lost in thought.

"Here," I said, reaching for the earphones, "let me get those out of your way."

"No," Carling said quickly, blocking my outstretched hand. "It's all right; nothing's in my way."

Carling removed and emptied Garth's colostomy and urine bags, replaced them with new ones. He again checked my brother's pulse, recorded liquid intake and outtake levels on a chart hanging from a cord attached to the foot of Garth's bed. He continued to appear deep in thought, and he frequently looked back into Garth's face. I still couldn't see any change in Garth's eyes or expression—but the trained eyes of Tommy Carling apparently did. My heart began to beat a little faster, and I could feel the muscles in my stomach tighten.

"So," Carling said at last as he let the chart drop on its cord and replaced his pen in the pocket of his white coat, "how are all the little LITs down at the children's hospital?"

"LITs?"

"Loonies-in-training."

"Oh," I said, and smiled. "They're loony, all right, and some of them aren't so little. How did you know I'd been down there?"

"I'm friendly with a couple of the cottage workers there. We were having a beer last night, and they mentioned this superdwarf who had come in to substitute. How many superdwarfs can there be wandering around here? You made quite an impression—on kids and staff."

"It's the natural ham in me," I said, and suddenly felt sad. It was the kind of thing my brother would say.

"You've got some very dangerous kids over there, Mongo," Carling said seriously.

"Yeah, but you've also got some very pleasant and bright ones—a lot of the suicidals are like that. I really enjoy working there, Tommy."

"A little different from college teaching, huh?"

"To say the least."

Being careful not to disturb the tape player or the earphones on my brother's head, Tommy Carling rolled Garth over on his right side, facing away from me. "Are you hungry, Mongo? I can bring you something to eat."

"No, thanks," I replied. The male nurse headed for the door. I cleared my throat, said, "Tommy?"

Carling paused in the doorway, turned back. "Yes, Mongo?"

"The music. Do you think I could be harming Garth in any way by playing it for him?"

Carling laughed good-naturedly. "There are some people who'd claim that listening to Richard Wagner would damage anybody's brain." He paused, continued seriously: "No. On the contrary; if I'm right about there being a bit more life in his eyes, it's probably good for him. What harm could music do?"

"In that case . . . I didn't ask anybody about this, and maybe I should have. If there's any possibility that Garth really is getting something out of the music, I'd hate to see it taken away from him just because I didn't ask permission and somebody's nose got out of joint."

Tommy Carling smiled easily. "I won't mention it to Slycke, Mongo. Don't worry about it." He gave me a thumbs-up sign and walked from the room.

I wanted to play the entire *Ring* cycle through, opera by opera, with as few interruptions during the course of each opera as possible, and nights seemed the best time to do this. The next day I stopped by the clinic early in the morning, before my third straight day of substituting, and sat and talked with Tommy Carling while he shaved and bathed my brother. I stopped by again after school, then left just before six.

I ate dinner in a pleasant Italian restaurant in nearby Orangeburg, then went back to the apartment, set my alarm clock to wake me at midnight, and went to bed. At midnight I rose, made myself some coffee and shaved, then packed the Walkman and tapes of *Die Walküre* into my leather shoulder bag, headed over to Building 26.

It seemed there was no guard in the kiosk outside the building at night, and I used my own keys to gain entry to the building, took the elevator up to the fourteenth floor. Three male nurses I hadn't seen before were standing and talking in the vestibule in front of the elevator, and they seemed startled when the elevator door sighed open and I stepped out. However, after one glance at the ID badge clipped to my shirt pocket, they resumed their conversation.

I couldn't find any psychiatrist around, so I signed my name on a piece of paper I got from one of the nurses, slipped it under Slycke's door. I didn't note the time.

I found Garth rolled over on his left side, staring—as always—at nothing. I covered his face with a towel to protect his eyes, then quietly closed the door and turned on the lights. I uncovered his face, put on the earphones, then loaded the cassette player with the first tape and turned it on. Then I sat down with a magazine to wait through the three hours of *Die Walküre*.

Siegfried.

The next night I checked the chart at the foot of Garth's bed; there was no indication that chemotherapy had begun. I put the earphones on Garth's head, snapped the first tape of the third opera in the *Ring* cycle into the cassette player, turned it on.

I'd brought a book with me to read, but I must have nodded off; when I woke up, the book was on the floor by my feet and I had the urgent, distressing feeling that something was wrong—no, not wrong; but different. Strange. I quickly got up, looked around the room; there was no one there, and the door was still closed. Garth, of course, hadn't moved; he was still in the same position, turned away from me on his side, with earphone and half his face hidden by the sheet. I yawned, stretched, glanced at my watch; it was almost time to put in the next cassette. I took the second tape out of my bag, walked around to the other side of the bed— and almost cried out.

Tears were streaming from Garth's eyes, dripping from his face, soaking the sheet beneath him.

"Garth!"

My brother's bloodshot eyes rolled, then came into focus on my face.

"Garth?!" I cried, snatching the earphones from his head. "Are you all right?! Can you hear me?! Can you talk?!"

The fact that he could indeed hear and understand me was now clearly reflected in Garth's eyes—but that was all. He still couldn't—or wasn't prepared to—talk.

But he was coming back, I thought, slowly riding wave after sonic wave of the most profoundly moving music ever written, dripping tears as evidence of his long, tortuous passage. I would settle for that, not be impatient.

After gently trying and failing for close to twenty minutes to elicit some response in addition to his tears, I put the earphones back on his head, changed the cassette, turned on the Walkman. I sat on the edge of the bed, holding his hand and smiling down into his tear-streaked face, until the opera was finished. I packed up the tapes and the Walkman, hugged and kissed my brother, then went back to Building 18 and contentedly went to bed. I was confident that I would see some change in Garth in the morning.

*   *   *

I was wrong, and bitterly disappointed.

At eight o'clock, it was impossible to tell that Garth was the same man I had seen copiously weeping only a few hours before; his eyes were once again glassy and vacant, and the only change was that he seemed even paler than usual. I debated whether I should tell Slycke, or Tommy Carling, about what had happened during the night, decided not to. It would have meant trying to explain why the *Ring*—and only the *Ring*—could elicit such a response from Garth, and I was not yet prepared to do that, at least not until the complete cycle of four operas was finished.

Despite Garth's present unresponsiveness, I had seen unmistakable evidence that the music of the *Ring*—combined with the images of horror and unrelenting cruelty that he and I would always associate with it—was a bridge that had reached across the unfathomable void in his mind and touched his consciousness. Now that bridge had to be maintained—and expanded. Now, more than anything, I was afraid of being second-guessed and interfered with. Charles Slycke might be a fine psychiatrist, if not so fine a person, and the D.I.A. facility might be a fine psychiatric clinic, but *Der Ring des Nibelungen* evoked a realm of consciousness shared by only Garth and me in a way no one else would ever be able to understand. I had now taken Garth back three-quarters of the way through that realm, and I felt I had no choice but to take him the rest of the way. Whatever happened at the end of the journey, if anything, would be my responsibility.

Götterdämmerung.

As the lush, revolutionary music of the final opera in the *Ring* cycle flowed through the earphones into Garth's brain and mind, he again began to weep. After a few minutes I realized that I, too, had begun crying. I brushed his wet cheek, then rose from the edge of the bed and walked to the Plexiglas window. I stood looking out over the moonlit grounds of the Rockland Psychiatric Center, remembering the horror . . .

"What are you doing?!"

I wheeled around, and was thoroughly startled to see Charles Slycke standing over my silently weeping brother and glaring at me. He abruptly snatched the earphones off Garth's head, ripped off the sheet covering him, and grabbed the Walkman. The psychiatrist's unruly gray hair stuck up from his head as if an electric current were running through him, and his rheumy eyes glinted with rage. I started to say something, but the man was obviously in no mood to listen to any explanations, even if he had requested them.

"What are you doing here?!"

"Just a minute, Doctor. I've signed in every time—"

"Signed in?! That didn't tell me you were here in the *middle of the night!* That was left for somebody else to tell me!" Slycke's moon face was almost crimson as he marched around the bed, marched up to me, and shook the Walkman in my face. *"Now* I see what you've been up to! What on *earth* do you think you've been doing?!"

"I think I've been playing some music for my brother," I replied evenly, stepping away from Slycke so that I could see Garth. "In case you haven't noticed, Garth is responding."

"The man is crying!"

"So what? Aren't signs of sorrow better than the vacuum that was there before?"

"That's not for you to say!"

"It's for anybody to say!"

"You're not a doctor!"

"And my brother isn't a Goddamn turnip!" I paused, took a deep breath, lowered my voice. "The tears show that Garth's mind is still there; it hasn't been burned out of him. Whatever door it's locked behind has been opened, even if just a little bit, by the music. I'd think you'd be pleased."

"What you've done is unauthorized! How do you know what effect that music has had on him?"

"We can both see the effect; he's awake, and he's aware."

"You had no right to do something like this! He is my patient!"

"He's my brother, and I've done absolutely nothing but play some music for him. Instead of standing around and screaming at me, why don't you consider the implications of the fact that the music elicited a response?"

"Just because you're a friend of Lippitt's doesn't give you the right to do something like this without my permission! This is *my* clinic, and in medical matters I have supreme authority! I'll have your pass *removed,* Frederickson!"

Garth settled the argument when he suddenly sat up in bed. Slycke and I stared, dumbfounded, as my brother swung his legs over the side of the bed and stood up. He swayed for a few moments, supporting himself with one hand on the edge of the bed, finally steadied himself. Then, without really looking at either Slycke or me, he walked forward, almost casually pried the Walkman from Slycke's stiff fingers, turned around, walked back to the bed, and got in. He put the earphones on his head, turned on the player, lay down on his back, and pulled the sheet up to his chin.

I let out a whoop of joy and excitement that must have been earsplitting, because it brought the three male nurses into the room on the run. They stopped just inside the doorway when they saw Slycke and me, exchanged puzzled looks.

Garth was going to be all right, I thought, elation welling up in me and overflowing as tears as I stared at my brother. I let out another whoop, even louder than the first, just for good measure, then did a little hopping dance of celebration. I picked up my shoulder bag, which contained the rest of the tapes and an ample supply of batteries, triumphantly set it down on Garth's stomach.

"Batteries for the Walkman and the rest of the tapes are in here, brother," I said.

I waited, my breathing shallow. Slowly, Garth's hands came out from under the sheet, wrapped themselves around the bag. I wheeled around to face Slycke, who was continuing to stare at Garth with an expression of disbelief.

"You want the tapes and the player, Doctor," I continued, unable to wipe a very large grin off my face, "you take them away from him."

"*Frederickson—?!*"

"Keep up the good work, Doctor," I said, skipping around the three stupefied male nurses and heading for the door. "I'll see you all later."

7.

AT seven fifteen I found Garth sitting up in bed eating breakfast off a tray by himself. He was wearing his earphones, and the Walkman was on the pillow just behind him; the leather bag was sitting at the foot of the bed. Tommy Carling was leaning against the wall, ankles and arms crossed, looking bemused.

"Yo, brother!" I shouted, running up to the side of the bed and pounding Garth's shoulder. "Welcome back to the land of the living!"

There was no response; Garth simply waited until I had stopped thumping his shoulder, then resumed eating his scrambled eggs. I leaned over the bed, waved my hand in his face. "Hey, Garth," I continued with just slightly less spirit, "it's me—your favorite only brother. Remember me? How about a little 'hello,' just for old times' sake?"

My brother stopped chewing, looked at me. His eyes were clearly in focus on my face, but it was as if he didn't recognize me—or simply didn't care. He studied me without interest for a few moments, then once again resumed eating. Chewing slowly and methodically, he finished his eggs, swallowed some coffee, patted his mouth with a paper napkin, lay back in bed. Bewildered and not a little hurt, I looked inquiringly at Tommy Carling.

"What can I tell you?" the burly male nurse said with a shrug. "What you see is what you get. I can understand how you might be a little disappointed at his lack of response, but you'll have to admit that the overnight change is absolutely remarkable. Garth just isn't ready to talk yet; it's what we call VMS—'Voluntary Muteness Syndrome.' We see it quite often in certain kinds of patients. But the improvement is incredible. I think I'll suggest that we pipe Wagner into the rest of the clinic so all the patients can listen to it."

"Garth?" I said in a voice that had suddenly grown hoarse. I found myself wanting to reach out and take the earphones off his head, demand that he acknowledge my presence, but knew that probably wasn't such a good idea. "Can you speak? *Will* you speak?"

Garth's eyes momentarily darted to my face, but then he went back to staring at the ceiling as he listened to the music. I peered in the plastic window of the Walkman, saw that Act One of *Das Rheingold* was playing; he was beginning the cycle of operas all over again.

"How long has he been like this?" I asked Carling.

"Since sometime after five this morning. I came on duty at six, and the night guys told me about what had happened earlier between you and Dr. Slycke. When they'd checked Garth an hour earlier, he'd been like you'd left him—lying on his back and clutching that bag. I came here first, and I found him sitting up in bed with his earphones on. He'd removed the tube from his nose and the needles from his arms, which I took as a not so subtle sign that he was ready for some solid food and wanted to feed himself. You saw how he handled breakfast—and that was his third helping of eggs. If he keeps this up for another day or two, I'm sure they'll remove the colostomy tube and sew him up."

"Does Slycke know?"

"He left about a half hour after you did. He's supposed to attend a symposium in New York today, but I called him right after I found Garth sitting up. He should be here any minute."

"Garth obviously knows what's going on," I said tersely, looking directly—perhaps a bit defiantly—at my brother. The hurt I'd felt was now melting into a sourish sense of betrayal; I knew I was losing sight of the proverbial big picture, and was ashamed of myself for my feelings. I'd found more than a bit of Charles Slycke in myself, and I didn't much like it. "Why won't he talk?"

Carling shook his head. "That's not a useful question at this point. We don't really know whether he won't talk, can't talk, or doesn't comprehend nearly as much as we think he does at the moment. I tried to get him to communicate by blinking his eyes, but I didn't get anywhere. He didn't *ask* me for solid food; I brought it to him, and he ate it. Right now, all we know for certain is that he can move, he can feed himself, and that he constantly listens to the tapes you brought him. Don't assume anything more. Remember that your brother was poisoned with a substance having properties we know virtually nothing about when it is ingested. Garth is obviously better, but he's a long way from being well."

"I understand that, but—"

"You may not understand it as well as you think you do," Tommy Carling interrupted gently. "Understandably, you're also dealing with a lot of emotion. Everything we know about the short- and long-term effects from this drug we're learning now, minute by minute and day by day, as we observe Garth. His EEG has never shown any signs of brain damage, so now we may be looking at just another stage of a chemically induced psychosis. It's quite possible he would have come out of his catatonic state—perhaps last night—even *without* the music. We can't be certain one way or the other. We can't be certain he recognizes us, understands anything we're saying, or even *hears* the same thing we'd hear if we were listening to the tapes.''

"He hears the same thing," I said, looking hard at Garth. Saw the same images, had the same associations.

Carling shrugged again. "You can never be sure what's going on in the mind of a psychotic, and Garth is still psychotic. Incidentally, I heard that Dr. Slycke was really upset when he found you here last night."

"Oh, yeah. And then some."

The first side of the tape had run out. Garth sat up, unhurriedly flipped the cassette, turned the player back on. Then he lay back, put his hands behind his head, and resumed his careful scrutiny of the square meter of ceiling directly above him. He didn't appear to me to be psychotic or disoriented, but like a man who was simply very, very deep in thought. Try as hard as I might, I couldn't shake my feelings of hurt and betrayal. Garth, I thought, was just being Goddamn . . . *rude*.

"You're taking Garth's behavior much too personally, Mongo," Tommy Carling said, as if he had been reading my thoughts. "You can't do that. Your brother is still a very sick man, perhaps just as sick as when he was catatonic; catatonia is just one symptom of psychosis, not the psychosis itself."

"Garth can speak," my brother said evenly.

The words, delivered as they were in a casual, matter-of-fact tone as he continued to stare at the ceiling, startled both Carling and me, and I found his speech almost as chilling as his previous muteness.

"Garth?" I said tentatively, leaning over him. There was no response, and my brother didn't even look at me. I could hear the Magic Fire Music motif leaking from the earphones. "Garth, talk to me, for Christ's sake. What are you feeling? Do you know who I am?"

I waited; although Garth's eyes were clear and in focus, he

didn't look away from the ceiling. I felt Carling's hand gently touch my shoulder.

"You have to be patient, Mongo."

Suddenly the pale blue telephone mounted on the wall next to the door rang. Carling answered, listened for a few moments; he mentioned my name and the fact that I was there, listened some more, then hung up.

"Dr. Slycke is waiting in the infirmary with an internist and a neurologist," the nurse said to me quietly. "He wants me to bring Garth there now; he's got a battery of tests lined up. They'll probably take all day." He paused, sighed softly, dropped his gaze. "He doesn't want you there, Mongo. That's a medical decision—his right to make. I'm sorry I can't invite you to come along."

I grimaced with frustration and irritation, kept my anger to myself. "It's all right; I'm scheduled to teach today, anyway. As I keep saying, I'm not interested in telling Slycke his business, or getting in his way. I'm just sorry this whole thing has become so confrontational."

"He's suspicious of you; he doesn't care much for the Director of the D.I.A., and he thinks the man may be out to get him by sending you here as a spy—notwithstanding the fact, of course, that Garth is here legitimately."

"So Slycke told me."

"Anything to it, Mongo?" he asked in a disarmingly casual tone of voice.

"You've got to be kidding me, Tommy."

"There's word on the grapevine that you, Garth, and the Director are old friends who go back a long way together."

"I haven't even been in touch with Mr. Lippitt since I got here."

"It's all wrong," Garth said to the ceiling. Once again, tears were streaming from his eyes.

"Garth?" I said, again leaning over him. "What's all wrong?"

There was no reply; but then, I knew the answer.

"Garth," Tommy Carling said as he walked around to the other side of the bed, "we have to take you to the infirmary so the doctors can run some tests on you. Can you walk there, or would you prefer that I get a wheelchair?"

Garth gave no indication that he had heard. Carling started toward the telephone, then stopped and turned back when Garth abruptly sat up and got out of bed. He picked up the leather bag filled with tapes and batteries, walked the length of the room and stood waiting by the door. Carling took slippers and a woolen robe from a wardrobe in the corner, slipped the robe over Garth's shoulders. My brother put his feet into the slippers.

"Why don't we leave the tapes and the player here?" Carling continued quietly as he gently slipped the earphones from my brother's head and took the Walkman from his hand. "You won't need them where you're going, and they'll probably get in the doctors' way. I'll hang on to everything myself, so you know they'll be here when you get back."

Garth didn't seem to think much of the idea; he turned, took back the Walkman, put the earphones on his head and the player in the pocket of his robe. I almost smiled.

Carling looked at me, shrugged. "He'll be back around dinnertime, Mongo—six, probably seven at the very latest. You want me to order you up a tray?"

"Order me up some time with Dr. Slycke, Tommy," I said, staring at Garth's back. "At his convenience, when all the tests are done."

"I'll tell him—and I will order you a tray. It's roast beef tonight, and it'll be good."

"See you later, Garth," I said loudly.

Garth did not reply. Carling put his hand on my brother's arm, and without any further prompting Garth walked from the room.

The big news on the cottage sheets was that Dane Potter had somehow escaped from the locked facility during the night.

Having a psychotic, potentially murderous teenager on the loose in the county wasn't anyone's idea of a happy event; the local police had been notified; and a search was in progress. RCPC wasn't exactly Folsom prison, and kids sometimes ran away—but usually when they were outside on the grounds. Potter wasn't allowed outside, and no one was sure how he had managed to get away. There was some speculation that the boy had stolen a staff member's keys, or that a door had inadvertently been left unlocked. Whatever had happened, Dane Potter was long gone.

Tense and anxious, wondering if I had done the right thing in exposing Garth to the *Ring* with all of its attendant emotional shocks and associations, I didn't have a particularly good day at the school. I was moody and snappish, and probably hurt the feelings of a number of kids who'd come to look for fun and games from me in addition to their lessons. It wasn't a performance that would win me a nomination for Mental Health Worker of the Year, and I tried to make amends by staying after school and going back to visit with some of the children in their cottages on the two floors at the rear of the building. I talked with Kim Trainor, Chris Yardley, and a few other older adolescents who were walking by the reservoir, and then played checkers with an eight-year-old boy by the name of Steven Wallis.

Steven, with his doe eyes and dark, silky hair, was a beautiful child who, for some years, had been the object of sexual abuse by both his father and his uncle. He had managed to tolerate the abuse until he entered the third grade, when his marks had begun to fall precipitously. A bright boy, Steven had been able to function in his nightmare world at home because of his success in school, and with failure had come a complete loss of self-esteem and desire to live. He had tried to kill himself by drinking close to a quart of gasoline.

Garth hadn't been too far off the mark when he'd said it was all wrong.

*   *   *

It wasn't quite four thirty when I left the children's hospital;
not feeling like hanging around Garth's room until he was
brought back, I headed for my apartment. Still anxious and
agitated, I was pleasantly surprised to find Veil waiting for
me outside the staff building. The yellow-haired man with
the glacial blue eyes was dressed in jeans and a T-shirt, and
he was lounging on a bench set on the grass a few feet back
from the sidewalk. He saw me coming down the street, stood
up and waved with his good arm.

"Hello, my friend," Veil said as I came up to him. "I
figured it was time to get out into the country for some fresh
air, so I rented a car, and here I am."

"Hi, Veil," I said, gripping his hand. "Hey, I'm sorry I
haven't been in touch."

"Don't be ridiculous. You've got a few things on your
mind."

"How's the arm?"

"The cast comes off next week." Veil's smile vanished.
"How's Garth?"

"You want a drink or something, Veil?"

"Not really."

"Neither do I," I said, and we sat down together on the
bench. I brought Veil up to date on everything that had
happened, shared my misgivings about Slycke's behavior—
and my own.

Veil was silent for some time when I had finished, staring
out over the grounds where patients and staff members were
walking in groups of two and three. "This is the first time
I've been back here," he said at last. "It's been more than
twenty years since I was committed. The place hasn't changed
much—except, of course, for the fact that we didn't have a
children's hospital then, and we were housed in these buildings with the adults." He paused, pointed down the street. "I
was in Building 11—just around the corner from the firehouse."

"God, you must feel spooky sitting here."

"Yes and no," Veil replied easily. "It's like something that happened to a different person, in a different world." He paused, looked at me. "My point is that I have a lot more experience being certifiably crazy than you do. I hear you loud and clear when you say you're worried about Garth. Of course you are. But you can't press. That nurse is right when he tells you that you really have no idea what's going on inside Garth's head. It sounds to me like something close to a miracle has happened virtually overnight, and you're bitching about it. Think of where Garth has been."

"I know where he's been, and I know I'm probably being childish and ungrateful. But to have Garth simply *ignore* me now that he's up and around is upsetting."

"Are you sure he recognizes you?"

"No . . . I'm not sure. But I *think* he recognizes me, and he just doesn't seem to give a damn. His responses are totally *flat*, if you know what I mean."

Veil nodded thoughtfully, then pointed to my forehead. "How's the cut?"

"Clean as a whistle. You do good work."

Veil reached out and gently peeled back the small bandage, grunted. "You should have listened to me and gone to see a plastic surgeon, Mongo. You're going to have a pretty nasty scar there."

"Veil, I really don't give a shit."

"Anyway, the wound seems to have healed. I think you can have the stitches taken out now."

"Can you do it? You'll save me the trouble of waiting around some doctor's office for two hours for five minutes' work."

Veil shrugged. "Hell, I put them in, so I may as well take them out."

I found a pair of small scissors in a drawer in the kitchen. Veil sterilized them with boiling water, sat me down over by a window, then proceeded to remove the stitches from the wound in my forehead.

"By the way," Veil said, "it looks like we won't have to wait around for Garth to tell us who poisoned him—assuming he knows."

I reached up, pushed Veil's hand away from my forehead. "Did you . . . ?"

"I didn't do anything."

"But the police have caught him?"

Veil shook his head. "Not him; them. Two men. The police don't even know about it yet, although they probably will by this evening. Chances are very good that they're K.G.B. They'd managed to infiltrate the manufacturing section of Prolix."

"How do you know all this?"

"Mr. Lippitt called earlier this afternoon to tell me. I was planning on coming up here anyway, so I said I'd tell you."

"Why the hell didn't Lippitt call me?"

"He said he tried to reach you a number of times, but you were never around. He also called your answering service in the city, but it seems you don't bother checking in with them anymore. He knew you'd be spending a lot of time up in the clinic, but for some reason he preferred not to call you there; he said it might make someone nervous."

I thought about it, nodded. It seemed Mr. Lippitt wasn't quite as oblivious to Charles Slycke's sensibilities as I'd thought. "He's right. I should have touched base with him, or made it easier for him to get hold of me."

"No problem. He wanted you to have the information as soon as possible, and now you've got it. Before I leave, it might be a good idea to set up some kind of system to make it easier for Lippitt or me to get in touch with you if we need to."

"Agreed. You say the police don't even know about these guys yet. Then how . . . ?"

"They took off; in effect, they fingered themselves. They

must have been feeling the heat, and got a bad case of nerves.

"Lippitt told me that the D.I.A. had been working on the case overtime—but keeping a low profile, because they didn't want what's happened to happen. There were a dozen people under surveillance; yesterday morning, two of those people failed to show up for work. The surveillance people let themselves into the men's apartments, found them both cleaned out. Both guys had split during the night without being spotted. But they were in such a big hurry that they left some tracks, and those tracks appear to lead out of the country, probably to Russia. Mr. Lippitt is pissed."

"The hurry and the sloppiness sounds very un-K.G.B.-ish."

"Agreed."

"Maybe they were just amateurs selling information to another company."

"Mr. Lippitt thinks not. I don't know what the evidence is, but he seems certain they were K.G.B."

I thought about it, frowned. "You say they may have been feeling the heat, but they were only two of a dozen people under surveillance. From what I understand, the K.G.B. is usually pretty good at making clean, orderly retreats. Why would they have suddenly panicked and taken off like that?"

"Mr. Lippitt has a rather interesting theory on that subject."

"Which is?"

"Think about it. What's been happening the past couple of days?"

"For Christ's sake, Veil, I haven't exactly been keeping up on current events."

Veil's response was to go back to work on my forehead. When he had removed the last stitch and cleansed the wound with peroxide, he leaned back against a counter and made a gesture which seemed to indicate the building—or the entire hospital complex.

"*Garth*?" I said.

Veil nodded. "That's Mr. Lippitt's notion. It was four

days ago that Garth first showed signs of coming around—after you started playing the *Ring* for him.''

"Wrong. Four days ago I played *Das Rheingold* for him, and he didn't respond at all. He cried two nights ago, but I was the only one who saw that. Nothing heavy happened until last night, and according to you these guys were gone by then.''

"To *your* eyes, Garth didn't respond to *Das Rheingold*. One of Garth's nurses made a note on Garth's chart four days ago that Garth had possibly displayed emotional reaction to a stimulus. The music, and your role, wasn't mentioned, but the possibility of increased awareness was.''

"How the hell does Lippitt know that?''

"It seems your old friend has his own means of keeping track of what goes on in that clinic. He's been closely following Garth's progress since the day he arrived here. He knows all about the conflict between Slycke and you, because Slycke has been bitching about Lippitt and you to anyone who'll listen.''

"That's almost funny,'' I said, and laughed without humor.

"What's almost funny?''

"Slycke has been worried about *me* being sent to spy on him, and all the while Lippitt must know every time the man farts. It makes me wonder if Lippitt gave me that high-powered pass to distract Slycke from the *real* spy, or spies, Lippitt has in there.''

"That seems unlikely, Mongo, judging from the way he obviously feels about the two of you. But you know Mr. Lippitt better than I do.''

"Nobody really knows Mr. Lippitt. I don't think anyone but Lippitt even knows how old he is; they just know he's old.''

"Mr. Lippitt's thinking is that Garth, in hindsight, would know exactly who it was who tried to kill him. The K.G.B.—if that's who was behind it—would be very much afraid of that. As soon as it looked like Garth might be coming around, the two agents were given hasty marching orders.''

"I told you: Garth hardly talks at all, and what he does say doesn't make a whole lot of sense."

"When the information was passed on, nobody knew what Garth would or wouldn't say; the source of concern was that he might be talking at all."

"That would mean Lippitt isn't the only one with eyes and ears in the clinic."

"Precisely Mr. Lippitt's concern. If his notion has any validity at all, it means there's a K.G.B. agent operating right under Slycke's nose."

Even paranoids could have real enemies, I thought. And valid reasons to be afraid. "Jesus," I said, "it could be Slycke himself. It would certainly explain the supersnit he's been in since Garth and I showed up, wouldn't it? Maybe he has damn good reasons for fearing that Lippitt sent me to spy on him."

Veil shrugged. "He's certainly made no secret of his distrust and suspicion of you. I think a trained operative would be a good deal more subtle."

"Maybe he's being subtle by not being subtle."

Veil smiled. "That's too subtle. Of course, it could be Slycke—but it could also be anybody with access to clinical information; it could be any of the psychiatrists, nurses, or other workers up there. It could even be a patient who'd been carefully planted; from what I understand, virtually anyone up there could have walked into Garth's room at any time, day or night, and seen the notation on Garth's chart."

"True—except for the patients in the secure unit."

Veil raised his eyebrows slightly. "People easily fall into predictable routines, Mongo, as you well know. People working at night often take naps at certain times. If *I* were an operative working a place like that, I'd *prefer* to be in a secure unit where my movements were supposedly severely restricted. I'd simply make certain I had a key."

"A good point. But all this talk is highly hypothetical, right?"

"Highly. Mr. Lippitt simply asked me to share his notion with you—and to tell you *not* to try to look into it on your own, in case you're curious."

"I'm much more skeptical than I am curious, but even if it were the other way around, I wouldn't do any kind of snooping while Garth is up there. He's too vulnerable."

"Yes. Lippitt didn't come right out and say so, Mongo, but I got the feeling he might like it if I rode shotgun for you for a while. Is there anything I can do for you or Garth?"

I shook my head, absently touched the slightly puckered, still tender flesh just above my eyebrows. "I really can't think of anything, but thanks for the offer. Besides, the more I think about it, the more I doubt there's any connection between Garth coming around and the two guys taking off. Any spy sneaking in to read the chart could see with his own eyes that Garth wasn't ready to give speeches. Garth was *nowhere* until last night. I say you were right the first time; the K.G.B. agents, if that's what they are, got wind of the surveillance and decided to leave while the getting was good."

"You could be right," Veil said evenly. "But you'll keep your eyes open, won't you?"

"Sure."

"You want to look at your scar?"

"Not really. I hope it's sexy."

"I'm sure."

"Thanks for coming up to see me, Veil, and for delivering the message. I'll call Lippitt as soon as I get a chance and thank him, too."

"How about letting me take you out to dinner?"

I shook my head. "I'd really enjoy spending some time with you, and it would be good for me, but Garth should be back in his room soon. They've been running tests on him all day, and I'm a little anxious to find out the results."

"Of course."

"Thanks again for driving up. I needed to see a friendly face."

"You'll see me again—soon. How about if I walk you to wherever it is you're going?"

"I'd like that."

8.

I was early, and Garth was going to be late. The guard in the kiosk had a note for me, from Tommy; Garth's testing was going to take at least an hour longer than anticipated, and the male nurse wanted me to come up to his apartment in the staff quarters for a drink and a sandwich.

It was kind of Tommy to extend the invitation; I didn't feel like hanging around the clinic for an uncertain amount of time with nothing to do but worry. But I didn't feel like hanging around with Tommy Carling either. It wasn't company I needed, but release from the anxiety and tension inexorably building inside me. I needed exercise.

I figured it would take me just about an hour to hoof it around the reservoir next to the hospital, if I didn't pause to watch the birds, and that seemed about right. Walking at a fast clip, swinging my arms like a drum major and not caring how comical I might look, taking deep breaths, I zipped down the center of the main thoroughfare, turned left after I passed through the gates on the eastern side of the hospital grounds.

Fifteen minutes later I had reached the bridge spanning the reservoir. The fast walking and deep breathing had leached away a lot of my tension, and I felt better. Not wanting to work up more of a sweat than I already had, I stopped to rest in the middle of the span, leaned on the metal railing and stared down at the surface of the water, which was glinting and moving like a chestful of living jewelry as it reflected the last slanting rays of the setting sun.

The harsh revving of an engine in the stillness, on an otherwise empty road, startled me and made me turn to my left—not a moment too soon.

The sun was almost directly in my eyes, so I couldn't see who was driving the pickup truck that was barreling at high speed down the center of the road, straddling the white line; but I definitely didn't like the looks of what I could see, and I tensed, both hands firmly placed on the top of the bridge railing, and waited, wondering whether the driver was just in a big hurry, drunk, hoping to put a bit of a scare into me, or all three. The pickup truck continued to accelerate; when it was about fifteen yards away it abruptly swerved, coming right at me.

I went in the only direction left to me—up and over the railing. I twisted in the air, and on the way back down once again grabbed hold of the railing, saving myself a dunking. The side of the truck banged into and scraped against the railing at the spot where I had been standing only a moment before. Sparks flew and I turned my face away—but not before I had seen a large decal of the familiar RPC logo on the door of the green truck; the vehicle was part of the hospital's maintenance fleet.

As the truck sped across the bridge, I clambered back up over the railing and stared after it as it fishtailed out of sight around a bend in the road. One of two things was true about the truck, I thought; either it was stolen, or it was not. If it had been stolen, I was unlikely to find out who—purposely or not—had almost killed me. But if the truck had not been stolen, it shouldn't prove all that difficult to find out which driver had brought back a truck with a badly damaged side panel.

But first things first, I thought as I started back the way I had come. I decided I'd had enough exercise; I definitely wanted to save some energy for a spirited interrogation of the driver of the pickup truck, if I ever found him.

"Hello, Mongo," Garth said to me when I walked into his room at seven fifteen.

Well, well, well.

Garth sat at a card table which had been set up by the window, eating his dinner. The Walkman, its wires snaking up to the earphones on his head, sat next to his tray. He was still dressed in his pajamas, robe, and slippers.

"Why don't you sit down and eat?" Garth continued, motioning toward a second, covered, tray on the table. "Tommy brought these in only a few minutes ago, so yours should still be hot."

"I don't think I'm hungry."

Feeling somewhat stunned by this second, abrupt change in Garth's behavior, I eased myself down into a chair across from him at the table. Only when I was already sitting did I realize that it had not even occurred to me to do what should have seemed natural—walk up to Garth and hug him. Garth had emerged from his long, silent journey to nowhere, but now he seemed like a stranger to me; I almost felt as if I should be introduced to this man who was my brother.

"It's roast beef," Garth said around a mouthful of food. "Very good."

"I'm sure it is."

"How did you hurt your head?"

"Just an accident." There were more important things than Henry Kitten to talk about. "I'm glad to see . . . you're feeling better, Garth."

"Garth told you he could talk."

"Why didn't you?"

"Garth had too many things on his mind; he couldn't talk through all the thoughts."

"What were you thinking about?"

Garth paused with his fork halfway to his mouth, suddenly

fixed me with a hard stare. Strange lights and shadows moved in his eyes. "You know," he said, and then put the forkful of food in his mouth.

"Yes," I said softly. "I know. That was a stupid question. I'm sorry if I brought you pain."

"The pain was already there."

"We have to talk, Garth."

"We are talking, aren't we?"

"Can you turn that thing off for a little while?"

"Garth would rather not," my brother replied evenly.

"Richard Wagner is a tough act to compete with for your attention."

"Garth can hear you."

"Garth, how *are* you feeling?"

"You know how Garth is feeling."

"No, I don't. I know what you were thinking about, but I don't know how you feel now."

Garth pushed his tray aside, once again fixed me with a hard gaze. "Once, you would have."

"Jesus, Garth, are you saying that you feel the same way now as we felt when Loge showed us his film?"

"Yes."

"Then you're feeling very bad."

"Yes. You could say that."

"If the music makes you feel bad, why do you keep listening to it?"

"Garth must."

"Why?"

"Garth must."

"Garth, I played that music for you because I'd hoped it would *help* you, not hurt you."

"It did help. Without the music, Garth would still be lying in bed. He would not be talking to you."

"Well, now that it's done its job, maybe it's time for you to stop listening to it."

"No," Garth replied evenly. "Not listening to the music

will not make the thoughts go away. That would be like killing the messenger. Siegmund Loge's message was valid when he delivered it, and it still is. He demonstrated not only that our species is doomed, but why; one proof was mathematical, the other emotional. The music makes Garth think of that, yes; but without the music, the thoughts would be worse and Garth would sink back to the place where he was.''

I smiled tentatively. ''Listen, brother, if I'd known how my little experiment in music therapy was going to work out, I definitely wouldn't have brought you anything stronger than 'Twinkle, Twinkle, Little Star.' ''

Once, Garth would have thought that funny; now the big man with the wheat-colored hair and piercing eyes who was my brother simply stared at me, a fixed, stony expression on his face. I decided it was time to change the subject.

''Why do you keep referring to yourself in the third person?'' I continued. ''What happened to 'I'?''

''Garth feels a great distance away, Mongo.''

''That doesn't seem like an answer.''

''Garth's 'I' is at the bottom of an ocean. It was too heavy. Garth had to leave 'I' behind in order to come back to the surface.''

''What ocean are you talking about?''

''Garth can say 'I' if it makes you feel more comfortable with him.''

''Jesus Christ,'' I said, then sighed and rolled my eyes toward the ceiling. I felt like laughing and crying at the same time. I forced myself to reach out and touch his hand, which was resting on the table next to his Walkman. The gesture felt unnatural. ''I don't want you to do me any *favors*, brother; I'm just trying to understand what you're saying and feeling. I want to help Garth get his 'I' back.''

''Garth's 'I' is dead, Mongo. If Garth ever went back down to look for it, he'd die too. The music keeps him from sinking.''

I sighed again, took my hand away from his. "Garth, I have to say something."

"Go ahead."

"I feel like I'm talking to a stranger, and I don't like it."

"Garth's sorry he makes you uncomfortable."

"Don't be sorry; it's not your fault. I've been making myself uncomfortable, because I've been searching for some new kind of way to talk to you. If you were somebody else's brother, I think I could do that without any trouble. I know how sick you've been, and I can't tell you how happy I am to see you out of that Goddamn bed, walking around and talking— even if I don't understand what you're talking about. I should be patient and understanding, grateful that you're talking at all; I should just sit here and listen, and nod my head a lot—but I can't, Garth. I've got too much feeling; I can't find a new way to talk to you. I don't care how—or even if—you respond; I'm going to speak the way I always have to the Garth I know and love—the brother who once had a very powerful 'I.' It's the only way I can deal with this situation, and with you."

"Garth understands," my brother replied evenly. "You should speak to him in any way that makes you comfortable."

"But I want you to feel comfortable with *me*."

"Garth is not uncomfortable with you, Mongo. Garth hasn't forgotten."

"You haven't forgotten what?"

"All that we've been through together, and what Garth owes you."

"You don't owe me anything; if anything, it's the other way around."

"Garth hasn't forgotten how you loved and cared for him when he was sick."

"I still love you, and you're still sick. And I'm still going to take care of you."

Garth cocked his head slightly, and a sad smile tugged at

the corners of his mouth. "Garth feels strongly that you love and miss someone else. Garth doesn't feel that you can love him when he has no 'I.' "

"Let me tell you something, brother," I said tightly. My stomach was hurting badly, and I had to fight back tears. "My old buddy Garth is going to get his 'I' back. That's a promise. If you can't do it, and the doctors here can't do it, then I am personally going to paddle to the bottom of whatever ocean you dropped it in and haul it back up. And I *still* think you should give Wagner a break for a little while. You won't sink anywhere; I won't let you."

"You should eat. The food's very good."

"I don't care how good it is," I said curtly. "I'm not hungry, and I don't want to eat. All I want to do is just sit here and talk to my brother."

Garth stared at me strangely for a long time, and then tears suddenly welled in his eyes and rolled down his cheeks. "You're a dwarf," he murmured.

"No shit," I said bitterly. I knew I was behaving atrociously, and couldn't help it. Garth's tears had startled and frightened me. Now, for the first time, I was struck with the realization that Garth really *could* be insane, and might stay that way. For some reason, I felt threatened, and my immediate, defensive response was anger—and shame for the thought that it might have been better if Garth had never regained consciousness. I had never lost hope for the unconscious Garth, and now the madman sitting across from me was draining that hope away from me. "Did you just notice?"

"But it doesn't bother you."

"What the fuck are you talking about, Garth?"

"You've never suffered because you're a dwarf."

"That's bullshit. I distinctly remember it bothering me when some of our nastier classmates in high school insisted on trying to use me for a medicine ball. *You* should remember, because you were the one who punched their lights out when they did it."

"You've had bad experiences, but they only made you stronger. You're a very strong man, Mongo; you would have grown up to be a strong man in any case, but being born a dwarf made you stronger. It gave you a great challenge, something to test yourself against constantly. You've won. You've always won, because you've never allowed yourself to be beaten. That makes it very difficult for you to understand . . . the rest of us."

"More bullshit, Garth. I've been beaten down a good many times, and you damn well know it."

"But you always got back up again. You've never been crushed."

"Neither have you."

"Now Garth has been crushed."

"You've always been as strong as me, if not stronger."

"No. Your 'I' could never be lost, because you would die before you gave it up. You don't really need anyone. You don't need Garth."

"I need Garth to be well. What do you need?"

"The reason you can't understand is because you've never really suffered any serious damage to the part of you that is *you*. If you weren't so strong, Garth believes you would understand what he is saying, and you would feel more comfortable with him."

"Garth, what do you *need*?"

"Garth . . . just needs."

"You need *what*?"

"Garth . . . isn't certain, Mongo. Right now, he knows only that he needs this music to stay on the surface."

"Listen, brother," I said through clenched teeth, "what Mongo feels right now is like punching you in the mouth, and maybe Mongo will do it if you don't stop talking crazy. I mean it. How's *that* for a therapeutic prescription?! You have to *fight* madness, and you're not doing it!"

Garth's response was to abruptly reach up and snatch off his earphones. His hands were trembling slightly as he set the earphones down on top of the Walkman, shut the player off. He clasped his hands together on top of the table, leaned toward me.

"Garth was lost before you brought him the music of the *Ring*," my brother said in a low, earnest voice. The muscles in his jaw and throat clenched, unclenched. "He was drowning. It is impossible to describe what it was like—what Garth really means when he says 'drowning.' Garth's mind was still working; he could remember killing Orville Madison, and wounding Veil Kendry, just before he . . . sank into this vast ocean of despair and unconsolable sadness. There was no hope in this ocean, Mongo—no reason whatsoever to live, much less to move or talk. Garth could hear voices; he knew what was happening all around him, but he couldn't move or talk under the *weight* of all that sadness. He couldn't—"

"That's because you'd been *poisoned*, Garth!"

My brother blinked slowly, as if momentarily disoriented, then leaned back in his chair. "Yes," he said in an odd, distant tone of voice. "Garth was poisoned by one of two men—possibly both of them. Their names—at least the names they were using—are Larry Rhodes and Michael Watt. When Garth first started working on the case, he thought it might be a matter of one company trying to steal secrets from another. Now Garth thinks that Rhodes and Watt are foreign agents."

"Then you *know*?! You *realize* you've been poisoned, and you even know who did it?!"

Garth shrugged, smiled faintly. "*Now* Garth realizes that he was being slowly poisoned, and who was doing it. The three of us were always bringing each other coffee. Garth was very stupid."

"It's the *poison* that's making you think the way you are, Garth! Realizing what's been done to you is the first step in fighting back."

"No, Mongo. It was the poison that sent Garth to the bottom of the ocean, yes . . . but the ocean was always there, before the poisoning, and it was the weight of the ocean that crushed Garth and destroyed his 'I.' "

"You're going to get better."

"Better?"

"Yes, *better*."

"You believe Garth will somehow get 'better' only because you do not understand how Garth is now."

I sighed, shook my head. "Rhodes and Watt took off yesterday, and they're probably already out of the country. Mr. Lippitt thinks they're K.G.B."

"Oh, really?"

"You don't seem all that interested."

"Who they really are, what they did, and where they are isn't important. They were two silly men doing silly things for silly reasons."

"Yeah, the problem is that they made you silly."

"Do you really find Garth silly, Mongo?"

"Damn it, you know I don't! But the poison they fed you screwed up your head, and it's *still* screwing up your head. You've *got* to understand and accept that if you want to get better. Unless you want the doctors here to start doping you up with psychotropic drugs, and unless you're ready for a lengthy stay in mental hospitals like this one, you'd better start giving a lot of serious thought to attitude adjustment. You have to *will* yourself to fight against the effects of the poison and get better. You have to *want* to get better. That isn't at all what I'm getting from you now."

"Garth understands what you're saying, Mongo, but you don't seem to be able—or want—to understand what Garth is saying. You don't even seem to want to hear it. When Garth was telling you about the ocean, you interrupted him to talk about unimportant things."

"I'm sorry, Garth," I said, feeling as if I were talking to a child. "Go ahead and tell me about the ocean."

'It's thousands of feet deep, filled with needless pain,

cruelty, stupidity, waste. It's the ocean Siegmund Loge showed us. All his life, he lived under that ocean, Mongo. All his *life*. He took the two of us down for only sixteen hours, and the experience almost shattered us. He'd lived there all his life, *feeling* all that pain, and yet he continued to function. And he functioned brilliantly. Siegmund Loge was a very great man, Mongo.''

"Yeah; a real prince, that one. I seem to remember a time—not all that long ago—when you weren't quite so impressed with his character. It was about the time you were growing fur and I was growing scales. You remember beastie time, Garth? You remember our nephew's funeral?''

"Garth hasn't forgotten what Loge did to us and others, Mongo, but that isn't the point. He's trying to explain something to you.''

"Go ahead.''

"The music brought him back to the surface of that ocean.''

"But the music just served to *remind* you of all the misery in the world.''

"You still don't understand. He didn't need to be *reminded* of the misery; it was all sitting on top of him, crushing him. It was the music that reached down into the ocean and allowed him to deal with the misery, bit by bit. Do you understand what he's saying?''

"I understand that I made a serious mistake—a criminal mistake—in bringing you *Der Ring des Nibelungen*,'' I said quietly, guilt and grief swelling in me and making it difficult to breathe. "Slycke was right; I had absolutely no business doing anything like that, and I damn well wish it could be undone. If I was going to bring you music, it should have been something you could associate with joy and hope, not despair.''

Garth shook his head. "It wouldn't have worked, Mongo. Joy and hope are illusions, and that kind of music could never have reached him; joy and hope would have dissolved on the surface of the ocean, and he would still be lying in that bed. The *Ring* was like a lifeline he could climb back to the surface precisely because it reminded him of someone who not only had survived at those great depths, but had at least done something to try to drain the ocean.''

"Jesus Christ, you're talking about Siegmund Loge again.''

"Yes. Everything must always come back to Siegmund Loge. He was our teacher, remember? He taught us what the world is really like, for the vast majority of people. But of course you remember; it's why you brought the *Ring* to Garth. You remembered the incredible power of that lesson, and you thought it might bring Garth back. You were right . . . and now you seem to want to deny the power of the lesson.''

"Loge was *crazy*, Garth! You *know* Loge was crazy!''

"Yes. And now Garth is crazy. Like Loge.''

"No, damn it, *not* like Loge! You don't want to destroy the world!''

"Siegmund Loge didn't want to destroy the world, Mongo, only change it so that we would not destroy ourselves. It was an impossible task. We can't change the world; we can only live in it until the end finally comes. And the best we can hope to accomplish as individuals is to drain just a little bit of that ocean off, or at least not make it deeper, while we're waiting for the end.''

"You sound like a Goddamn street-corner evangelist, Garth, the only difference being that at least the evangelist tells people they can be saved if they repent.''

"You know that nobody will be saved, Mongo.''

"I don't know any such damn thing. Nobody's ever been able to get those human extinction numbers out of the Triage Parabola but Loge, and we both agree that Loge was crazy.''

"Despair drives people crazy, Mongo. You may think you understand that, but you don't. For example, what do you smell here?''

"Roast beef.''

"Despair. It's very, very thick in this place.''

"You're telling me you can *smell* despair?"

"Garth can; and he can see it. And it's not only here; despair is all around us. It's suffocating the world."

"But there's also *hope*, Garth. *Hope* is the antidote to despair."

"Hope is an illusion."

"Hope is no more an illusion than despair; both are feelings. Feelings affect attitude, and attitude affects behavior."

"Hope is for strong people like you, Mongo."

"Garth, you don't have *any* hope?!"

"No. Only need."

"But for *what*?!"

"Garth has told you that he doesn't know yet. It's like a hunger for some food with a name he can't recall. Eventually, he'll know what he needs."

"What about love? Love is also a pretty good antidote for despair."

Garth slowly shook his head. "Mongo, Garth remembers the word, 'love,' but he can't remember what it feels like."

"Oh, Jesus, Garth," I said, my voice breaking. "That's so sad."

"Garth doesn't want you to feel bad because of him," my brother said soothingly. "Garth doesn't feel bad about himself."

"You don't, huh? Funny, I'd have sworn you sounded depressed."

"No. Depression is something which a person who has hope feels when that hope temporarily wanes. *You're* depressed."

"All right," I said, fighting back tears. "I'll try real hard not to feel bad about you."

"Good. That would only add depth to the ocean."

"Garth, there's a kid over in the children's hospital who's totally convinced that he's Jesus. I told him he'd be a whole hell of a lot better off if only he'd stop going around *telling* people he was Jesus. He explained to me that he couldn't do that; it seems God insists that he witness to the fact that he's Jesus. You remind me of him.''

Garth raised his eyebrows slightly. "Why? Garth doesn't even believe in God or gods.''

"You used to.''

"God is part of the 'I,' and it's just another illusion—a very dangerous one. That illusion is a large part of the reason we're all going to die.''

"You still remind me of the kid.''

"Have you ever heard Garth claim to be Jesus?''

"Both you and that kid are irrational; you refuse to *think* in a way that's in your best interests. You understand that you've been poisoned, and you understand that the poison has altered the way you think, the way you feel about yourself, and the way you perceive the world; yet, you seem quite willing to accept the changes as permanent.''

"Garth accepts things the way they are, and you call that irrational. What you really mean is that you cannot accept Garth the way he is—without his 'I.' ''

I started to say something, then turned in my seat when I heard a knock at the door. A male nurse I hadn't seen before leaned in the open doorway.

"Dr. Frederickson?''

"Yeah.''

"You told Tommy you wanted to speak with Dr. Slycke?''

"Yeah.''

"Dr. Slycke can see you now, for a few minutes.''

"Tell him I'll be right with him," I said, then turned back to Garth. My brother had put his earphones back on, turned on the player, and was staring out the window with a distant expression on his face. "If you haven't already," I continued quietly, "and if you feel up to it, you might call Mom and Dad. They've been just a little bit worried about you.''

Garth didn't respond. I rose from the chair and, feeling as if I were trudging along the bottom of my own ocean of sorrow, walked from the room.

9.

"WHAT'S the matter with my brother, Doctor?"

Dr. Charles Slycke sat half in and half out of a harsh pool of light cast by a gooseneck lamp set off to one side of his desk. The psychiatrist looked tired; there was thick, black stubble on his puffy cheeks, dark shadows around the dark, puffy bags beneath his eyes, and his gray hair stuck out from his head at odd angles. Perhaps because he was obviously near the point of exhaustion, I didn't sense the usual hostility from him.

"At this point, that's difficult to say with any certainty, Frederickson."

"I'd appreciate your best guess," I said quietly. "Also, I want to thank you for agreeing to see me now. I know you're very tired, and I appreciate the fact that you're tired because of the many hours you've spent with Garth."

"So have a lot of other people," Slycke responded with a slight nod. "Physically, you can see that he's made a remarkable recovery."

"To all outward appearances, yes. Do your tests confirm that?"

"Yes. Physically, he appears no worse off than anyone who has spent a couple of weeks in bed. However, there are still traces of nitrophenylpentadienal in his tissues and in his urine, which means that the drug is still in his system. That tells us that NPPD metabolizes very slowly—but it does metabolize. We may also surmise from his behavior that the chemical transits the blood-brain barrier and forms chemical bonds with the molecules of the brain. There's no indication that it's addictive, but like heroin, alcohol, or any one of a number of other drugs that transit the blood-brain barrier and form chemical bonds, it apparently has a profound effect on mood, perceptions, and behavior.''

"Doctor Slycke," I said, leaning forward in my chair, "I love the man in the room back there, but that man isn't anything like the brother I used to know. That man is a stranger to me."

Slycke passed a thick hand over his eyes. "Your brother is showing marked tendencies of having developed a schizoid personality as a result of the chemical bonding I mentioned. The tests don't indicate any organic damage, but that doesn't mean there isn't any. He's developed a number of bizarre fantasies.''

"Like what?"

"For one thing, he insists that he murdered the late secretary of state; he claims that he shot the man down in cold blood.''

Terrific. I could feel muscle tighten across my chest like a band of steel. "That is a bizarre fantasy," I said carefully. "When did he tell you all this?"

"Early on. Once he decided to talk, he spoke quite freely."

"Why would he tell you such a thing? I mean, what was the context of the conversation?"

Slycke shrugged his broad shoulders. "He believes very strongly that the human race is doomed to extinction, perhaps in the very near future, but certainly within four hundred years. This extinction fantasy involves Dr. Siegmund Loge, the triple Nobel laureate who disappeared some years ago and is presumed dead.''

"Yeah. The name is familiar to me."

"Dr. Loge was awarded one of his Nobels for inventing the Triage Parabola, a mathematical model that is very effective in predicting which endangered species are inevitably doomed to extinction, and which could most benefit from

human intervention. The Triage Parabola has been most useful to zoologists and conservationists in helping them to
make decisions as to how best to allocate their limited resources in trying to preserve endangered species. Part of
Garth's fantasy is that Dr. Loge determined from his model
that the human species itself is in imminent peril of extinction, and that he then embarked on some fantastic scheme to
alter human DNA—not only in future generations, but in
people now living. Of course, the human species is far too
complex ever to be accurately measured by a mathematical
model.''

"Of course.''

"Garth further fantasizes that the two of you became
involved in a protracted struggle with Dr. Loge because
you'd been injected with some deadly serum Loge had developed. From what I can tell, these beliefs compel Garth to
witness to the danger to our species, and to unburden himself
of guilt for crimes he imagines he has committed. It's a
remarkably rich fantasy—the one involving Dr. Loge—and it
combines elements of classic Western mythology, as reflected in works like Wagner's *Ring*, or Tolkien's *Lord of the
Rings*. Obviously, your brother is very familiar with the *Ring*
cycle, and its various motifs. Do you know if he's read
Tolkien?''

"I'm sure he has. Garth's quite a reader.''

"It wouldn't surprise me. Garth's fantasy comes complete
with a great quest, giants, fearsome creatures, sentient ani-
mals, death and destruction; there's even a kind of magical
sword—a knife, really—which he believes you found, and
which you dubbed Whisper.''

"Garth has a remarkable imagination,'' I said dryly. "Now
he seems to have turned it against himself.''

"We know, of course, the stories the music conjures up.
Do you know of any real incidents Garth experienced which
could form the basis for this kind of fantasy?''

"Which one? Killing Orville Madison, or doing battle with Siegmund Loge?"

"Either."

"No," I said in a flat voice. Garth had certainly been downright chatty with the doctors who'd examined him during the day, and he was blithely letting a lot of ugly cats out of a lot of ugly bags. These cats had poisonous fangs and claws, and letting them loose wasn't going to do anyone any good. "What does the murder fantasy have to do with the end-of-the-world business?"

"I'm not sure there is a connection. However, your brother insists that he shot Madison."

"Everyone knows that Orville Madison died in a hunting accident."

"Garth says that the hunting accident never happened, that it was a cover-up engineered by, among other people, no less than the president of the United States."

"Well, certainly no one can accuse Garth of not casting his fantasies with the biggest names in show business."

Slycke glanced up sharply at me. "Do you find this amusing, Dr. Frederickson?"

"No, Dr. Slycke, I most certainly do not. I apologize if I sounded flippant. It's just my way."

Slycke thought about it, apparently decided to accept my apology. "In Garth's mind, the murder of the secretary of state is somehow tied in with a search for an angel. This aspect of the fantasy isn't quite clear to me, and I'll have to listen to the tapes when I'm more rested."

"What about his constant use of the third person when he's referring to himself?"

"A loss of identity—diminishment of ego and the persistent feeling that one is living in someone else's body—isn't all that rare in certain schizoid types."

"Didn't Garth explain his angel fantasy to you?"

"Not exactly. He simply said that the two of you—yes,

you're involved in this fantasy, also—were searching for an angel that the secretary of state wanted to kill. Garth had a lot of things to say about all sorts of incidents, but his method of telling them was . . . well, perfunctory. He seemed to have a need to talk about these fantasies, but not to explain them in any detail; once he had said something, no matter how bizarre, that seemed to be the end of the matter. He resisted answering questions—another reason why I have to listen carefully to the tapes. I was hoping you might be able to shed light on some of these matters. Wagner's music is clearly connected to his quest fantasy, but it doesn't seem to explain the murder and angel fantasies. There must be *some* basis in reality for these fantasies.''

"I guess maybe I should listen to the tapes too, Doctor."

"Surely you understand that records of conversations between doctor and patient must be kept confidential."

"I'd just like to be helpful." And find out just how much, about how many things, Garth had told these doctors—one of whom could be a K.G.B. informant. Mr. Lippitt was not going to be pleased.

Slycke grunted noncommittally. "Garth has also developed a most intense empathic facet to his personality. Indeed, it's the most powerful sense of empathy I've ever encountered. Most unusual."

"Meaning what, Doctor?"

"Your brother is obsessed with human suffering, virtually to the exclusion of everything else. Human misery is all he seems to think or really care about."

"Garth has always been a kind and sympathetic man."

"This is more than mere kindness and sympathy, Frederickson. This is *empathy*—almost total identification. Any decent individual is sensitive to the suffering of others, but with Garth this goes a step—or many steps—further. With Garth, it's almost as if he not only imagines but actually *experiences* the suffering of others. This intense empathy clearly seems to be linked to the music of Richard Wagner—specifically, *Der Ring des Nibelungen*."

"Yes," I said softly.

"Yes?"

"I can see that."

"Can you explain why this should be? Does that music have specific associations for him?"

"What does Garth say?"

"Nothing edifying, since it's bound up in his quest fantasy. He claims that Siegmund Loge used that music to torture the two of you in some way."

"The *Ring* has always had a powerful effect on Garth."

"The anomalies in Garth's blood which I mentioned previously: Do you suppose the same unique antibodies would show up in your blood, Frederickson?"

"I don't know."

"Your brother says that both of you were tortured and infected with this strange disease. If that were the case, you would also carry those same antibodies."

"Are you saying that you believe Garth's stories may be true?"

Slycke shook his head impatiently. "Of course not. The point is that *he* believes them to be true, and I'm trying to establish whether there may be some basis in reality for that belief. His fantasies are highly complex and structured, and he holds to them with remarkable consistency."

"Even if I did carry the same antibodies in my blood, it wouldn't mean anything, would it? It would just indicate that I'd picked up whatever Garth had had, but it was such a mild case that I wasn't even aware I had it."

"But you don't recall Garth ever suffering from any exotic disease?"

"No."

"I hope you're not concealing anything from me that could be useful in the treatment of your brother, Frederickson."

"I'm sorry I can't be more helpful, Doctor."

"So am I, Frederickson, so am I." Slycke paused, rubbed his temples with his middle fingers, grimaced as if he had hurt himself. "You shouldn't have brought those tapes of the *Ring* to your brother."

"I think I might agree with you. But that's a moot question now, isn't it?"

"We're looking at symptoms; we still don't know the deep structure of Garth's psychosis, or the mechanics of what's causing it. We could speculate that one effect of NPPD poisoning is to wipe the mind clean of most emotions associated with people and events, past and present. In essence, the mind becomes a kind of emotional blank tape, and the result is a state of profound depression leading to a paralysis of thought, will, and movement which closely mimicks classic catatonia. But that blank tape can be imprinted—if a stimulus can be found that is powerful enough to pierce the profound depression. You pierced the depression, and imprinted the tape, when you played the *Ring* for him. But that's all you did; you didn't reawaken the whole person, or heal the real hurt. Indeed, you've probably compounded the injury."

"Why do I get the impression that you're trying to make me feel bad?"

"I'm trying to construct a psychiatric model of your brother's problem that I can work with, Frederickson. If you get the impression that you've made my work more difficult, and possibly endangered your brother's health, by taking unauthorized actions, it's a correct one. But what's done is done, and recriminations are useless. We have to go on from where we are."

"I'm glad you feel that way."

"Whatever experiences and feelings Garth associates with that music now form the core of his emotional being, and he behaves accordingly. As a result of that imprinting, Garth's personality is now focused almost completely on physical and emotional pain. You know, your brother actually *suffers* when he listens to that music.''

''So you told me.''

''Yet he won't stop listening.'' There was a faint note of disbelief in the psychiatrist's voice.

''Maybe the music is the only thing that's holding him together,'' I ventured carefully.

''Then he's holding himself together with barbed wire; eventually, that will shred him.''

''What are you going to do about it?''

''I'm not sure, frankly, that there's anything we can do about it,'' Slycke said with a heavy sigh. ''Psychiatry is very effective with neurotics, but—I'm sad to say—not so effective with psychotics. At the moment, your brother is definitely displaying psychotic symptomology. Usually, the best we can do with psychotics is to attempt to change their brain chemistry in order to alleviate their symptoms and allow them to function to whatever degree they're capable of.'' The doctor smiled thinly, without humor, and for a moment frustration and real pain moved in his eyes. ''We dope them up.''

''I appreciate your candor, Doctor, and I'm beginning to understand why you . . . come so highly recommended. All right, then, what about medication? Antidepressants?''

''They might work to some degree,'' Slycke said thoughtfully, ''but it's doubtful that they'd provide any significant or long-lasting relief for the sort of core personality disorder your brother is displaying. I may approach Garth on the subject; we'd need his permission to medicate. My guess is that he'll firmly reject the idea.''

''Nobody's going to dispute the fact that Garth is seriously disturbed. Why do you need his permission to medicate him? I'll give you permission, if you think it might help in any way.''

''You can't. He's now conscious, aware of his surroundings, not a threat to himself or others, and functions rationally within a construct of reality that includes this facility and his own treatment. Even if correct therapy didn't dictate that he participate in a decision concerning chemotherapy, which it does, state law insists on it.''

"Then what happens now?"

"We wait, and we continue to observe closely to see if more changes take place. Also, we hope. As long as traces of nitrophenylpentadienal show up in his urine, we know that the drug is continuing to pass out of his system as it metabolizes. If Garth's brain chemistry were eventually to return to normal—" Slycke paused, shrugged. "Who knows?"

"You mean we may simply be waiting for him to get over one long, humongous hangover?"

There was a quick smile, reflecting genuine amusement. Then it was gone. "I don't want to raise any false hopes, Frederickson."

"You're not."

"Your somewhat bizarre analogy may not be beyond the realm of possibility. We're just going to have to wait and see, and in the meantime deal with Garth honestly."

"Thank you very much for your time, Doctor," I said, rising to my feet. "You've been very kind, and I appreciate your concern."

"Frederickson . . . ?"

Slycke had begun to shuffle nervously through some papers on his desk. Finally he looked up at me, said: "Mr. Lippitt really is a close personal friend of yours, isn't he?"

"Yes, he is," I replied evenly. "Why?"

The psychiatrist shuffled more papers. "Have you spoken to him, uh . . . lately?"

"No," I replied, my curiosity aroused. None of the former hostility, resentment, or suspicion remained in the psychiatrist's voice; it had been replaced by what sounded like anxiety, and not a little uncertainty. "I haven't spoken with Mr. Lippitt since the arrangements were made for placing Garth here."

"I see," Slycke said quietly, then cleared his throat. "I thought . . . maybe you had."

"Is there some reason why you think I would—or should—have, Dr. Slycke?"

Slycke looked at me sharply, and something dark moved in his eyes. "No," he said curtly. "Why do you say that?"

"I know that somewhere you got the notion that I might be spying on you for Mr. Lippitt, but that was never true. It got us off on the wrong foot at the beginning, which is something I still regret. As I've said repeatedly, my only concern is that Garth get well; I don't care about anything else." I paused, wanting to choose my next words carefully. "Even if there were something funny going on here, I wouldn't want to know about it. That's not to say that I think there is; I'm just trying to make my priorities and position crystal clear."

Slycke studied me for some time, his face a blank, then abruptly looked down at the papers on his desk. "Good night, Dr. Frederickson," he said tersely.

"Good night, Dr. Slycke."

After my talk with Slycke, I returned to Garth's room. I'd been concerned that some of the things I'd said earlier might have upset my brother, but I found him where I'd left him—contentedly sitting at the table, staring out the window and humming softly along with the music coming through his earphones. *Siegfried*. I sat with him for a half hour, until it was time to change the tape. Forcing myself to flash a big smile, I rose, patted him on the shoulder, and told him I'd stop by next day to see how he was doing. Garth said that would be fine, and then went back to listening to his music.

Distracted, self-absorbed, and decidedly upset about Garth's condition and my possible role in causing it, I could easily have been killed if my knife-wielding attacker had been slightly more skilled and slightly less impatient. I was half-way back to the staff building, taking a shortcut around the back of the chapel, when a figure wearing a gray, hooded sweat shirt leaped out at me from behind the trunk of a huge oak tree. The man's right hand described an arc heading for my chest, and moonlight glinted off the six-inch blade of the hunting knife he held. I dropped to my knees; as the blade passed through the air over my head, I planted both hands on the ground, kicked up and back at the man's midsection. I missed his stomach and groin, but caught him solidly on the left hip. The man cried out in surprise and pain as he flew backward through the air and landed hard on his back. The knife landed on the grass in the darkness somewhere off to my right, and I decided not to waste time looking for it. I scrambled to my feet, darted back to where the man still lay on the ground, and kicked him in the head. Then I sat down hard on his chest. With my left hand I pulled back the hood, brought back my right with the index and middle fingers stiffly extended, ready to strike at his eyes or larynx. I stopped when I found myself looking down into the startled, frightened face of Dane Potter. Blood was running from his mouth. He coughed, turned his head to one side, and spat teeth.

"You hurt me," the boy mumbled thickly, gasping for breath.

"Just what the hell do you think you're doing, Dane?"

"You're not allowed to hurt me! My parents will sue you!"

"Dane, that's a really crazy thing to say to me," I replied, and stomped on his stomach as I was getting off him. He doubled up, turned over on his side, gagged, and threw up.

When Dane Potter had finished being sick, but before he could completely catch his breath, I stripped his sweat shirt off him, used it to tie his hands firmly behind his back. I pulled him to his feet, gripped the folds of the sweat shirt, and dragged him backward along with me as I searched in the grass. I found the knife, slipped it into the waistband of my jeans. I also picked up his teeth—three of them—and put them in my pocket. Dentists can do wonders these days.

"I want to go back to the hospital now, Frederickson," the boy wheezed over his shoulder in a kind of mewling, simpering moan. His breath whistled through the gaps where his teeth had been.

"That's where you were headed before you decided to take this little detour and try to kill me, right?"

"Frederickson, I—"

"And that was you in the pickup trying to add me to the paint job on the bridge this afternoon, right? Don't try to bullshit me, Dane, or I'll kick out some more teeth."

The boy swallowed hard, nodded. "I'm sorry, Frederickson. Please take me back."

"In a few minutes," I said, dragging the limping teenager into the moon shadows at the rear of the chapel. "Maybe. Then again, maybe I'll break your arms first. I hate to think of what would have happened to me if you'd gotten your hands on a gun. That's your weapon of choice, right?"

The boy's eyes were wide with pain and fear; I decided my words were having a therapeutic effect on him.

"You can't do this," the boy whimpered, craning his neck back and spraying blood over me. "It's against the law; it's abuse."

"If it's abuse you want, you big, stupid shit, I'll give it to you. What I've done so far is called reality therapy—and if I think the reality therapy isn't working, then I may *really* beat your ass. People have a right to defend themselves, Dane. If you want to be crazy and try to hurt people, don't be surprised or offended if someone hands you your head. This is the real world out here, my young friend, and you made the wrong move with the wrong person. You're extremely lucky you're not dead or permanently crippled right now, and I'm debating how I should drive that lesson home. What do you think? Should I knock out some more teeth, or just break your nose?"

The boy bowed his head, sobbed. "Please don't hurt me any more, Frederickson."

"I won't if you answer my questions and tell me the truth. Have *you* hurt anybody since you ran away?"

"No."

"Everyone thought you were long gone. What the hell are you doing here, and why did you try to kill me? I certainly don't think it's because you miss your desk. I never hurt you, and I even thought you and I were beginning to establish something of a working relationship."

The psychotic teenager shook his head, sobbed again. "I didn't want to do it, Frederickson."

"Then why did you?"

"Marilyn made me do it. She said I had to kill you if I wanted to stay with her."

"Dane, I really hope for your sake that this isn't crazy talk."

"It's not crazy talk, Frederickson."

"Who the *hell* is Marilyn?"

"She's my woman, man," the boy replied, raising his head. His voice had become considerably brighter. "She's *beautiful*, man. She helped me escape and then took me to live with her. Man, we've been blowing dope and fucking like bunnies."

I yanked on the sweat shirt, slinging Dane Potter none too gently up against the brick wall of the chapel. I anchored him there with my finger on his solar plexus. Now I could see that his eyes were cocaine-bright.

"What horseshit are you trying to hand me, Dane?"

The boy swallowed, grimaced, spat blood. "You hurt me bad, Frederickson."

"Who's this Marilyn? Some old girl friend?"

"Marilyn's no *girl*, Frederickson; she's a *woman*."

"How old is she?"

"I don't know how old she is."

"But she's not a kid?"

"*No*, man. I told you she's a—"

"How'd you meet her?"

"Two days ago I got a call down in the cottage. There was this woman on the line, and she talked in this low, real sexy voice. She told me she was dying to fuck my brains out; she actually *said* that. She told me she worked at the hospital, out in the records department at the front. She said I'd never seen her, but that she was always watching me. She said that she was in love with me, and she wanted to help me run away so that I could come and live with her. She told me she needed a big stud like me to keep her satisfied, and she wanted me around so she could fuck me any time she wanted. Recreation was showing us a movie that night, and she told me to slip out whenever I could and go down by the gym; the exit door there would be unlocked. That's what I did. The door was unlocked, just like she'd said it would be, and she was out there waiting for me in her car. Whooee! She drove me to her place, and we got right into bed. Man, I ain't *never* had a woman like that. And she had lots of coke—a whole pile of the stuff. We'd screw, blow some dope, then screw some more. Today, just after lunch, she said that I had to do something for her if I wanted to stay with her. I had to kill you."

"Kill me?"

Dane Potter nodded. "She drove me back here, and we parked and just kind of watched and waited. When you started walking off the grounds, she made me steal the truck; she said I should run you over first chance I got."

"Nobody *made* you do anything, Dane. You were just afraid of losing your meal ticket and a piece of ass."

The boy shook his head. "Marilyn's a spooky broad, Frederickson. Some of what you say is true, but it's also true that she kinda scared me."

"Tsk. Tsk. Poor you."

"When she found out that I missed you, she was pissed. She said that I didn't deserve a real woman like her, and that maybe she should kill me. She gave me that knife. She told me you'd eventually be coming out of that building tonight, so I just waited. I really am sorry, Frederickson."

''Why did she want you to kill me?''

''She didn't say.''

''And you didn't ask?''

''Hey, man, I was high—you know what I mean? I wasn't really thinking about anything except getting more of Marilyn's dope and back into her pants.''

''What kind of car did she drive?''

''A Mercedes; a red convertible.''

''What does Marilyn look like?''

''Tall, long blond hair. She's got these great long legs, and *big* tits.''

''Dane, what did the social worker you tried to rape look like?''

''Now that you mention it, she kinda looked like . . .'' Dane Potter paused, frowned. ''You know about that?''

''Yeah. I know about that. I also know that you have a lot of sexual fantasies, most of them associated with violent acts.''

The boy blinked slowly. ''You don't believe me?''

''Where does Marilyn live?''

''Somewhere around here. It's about a half hour away. She's got this beautiful house, and a waterbed with—''

''Where around here?''

''Hey, man, I don't know. It was night, and I had my hand up her dress all the time she was driving. I wasn't exactly looking at the scenery.''

''Do you think this story you're telling me gives you some kind of *excuse* for attacking me with a knife?''

''What do you mean?''

''Let's start all over again, Dane. Begin with how you managed to get out of the hospital, and then tell me where you've been.''

''You *don't* believe me!''

''Let's see if I've got this straight. A tall, beautiful woman with long blond hair, long legs, and large breasts who drives a red Mercedes convertible and lives in a big house with a waterbed lusts after you so badly that she helps you run away from the hospital so that you can live with her and have all the sex and dope you want. Then she says you have to kill me if you want the sex and dope to keep coming. Right?''

"Right!"

"How did you know I'd be coming out of the building? Or did you just happen to see me walking across the lawn and then decided to have a go at me?"

"*She* told me where you'd be! It's the truth!"

"Dane, let's just say that I enjoyed the account of your adventures so much that I want to hear it all over again."

"Are you going to hurt me anymore?"

"No, Dane," I said wearily. "I just want you to tell me the truth."

The boy swallowed hard, shook his head. "I'm telling you the truth, Frederickson. Marilyn's waiting for me right now."

"Where?"

"Down the street. She's parked on the other side of the firehouse."

"She's sitting there in her red Mercedes convertible waiting for you to go back with her to her house for more sex and dope."

"Right. Go see for yourself."

Keeping a firm grip on Dane Potter's belt, I marched him the two blocks to the firehouse, where we stopped and looked down the side street. The street was empty, as I'd been certain it would be. Dane Potter looked genuinely bewildered, as if he really had been expecting to see a blonde in a red Mercedes convertible waiting for him.

"She left," the boy said in a tone of hurt and disbelief.

"It certainly looks that way," I said with a sigh. Despite myself, I was beginning to feel just a bit guilty. Dane Potter had indeed come at me with a knife—but then, Dane Potter was a certified loony; I'd beat on him badly, and scared him probably more than I had to. The boy had done some bad things to a few people, but his file also indicated that a few people had done some very bad things to him. "I'm taking you back to the hospital now, Dane," I continued as I steered him around and headed back the way we had come. "You're going to tell the staff there exactly what happened here tonight; whether or not you want to tell them about Marilyn is up to you. Then we'll see if we can't find a dentist on call who'll be able to put your teeth back in your head."

"Frederickson?"

"What?" I answered curtly. Suddenly I felt so tired, emotionally and physically drained, that I could hardly keep my eyes open. Having a crazy teenager jump me with a knife had been an aggravation I hadn't needed.

"Do you really think that business with the woman was all in my mind?"

"You tell me, Dane."

"I thought it happened."

"Okay."

"Now maybe I'm not so sure."

"Talk it over with your therapist, Dane. He or she will help you try to sort it out."

"What will happen to me?"

"I don't know."

"I don't want to go back to DFY."

"If people thought you were responsible for your actions, you wouldn't have been sent to the hospital in the first place. It's your job to *become* responsible—listen to the doctors, study hard in school, and try hard to keep your head together. They just want you to get well. Me too."

"Frederickson?"

"What?"

"I hope you believe me when I say I'm sorry I . . . did what I did. I really am."

"Yeah. Thanks, Dane. That's really sweet of you. If I think about it long enough, I'll probably be sorry I kicked you in the mouth."

10.

THE next day, a Wednesday, I wasn't called to teach; I was called to answer a lot of questions from hospital officials and the police in connection with the attack on me by Dane Potter. I was asked if I wanted to prefer charges. I did not.

Continuing anxiety concerning Garth's bizarre behavior combined with my tussle with Dane Potter the night before had left me feeling out of sorts, and I decided to give myself a break from tension for the rest of the morning. I read the *Times* over brunch, took a long walk, and then a nap. In the late afternoon I went to see Garth.

My brother wasn't in his room. I waited around for a half hour, and when he didn't show up I went looking for him. I was on my way to the nurses' station to ask if he'd been taken for more tests when I passed the Day Room and saw Garth inside sitting at a card table and talking with three other patients. There was a deck of cards in the center of the table, but the men seemed more interested in their conversation than their game. Garth was dressed in new clothes; jeans, a wool plaid shirt, and moccasins. He had his Walkman clipped to his belt, but the earphones were hanging around his neck. I watched them for a little while, and saw that it was Garth who was doing most of the talking; the others were leaning forward over the table, apparently listening intently to whatever it was he was saying. All four men looked over at me as I came into the Day Room and walked up to them, and I had the distinct feeling that I had interrupted some personal, intense, private conversation.

"Hi, Garth," I said brightly, feeling very much like an intruder.

"Hello, Mongo," Garth replied easily. "How's your head?"

"It's okay," I said, resisting the impulse to tell him that it was his head I was worried about. "How are you feeling?"

My brother put the earphones back on his head, turned on the Walkman, and adjusted it to low volume. "Garth is feeling fine. Thank you."

There was a long, uncomfortable silence, during which Garth and the other men simply stared at me. "I'm Bob Frederickson," I said at last to Garth's audience, smiling and extending my hand.

One by one the men introduced themselves, shook my hand—and then turned their heads toward Garth, as if looking for direction. I expected Garth to excuse himself from the group and come back with me to his room to talk. Instead, he simply sat and stared at me, a curious half smile on his face. I tried a few conversational gambits, none of which produced anything more than perfunctory responses. I was growing increasingly uncomfortable.

"I've interrupted your card game," I said as I rose to my feet. "You guys go ahead and play."

And they did; whatever it was they had been discussing before I'd come in, they weren't going to resume the conversation while I was there. Garth turned up the volume on his Walkman slightly, then shuffled the deck of cards and started dealing. I turned and left.

After kicking Dane Potter's teeth out of his head, I thought the children's hospital wouldn't be too anxious to use me again. I was wrong. I got a call early the next morning asking me to come in and substitute for the English teacher. Dane Potter, his teeth surgically reimplanted and wired in place, was in one of my classes; he was properly subdued and respectful, and even joked with me a couple of times. Word of the incident had gotten around, and I got a lot of attention from all the kids in the hospital. I responded as best I could, but I was still feeling distinctly out of sorts.

I felt as if a crucial decision I had never expected to have to make was being forced on me, and my dilemma was generating a good deal of internal pressure.

After school I traipsed across the field at the back of the children's hospital toward the main complex—and was startled to see Garth, earphones on his head, walking down the hillside toward me, holding the hands of an old man and old woman who were determinedly, eagerly, shuffling alongside him. Garth was smiling; the old man and woman were smiling. Tommy Carling, a bemused expression on his face and looking like nothing so much as a chaperone or mother hen, was walking down the hillside about twenty yards behind the trio.

Garth merely nodded to me as we came abreast, and then continued on with his two elderly charges, speaking to one and then the other. Both the old man and the old woman had rapt expressions on their faces.

I waited for Tommy Carling, then fell into step beside the ponytailed male nurse. "I'm surprised to see Garth outside," I said.

Carling shrugged his broad shoulders. "Why shouldn't he be? He's not violent, and he's given no indication that he's a threat to himself or others; if gentleness was radioactive, Garth would glow in the dark. Patients who aren't violent or too unpredictable are given outside privileges to walk around the grounds as long as they have a nurse, aide, or male relative with them."

"If Garth is functioning so well," I said carefully, "maybe it's time I took him home."

Carling looked at me, raised his eyebrows. "Just because he's functioning doesn't mean he's healthy—or that he might not suffer a relapse and go catatonic on us again."

"Granted."

"With Garth, you can never be quite sure where he's going to be from one day to the next."

"Granted; but maybe he can heal just as well—or better—at home. If he has a relapse, I can always bring him back here."

"Where would you take him?"

"Back to his own apartment; I'd stay with him. I moved in with him after I got burned out of my own apartment. I've been looking for a new apartment, but I'll just put that off until everyone agrees that Garth is well—or as well as he's likely to get."

"Mongo," Tommy Carling said in a low voice, "Garth's only been *conscious* and out of bed for a couple of days. Why are you in such a hurry to get him out of here?"

I looked down at the grass, debating how much of the basis for my concern I could—should—share with Tommy Carling. Despite his disarming, often foppish, manner, and despite his healing skills and his obvious concern for Garth, Tommy Carling was, above all else, a Defense Intelligence Agency employee with a high security clearance, and the D.I.A., was not the Little Sisters of Mercy; in a crunch, there was no doubt—or little doubt—in my mind where Carling's loyalties would lie. The first horn of my dilemma, made even sharper by the fact that the K.G.B. wasn't the Little Sisters of Mercy, either. The second horn was the fact that, despite the first horn, the D.I.A. clinic, with its decidedly mixed bag of what could be conflicting interests, not to mention the possibility of Russian infiltration, might still be the best place for Garth. I didn't even want to think about how I would feel if Garth suffered any more damage because of a wrong move I might make, or a right move I might not make, so I decided to dance around the subject a little while longer, and see where the conversation might lead.

"I'm just not sure he wouldn't be more comfortable in his own place, in familiar surroundings," I said.

Carling was silent for some time. Finally, he said quietly: "I think it's you who's not comfortable here, Mongo. And it's Garth who's making you uncomfortable. Am I right?''

"There's some truth in what you say."

"But you're not the patient, Mongo. Garth has given no indication that he wants to leave. I'm sorry if I sound rude, but I have to ask if you're certain that you have Garth's best interests in mind when you talk about taking him out of here."

"He's up and about, and it occurs to me that he might begin to act more normal if he were placed back in normal surroundings."

Garth had sat the old couple down on swings outside one of the children's cottages and was gently pushing them. All three mental patients looked perfectly content, and no staff from the children's hospital had come out to complain of their presence. Carling sat down on the grass, and I sat beside him. I declined his offer of a cigarette, and he lit one for himself.

"Garth has a great gift," the male nurse said, picking a speck of tobacco off his lower lip as he exhaled.

"For what?" I asked in a tone that was more curt than I'd meant it to be. "As a companion for old people, or as a budding music critic specializing in Wagner?"

Carling, resting on his elbow, turned his head and looked at me. "You're upset because I suggested that you might be more worried, even if unconsciously, about your own feelings than you are about your brother's welfare."

"No, Tommy, I'm not upset," I said evenly. "It shows me that you're thinking about Garth, and I like that. You continue to worry about Garth, and I'll worry about my feelings."

Carling dragged deeply on his cigarette, pointed down the hillside at the trio on the swings. "Look at him down there. Those two old people listening so intently to whatever it is your brother is saying to them are considered hopelessly senile, with virtually no attention span for anything. I was told when I signed them out from the geriatric section that they didn't respond to anybody. Obviously, the staff who told me that were wrong.''

''Are they from the clinic?''

''No; they're just regular patients at the hospital. But you see how they respond to Garth; a lot of very sick people respond remarkably well to Garth. He seems able to relate to them in a way no one else can.''

''He just doesn't relate to normal people.''

''That seems to be true, unfortunately, at this point. That doesn't diminish his gift, or the power of that gift. I've spent a lot of years trying to do what little I can to alleviate the suffering of others, and I've never seen anything like it.''

''How did those two end up with my brother?''

''Garth asked if he might be allowed to volunteer to work with other patients in the hospital. Geriatrics is *always* looking for volunteer companions two or three hours a day. I got Dr. Slycke's permission to take him out, and here we are. I think it's remarkable the way Garth is able to calm and communicate with them. This gift he has even works with the men in the secure unit.''

''What was Garth doing in the secure unit?'' I asked, feeling a sudden sense of alarm. I was not sure Garth would—or could—defend himself anymore.

''He walked in; voluntarily. I explained to you that the other patients can go in there and use the facilities, as long as things are quiet there.''

''What did he do in there?''

''Talk—for hours. And the others just sat and listened.''

''What was he talking about?''

''Who knows? I didn't stay in there with him, but the other nurses tell me he always spoke in a low voice, and tended to clam up whenever one of them got too close. He wasn't causing a disturbance, or stressing the men—quite the opposite—so nobody objected. Hell, even Mama Baker sat and listened to him, and for Mama Baker to sit still for fifteen minutes without cursing somebody out is quite an accomplishment." Carling paused, smiled thinly. "Still, I wouldn't advise you to visit there again. Mama still hears voices commanding him to kill dwarfs. Incidentally, I'm really sorry about what happened that day."

"It wasn't your fault."

"Yes, it was; it's my responsibility to be aware of any situation that can unduly stress a patient. At the time I wasn't aware of Mama's obsession with killing dwarfs, and I should have been. Anyway, it seems that Garth has developed a marked talent for communicating with the sick and the hopeless. He's able to break through all sorts of psychic walls, and he gives them comfort."

"Dr. Slycke told me about his empathy."

"I don't think 'empathy' is a strong enough word to describe it; I'm not sure there is a word. The other patients seem to believe that Garth *knows exactly* how they feel, and that gives them comfort. We're both watching him right now bring a senile old man and woman out of their shells, but I've also watched him calm violent patients. He not only cries when he listens to that music; I've seen him cry when other patients talk to him about their troubles. But, like you said, he doesn't relate to normal people. He'll talk or really listen to you only if he perceives you to be suffering. It's almost as if the rest of us aren't really there. Or we don't matter to him. It's not only you he treats that way, Mongo. His attitude toward Dr. Slycke, the other staff, and me is one of benign neglect. He functions, will do what he's asked to do without question, and will listen to you politely; but you can tell that he's not actually relating. You know what I mean."

"I know what you mean. I also know that Garth and I have gone through a hell of a lot of good and bad times together. I'm not just anybody; I'm his brother."

"Yes," Tommy Carling said quietly as he blew a smoke ring, then butted out his cigarette in the grass. "But, again at the risk of being rude, I might suggest that an outside observer could conclude that you're envious of all the attention Garth is lavishing elsewhere.''

"I won't deny that I'm hurt by Garth's reaction—or lack of it to me, Tommy. I also won't deny that I'm more than just a bit egocentric, but I'm not so self-centered that I can't separate my interests and needs from Garth's." I paused, trying to decide where I wanted to go next. I sensed that the conversation had reached a critical juncture, and I would either have to back off or go ahead. I went ahead. "After a certain point, which I think may have been reached, I have some doubts about the staff of this clinic being able—or even wanting—to make the same distinctions.''

The male nurse slowly removed another cigarette from his pack, lit it with a butane lighter. When he spoke, his tone was flat. "You question the quality of the care Garth's been receiving, Mongo?''

"I'm not talking about you, Tommy. You have quite a gift yourself for working with the sick and helpless; I believe that you truly care for Garth, and have only his interests in mind. You're a good man and a good nurse, but you don't do the strategic thinking or make the final decisions around here.''

"I have a lot of input, Mongo.''

"I'm not talking about strictly medical decisions.''

"Then I'm not sure what you're talking about.''

"You don't know what's going on in the minds of Dr. Slycke and the other psychiatrists here, or what their long-range concerns may be. I'm suggesting that Garth's best interests and the interests of the Defense Intelligence Agency may begin to diverge, if they haven't already. After all, what's Garth doing in this secret clinic in the first place?''

Carling tugged absently at his ponytail, then nodded. "Now I see what you're getting at. But the doctors here are good, Mongo.''

"I'm not questioning their medical skills, Tommy; just their loyalties. Their paychecks come from the D.I.A.''

"Like me,'' Carling said with a thin smile.

"Like you."

"Yet, you're willing to have this conversation with me?"

"Obviously. Can you see me trying to have it with Slycke?"

"I thought this Mr. Lippitt, the big poohbah who authorized Garth's admittance here and gave you the Z-13 pass, was a personal friend of yours and your brother's."

"He is, and I'm not questioning his motives in placing Garth here; indeed, I'm grateful to him. But we were all dealing with an emergency then; now, things are different."

"How are things different?"

"For one thing, obviously, Garth isn't catatonic any longer. Now, Garth has gone through any number of changes as a result of being poisoned with that shit; what worries me is that certain D.I.A. personnel might consider it imperative, for security reasons, to keep Garth here for close observation, even if it might be better, for medical reasons, to send him home. Those same personnel would consider it more important to observe the long-range effects of NPPD poisoning than to get Garth's head working right; they're going to be thinking about national security implications, and how they can use what they're learning from Garth."

Tommy Carling laughed good-naturedly. "What national security implications?"

"For one thing, we're talking very serious behavior modification. Want to quiet some dissidents, calm down some political prisoners—or maybe pacify an entire population, for that matter? Sprinkle a little NPPD on their cereal every morning. I'm not being facetious."

"I can see that," Carling said evenly.

"Also, you have what you're looking at down there on the swings."

"An empath fixated on alleviating human suffering? You think our intelligence services, or anyone else's, would be interested in that? We should all be so fortunate."

"I'm talking about imprinting. What you see isn't necessarily what you would have gotten in different circumstances."

"You're losing me again, Mongo."

"Garth was thrown into a profound depression as a result of NPPD poisoning; Slycke thinks it literally erased all sorts of emotional valences and connections to things in the past. He came out of it when I stimulated him with music which had very strong emotional associations to human suffering, and the need to do something about it. So Garth winds up thinking about nothing *but* alleviating human suffering. Now, what would have happened if I'd imprinted Garth in some other way?"

"Yes," Carling replied quietly. "Your point is well taken."

"The NPPD wiped out, or repressed, a major part of his personality, and I unwittingly helped to give him a new one. I hate to think of what would be happening with Garth now if I'd imprinted him with something deeply associated with rage, or hatred. Now, I'm not saying anything to you that hasn't already occurred to the strategic types of personnel I mentioned earlier. I absolutely guarantee you that a lot of wheels are turning in the heads of people who don't give a shit about Garth as a person, and I don't want Garth to get crushed in the gears. I don't want him used, and I have to do what I think is in his best interests."

It was certainly true that I didn't want Garth to be used as a guinea pig—firsthand by the D.I.A., or secondhand by the K.G.B. But it was also true that Garth was simply talking too much, about things he shouldn't be talking about at all, and that was information I couldn't share with Tommy Carling, or anyone else. It was certainly a convenient irony that Charles Slycke and the rest of the staff at the clinic should dismiss Garth's stories about Orville Madison and the Valhalla Project as the fantastic delusions of a madman, but the fact that Garth wasn't believed when he told the simple truth about things which obviously still troubled him very deeply could only complicate his therapy.

If Garth's little tales got out—which they certainly would if the K.G.B. had ears in the clinic and they decided to do some serious digging for facts—and if he *was* believed, Mr. Lippitt, Veil, and I could end up in prison for a very long time, and the administration of Kevin Shannon would fall.

A third horn on the head of my curious, and increasingly ugly, dilemma.

"You seem to know a lot about intelligence work, Mongo," Carling said in a neutral tone.

"I know a lot about the kinds of people in whose heads those wheels are turning; they relate best to scenarios, not people."

"But, in the end, you still have Mr. Lippitt to protect Garth's interests."

"Mr. Lippitt might not agree that the agency's interests and Garth's aren't the same. Besides, he's only one man; he's a powerful man, but there are a lot of powerful men in the intelligence community. He's in Washington, not here, and he could die—or be dismissed—tomorrow."

"Assuming these so-called strategic types are thinking what you say they're thinking—"

"They are."

"Then there would still be problems, even if you did take Garth out of here. The interest of these people wouldn't stop just because he wasn't here; if anything, they'd just get very nervous. How would you protect Garth from that . . . continuing interest?"

"I'd just take him home and lock the door," I said, only half joking.

Carling sighed, lit a third cigarette. "Some of your points are good, Mongo, but I still think the doctors here are doctors first, and agency employees second. They would resist pressure from those strategic types. Maybe you're being just a bit paranoid."

"That could be, and if so there's no harm done by talking to you. I have to deal with scenarios, too."

Tommy Carling was silent for some time, and together we watched Garth talking with the old man and woman down by the swings. I wondered what they were talking about.

Carling finished his cigarette, tossed it away. "Mongo?"

"What?"

"I'm supposed to report on anything we discuss. It's a rule covering all conversations with visitors."

"That doesn't surprise me," I said evenly, still watching Garth. He had said something to make the old woman laugh. "I understand that this is a D.I.A. clinic, not the Mayo. I'm glad I talked with you, because it's helped me to clarify a lot of my thoughts and focus my thinking. I don't care what you tell Dr. Slycke, or anyone else. I told you; I won't be giving them any new ideas, and it may be just as well that they know what I'm thinking."

"I don't think I'll report this conversation."

"Do what you think you have to do, Tommy. In the meantime, I'd like to ask for your personal and professional opinion on something."

"Which is?"

"Should I discuss any of this with Garth? In particular, should I discuss with him the possibility of his going home?"

"You're Garth's brother, Mongo; even more germane to this situation, you have a Z-13 badge. You can talk about anything you want, with anyone you want, any time you want."

"That doesn't answer my question, does it?"

"Mongo, I'm truly flattered that you should ask for my advice on something which is so important to you—but I can't give it to you. It's clearly a medical question about something that could have a large bearing on Garth's state of mind, and I wouldn't feel right about advising you. I can't take the responsibility. That's a question you'll have to take up with Dr. Slycke—if you care to."

"All right. I understand."

"I will say that, despite the concerns you've brought up, I still believe this is the best place for Garth—without question. What you're witnessing now could be just one more phase Garth is going through. You don't know what may happen, how he may be acting tomorrow, or the next day. As you pointed out, you might only have to bring him back here, anyway. What would happen if he suddenly turned violent, or uncooperative, and you couldn't handle him? We're an hour away from the city—when there's no heavy traffic. This clinic is still a government installation, and the results of all tests done on Garth—even the description and causes of his condition—are highly classified. Nobody here will share any information about Garth's condition or NPPD with any other hospital. I think you'd be shouldering a very heavy responsibility if you decided you wanted to take him out of here just yet—assuming he would want to go, which may be a very large assumption.''

"Thanks, Tommy. I'll bear all that in mind.''

When I did broach the subject of going home with Garth, he gave no indication that he cared one way or another what was done with him. Indeed, I couldn't even be certain he was listening to me; he was playing his Walkman so loud that I could hear Siegfried's Funeral March, from *Götterdämmerung*, clearly through the earphones.

Without going into the reasons for my concern, I asked Charles Slycke what he thought of the idea of Garth's going home. He told me he would advise against it, and he gave the same reasons Tommy Carling had. It didn't surprise me. I tried to tell myself that my fears for Garth were ill-founded, and that I had no real choice but to leave Garth where he was, regardless of the fact that there might be a K.G.B. informant in the clinic, and regardless of the fact that Garth was continuing to chatter away about the Valhalla Project and the shooting of Orville Madison. I remained anxious and undecided.

That didn't surprise me either.

11.

THE next day, I met Tommy Carling in the corridor on my way to Garth's room.

"Garth's visiting in the secure unit," the male nurse said. "It looks like he's in a pretty heavy conversation with Marl Braxton, so he'd probably prefer that you go down there. Besides, I know Braxton would like to talk with you. It seems he's a fan of yours."

"What about Mama Baker?"

"Mama went off last night, and they had to put him in a camisole and give him a needle. He'll be in the Critical Care room all day, so he's not a problem. It's very quiet in there. That key you have will let you in."

"I'd rather not do that—use my key."

"Then just knock on the door. One of the nurses will let you in."

Just to be on the diplomatic safe side, I checked back with Slycke to make certain he had no objections to my going into the secure unit. The director of the clinic seemed very distracted, and he merely waved a hand at me in what I took to be a gesture of approval. I went out of his office and down the orange corridor to the secure unit, knocked on the thick Plexiglas door.

Marl Braxton was sitting with my brother at the far end of the huge commons room, near a bank of barred windows. Garth had his earphones around his neck and was leaning toward Braxton as he spoke, occasionally waving his arms for emphasis. The animated discussion stopped when I entered, and both men rose as I walked toward them.

"Dr. Frederickson," Marl Braxton said, extending a large hand. His large, piercing black eyes gleamed with pleasure. "*Now* I'll shake your hand."

"Then you'll have to call me Mongo," I replied, taking his hand. His grip was firm, the muscles in his hand and forearm sinewy and clearly articulated; the man with the glittering black eyes and pronounced widow's peak kept himself in excellent condition.

"I'm glad we can get together under more pleasant circumstances than when you were in here the last time. It's a real pleasure to meet you."

"It's a pleasure to meet you, Marl. Anybody who has the patience to wade through my monographs can't be all bad."

"I find your work intriguing. I feel like the pieces you've done on the so-called criminally insane speak directly to me."

The man was smiling; since most of the research I'd done recently was on serial murderers, I hoped this was Marl Braxton's idea of a joke. I managed to smile back. "Are you keeping my brother entertained, off the streets, and out of trouble?"

"On the contrary," Braxton replied seriously. "It's been Garth who's been keeping a lot of people around here out of trouble."

"Hi, Garth," I said to my brother as Braxton went to get a chair for me.

"Hello, Mongo," Garth said easily, smiling. He was looking directly into my eyes, and he seemed perfectly at ease, but I noticed that—unlike Marl Braxton—I was once again competing with Richard Wagner; Garth had put his earphones back over his head and turned on the Walkman.

"How are you doing?"

"Garth feels fine, Mongo. Thank you. And you?"

"I'm fine. Uh, how was lunch?"

"Lunch was very good. Garth ate in the dining room here; Garth thinks the food in the secure unit is just slightly better."

Feeling decidedly uncomfortable engaging in this vacuous chitchat with my brother, I was relieved when Marl Braxton returned. I sat down in the chair he had brought me, and he sat down across from me. Garth sat, then shifted his gaze toward the ceiling as he listened to his music.

"Frederickson," Braxton said easily, "I was an admirer of yours even before Garth told me some fascinating things I hadn't known."

I looked at Garth, but couldn't tell whether or not he was listening to anything but *Die Walküre*; at the moment, he seemed to have opted out of the conversation. "Garth's been talking about me?"

"He's told me all about the horrors the two of you went through with Siegmund Loge and the Valhalla Project," Braxton said, his intelligent, expressive eyes suddenly flashing with excitement. "I'd certainly love to see that knife you call Whisper. Damascus steel. Incredible. It must be some weapon."

"Garth has taken to talking a lot since he got here," I said, looking at my brother with what I hoped was a most eloquent expression of disapproval.

"He also told me how he shot Orville Madison a few weeks back; blew his head off. What a son-of-a-bitch *that* guy was."

I said nothing, stared at the floor.

Braxton continued, "What's funny is that Slycke and the other shrinks around here don't believe him."

"But you do."

"I do," Braxton said with sudden intensity. "I know it's true, Mongo. All of it."

"Assuming it is true," I said in a low voice, looking up to

meet Marl Braxton's gaze, "I think you'd agree those are stories he should keep to himself."

"Don't worry, Mongo; the patients are the only people around here who believe him. And we're crazy, remember?"

"What the hell do you think you're doing, Garth?" I said to my brother in a low voice. "Do you have any idea?"

"The world as we know it is coming to an end, Mongo," Garth replied evenly, in a clear, strong voice. "You and Garth know it, because Siegmund Loge taught us. Now others know it."

"Loge could have been wrong, Garth; the Triage Parabola is no crystal ball. Besides, he never said it was going to end tomorrow. The human extinction he predicted could be hundreds of years away."

"But it *could* end tomorrow, and the only way to change that outcome is to change ourselves—person by person, heart by heart. Lippitt, you, and Garth thought it was best to keep everything that had happened and that we had learned a secret, but we were wrong. We've already wasted years, and now there's no time left for anything but the truth—no matter what that truth might cost."

The words struck me, perhaps because of his intense manner of delivery, as probably the most coherent, focused thing Garth had said to me at one time since he'd regained consciousness. I knew I should probably feel encouraged, but I didn't. "Has it occurred to you what could happen to all of us if people *did* start believing you killed our late secretary of state? And remember that it was Lippitt who killed Siegmund—"

I abruptly stopped speaking when Marl Braxton quickly shifted in his chair in what I took to be a warning signal. I turned around just as Tommy Carling came up behind me.

"Time for therapy, Garth," the male nurse said brightly. "Dr. Slycke is waiting for you."

Garth immediately rose, walked off with Tommy Carling.

I started to rise, intending to leave, but Marl Braxton put his hand on my arm.

"Relax, Mongo," Braxton said in a curious tone of voice that sounded something like a plea. "Garth won't be back for at least an hour—maybe two, if he's feeling talkative. We don't get that much intelligent company in here. If you've got nothing better to do, I'd like to buy you a beer."

He hadn't been kidding about the beer. His room, radiating off the commons area just to the right of the entrance, was pleasant and spacious, decorated with prints of impressionist paintings. Bookcases, filled to overflowing with well-worn books and magazines, lined all four walls. In one corner was a small electric cooler, and from it he produced two frosted bottles of Coors. He opened one, handed it to me.

"We get a six-pack a week," Braxton continued, reacting to my somewhat surprised look. "That is, if we've behaved ourselves, and if alcohol isn't contraindicated by our medication. Since Garth has been coming around, the clinic has had to up its beer budget. There's just something about the things he says and does that's very soothing."

"You find predictions of human extinction soothing?"

"It's soothing to know that there's a man alive today on the face of the planet who can prevent that extinction."

"Garth?"

"Yes. Your brother has a great gift."

"So I've been told."

"He *is* a great gift."

"I'd agree that he's become something else, and that's for sure."

Braxton looked at me oddly for a few moments, and he looked as if he wanted to say something. Instead, he finally nodded toward the one chair in the room. I sat down in it, while he sat on the edge of his bed. He opened his bottle of beer, sipped at it.

"This bottle of beer I'm drinking represents a heavy percentage of your weekly allotment," I continued. "That makes it taste even better."

"It's my pleasure to share it with you."

"Thank you."

Braxton drank some more of his beer as he studied me with his bright eyes. "Garth really does have a very calming influence on the patients here, Mongo," he said quietly. "He certainly does on me."

"You always seem pretty calm, Marl—at least to me. It's hard for me to imagine you losing control of yourself the way Mama Baker does. Why do you have to stay here in the secure unit? If you don't mind my asking."

Braxton smiled thinly. "I don't mind you asking—in fact I appreciate your candor in asking me about things which interest you, without worrying that I might be offended because I'm a patient in a funny farm. It makes me feel that you're comfortable with me, and I like that."

In fact, I felt far more comfortable with Marl Braxton than I did with Garth. The realization made me sad. "I guess I'm saying that you don't seem all that crazy to me."

"I take that as a compliment, and I thank you."

"It's just an observation, Marl."

"What you observe on the outside is not necessarily a reflection of what's going on inside."

"That's true of many people."

"With me . . . I don't act out. Not in here. But Dr. Wong—he's my therapist—understands what could happen if I were let out of here. He's the only person besides Garth who fully appreciates the relationship between me and my maid of constant sorrows."

"You've told Garth about your maid of constant sorrows?"

"Oh, yes. Garth knows everything about me."

"Your maid of constant sorrows is your madness?"

"No. It's personal, Mongo, and I don't want to talk about her with you."

"I'm sorry, Marl. I didn't mean to pry."

"Don't apologize; I told you I'd like you to feel free to ask me anything you'd like. When you ask me a question I don't want to answer, I'll just let you know."

I smiled, nodded. "Like I said; you don't seem all that crazy to me."

"You seemed a bit nervous when you first walked into the unit. You don't now."

"I was never nervous for myself. Frankly, I don't much like the idea of Garth hanging out in here. All of the patients in this unit, including you, are potentially violent. I'm afraid Garth could be hurt—if not by you, then by somebody like Mama Baker, who doesn't have your kind of control."

"If Garth had been in here last night, Mama wouldn't have gone off."

My response was to shrug.

Braxton smiled, continued: "Don't you think your brother can take care of himself? He certainly has in the past. In fact, he came within a punch or two of busting up Jake Bolesh and a jailful of deputies when Bolesh had you locked up in Nebraska. I believe that was just before Bolesh injected you with the stuff that caused your bodies to change."

"Obviously, Garth has gone through some radical changes," I said, ignoring the clear invitation to discuss Valhalla—while taking note of the fact that Garth had indeed been telling Marl Braxton all about it, in detail. "He's a bit mellower now, to say the least. If he was attacked, I'm not even sure he would make a move to defend himself."

"Don't worry. I'd never let anything or anybody hurt Garth. But he won't be attacked; it's not meant that he should be harmed."

Something in the other man's voice made me sit up straighter. "Why not?"

Marl Braxton set his half-empty bottle of beer down on the floor, then folded his hands in his lap. "Because Garth is the son of God."

I was sorry I'd asked, and I tried to cover my embarrassment by taking a long swallow of beer.

"Garth is the Messiah," Braxton continued evenly. "He's been sent by God to save us from ourselves."

"Oh," I said, wiping my mouth with the back of my hand. And I couldn't resist adding, "Son-of-a-bitch."

Marl Braxton laughed loudly and easily. "All of a sudden I'm seeming a little crazier to you, aren't I, Mongo?"

"Yep. That you are."

"Well, at least you're not trying to patronize me by denying it. I can see that what I've said comes as a shock to you; it came as a shock to me when I first realized the enormity of just what it was Garth represented."

"It will come as a shock to my mother and father. Listen, Marl, I've got a flash for you. Garth doesn't even *believe* in God."

"I know that," Braxton said evenly, apparently unperturbed by my revelation. "Garth told me. It doesn't make any difference."

"It doesn't make any difference that the man you believe is a messiah doesn't even believe in God?"

Braxton shook his head, ran his hand back over his widow's peak. "Garth is still God's messenger, the Messiah, whether he chooses to believe it or not. Do you believe in God, Mongo?"

"I certainly don't believe in messiahs, or divine intervention. I consider them primitive notions—answers to human longing, fear, and suffering that have always been a big part of the problem. Garth's got one thing right; any help we get is going to have to come from ourselves."

"Can you see his aura?"

"Whose aura? *Garth's*?"

"So you can't. There's a blue-white light all around him; he literally glows with holiness. Eventually you'll be able to see it, as will others."

Marl Braxton paused and looked at me, as if waiting for a

response. His casual assertion that my brother was some kind of divine messenger had indeed shocked me, precisely because he had seemed so rational up to that point. I did not want to begin to condescend to Braxton's insanity, or appear to be mocking him, so I decided it was best to leave the subjects of my brother's divinity and his blue-white aura alone. I said nothing.

"But you've certainly witnessed Garth's healing powers," Braxton continued.

"I'm not sure what you mean by 'healing powers.' "

"Oh, I think you do. You just don't want to talk any more because I've made you uncomfortable, and you're no longer certain how to deal with me. You shouldn't feel that way. Everyone around here has witnessed Garth's healing powers; they just don't understand where his gift comes from. Like you. It occurs to me that you're now caught in a curious kind of netherworld between this world of madness and the other world of madness you come from. Garth will tell anyone who cares to listen about the Triage Parabola and the Valhalla Project. They don't believe him, but *you* know that everything he says is true. The fact that Garth is the Messiah is obvious, and it's just as true as the things that were done to you by Siegmund Loge. But you can't accept it."

"You're confusing two different things."

"Am I? The kind of healing power Garth displays could only come from God; there's no one else on earth who can bring about the changes in people the way he does, with a few simple words or a gesture. I believe he's healed me; because of Garth, I believe I can now escape from my maid of constant sorrows and function away from here. I'm in no hurry to prove it, and I don't even intend to tell Dr. Wong. Garth's in no hurry to carry out his mission, and his time is my time."

"What's Garth's reaction to this belief of yours that he's the Messiah?"

Again, Marl Braxton laughed. "He says I'm crazy."

Suddenly I felt a wave of affection for the other man, and my unease fell away from me. It didn't matter what he believed; what he believed might be insane, in my view, but in my view it was no more insane than the religious fantasies of millions of other people around the globe. The only difference was that the others banded together and received tax waivers.

I grinned, cocked my thumb and forefinger like a gun, pointed it at him. "There you go."

Braxton stood up and stretched. "You want another beer, Mongo?"

"I'm still working on this one. Thanks."

"You know, the proof of what Garth is can be seen in what he says and does, but it's also easy to see a pattern in Garth's life over the past few years as God was preparing him for his mission."

"What pattern?"

"First, his trials at the hands of Siegmund Loge, and then his involvement in the hunt for Veil Kendry—Archangel."

"So he's told you all about Archangel, too," I said with a sigh.

"Yes."

"You know, Marl, I just happened to be slightly involved in those matters, too."

"Yes," Braxton replied easily, "but it's also now clear that your involvement was incidental to God's plan for awakening His son. You're not the Messiah; Garth is."

"Loge's Valhalla Project and the Archangel affair had nothing to do with each other," I replied, aware that I was probably crazy for carrying on such a crazy conversation with a bona fide, card-carrying crazy man. Yet, I not only found myself liking and respecting Marl Braxton, but increasingly curious about the pathology he was now clearly displaying. I remembered Chris Yardley, and my inability to convince him that it was in his best interests not to tell everyone he met that he was Jesus. Marl Braxton's pathology was different, inasmuch as his fantasy was projected onto Garth, but I was still curious to see what effect, if any, my rebuttals of facts and common sense would have on him. The fallen D.I.A. operative with the top-secret past was intelligent and articulate; as long as he didn't suddenly decide to try and hand me my head, I found I was perfectly content to sit and discuss his nonsense with him.

"The doors of perception—true perception—were opened for Garth at the hands of Siegmund Loge," Braxton patiently explained to me as he sat back down on the edge of his bed. "The naked truth of our situation was deeply implanted in him, and it exploded into full bloom in his consciousness when you brought him *Der Ring des Nibelungen.*"

"Marl, I had exactly the same experiences—and I'd be just as happy if I never heard the *Ring* again."

"Nobody ever has exactly the same experience as someone else. You were simply God's tool, your role to be Garth's companion and solace on his two great spiritual odysseys. The proof is in the fact that, even though you triumphed over Siegmund Loge, you didn't change the fact that our species was doomed. In fact, all during the time when you were resting on your parents' farm, you had to wrestle with the possibility that the two of you, with Mr. Lippitt, had doomed humanity when you destroyed Siegmund Loge."

That touched a sensitive nerve, and I slowly finished my beer before I spoke again. "What does the Archangel affair have to do with it?"

"The seeds for Garth's awakening had been sown by Siegmund Loge, but they lay fallow for years. They had to be watered by the nitrophenylpentadienal—which would have killed him, if it had not been cut off when it was. The Archangel affair not only saved his life, but provided the emotional catalyst which sent him into the holy sleep from which he awakened as the Messiah. In Garth's body, nitrophenylpentadienal became a holy substance."

"Oh, come on, Marl; this is getting more complicated than Revelations."

"The pattern is there," the other man said earnestly, "for those with eyes to see it. Like you, Siegmund Loge was a tool of God. He provided the crucible in which the soul of the son of God would be fired and reshaped. Also, he set up communes around the world. The people who were in those communes are out there, waiting; *they'll* know that Garth is the Messiah, and they'll form the first troops in an army of love and compassion that will change the world, and save us from extinction."

"Bullshit," I said with more feeling than I'd intended to show. "Believe me, Marl, even the Messiah wouldn't want anything to do with the people who were in those communes. I mean, I'm talking about *seriously* stupid, absolutely mindless people—which is why Siegmund Loge was able to suck them into his operation in the first place. I've met and talked with some of those people, Marl; you haven't. You wouldn't be able to tolerate the company of any one of them for more than five minutes. Hell, they thought *Loge* was the Messiah; a few of them thought Loge was God."

"Loge was a false Messiah; his true mission was to prepare the way for Garth, and this was accomplished."

I shook my head. "Garth told you you were crazy for thinking he's the Messiah. Does my brother believe any of this other business?"

"No," Marl Braxton replied easily. "In fact, he said the same things about the commune people you did."

"But that doesn't make any difference?"

"That doesn't make any difference. Garth doesn't fully understand yet."

"Then how can you be so damn sure that you understand so much? Does God speak to you?"

Something that might have been dangerous glinted for a moment in Braxton's dark eyes, then was gone. "God doesn't speak to me, Mongo,'' he said calmly. ''In fact, God doesn't speak at all. Hearing voices is Mama's problem, not mine; my maid of constant sorrows is—was—my problem.''

''Speaking of voices, Garth hardly says ten words at a time to me. Why does he spend so much time talking to everybody else?''

''Not everybody else; only those who understand pain.''

''If Garth has told you about Valhalla and Archangel, then you must know that I understand a few things about pain.''

''It's true that you've suffered great pain, but you've never been broken like Garth and me. For now, Garth's words are only for broken people.''

''The world isn't made up of broken people, Marl. Loge's lesson—if it can be called that—is that there are far too many insensitive, *stupid* people in the world, and they'll destroy us all.''

Loge's lesson was that people with fantastic notions like Marl Braxton's would destroy us all, but I thought it better to keep that thought to myself.

''Garth will change that,'' Braxton said.

''How's he going to do that if he can only speak to broken people?''

''There are many more broken people than you think. Not all broken people end up in mental institutions. They're all around you, but you can't see them because you've never been broken. Garth knows who they are; he'll find them, and they'll find him.''

''Okay,'' I said quietly, looking down at the floor. I was rapidly losing interest in Marl Braxton's pathology, and couldn't see any way in which it could help Garth. Quite the contrary.

''I guess we'll just have to see what happens.''

''What do you think is going to happen?''

''Garth will carry out his mission, and bring his message to the world. We will all be changed.''

''Okay. I can use a change.''

"Thanks for sitting down and talking with me, Mongo. I really appreciate it. In a nut house, time tends to drag."

"You're welcome."

"How did you get that scar on your forehead?"

"A bad guy cut me. With the help of a friend, I changed him."

"You killed him." It wasn't a question, and there was a faint hint of amusement in the other man's voice.

"I changed him."

"The scar is fresh. You were cut fairly recently, right?"

"Right. Why?"

Braxton shrugged, but he continued to stare thoughtfully at my forehead, as if he were reading some message there. "Just curious," he said at last. "Are you in a hurry? Do you have to be any place?"

"No."

"Would you mind hanging around a while longer? I really enjoy your company." He paused, laughed easily. "There are too many crazy people around here who *do* talk to God."

"I don't mind hanging around and talking, but I'm a little tired of the subject of my brother's divinity," I said seriously.

"Then we'll drop it."

"Why did you bring it up in the first place, Marl? Somehow, I have the sneaking suspicion that you knew what my reaction would be."

"I wasn't sure. I wanted to see if, by now, you'd come to realize that Garth is the Messiah. You haven't, so that's that. I'd love to discuss some of your monographs with you, and have you sign my copies."

"You've got it."

"And you'll help me finish up my weekly allotment of beer?"

"I'll drink to that."

Which I did. Marl Braxton and I talked easily for another hour or so, until Garth came back and joined us in the room. I left shortly afterward, depressed by the sight of Marl Braxton's Messiah sitting on the floor, head bowed, seemingly oblivious to both Braxton and me while he listened to his music.

I was skittish and ill at ease when I left the clinic, and I didn't feel like going back to my small apartment in the staff building. I drove into New York to see a show, just for something to do, and then treated myself to drinks and a good dinner before driving back to Rockland County.

But my sense of foreboding wouldn't leave me, and I couldn't sleep. I knew I had to make a decision one way or another on what to do with Garth, and then learn to live with it. I thought of calling my parents, which I had been doing every other night anyway, to ask for their advice, then decided against it. They were old, and it didn't seem fair for me to lay on them all of my doubts and conflicts, especially when they weren't around to judge the situation for themselves. They would only tell me to do what I thought best.

I wondered how many other patients, either in the clinic or the larger facility, believed with Marl Braxton that my brother was the Messiah, and would begin to act toward him accordingly. I suspected there were quite a few, and the number would grow. Certainly, Garth didn't need that.

All through the night I paced, trying to weigh the obvious risks of taking him out of the clinic against all my other misgivings. I didn't want him in a place where people were thinking he was the Messiah; if he couldn't live with me in his own apartment, then I at least wanted him in a nice, quiet sanitarium where there were no potential conflicts of interest among the staff, where Garth could simply rest, and where I might eventually be able to bring about a change in his musical diet.

I also decided against calling Mr. Lippitt, because he would also have a potential conflict of interest and I did not want him to be put in an embarrassing situation; I didn't want to complain about Slycke and the clinic, and I certainly didn't want to get involved in D.I.A. politics.

All I wanted, I finally decided, was to get Garth someplace else.

Having made my decision, I finally fell asleep just before dawn. I was jarred awake slightly before eight by my telephone ringing—the school calling to ask if I could come in. I declined, thanked them for using me, and expressed regrets that I would not be available for any more assignments; I was taking my brother home with me to New York City.

I made a series of phone calls to check on Garth's rights and mine, and to make preliminary contingent arrangements for Garth's psychiatric treatment in the city. Then I got dressed, ate breakfast, went out into the morning, and headed toward Building 26.

12.

"THIS badge has been cancelled," the harelipped guard inside the kiosk said as he placed the square of beige plastic I had given him somewhere behind his desk. "May I have your keys, please?"

"You may not," I replied curtly as anger—and anxiety—welled up inside me. "That's a Z-13 badge, in case you didn't notice, and I'm ordering you to give it back to me."

"It's been canceled. You no longer have authority to enter this building or to carry your keys, Dr. Frederickson."

"On whose authority was that badge canceled?"

"Dr. Slycke's."

"He doesn't have that authority!"

"You'll have to take that up with him, sir. Please give me your keys."

"I'll give them back to the man who gave them to me," I said as I pointed a trembling finger at the green telephone beside the guard's right hand. "You call Slycke and get him down here. You tell him that if he won't talk to me right now, a lot of high-level shit is going to hit a high-level fan."

The guard picked up the phone, dialed a single number; he spoke into it, listened for a few moments, hung up. "Dr. Slycke will come down to speak to you," he said in a flat voice.

It took Slycke, accompanied by two burly male nurses I didn't recognize, five minutes to come down from his aerie on the fourteenth floor. In that time, two RPC Security patrol cars had appeared on the scene and were parked ostentatiously on the street at the foot of the walk leading to the entrance.

"Where the hell do you get off canceling my badge, Slycke?!" I shouted at the portly, round-faced psychiatrist as he emerged from the building, squinting against the bright sunlight.

Slycke flushed, swallowed hard. He looked decidedly uncomfortable. "Your brother has suffered a serious relapse, Frederickson," he said quietly.

That brought me up short, and suddenly my mouth and throat were very dry. "What? What do you mean, a relapse? He was fine yesterday."

"That was yesterday. During the night he lapsed back into a catatonic state which is perhaps worse than the previous one. Now his physical condition is deteriorating. We're monitoring him very closely."

"Oh, Jesus," I said as my heart began pounding in my chest. "Oh, Jesus Christ. Let me see him, Dr. Slycke."

"I'm afraid that's impossible," Slycke said stiffly. "I'm not allowing him any visitors—and especially not you. I canceled your badge because, from the beginning, you have interfered with your brother's medical treatment, and I will no longer have you endangering my patient's health.''

"I didn't put him into a catatonic state, Slycke; I brought him out of the first one."

"And what we're seeing now may be the price your brother is paying for your interference. The first priority now is to stabilize his physical condition. Then we're going to have to begin all over again with a therapy program. I'm responsible for this man's health, and in my judgment he must be treated in a strictly controlled environment, without any distractions or outside influences."

"You have no right to cancel my badge," I said in a trembling voice, fighting against a sudden wave of nausea that made me want to gag. I was thoroughly frightened.

"On the contrary," the psychiatrist replied tightly. "This is strictly a clinical decision, Frederickson, not a personal or political one. When you call Mr. Lippitt, as I'm sure you'll do the moment you leave here, he'll tell you that I've acted within my authority, which takes precedence in all medical matters. I'm not barring you as an administrator; I'm barring you as a physician."

There was something in the other man's voice that just didn't ring true to me. Struggling to contain my fury against Slycke, and my piercing anxiety over Garth, I clenched my fists and glared at the psychiatrist. Slycke refused to meet my gaze. Despite the fact that it was a cool morning, he was sweating through his lab coat.

"My God, you're lying," I breathed. "You son-of-a-bitch, you're lying!"

Now Slycke glanced at me; I could see the confirmation in his eyes . . . along with not a little fear of his own. He tried—too late—to cover his reaction by spluttering, "That's preposterous!"

"Prove it to me! I don't want the badge back! Just let me see my brother for five minutes so that I'll know you're telling the truth!"

"How dare you call me a liar!"

"You listen to me, Slycke," I intoned in a voice I hoped was sufficiently threatening to bring him up short the way he had brought me up short. "I don't know what games you're playing upstairs, but you're not going to use my brother for them. I don't need to call Mr. Lippitt—at least not until I'm ready to level some pretty heavy accusations against you. My brother wasn't committed here by any court; he was admitted on a voluntary basis, and I was the one who signed the papers. That means I can get him out seventy-two hours after filing official notice that I want him out. When I walk away from here, the first call I make will be to my lawyer. RPC, under whose aegis you operate, will have my official request for Garth's release on file before noon. In three days, exactly at the appointed hour, a private ambulance is going to pull right up to the entrance to this building. Then, no matter what shape my brother is in, he's coming out of there. You got that, pal?"

Slycke's face had gone pale, and the dark pouches beneath his eyes began to quiver. "I wouldn't do that, Frederickson."

"Let me go up to see him!"

"I . . . can't."

Struggling to keep my voice and emotions under control, I took a deep breath, slowly let it out. "Then there's something you should know, Slycke, and I'm saying it in front of these witnesses so that you will most definitely take it as a threat. If anything happens to my brother before that private ambulance can take him away—if he's in any kind of damaged state which I even suspect could have been caused by your games—I am going to take it *very* personally. You were worried about me spying for Lippitt when I wasn't; now you're just likely to have cause to worry. If I don't like what I find when I see Garth, if I think there's been any monkey business with his head or body that I think *you're* responsible for, then I'm going to *start* spying on you with a persistence you won't believe. If I ever start digging, Slycke, then your personal life and your stewardship of this clinic had better be purer than the Virgin Mary. If you don't want to find yourself up to your ass in alligators, you make damn sure Garth Frederickson is in good shape when I pick him up in three days.''

And then I turned on my heel and stalked away. When I was certain I was out of sight, I ducked behind some bushes and threw up.

By the end of the day I had filed official notice that I wanted my brother released from the clinic within seventy-two hours. I'd also made arrangements for a private ambulance to transport him, and booked a room in a private sanitarium in New York just in case Garth really was out of it when I got him back.

Then there was nothing more to do but wait—which I didn't like at all. I tried to call Lippitt, just to keep him informed, but he wasn't in his office. By using "Valhalla" as a password, I could have been put in touch with him, no matter where he was, almost immediately, but I did not choose to use this emergency procedure. There wasn't an emergency—yet. I felt I owed him the courtesy of telling him I was removing Garth from the clinic, and why, but I wasn't yet ready to push any panic buttons. I left a message asking him to call me, at his convenience.

Everything that could be done had been done, I thought. And so I continued to wait.

I no longer had access to the secret clinic, but I still had my apartment on the grounds of the hospital complex, and that's where I waited after filing notice that I intended to take my brother home. Slycke called me early in the evening of the second day.

"Frederickson, this is Charles Slycke." He sounded out of breath, as if he'd been running.

"I know who it is," I replied curtly. "Is my brother all right?"

"I must speak with you."

"I asked you about my brother!"

"He's . . . all right," Slycke said with what I considered rather ominous hesitation.

"He damn well better be."

"I must speak to you, Frederickson. Alone."

"Come on over. You know where I am."

"No. I must meet you here. There's something I have to show you."

"What?"

"Not over the phone."

"I'm on the way."

"No!" Slycke said quickly. There was a lengthy pause, during which I could hear the psychiatrist breathing heavily. Finally he continued, "There are too many people around now. Tonight there won't be so many, and I can arrange to keep the night staff busy elsewhere. Will you come to my office at eleven?"

"You took my badge, remember? I've still got my keys, but I can't get in the building without the electromagnetic strip on that badge."

"All right, I'll come down and let you in at eleven."

"Why do we have to meet in your office at eleven? Why can't we meet someplace else right now? For that matter, why can't you tell me what's on your mind over the phone?"

"I just can't speak over the phone about this, and I can't remove what I want to show you from the building. You have to come here; eleven o'clock. We won't be disturbed at that time."

"Put my brother on the phone."

"I can't do that, Frederickson."

"Why not?"

"It would look suspicious."

"To whom?"

"Not over the phone, Frederickson."

"But he *is* awake."

"Yes . . . he's awake."

"All right, Slycke. I'll see you at eleven."

"And you'll come alone?"

"I'll come alone."

Slycke hung up. I pressed down the receiver bar, released it, and got a dial tone. I called Veil, grimaced with frustration when his telephone answering machine came on. I was starting to leave a message that I needed to speak to him as soon as possible when there was a click and he came on the line.

"Hi, Mongo. I was painting, and I didn't want to be bothered by some idiot trying to sell me something."

"Sorry for the interruption, Veil."

"You're never an interruption. What's up?"

"I could use some help tonight. Can I pick you up?"

"No. I can get hold of a car and save you the trip into the city. What's the problem?"

Quickly, I filled Veil in on what had been happening with Garth, my banning from the clinic, my filing of the seventy-two-hour notice, and Slycke's phone call.

Veil's laugh was sharp, without humor. "He's got to be kidding. He really said that he wanted to meet you at eleven, and you should come alone?"

"Maybe he thinks I never go to the movies. But he could be on the level, and in any case it's an opportunity for me to try and see if Garth's all right. I have to go. I want you to ride shotgun."

"You've got it. I'll be there in an hour or so."

"We've got plenty of time, so you don't have to rush. Can you make a stop in an electronics store?"

"What do you need?"

"A miniature tape recorder, and a pair of paging beepers with matching frequencies and signal buttons."

"I'm not sure I like the idea of using beepers," Veil said as he sipped coffee at my small kitchen table and nodded at the two pocket-sized instruments in front of him. "Why don't I just come up with you?"

"He's going to be meeting me downstairs."

"You're going to have to find a way to leave the door wedged open, anyway. I'll follow the two of you up. He said he'd be keeping the staff busy elsewhere."

"Yeah, but we don't know where 'elsewhere' is. There's too much open space up there, Veil, too many long corridors. It would be hard for even a *ninja* to keep visual track of me without risk of being spotted."

"I can do it, Mongo," Veil said evenly. "Nobody will know I'm there."

"Let's stick with the beepers. I'm pretty sure I can distract Slycke with a little sleight of hand, and I'll use a credit card to wedge the door open. If I do need you, then you can come running. Did you bring a gun?"

Veil patted his right ankle.

"Well, let's hope neither of us will be needing it," I said, shoving my keys across the table to him. "You take these. The little one will open and operate the elevator; the one with the M on it will open any other door in the clinic once you get up there. You've got the floor plan I drew for you, and I've put an X over Slycke's office—which is where I assume we'll be."

"Are you taking your gun?"

I shook my head. "In my situation, I don't think it's a good idea to take a gun into a mental ward. If something does happen to me, it's conceivable that a patient could get hold of it and start spraying bullets around for no reason at all. I don't want to be shot with my own gun, and I don't want to take any undue risk of innocent people getting hurt or killed. You'll be my gun—if I need you.''

Veil nodded, then slipped my keys into his pocket.

"I'll be at the entrance to Building 26 exactly at eleven," I continued. "Precisely ten minutes later you'll get a beep—if everything is okay. You'll be in your car out on the street. After that, if I'm in there for any length of time, I'll beep you once every half hour to signal that I'm all right.''

"Let's make it every fifteen minutes, Mongo.''

"All right, twenty. After the first beep to signal I'm in no danger, twenty-minute intervals should be enough. If Slycke is dealing with me straight, and if I have to pay attention to something he's saying or showing me, I don't want to have to keep looking at my watch. One beep means that Slycke and I are having tea and crumpets and don't wish to be disturbed. Two slow beeps means I don't like something I'm seeing, but that there's time to involve RPC Security and bring some cops up with you; those keys you're carrying should get their respectful attention. Three quick beeps—or no beep at the proper interval—means that the bad guys are tying me across the railroad tracks, and the train's coming around the bend; I'll need you in a big hurry.''

"Got it," Veil said evenly as he came around the table to synchronize his watch with mine while I buttoned my shirt over the miniature tape recorder taped to my chest. The wall clock read 10:55. "You watch your ass, Mongo.''

"Yep," I said, rising to my feet and reaching inside my shirt to turn on the recorder. "Let's do it.''

We left the staff building thirty seconds apart, with Veil going to his car while I cut behind the chapel to Building 26. I'd been expecting Slycke to be waiting for me outside, by the empty kiosk. He wasn't there. I gave it three minutes, then tried the door. It was open. I stepped inside, stopped in the vestibule in front of the elevators, looked around. The

lights were on in the corridor, but they were decidedly dim-
mer than usual.

Suddenly I wished I had brought my Beretta.

"Slycke?"

There was no answer.

I'd done a few stupid things in my life, but over the years I
hoped I had learned not to confuse stupidity with courage. I
was getting too old for heroics, stupid or otherwise, and I'd
already seen enough of this dimly-lit-corridor nonsense to
convince me that I was walking into a trap. I wasn't going to
walk any farther. It was certainly a classic two-beep situation
if ever I'd seen one, but I didn't even plan on signaling Veil
and waiting until he showed up with the cops. I'd go with
him to get RPC Security, and would give Mr. Lippitt an
emergency call for backup troops.

I was heading back to the main entrance, feeling quite
smug with myself for displaying such obvious good sense,
when something very hard hit me on the back of the head,
and even the dim lights in the corridor winked out.

13.

SOMEONE was singing, "*Heigh ho, heigh ho, it's off
to work we go . . .*"

I'd never much cared for that song, and I particularly
disliked it now that it was being sung in a low, rasping,
ominously familiar voice.

"The voices will stop after I kill you, dwarf," Mama
Baker said.

"Blauugfh," I said—or something to that effect. My ears
seemed to be working perfectly well, but not my tongue.

The fact that I couldn't make my tongue and lips form words didn't really make any difference, since Mama Baker obviously wasn't interested in hearing anything I had to say, but only in sacrificing me to the cruel, demanding, maliciously chatty gods he carried around with him inside his head.

"Heigh ho, heigh ho, it's off to work we go . . ."

Nothing else seemed to be working right, either. My vision consisted of blurred, wavering images that only occasionally came into focus, then exploded or dissolved into wisps of luminous vapor that were sucked down long, multicolored DayGlo tunnels. My head felt as if the skull had melted and fused with my brain into a ball of thick rubber that was rolling around on my shoulders; I was very conscious of my own breathing, slow and deep, and the air in my lungs bubbled, fizzed, and popped like sparkling champagne; I imagined I could feel my blood, like warm milk, coursing through my veins and arteries, hear my heart pumping.

Somebody had shot me up with something seriously psychotropic, I thought, and wondered if this was how some psychotics experienced the world *before* they were medicated.

I was floating in the air face down, gently bobbing up and down like a toy blimp caught in a light breeze. I could feel my legs, and even managed to move them, but my feet weren't in contact with the ground, and so my feeble kicking was futile. My arms, however, weren't hanging in their accustomed places, and I wondered where they could have gone.

"I'm going to hang you up and slit your throat, dwarf," Mama Baker said. "When all the blood has drained out of you, I'll be free."

"Mmfltelkpt!" I replied as I rolled the ball of rubber that was my head to the left and, just for an instant, clearly saw the figure of Charles Slycke slumped against the wall just outside his open office door; the thick plastic barrel of a good-sized hypodermic needle was protruding from his right eye.

Somebody had shot Slycke up pretty good.

"Heigh ho, heigh ho, it's off to work we go . . ."

Human shapes appeared, dissolved, reappeared in the rainbow mists swirling around me. Patients I recognized.

"Fmmlptzxchpht!" I cried, shouting for help and feebly kicking my legs.

But, of course, nobody was going to help me—certainly not if it meant getting in Mama Baker's way. The freed patients of the D.I.A. clinic were content to wander aimlessly through their own private, tormented worlds, leaving Mama Baker alone with his sacrificial dwarf. The men were stepping around or over the corpses of two male nurses; one nurse had had his skull bashed in by something very heavy, and the other appeared to have been strangled.

I just kept bob-bob-bobbing along through this Hieronymus Bosch world, and I finally managed to deduce that my upper body was wrapped in a canvas camisole and Mama Baker was schlepping me around by the back straps; I deduced this just before my bearer hung me up on a prong of a wooden coatrack he'd gotten from somewhere, and placed in the hallway near the elevator. All the doors in the place seemed to be wide open.

"I'll be right back, dwarf. I gotta find myself something real sharp to cut you with."

"Tegelmimp!"

"*Heigh ho, heigh ho,*" Mama Baker sang as he walked away.

The circus was definitely in town and playing to a full house inside my skull, with everybody using my brain as a trampoline. Still, if I hoped to survive my visit to the most peculiar madhouse that the D.I.A. clinic had become, I knew that I was going to have to find *some* relatively quiet and stable corner in my drug-sotted brain where I could think, plan, and will myself to act.

I vaguely remembered making some kind of arrangements for my safety with Veil Kendry, but I couldn't remember what the arrangements had been. I kept thinking of Road Runner cartoons: *Beep-beep-beep*. It didn't make any difference; obviously, Veil wasn't around. I hoped he wasn't dead—but, no matter what he was, he couldn't help me at the moment; it would undoubtedly be a matter of only a few minutes before Mama Baker found something he considered appropriately sharp and ceremonial with which to slit my throat.

Or, if he got impatient, he might simply stick a hypodermic needle through my eye into my brain.

I couldn't understand why Veil hadn't come to rescue me. I also couldn't understand why Garth or Marl Braxton wasn't helping me. All of the patients seemed to be wandering at will through the wide open spaces of the clinic, and I had to assume that Garth and Braxton were among them. It definitely seemed an appropriate time for Garth to employ some of the soothing words and gestures that had so impressed Braxton to calm down Mama Baker. Nor would I be displeased if somebody had taken the more expedient measure of simply smashing a chair over the man's tattooed head.

And I knew I was wasting precious time for thought by engaging in petulance and speculation as to why people I'd thought I could count on had not arrived to save me from the man with the crown of scar thorns around his head and JESUS SAVES carved into his cheeks.

"Heigh ho, heigh ho, it's off to work we go . . ."

Ah, yes; thinking and planning time was over, and if I hung around on the coatrack any longer I was going to end up dead. Snow White was on his way back.

The coatrack had been set up near the elevator, which I couldn't use—but the elevator was near the stairs.

"Heigh ho, heigh ho . . ."

I bucked and wriggled in the air until I got my hips and legs swinging back and forth. At the apogee of a forward swing I bent my knees, then kicked up as high as I could; the coatrack tipped over, and I flew through the air to land hard on my back, with my head banging painfully against the floor. The wind was knocked out of me, and stars began to fill the DayGlo tunnels swirling around me. Just what I needed.

*"Heigh ho, heigh ho—*hey, dwarf!"

Mama Baker's voice seemed to be right above me—and that had a remarkably galvanizing effect on my muscles and mind.

"Sugtelmptph!" I shouted in panic as I struggled to my feet and wobbled off down one of the tunnels, through an open door, toward the stairs.

Footsteps were coming up fast behind me; with the drugs in my brain and my arms strapped around my body, there was no way I was going to outrun the other man on the stairs. Baker was going to nab me, unless I did something ingenious— like trust that I maintained what in normal times was a pretty keen sense of balance, jump, drape the canvas-shrouded upper part of my body over the steel guardrail on the stairs and slide down. I banged painfully into the knob at the end of the first section of railing, fell back, and landed on my side.

"Goddamn you, dwarf!" Baker was shouting as he scrambled down the stairs toward the first landing. "Stop! Stop, dwarf!"

Stop, dwarf? He had to be kidding me. "Mflkmpiph!" I screamed as I got to my feet, did another perilous dive and bellyflop up onto the railing, and slid down to the next landing. This time there was no knob to halt my descent— which simply meant that I sailed right off the railing and slammed hard against the opposite wall in the stairwell.

Baker's shoes clattered on the steps, descending on me. I looked up, saw something flash in his right hand as he raised it to strike . . .

I ducked under the swinging scalpel blade, once again managed to get to my feet, and flung myself on the railing. But this time I had been off balance, and had lunged too hard; I was sliding down the railing, but I was leaning too far over, slipping . . .

An instant before I would have slipped over the railing and escaped from Baker the hard way, in death, strong hands gripped the straps on the back of the straitjacket and pulled me back over the railing, set me down on the stairs.

"Mongo!"

"Elmptak!"

"You son-of-a-bitch, I'll kill you too!" Mama Baker screamed as he rushed the rest of the way down the stairs and slashed at Veil.

There was a most satisfying sound of Veil's fist colliding with Mama Baker's jaw. I savored that sound for a few moments, then decided to reward myself for my strenuous labors with a little nap.

I had vague recollections of very nasty things, but they all seemed to have happened a long time ago, in a prehistoric nightmare time. At the moment the most pressing thing I had to deal with was a splitting headache. Very gingerly, I opened one eye—and winced as a pinkish-white razor blade of light stabbed through to my brain. Gradually, I became accustomed to the light and saw Mr. Lippitt and Veil floating in the middle of it, at the foot of my bed.

And then I remembered what had happened.

I started to sit up in bed, and almost fell out of it when pain exploded inside my skull, momentarily blinding me. I cried out, and hands grabbed me and pushed me back up on the bed, eased my head back on the pillow.

"Take it easy, Mongo," Lippitt said. "You'll be all right, but you're not ready to jog around the park yet. First you have to recover from that psychotropic cocktail of LSD, Thorazine, and scopolamine Slycke shot you up with. Also, you have a slight concussion. You've been out of it for close to two days."

"Two days?!" That got my eyes open again. This time I found myself looking up into the smiling face of a handsome woman I judged to be in her early fifties. She winked at me.

"You're in the clinic infirmary," Lippitt said. "This is

Dr. Fall—the new director of the clinic. You'll be in good hands here."

"You can call me Helen, Dr. Frederickson," the woman said. "I believe you'll be feeling fine after a few more days of rest. In the meantime, if you need anything, just push the button at the side of your bed."

Helen Fall patted me reassuringly on the arm, then walked from the room. I glanced back and forth between Lippitt and Veil, who had taken up positions on opposite sides of the bed. "What the hell happened?" I croaked.

"What do you remember?" Lippitt asked, running a leathery hand back over the top of his completely bald head.

"I was supposed to meet Slycke at eleven at night up in his office. I found the door to the building open, and I went in. I didn't like the feel of the situation. I was on my way out to go with Veil to get RPC Security and call you when I got cold-cocked. I remember being carted around in a straitjacket by a psychotic patient by the name of Mama Baker who was getting ready to open up my throat. I remember taking myself off the hook, so to speak, and then getting down the stairs . . . to Veil."

"I was almost too late," Veil said tightly. "Mongo, I got the first beep, at ten after. And then I got another beep twenty minutes later. It was when I didn't get a third one that I ran to the building, and found the front door open. I figured the elevator might be just a bit too public, so I started up the stairs. I was about halfway up when I heard all this shouting and commotion above me, so I decided I'd better put a move on."

"The son-of-a-bitch had my apartment bugged," I said with disgust. "Slycke knew all about our security arrangements; he was the one sending you the signals, while he was giving me that hot shot and otherwise taking care of business upstairs. What happened serves me right for being so stupid. When I get out of here, I'm going to order myself a custom-made dunce cap."

"Better order two," Veil said. "I should have considered the possibility of your apartment being bugged."

"No dunce cap for you. But it's a damn good thing you got there when you did; about two seconds later, and you'd have had to mop me up off the ground floor."

Veil smiled thinly, shook his head. "You and your buddy were putting on quite a show, Mongo. I could see you while I was running up. There you were sliding down the railing, falling off, and sliding down another one . . . and all the while this maniac with a scalpel is clomping down the stairs, trying to catch you. It was a sight to see."

"I'm really happy Mama Baker and I kept you amused, Veil. Sprinting up those stairs must have been tiresome."

Veil laughed. "You should have seen the look on his face; he was really getting frustrated."

"The look on Mama's face was the last thing I wanted to see, Veil, I assure you. And he wouldn't have been frustrated much longer if you hadn't gotten to me when you did."

"Yeah, well, I should have followed you in like I'd wanted to in the first place. It's the last time I ever listen to you."

I turned to the old man with the soulful eyes and bald head. "So Slycke was K.G.B.?"

"An informant, not an officer," Lippitt replied with a faint note of anger in his voice. "A traitor. He'd probably been feeding information to the Russians for years. They were blackmailing him. From what we've been able to turn up in the past twenty-four hours, it looks like they had the goods on him as a homosexual; he frequented some pretty heavy leather bars in the city. They probably entrapped him with K.G.B. personnel, took photographs and made tape recordings, and then threatened to expose and ruin him if he didn't cooperate by giving them information about who was in the clinic, and what went on there. That's the way these things usually work."

"What the hell's such a big deal about being a homosexual?"

Lippitt shrugged. "It's no big deal, as long as you don't care if people know you're one. Slycke cared very much; he had a wife and four children. The bars he patronized specialize in some pretty gruesome activities. It means I was almost certainly right about the connection with Prolix; it was Slycke who provided the information about Garth—"

"Garth!" I said, sitting up. Pain sloshed around inside my head, and I swayed. Veil grabbed for me, but I pushed his hands away. "Where's my brother?!"

Lippitt and Veil looked at each other. "He's missing, Mongo," Veil said at last.

I looked at Lippitt. *"Missing?"*

The Director of the Defense Intelligence Agency nodded. "He's not here, and he's not anywhere on the hospital grounds. He's missing, along with another patient by the name of Marl Braxton."

"Oh, shit," I said.

"Lie down, Mongo."

"You're sure . . . he's not . . . ?"

"We're not sure of anything, Mongo—except that he's not here at the hospital, and the police haven't found him wandering on the roads in Rockland County. The same with Marl Braxton. Everyone else is accounted for, so we're assuming for now that Garth and this Braxton took off together. There's also a male nurse who hasn't shown up for work for two days, and who doesn't answer his phone—but we're not sure if that's connected with any of this. He wasn't on duty when all of this happened."

"Tommy Carling?" I said.

"Yes," Lippitt replied, his eyes and voice registering surprise. "How did you know?"

"Just a guess; Carling was Garth's nurse on the day shift. You know, Braxton's supposed to be very dangerous. *I* never saw him do anything violent, but—"

"Marl Braxton is indeed dangerous," Lippitt said in a flat voice. "I've reviewed his file."

"What's his story, Lippitt? I know information about Braxton is classified, but—"

"Marl Braxton is fifty-five years old, although he looks at least a decade younger," Lippitt said evenly. "During the Korean War he organized and operated in a special, very secret unit which came to be known as Reprisals."

"He was an assassin?"

Lippitt nodded. "Of sorts. Reprisals could include assassinations, but they could also be other things—depending on what it was the North Koreans had done that called for reprisals. The North Koreans are a tricky bunch, and they started doing sneaky little things to annoy us and our allies *after* we sat down to negotiate with them at Panmunjom. That's when the Reprisals unit was set up. Marl Braxton was the principal operative in his own unit, and he was very good at what he did. Then the North Koreans caught him. They had him for five years, and he was severely tortured—with acupuncture techniques, of all things. First they ruined any chance he would ever have for a sex life, and then they ruined his mind. We eventually got him back in a swap of prisoners, but by then he'd become hopelessly damaged goods. He continued to carry out reprisals—killings; but he was carrying them out against our own people—people Braxton felt had betrayed him, or who were guilty of crimes that were only fantasies in Braxton's mind. When he does decide to kill, he's cold and calculating—which makes him far more dangerous, in a way, than the patient who wanted to kill you, Mongo. Marl Braxton gives no warning; but when he decides that a person should die, for whatever reason, that person usually dies. Over the years, the prognosis hasn't changed; he will never respond to treatment."

I swallowed hard, found that my mouth had gone dry. "And this is the man who's with Garth."

"Maybe they're together, maybe not. The police in the county have been notified, as well as the NYPD. There's a Missing Persons bulletin out for both Braxton and Garth."

"I would think you'd have them put out an APB for Braxton."

"We can't have the police put out an APB for Braxton without questions being asked about his background, and things like the Reprisals unit aren't matters we like to see discussed in the newspapers. Also, the police might want to try and interrogate Braxton after they picked him up; not good for Braxton, not good for us—and potentially deadly for any police officer who tried too hard to pick him up, or pushed him too hard afterward. Let's see how far we get with the Missing Persons bulletin. The police are simply supposed to notify us immediately if they spot either Garth or Braxton."

"I have to call my parents," I said huskily.

"I already have," Lippitt said. "They're taking it well. Your parents, as you well know, are strong and positive people. They're grateful for the fact that you're alive. I apologized to them for not removing Garth from the clinic as soon as I suspected something might be wrong. I apologized to them, Mongo, and I now apologize to you."

"You don't have anything to apologize for, Lippitt. You immediately let Veil know what your suspicions were, and he let me know. At the time, I thought you were out of your mind. You gave me the information, and I should have paid more attention to it. It certainly does explain why Slycke was so paranoid about me."

Veil said, "Sure. Slycke was caught between a rock and a hard place. He was forced to take orders from, and feed information to, his K.G.B. controller. In the beginning, he may have thought that Mr. Lippitt was on to him."

"Which I wasn't," Lippitt said, anger and disdain resurfacing in his tone. "I only became suspicious when Garth first showed signs of regaining consciousness, and then the two operatives at Prolix took off."

Veil grunted. "The K.G.B. must have been leaning on Slycke hard from the beginning to keep them up to date at all times on what was happening with Garth. But you were right here all the time, Mongo, keeping a close eye on things, and they perceived you as a threat to their interests—for whatever reasons. You even mentioned to Slycke the possibility of removing Garth from the clinic, and that must have had the Russians climbing the walls. They didn't miss any of the implications of what was happening to Garth as a result of the NPPD poisoning, and they wanted to keep a close watch on all developments. They ordered Slycke to cut you out of the picture, which he tried to do.''

"And then you started to make some very heavy noises, Mongo," Lippitt said. "Not only did you make it clear to Slycke that you *still* intended to remove Garth from the clinic, but you threatened to investigate his private life. You must have really rung his bell with that one, and he couldn't tolerate the danger of being exposed a second time.''

"Which was why I ended up being carted around by Mama Baker," I said. I was thirsty. Veil poured me a glass of water from a pitcher on a table beside my bed. I drank it down, sighed. I was feeling better—better, for certain, than the man who had tried to kill me would ever feel. "I thought I saw Slycke with a needle stuck in his brain. Was that real?"

Lippitt nodded. "We don't know whether his controller ordered him to kill you, or whether it was his own idea. We're leaning toward the theory that Slycke thought it up on his own, since he was the one who felt most immediately and personally threatened; the K.G.B. could have gotten rid of you in a number of other ways. No matter whose idea it was, it seems that Slycke got caught in the same trap he'd set up for you. He knew about this Baker's obsession with killing dwarfs, and he figured he'd simply arrange for Baker to nab you 'by accident' after you'd sneaked into the clinic for an unauthorized visit to Garth. He probably sent the nurses off on some errand before he went down to ambush you. He used your beeper to signal Veil at the appropriate times while he took you upstairs and shot you up with those drugs. Then he opened up the secure unit—and got ambushed himself, with nobody around to help him. He'd juiced up the men in that unit beforehand; the blood of Baker and the other patients in the secure unit showed definite traces of amphetamines . . . definitely not the medication of choice for disturbed and violent men.''

"He'd primed them to go off beforehand," Veil said quietly, "and one or more of the patients in that unit blew up in his face. One of them got hold of Slycke's keys and—fortunately for you—opened up the whole place. Then the nurses came back and saw what was happening, but they were too late to save Slycke—or themselves. You were lucky Baker felt he had to make a special, ritual sacrifice out of you, or you'd have been killed right away, like the others.''

"I don't understand why Garth didn't try to help me," I said, looking away from the two men.

"You don't know whether or not Slycke medicated the nonviolent patients," Veil said quietly. "He may have doped everybody up, and Garth slept through it all."

"Then where is he now?"

"There's no sense in speculating on what he could or couldn't have done until we find him, Mongo," Lippitt said. "And we will find him; or he'll turn up on his own. How far could he have gone?"

PART II

Missions of Mercy

14.

ABOUT thirty-three miles, depending on construction detours.

I was out of the hospital two days later. There was no word on Garth or Marl Braxton. There was also no sign of Tommy Carling; I made it my business to check on his apartment in the staff quarters, and he was gone, the apartment stripped of his personal belongings.

There seemed nothing more to be done in Rockland County, so I moved back into Garth's apartment in the city—which by now seemed as much my home as his. I called my parents every few days, even though there was nothing to tell them; they had not heard from Garth, either.

As first the days, and then the weeks and months, went by, I tried to accustom myself to the strong possibility that my brother was dead, perhaps killed by Marl Braxton during one of the fallen D.I.A. operative's psychotic episodes. Then, on a bitterly cold afternoon in mid-fall, a Wednesday four months later, while I was standing in the express line in a Gristede's supermarket, I found a grainy picture of Garth staring back at me from the front page of one of the lurid, always ridiculous, tabloids sold at the checkout counter. With trembling hands I lifted the paper out of the rack, stared in disbelief at the photograph and the blurb under it. Disbelief and a growing disorientation. I felt as if I had been struck, or drugged again, and for a moment I feared I would loose consciousness. Slowly, I became aware of a kind of Greek chorus of cursers in the stalled line behind me, and when another cart "accidentally" banged into mine I snapped out of it. I pushed my cart ahead. Then I flipped to the two-page spread and blaring but skimpy text inside the newspaper, cursed aloud when I could not find what I wanted.

Leaving my groceries in the shopping cart, I dropped two dollars on the checkout counter, then ran the three blocks back to the apartment. I was just reaching out to pick up the telephone to call the editorial offices of the tabloid when the phone rang. Irritated, I snatched up the receiver.

"Yeah?"

"Frederickson, this is Sergeant McIntyre."

"Ah, yes, Sergeant McIntyre," I replied tightly, still fighting a sense of disorientation and dizziness, trying and failing to mask the deep scorn and anger I felt. "Perchance, would you be calling to fill me in on what the massive forces of the NYPD have been doing in their attempt to find a missing colleague?"

There was a prolonged silence on the other end, and I half expected Sergeant Alexander McIntyre, who had been in Garth's precinct and whom I considered a friend, to hang up on me. "You've seen *The National Eye*," he said at last in a flat voice.

"As a matter of fact, I just picked up a copy at Gristede's. There's nothing like going out for a few groceries and finding out that the brother you'd feared dead has become a local celebrity, of sorts. McIntyre, can you explain to me how, with a Missing Persons report in the hands of the NYPD, I end up finding Garth's picture on the front page of a Goddamn fish wrapper like *The National Eye*? You worked with him for twenty years! What the hell's the matter with you people?! What the fuck have you been doing for the past four months?!''

"Just hold on a minute, Frederickson." McIntyre's voice had grown cold, hard. "New York City, in case you haven't noticed lately, is a very big place which is easy to get lost in—if that's what you want to do. Also, in case you haven't noticed, we're in the midst of a crime wave caused by a crack epidemic; we don't have a lot of resources to look for a grown man who's just happened to have dropped out of sight. If their picture isn't on a milk carton, we don't spend a lot of time looking for them. We thought from the beginning that there was something not quite right about that MP request, and we kind of filed it away; we figured if Garth and this other guy they were looking for wanted you to know where they were, they'd have told you. Like I said, your brother's a big boy."

"Okay," I said curtly. There was no percentage in arguing with the other man.

"One of the uniformed officers in the precinct saw the picture, and he recognized Garth. That's why I'm calling you."

"Okay. I appreciate it, Sergeant."

"Did you read the story about Garth and the other guy in the picture with him?"

"The story was long on horseshit and short on facts. It didn't tell me what I need to know. Where the hell is that place Garth is supposed to be living?"

"There was a cop on the scene when that incident happened; he didn't recognize Garth, and he didn't know there was an MP blip floating on him."

"I don't care about that crap, McIntyre. Where is he?"

"It's a big, converted bathhouse down in the Bowery—five blocks south of St. Mark's. The city shut it down when the AIDS scare first started. You'll recognize it right away by all the people hanging around it." McIntyre paused, and when he spoke again, his tone had become softer. "Like I said, there was a cop on the scene when that business happened—and the cop drew the photographer. A report was filed, and maybe I can let you see it if you're interested; you stop around, and I'll see what I can do for you. I can understand how you'd be pissed, and maybe we could have done a little more than we did. Don't quote me."

"Thanks for the offer, Sergeant, but I'm not really interested in that nonsense. See you."

"Frederickson?"

"Yeah."

"What the hell's the matter with Garth?"

"Your guess is as good as mine," I replied carefully.

"The way he's acting . . . it's why the Missing Persons report was filed, right?"

"Right."

"Is he crazy?"

"Aren't we all?"

"He's sure got some funny stories to tell."

"Yeah."

"He told me he killed Orville Madison. Can you believe that?"

"*You've* talked to him in person?"

"He was—is—my friend. After I heard about the newspaper story, I drove down to check out the situation. I called you before, but you weren't in. I didn't want to just leave a message on your answering machine."

"Why didn't you bring him in, Sergeant?"

"On what charges? He was reported missing, and now he's not missing anymore. There's definitely something the matter with Garth's head, Frederickson; you wouldn't believe the collection of people he's got down there in that mission of his.''

"Mission? I thought you said he was living in a bathhouse."

There was a pause, then: "You'd better go down and see for yourself, Frederickson."

That was precisely what I intended to do. I thanked McIntyre again, hung up.

I took the subway down to the Bowery, went up to the street, and walked five blocks south, until I came to a large traffic circle. Darkness had fallen, and I stood across the street, huddled against the cold in my parka, watching the proceedings on the opposite side of the circle, in front of a building of freshly scrubbed stone which took up half the block. There appeared to be a lot of construction going on inside and on top of the building, where the roof seemed to have been torn away, but business was obviously going on as usual. It was eerie, seeing the huge symbol painted above the entrance—four interlocking rings, skewered by a great knife with a jewel-encrusted handle. Valhalla and Whisper. I wondered if the logo had been designed to Garth's specifications, somehow doubted it. Unless Garth had changed once again, my brother certainly wasn't into symbols of any kind.

A line of bedraggled people snaked down the street and disappeared around the corner. The men and women, some cloaked only in rags and pushing rickety shopping carts or carrying shopping bags filled with their personal belongings, patiently shuffled forward, waiting their turn to be ushered into the bathhouse. A number of well-dressed people—young and old, black, brown, white, and yellow—moved up and down the line, clasping hands, occasionally hugging the bag people, evidently offering hope and encouragement. All of the aides wore green jackets or headbands—sometimes both—emblazoned with the rings-and-knife logo.

Tommy Carling, still wearing an earring and his long,

blond hair in a ponytail, was there, wearing a green jacket. He was standing near the entrance, talking with a woman who also wore a green jacket, along with a black nun's cowl that fell over her shoulders.

There was no sign of Garth, and I assumed he was inside the building.

As I stood in the night shadows and watched, a television news truck pulled up to the curb in front of the entrance. A well-known local news reporter, accompanied by sound and camera men, got out and went up to Carling and the nun. The reporter said something to Carling, who shrugged his shoulders and made a gesture with his hands that seemed to indicate the line of people. There was a conference between the three people, and then the nun turned and went into the building. Lights were set up, and the reporter and his team began walking down the line of people, interviewing those who were willing.

Five minutes later the nun returned with a short man with long, greasy black hair liberally streaked with gray, who walked with a slight stoop. Even from where I was standing, I could see the ugly red and white scars on the man's face, and he wore dark glasses—which he slowly and dramatically removed as the lights came on, the camera focused on him, and the reporter stepped up to him with a microphone.

That, I thought with a grim smile, would be Harry August, obviously a con man *par excellence*. Untold numbers of readers of *The National Eye* no doubt believed that my brother had cured Harry August of total blindness, and now the credulity of a broader television audience was to be tested; there was no doubt in my mind that a lot of them would believe it too. As my mother was fond of saying, some people will believe anything.

I waited across the street for more than an hour, but still saw no sign of Garth. People continued to file into the building, and very few came out; those who did were dressed in clean clothes, looked as if they had washed, and walked considerably straighter. Finally the line of people began to thin out and shorten, and Carling seemed ready to take a break. He stepped over to the curb, lit a cigarette.

Now I stepped out of the shadows and walked quickly across the traffic circle. Carling saw me coming, flicked away his cigarette, and held out his hand.

"Mongo!" Tommy Carling said brightly.

"Where's my brother, Carling?" I said coldly as I stepped up on the curb outside the entrance to the bathhouse, ignoring the other man's outstretched hand.

Carling shrugged, then made the same gesture I had seen him make earlier with the television reporter. "I don't know. He's not back yet."

"Back from where?"

"He's walking the streets with Marl and a few of the Guardian Angels; they're looking for more people to take in for the night."

"*Marl*? Braxton's here?"

The male nurse nodded.

"Braxton's *dangerous*, Carling. You told me that yourself; you said he was the most dangerous man in the clinic. You're supposed to be a Goddamn mental health professional. What the hell are you doing parading around with this freak show?"

"Freak show, Mongo?" Carling said softly.

"I'm not talking about these poor people, Carling, and you know it! I want to know why you let my brother go off walking the streets with a potential killer!"

"Marl isn't dangerous any longer, Mongo," he replied easily. "Except, perhaps, to anyone who tried to harm Garth. That hasn't happened yet, and I don't believe it ever will. Marl is Garth's protector, not his enemy."

"Carling, you son-of-a-bitch, why couldn't you at least have picked up a phone and told me that Garth was with you, and that he was all right?"

The big man with the ponytail flushed slightly, dropped his gaze. "I guess I should have," he said softly.

"You're damn right you should have! How the hell do you think my parents and I have *felt* all these months, not knowing whether Garth was dead or alive?"

"I . . . wasn't sure what your attitude would be, or what might happen if the D.I.A. got hold of him again. I knew . . . what Slycke was planning to do, and I just couldn't let that happen. If there was any chance that Dr. Slycke might somehow still manage to—"

"What the hell are you talking about? Slycke's dead."

Tommy Carling looked at me, his mouth slightly open. He shook his head, swallowed. "What did you say?"

"You didn't know?"

"That Dr. Slycke is dead? Of course not. How did it happen? When?"

"Is there someplace we can talk?"

Carling nodded, then gestured toward the entrance to the bathhouse. I followed him inside, through a group of bag people who were still clustered at the entrance. I stopped just inside the entrance and looked around, stunned by what I saw.

The interior of the building, that part which I could see, was huge; with all of the interior walls gutted, the space I found myself in looked as big as an airplane hangar. There was a lot of scaffolding spiderwebbing the interior space, and anchored to a stone balcony which went all around the hall. The entire roof of the building had been removed, and was now covered with layers of heavy plastic sheeting. Everything looked spotless—scrubbed where it was stone and freshly painted where it was wood. The line of people outside led directly to a long, gleaming counter where stew was being served out of huge, steaming cooking pots by men and women in green, logo-emblazoned jackets or headbands. People ate off paper plates in one section of the vast hall, while in another people rested in neat, tightly packed rows on air mattresses, covered by khaki army surplus blankets which looked new. At the far end of the hall, men and women wearing pale brown robes and paper slippers, with towels draped over their shoulders, emerged from two sets of swinging doors which exuded faint wisps of steam. The men and women filed behind separate partitions, emerged dressed in clothes that were obviously used, but clean. Then they left, or went to get food, or went to rest on an air mattress and blanket, which were being distributed by the nun.

Music, unobtrusive but still clearly audible, filled the hall, piped in through at least a dozen loudspeakers hanging from the stone balcony. *Siegfried.*

Men and women who were either doctors or paramedics moved quietly among the people on the air mattresses, checking throats, answering questions, listening to heartbeats, occasionally giving out something from the black leather bags they carried. Like the other workers, the medical people wore the distinctive green jackets or headbands.

There was a strange odor in the air, rising above all the other odors, which caught my attention, but which I could not immediately identify. Outside the building, there had been the smell of the streets and unwashed bodies; inside was the smell of soap, disinfectant, steam, paint, washed stone, medicine, plastic, coffee, hot food—but the smell that had caught my attention was none of these. I found the odor vaguely ominous.

"What the hell?" I murmured.

"Are you impressed, Mongo?" Tommy Carling asked quietly.

"Who runs this place?"

"Everybody; nobody."

"Who owns the building?"

"It belongs to Garth; the deed is registered in his name."

"Oh, yeah? Not bad for a guy who's never had more than two thousand dollars in the bank, and who hasn't even been bothering to pick up his disability checks."

"The money comes from many sources, Mongo. God provides. Shall we go someplace where it's quieter?"

I followed Carling across the hall, through a maze of pipe scaffolding, through a door and into a medium-sized office. Like everything else, it had been freshly painted. There was a desk, and a couple of chairs. The entire wall behind the desk was covered with a rendering of the rings-and-knife logo. *Siegfried* was playing here, too.

"You mind turning off that music?"

Carling sat down behind the desk, turned a rheostat on the wall; the music grew softer, but continued to play. "It always plays," Carling said simply, motioning for me to sit down in one of the straight-backed chairs. "We prefer it that way. We've learned from Garth to let that music serve to remind us of all that needs to be done; it focuses the concentration."

"I find it distracting."

Carling shrugged. "Yes, well; there's the difference, I guess."

"What difference?"

"Between you and us."

"How does God provide, Tommy?"

"You seem fixated on financial questions, Mongo."

"I'm curious; I'm curious as to what Garth is a part of, and who's financing it. If the deed for this place is registered in Garth's name, it could make him legally, or morally, responsible for things he might not want to be responsible for."

"Did you see anything illegal or immoral happening out there?"

"I just got here."

"Some people might say that it's none of your business," the other man said evenly.

"Some might."

"Would you believe that we picked up this place for a ten percent down payment against the back taxes owed by the previous owners?"

"I don't know. Why shouldn't I believe you?"

"Because you're a very skeptical man, Mongo—some people might even describe you as cynical."

"Yeah, but I've never tried to buy a bathhouse."

"It was foreclosed some years ago by the city after they closed it down. At the time, this wasn't exactly a target area for real estate developers, and the city was more than happy to unload it. It was a white elephant."

"There are a lot of other things going on around here that aren't financed by payments against back taxes."

"Word gets around."

"Word of what?"

"Word of good people with good intentions doing good things. Most people really do want to help people who are less fortunate than they are, Mongo, if you only give them a chance—and if you set an example and lead them. There are individuals and corporations, as well as various relief and funding agencies, which heartily approve of what we're doing, and they've been contributing substantial amounts of money, goods, and services. They like what's happening here. Most of the construction and mass organization you saw out there has only begun to happen in the past month or so."

"What is it that's happening here?"

"What you see."

"I'm not sure what I see."

"That doesn't surprise me, Mongo," Carling said in the same even tone—which was beginning to irritate me. "Each person must finally be responsible for what he sees—or doesn't see—with his own eyes, how he feels about what he sees, and what he does about it. That's one of Garth's lessons; it seems simple, but it certainly isn't."

"I'm Garth's Goddamn brother, Tommy, and I've been searching for him for four months! Why is it that none of this great 'word' ever got around to me?!"

Tommy Carling studied me with his expressive, hazel eyes. "Perhaps you didn't have the ears to hear, Mongo," he said at last in a very soft voice. "Somewhere it's written, 'Seek and ye shall find.' "

"You've got to be putting me on," I said in a low voice, feeling my anger begin to swell in me.

"I don't understand what you mean."

"No? Let me tell you who else has been just a tad concerned about Garth, my friend. Did it ever occur to you that his mother and father might have liked to receive just one little ring-a-ling to inform them that their son wasn't dead or lying comatose and unidentified in some strange hospital?!"

"But, if Garth chose not to—"

"Garth's sick!" I snapped. "He's not responsible for anything he thinks, says, or does. *You're* the one I hold responsible, Tommy!"

"Garth is not sick," Tommy Carling replied somewhat petulantly. "He's probably the healthiest person on the face of the earth."

"You've got to be kidding me."

"I admit I—we—may have handled things badly, and that maybe I should have pressed Garth to contact you and your parents; but I told you that I was very concerned about what could happen if Dr. Slycke ever got hold of Garth again."

"And I told you that Slycke was dead."

"I didn't know that, Mongo. It's the truth; if I had known, I would have handled things much differently. Do you care to tell me what happened to him?"

"Why don't you tell me how you come to be here with Garth and Marl Braxton in this super–Salvation Army operation."

"The Salvation Army totally supports our work here, Mongo, and they might not think much of your attitude. You tell me your story first. How did Dr. Slycke die?"

Watching Carling's face very carefully, I told him what had happened up in the clinic the night I had gone there in response to Slycke's phone call. When I had finished, Carling tugged absently at his earring and shook his head.

"That's incredible, Mongo; you were incredibly lucky to get out of there alive."

"So I've been told."

"I didn't know about any of this. Naturally, since the clinic is a secret facility, news of Dr. Slycke's death wouldn't have been in the newspapers—even if I'd been reading them."

"Your turn, Tommy. The three of you took off even before Slycke called me, which means you must have snuck Garth and Braxton out from under Slycke's nose."

"Yes."

"Why?"

"Garth never had any kind of relapse, Mongo. Slycke was lying."

"I'd gathered that," I said dryly.

"You talked to Slycke after you talked to me, about the same thing—the possibility of removing Garth from the clinic. You shouldn't have done that. It was why I didn't plan to report the conversation to Dr. Slycke; I knew it would make him very nervous. In fact, he panicked. I'm not sure why he reacted as severely as he did, but my guess is that he was under pressure—as you suspected might happen—from his superiors in Washington to keep Garth under close observation at all times, in order to monitor the effects of NPPD poisoning." Carling paused, seeming to study the opposite wall for a few moments, then continued: "Still, he was *so* upset that you might even be *thinking* about taking Garth out. I'm not sure I understand it. How could his superiors hold him responsible for potential actions of yours which you had every right to make? It doesn't make sense."

"Slycke's problems weren't with the D.I.A., Tommy, and they weren't the ones putting the pressure on him. He was an informant for the K.G.B., and they had their hooks into him good."

Carling's eyes opened wide, and he blinked slowly. "What?"

"Slycke was passing on information to the Russians, as

well as taking orders from them. It was the K.G.B. making him nervous.''

''Ahh,'' Carling said distantly, once again focusing his gaze on the wall behind me. ''That could certainly explain a few other things.''

''Like what?''

''I'd told you that Charles Slycke was a good doctor—and I sincerely believed that. It was why what he was planning to do came as such a shock to me.''

''What was he planning to do?''

''He was going to institute a clearly experimental—and potentially dangerous—drug therapy program with Garth. There was absolutely no reason to do that, and it was unethical; he planned to do it in secret, without informing either Garth or you, or even trying to get permission. That made it illegal, as well.''

''Just what kind of a program was this?''

''He was going to medicate Garth with a whole series of very powerful psychotropics. In effect, from what I could understand, his only motive was simply to see what might *happen*. I couldn't believe my ears when he told me what he was planning to do, or my eyes when I saw the medication orders on the daily sheet.''

''He came up with this plan just before he barred me from the clinic?''

''Yes. Even a layman could see that Garth had made tremendous progress in a very short time. He wasn't violent, certainly no threat to himself or others, and he was lucid. Under *no* circumstances would any responsible psychiatrist want to do absolutely anything but continue to observe patiently, listen, and perhaps counsel. Yet Dr. Slycke was planning to *saturate* Garth with these *drugs*. I couldn't make any sense out of it—and then I remembered some of the concerns you'd expressed to me during the course of our conversation outside on the grass. I realized then that you'd been absolutely right. I also understood then why you'd been barred from the clinic. I guess I panicked.''

''Why didn't you call and tell me about this when it happened, Tommy?''

''There was so little time. I was to begin administering doses to Garth—in any way I could manage—that very evening. I didn't know if you'd be able to stop Slycke, or what would happen to Garth, or me, if I tried to stop him. I'm just a nurse, and he could have ordered me off the premises out-of-hand—and had me locked up, to boot, as a suspected security risk. I was . . . very upset. By that time, as I think you know, I'd become very attached to Garth—and to you, if I may say so. I just couldn't let Dr. Slycke do something that could destroy Garth's mind. So I did the only thing I could think of at the moment.''

''You took Garth out.''

''Yes,'' Tommy Carling replied quietly. ''I just had to do *something*. I hadn't even thought about what I was going to do afterward . . . I just acted.''

''Thank you, Tommy,'' I said simply. ''Garth and I owe you more than we can repay.''

''Oh, no,'' the other man said quickly—and then looked at me in a way that made me slightly uncomfortable. I'd seen a similar look before—on Marl Braxton's face, when he had started to talk about Garth. ''It's I who owe the two of you. Garth is . . . very special.''

''How did Marl Braxton get to join the party?''

''I took him out with Garth. Garth wouldn't leave without him, and . . . well, there just wasn't a lot of time to argue; I only had two or three minutes' leeway. If I didn't take Garth out then, the chances were slim that I would be able to do it at all before he was drugged.''

''A hell of a big decision, Tommy.''

''Yes,'' the male nurse replied simply.

''How did you know Braxton wouldn't kill you the moment you got them away from the clinic? For that matter, how do you know he still won't kill Garth or you one of these days?''

Carling shook his head. ''Garth assured me that Marl would be fine, and that he wouldn't cause any trouble. It's hard to explain, Mongo, but somehow I knew *instinctively* that Garth was right. He was.''

''So far.''

''He was right.''

''Garth has an apartment.'' I said tightly. ''I happen to be living in it. Why didn't you bring him back there?''

''For the same reason I didn't contact you; I was afraid the authorities would catch us, and somehow force Garth to go back to Slycke. Besides, Garth didn't want to go back there. He told me he wanted nothing more to do with anything in his past.

''We ended up in a flophouse not too far from here. I had some cash with me, but it wasn't going to go very far with the three of us.'' Carling paused, spread his hands on the surface of the desk. ''Mongo, I don't really know how to explain easily all that's happened since then. Four months is such a short time, but . . .''

''Just tell me what happened, Tommy.''

''On that very first night, Garth started his work—talking to and comforting some of the others in the flophouse, walking the streets and talking to drunks, bag people, people living in cardboard boxes. Those people responded to him the same way the patients in the clinic responded to him. Garth explained to me that he had to do these things, that it was the only way he could keep from crying.

''The next day, Garth went to the bank and emptied his savings account. He thanked me for taking him out of the clinic, and told me I should leave and go back to my old life. He and Marl were going to spend all his money on food and clothing for the street people, and then just do whatever it was they had to do. He wasn't worried at all about the future.

Mongo, I just got caught up in the spirit of what Garth was trying to do. You may say I'm crazy, or a fool, but I didn't want to leave. I just had this feeling—and it's impossible to describe—that something wonderful and very important was about to happen, and I wanted to be a part of it. I had my own savings, and a trust fund with a not inconsiderable amount of money in it. I used that money to put the down payment on the sacred bathhouse to use as a base of operations for what Garth wanted to do, as well as buy the first food and clothing supplies to give out to those who needed it.''

"If you used your money to buy the bathhouse, why did you put it in Garth's name?"

"Because I wanted to." Carling paused, smiled thinly. "You still don't understand. It was *Garth* who was going to make this wonderful, important thing happen, not my money. Although I didn't fully realize it at the time, I'd made a commitment, like Marl, to give everything I had—including my life—to whatever it was Garth wanted to do."

"Go ahead."

"After we moved into the bathhouse, things just began to snowball. Garth and Marl were out all the time, walking the streets and bringing people back here for food, shelter, clothing—or just comfort. We were quickly running out of everything, including money, and then the wonderful things started to happen. The 'word' that I mentioned had already started to get around. The Salvation Army, as well as a number of other relief agencies that operate down here, began to help us and share their resources. Lines began to form, and still Garth and Marl walked the streets to bring more people here. I think what most impressed the other agencies was Garth's *effectiveness*; some of the men and women he got to come to us for help would never think of going anywhere else. Nobody had ever been able to get them to accept help; they had always been afraid to go to city shelters, even during the winter."

"Afraid with good reason," I interjected. "They get ripped off in those shelters. Who keeps order here?"

Carling thought about it, as if the question hadn't occurred to him before. "There's Marl, of course," he said at last. "He can be very intimidating—to anyone who's looking for trouble. Also, we have a couple of dozen Guardian Angels who work for us. But we've never really had any trouble. There's just this feeling of *goodness* and good feeling around here that's almost palpable, at least to some of us, and I really do believe that it's this sense of goodness that radiates from Garth which keeps away evil." He paused, flushed slightly. "Silly, I know."

"Maybe not so silly," I said quietly. I was indeed most impressed with what was going on in the bathhouse—and terribly proud of my brother, despite all my other concerns and misgivings.

"Anyway, almost before we knew it, we were getting all sorts of offers of money, goods, and services from other relief programs, wealthy individuals, and corporations; the jackets and headbands you see everyone wearing are donated —no advertising strings attached—by a sporting goods manufacturer. You want a jacket, Mongo? I'm sure we can find one that will fit you."

"Let me think about it."

"The point is that we ended up, virtually overnight, with a sizable financial structure—and the responsibility that goes along with it. Thank God for Sister Kate."

"Sister Kate, I take it, is the nun outside?"

Carling nodded. "She's with the Sisters of Mercy. They donated her, in a manner of speaking, and it was a most significant contribution. Besides being a nun, she's a C.P.A., with an M.B.A. from Wharton. She helped us organize, and she keeps the books. Without her, we'd have been swamped long ago. She's just wonderful. She's a gift from God— Who, as I said, provides."

"But she's still a Catholic, in good standing with her order?"

"Of course; as I said, they 'donated' her. Why shouldn't she be?"

I pointed to the rings-and-knife mural on the wall behind the desk. "Is that a religious symbol?" I asked in what I hoped was a neutral tone.

"No. It's just . . . well, it's just kind of a sign that identifies. People seem to like it. Kind of 'catchy,' don't you think?"

"It seems kind of militaristic for an organization like yours."

"Not at all; not when you understand what the rings symbolize."

"Wagner's operas."

"The Four Horsemen of the Apocalypse. The great knife is Garth, struggling to defeat them."

"Who understands that?"

"People who understand it."

"Who designed it?"

"A Guardian Angel who used to be a graffiti artist. He'd been listening to Garth's stories about the Valhalla Project, and he came up with it. Everyone thought it was just super, so we adopted it as a logo. Why?"

"Just curious."

"Incidentally, I know now that all of Garth's stories about Siegmund Loge and the Valhalla Project are true, Mongo. Garth was never psychotic. He was simply telling the truth to the doctors, nurses, and patients in the clinic—but the patients were the only ones who sensed that it was the truth. Interesting."

"Yeah, interesting. What do you call yourselves?"

"We don't call ourselves anything. Others are starting to call us Garth's People."

"Lousy name," I said as I felt a sudden chill.

"Why?" Carling asked, and smiled thinly. "Because it reminds you of the name given to the people in Siegmund Loge's communes—Father's Children?"

"Something like that." The notion that Garth, even inadvertently, might be taking up where Siegmund Loge had left off in the overall scheme of things was just too sour an irony to dwell on. The Triage Parabola. Human extinction. Loge had said that, given our present state of *being*, nothing could be done; history would keep repeating itself over and over and over, until . . . "Forget it. What difference does it make what you're called?"

"No difference. Names aren't important. The only important thing is Garth's mission on earth."

"His 'mission on earth,' Tommy?"

"Yes."

I spread my arms in a gesture meant to encompass the room, the bathhouse, the streets outside—and perhaps beyond. "What's your thinking about how Garth fits into all this?" The sudden chill I had felt hadn't gone away; indeed, I was growing colder by the moment.

"I don't understand your question," Carling said, leaning forward on the desk. His ponytail had fallen over his right shoulder. "Without Garth, *this* wouldn't exist. Garth *is* 'this.' "

"Tommy," I said as I breathed a small sigh, "from the very first time I saw you working with Garth, I knew you were a hell of a good nurse, a solid professional. I also pegged you as a man with his head and heart in the right place, and both feet solidly on the ground."

"But now you've changed your opinion of me?" the other man asked in a mild tone.

"Tommy, I can't begin to tell you how much I appreciate —am grateful to you for getting Garth away from that clinic when you did. If you hadn't done what you did, Garth could have lost his mind, and maybe his life. But now I have to ask you a question."

"Please do," Tommy Carling said in the same mild tone.

"Anyone can see that you're helping all sorts of people, doing all sorts of good works . . ."

"But?"

"Is what you're up to here good for *Garth*? Once, that would have been the first question you asked yourself."

Carling looked vaguely surprised. "*Good* for Garth? This is what he wants and desperately *needs*, Mongo. You don't seem to be able to understand—or accept—that. He's a man who feels the suffering of others to the very core of his soul. You know that he *cries* when he sees someone—man, woman or child—hungry, cold, or in pain? To help other people is not only a spiritual need for Garth; it is, without exaggeration, a *physical* one."

"Tommy, my brother's an escaped mental patient, with his thinking seriously out of joint. I know this is selfish, and not at all in the spirit of the way things are done around here, but I have to think of my brother's welfare first. It occurs to me that all the business I see around here just feeds into his fantasies."

"Fantasies, Mongo?" the male nurse said, raising his eyebrows slightly. "Just what fantasies of Garth's are you referring to? Siegmund Loge, the Triage Parabola, and the Valhalla Project? Or maybe you mean his fantasy that he killed Orville Madison—and tried to kill somebody named Veil Kendry—because of the hurt inflicted on you?"

I quickly looked away, angry for having trapped myself. "Maybe 'fantasies' was a poor choice of words. What you're doing is feeding into his problem—which is a badly distorted self-image and perception of reality. He belongs back in a mental hospital, not walking the streets playing Mother Theresa."

Tommy Carling slowly shook his head, then absently brushed his ponytail back over his shoulder. "You're a hard man, Mongo. I honestly believe there's no sense of wonder—of awe or mystery—in you. I think I feel sorry for you."

"Thanks, Tommy. Believe me, I can use all the sympathy

I can get. I'd like you to feel a little pity for my brother.''

"Garth doesn't need my pity; he's the man who's given *me* a renewed sense of wonder, awe, and mystery.''

"Garth is very seriously mentally disturbed.''

Again, Carling shook his head. "You truly believe that, Mongo? Still?''

"Still? Not so long ago you would never have questioned it. You didn't help Garth escape from the clinic because you thought he was well; you took him out because you couldn't bear to see a sick man made even sicker at the hands of a fool.'' I paused, swallowed, put my own hands on the desk. "I guess what I'm doing is asking for your support in trying to convince Garth that he should go back to the D.I.A. clinic. He'll be all right there now.''

"Garth doesn't belong in a mental hospital, Mongo,'' Carling said evenly. "Nor does Marl—not any longer, thanks to Garth. Garth is carrying out God's design for him.''

"What does that mean, Tommy?'' I asked, feeling my stomach muscles tighten.

Tommy Carling's easy, loud laugh startled me. "You've really been having a problem getting around to asking me what's really on your mind, haven't you? Well, the answer is yes, I *do* believe Garth is the Son of God, the Messiah. I believe just as Marl believes—and yes, I know about the conversation you had with Marl. If my thinking—knowing—that Garth is God's son, His personal messenger and our Savior, makes me crazy in your eyes, then so be it. I'm filled with more joy than you can possibly imagine, and what you think just doesn't matter to me.''

"Tommy, your brains have run out your ears.''

Carling merely smiled. "You hear something which disturbs you, and the only way you can react is with an insult. As I said, I feel sorry for you. I don't mean any offense, Mongo, but I can't help but wonder now if that scar on your forehead wasn't put there when it was for a reason.''

"That's cute, Tommy; it's a new twist, and I love it. When did this great revelation about Garth come to you?"

"Now that I think back, I think I was beginning to realize it back at the clinic, even before I took Garth out," he replied, totally oblivious to—or choosing to ignore—my heartily felt sarcasm. "I began to realize it when I saw the incredible impact Garth had on sick people. Now . . . I'm just grateful that God chose me as His tool to save His son from destruction."

"Marl Braxton didn't plant this notion in your head?"

"No. I believe you were the only person Marl broached that subject to—and only because you're Garth's brother. I was the one who went to him with . . . my conviction. That was when he told me about his. We had quite a laugh over it."

"I'll bet you did. Tommy, you don't really believe that Garth made a blind man see again, do you?"

"Absolutely," Carling said without hesitation. "There's no question that it happened. In fact, you had witnesses—including a New York City policeman, and a photographer. And there have been other miracles. The transformation of Marl Braxton is one—perhaps that was Garth's first miracle. Considering who—what—Garth is, it really isn't surprising that he should be able to perform miracles, is it?"

"Tommy, are you people running around advertising that Garth is the Messiah?"

"No. Even if we wanted to do that, Garth wouldn't permit it."

"Because he doesn't believe it himself."

"What Garth says and does is proof of who he is. Many people have already come to realize the truth, and their numbers will grow. Do you totally discount the possibility of miracles, Mongo?"

"In the sense that you mean the word, yes."

"Why?"

"Because I had to take science courses, beginning in grade school."

"What about the existence of God?"

"I don't know what you mean by 'God.' If you mean a kindly old fellow who periodically sends one of his offspring to earth to do magic tricks, the answer is no. The notion of divine intervention is a very old superstition, as old as our species. In its various manifestations down through the ages, the business of looking for, and finding, messiahs has caused us a lot of grief."

"That doesn't mean it couldn't happen."

"It's silly on the face of it."

"How do you explain Garth's impact on people?"

"How do you explain the impact Jim Jones or Adolf Hitler had on people?"

"Are you comparing your brother to mass murderers?"

"I'm saying that I have no way to explain why all of us occasionally think and behave in an irrational manner. I can't explain why people believe the things they do, or why they react to certain people the way they do. If somebody like you, who's intelligent and well educated, begins touting miracles and messiahs, what can we expect of people who aren't as intelligent and well educated?"

"But you don't understand," Tommy Carling said softly. "Garth really *is* the Messiah. When that sinks into your head, you'll feel the same joy and sense of wonder the rest of us feel. And your life will be changed forever."

"If this Harry August tells you he was totally blind and Garth made him see again, he's bullshitting all of you. You tell him I said that when you see him."

There was a soft knock on the door. Carling rose from behind the desk, walked across the office, and opened it. In the doorway stood the nun and the scar-faced man with the long, greasy black hair and dark glasses.

"Excuse me," the woman said, curtsying slightly in my direction. "I hope we're not interrupting anything important. Harry and I just wanted to meet Garth's famous brother.''

Carling opened the door wider, stepped aside, then turned to me. ''Mongo,'' he said evenly, ''perhaps you'd like to deliver your message to Harry in person.''

15.

I put Sister Kate in her late thirties or early forties. The hair that peeked from beneath the tight white band securing her black cowl was red. She had a sculpted face, with bright green eyes, high cheekbones, and a full mouth which was now set in a pleasant, expectant smile. She wore no makeup. Aside from her nun's cowl, the rest of her clothing was strictly secular; the green jacket over a Mets sweat shirt, jeans, and sneakers. She was a handsome woman, with an unmistakable, no-nonsense air of authority: I certainly wouldn't want to skim money from any outfit whose books she was auditing, and the fact that all the money and goods that were swirling around Garth at the moment were being properly accounted for made me feel slightly better.

The feelings Harry August stirred in me weren't quite so benign or reassuring. As far as I was concerned, despite his misshapen face, he had ''phony'' written all over him. His greasy hair and generally unkempt appearance made him an eyesore in a place where the watchword seemed to be cleanliness; obviously, he wasn't taking advantage of the shower facilities at the rear of the building. He was unshaven and looked thoroughly grubby. His facial features were twisted horribly out of shape by scar tissue which ringed both his eyes and radiated up over his forehead, down over his cheekbones. One milky brown eye was permanently tugged half shut by the scar tissue. I stared back into the one fully open eye of the "blind man" responsible for getting my brother on the front page of *The National Eye*.

"Pleased to meet you, Dr. Frederickson," the nun said in a low, pleasing voice. "I'm Sister Kate, and this is Harry August."

"You could have met me a lot sooner, Sister," I replied coldly, "if somebody in this organization had extended me the courtesy of picking up a telephone and calling me to let me know where my brother was."

Sister Kate looked inquiringly at Tommy Carling, then back to me. "Then I must apologize for all of us, Dr. Frederickson," she said in the same mild, disarming tone. "Not all of us were aware that you didn't know; I guess we all just assumed that Garth had been in touch with you."

"You assumed wrong."

The nun's silence and slightly downcast eyes comprised a most eloquent response; other people shouldn't be blamed for failing to do something that should have been my brother's responsibility. She had a point.

"There's something you wanted to say to me, Frederickson?" Harry August asked, peering at me with his one good eye.

"I have nothing to say to you, Mr. August," I replied sharply. I was feeling colder, angrier, increasingly helpless and frustrated. "I came here for one simple reason—to see my brother. I believe I've outstayed my welcome, and I'd appreciate it if one of you good people would tell Garth that I was here. Now you'll have to excuse me."

"Garth is here, Mongo." My brother's head and broad shoulders suddenly appeared in the doorway, framed by the nun and Harry August. Sister Kate and August moved aside at the sound of my brother's voice, and I could see that Marl Braxton was standing next to Garth. Behind them, crowded in a semicircle, were a number of tough-looking young men, all dressed in green jackets. "Welcome."

"Hello, Garth."

"You look well, Mongo," Garth said evenly as he and Marl Braxton entered the office. The stony-faced young men remained outside—as if standing silent vigil. From Garth's tone and manner, one would have thought that no more than a day or so had passed since we'd last spoken. He didn't seem at all surprised to see me; indeed, his expression seemed oddly blank to me.

"Hi, Mongo," Braxton said to me, his tone curiously flat.

"Hello, Marl," I said curtly, then turned my attention back to my brother. "Garth, I'd like to talk to you alone."

"Why alone, Mongo? All of us here are like a family."

"Not my family." I paused, watched as Marl Braxton leaned close to Garth and whispered something in his ear. Garth shook his head, smiled thinly, and made a deprecating gesture with his hands. I continued tightly, "Have you got something to say, Marl?"

Now Braxton shifted his gaze to me. "I've told Garth that I believe you may have been marked by God as a warning, Mongo," he said evenly, the expression on his face curiously bland. "I mean no offense."

"Marked?"

Slowly, Marl Braxton lifted his hand and pointed his index finger at my forehead. "That scar may have been put there by God as a warning to Garth's followers to be wary of anything you do or say. I've told Garth that I'm not sure it's a good idea for him to be alone with you."

I glared back into Marl Braxton's impassive face for a few moments, then bit off what I wanted to say as I reminded myself that Braxton was a certified madman. "Do you honestly believe I would do anything to hurt my brother, Marl?"

"You have been marked."

"Garth, do you believe that?"

"No," my brother replied matter-of-factly. "Garth doesn't believe you'd ever try to hurt him, and Garth doesn't believe you've been marked by God. There is no God."

"Everyone around here seems to disagree with you. They

not only believe in God, they believe you're His son.''

"What difference does it make what my friends believe, Mongo? Actions are what are important, and all of us here work toward a common goal.''

Slowly, I swept my gaze around the office—meeting the gazes of Sister Kate, Harry August, Tommy Carling, Marl Braxton, and the silent guardians outside the doorway. "I've got a flash for all of you," I said tightly. "Marked or not, I'm still Garth's brother; he's my flesh and blood.''

"He belongs to all of us now," Tommy Carling said evenly. "He belongs to the world.''

"Well, I want your Messiah all to myself for a few minutes. After I've talked to him alone, I don't give a damn what all of you do. But if everybody but Garth isn't out of this room in twenty seconds, and that door isn't closed behind you, I'll tell you what *I'm* going to do. The Messiah's earth brother is going to walk out of here and do something really crazy just so he can get some newspaper space and a few minutes on the evening news. I'll see if I can make a big enough fool out of myself, so that maybe people will begin to see what fools all of you are; I'm not sure Garth's People are ready for the kind of publicity I plan to get you. I'm not sure yet just what stunt I'll pull, but I'm already giving it some serious thought.''

Only Garth, who was smiling benignly, seemed unperturbed by my patently ridiculous threat to try to embarrass a group of volunteers whose only crime was trying to feed, clothe, and otherwise care for the countless numbers of the homeless, helpless, and hopeless who lived on New York City's streets. Harry August took a step backward, as if I had physically struck him; Marl Braxton's dark eyes clouded, and I could see the muscles in his neck and jaw begin to move: Sister Kate and Tommy Carling exchanged a quick glance.

"Garth?" Tommy Carling said. "Is it all right with you? Do you mind talking to your brother alone?''

"Of course not," Garth replied, and shrugged. "Why should Garth mind?"

It seemed an eminently sane response. Now Sister Kate took charge, ushering August, Braxton, and Carling out the door before leaving herself and quietly shutting the door behind her. I was left alone with the strange stranger who was my brother, who simply stood in the center of the room, his heavily muscled arms crossed over his chest, smiling at me. His wheat-colored hair had grown very long, and almost reached his shoulders; his brown eyes seemed full of strange lights, and the expression on his face was inscrutable.

"I almost didn't recognize you without your earphones," I said.

I'd hoped for at least a chuckle; instead, I got a serious reply.

"Garth doesn't listen to the music when he's on the streets. It isn't needed out there. Garth goes out to hear and be heard. The people living on the sidewalks are the music."

"What does Garth hear, and what is it that he wants to be heard?"

"We talk of need, loneliness, and pain. Then Garth tries to bring them back here so that we can do something about those things."

"You're doing good work, brother."

"Yes; Garth knows that. As you see, Garth has a lot of help."

"How did all those volunteers out there find out about you?"

"Garth doesn't know. They just come in off the street and ask if they can help."

"How come I didn't hear about you?"

"Garth doesn't know."

"Garth . . ." I took a couple of steps forward, then stopped. I wanted to hug my brother, tell him that I loved him and was proud of him; and tell him just to *stop* being crazy. But my heart wasn't in it. There was a wall between us that I

couldn't find a way to cross over. Besides, Garth no longer
seemed all that crazy to me. Carling now sounded crazier
than my brother. Everyone in the world, I thought, should be
as crazy as this big, gentle man who, with no thought whatsoever of earthly or heavenly gain, simply walked the streets
to gather in the mentally and physically crippled. Garth no
longer seemed crazy, only . . . different. Perhaps unalterably
changed. He was now a stranger I would probably never get
to know, because I would never be able to hear the music he
heard, the way he heard it. Which was probably the reason
neither the NYPD nor I had heard anything about him until
he had turned up on the front page of *The National Eye*.

"Why didn't you call me?"

Garth frowned. "Have you been ill?"

My brother now existed, almost literally, in another world.
And there were more of "them" than there were of "us."
The Lessons of Siegmund Loge.

"*No*, I haven't been ill. Did it ever occur to you that I
might have been worried about *you*?"

My brother thought about it, then slowly shook his head.
"No. That didn't occur to Garth."

"At the very least, you should have called Mom and Dad.
They've been worried sick about you. We thought you might
be dead."

"Garth has been all right."

"You should have called and told them that."

"Garth will call them if you think it's a good idea."

"Garth, don't Mom and Dad even *mean* anything to you
anymore?"

"Yes. Of course."

"Then why didn't you think of them—or me—during
the past four months? I'm trying to understand."

"But Garth *did* think of you," my brother replied evenly.
He paused and studied my face, may have noticed the beginning of tears. "Garth is sorry for the pain he has caused you,

Mongo. He just didn't . . . you, Mom and Dad . . . Garth knows who you all are, but you don't really have anything to do with him, the way he is now. It's as if Garth's parents and brother belonged to some other person's life.''

"But you *do* remember things from the other person's life?"

"Yes. But it's as if they happened to someone else."

"Do you feel any different now—physically or mentally—from the way you did the last time I talked to you, at the clinic?"

"No."

"Are you sure?"

"Garth is sure. Why do you ask?"

"The last time the doctors ran tests on you, you were still passing NPPD in your urine. The drug was still metabolizing in your system."

"So what?"

"So, maybe the damn stuff is *still* in your system, and that's why you don't feel any different; so maybe when it all breaks down and is pissed away, you *will* feel different—like *you*. Will you let me take you to a medical lab for a urinalysis?"

"Garth thinks not."

I sighed. "Why does Garth think not?"

"Garth is the way he is. The idea that he will one day change back to the way he was before is a hope of yours—a false one. Garth does not want you to be hurt anymore."

"You let me worry about that. How about it? One little pee in one little bottle is all I'm asking. How can that hurt?"

"Garth's time is better spent doing other things. He thinks not."

"Do you believe you're some kind of messiah?"

Garth abruptly laughed. It was the first time I had heard him laugh in what seemed like years, but was only months; it was a rich sound, and it made me feel very good.

"You *still* think Garth is crazy, don't you, Mongo? There can't be any messiahs when there is no God. The reason Garth is doing what he's doing is because there is no one else to look to for help outside ourselves."

Garth and I studied each other for a few moments, and then I pointed toward the door. "Some of the people out there think you're the Messiah. Braxton and Carling do, and I'll bet there are a lot of others."

"That's not Garth's problem, is it?"

"But do you ever tell them you're *not* the Messiah?"

"If the subject comes up, yes. Otherwise, it's not something Garth gives any thought to. Garth tries not to concern himself with silly things. What Garth thinks about is telling the truth, even if no one listens, and helping those who need it and who will allow Garth to help them. Is Garth doing wrong?"

"No, Garth," I said quietly, "you're not doing anything wrong. As a matter of fact, you're doing an enormous amount of good, and I'm terribly proud of you."

"Are the people working with Garth doing wrong?"

"Not intentionally. But I think they may be harming you, even if they don't mean to."

"No one is harming Garth, Mongo."

"What do Braxton and Carling *say* when you tell them you're not the Messiah?"

"They don't believe Garth." My brother paused, smiled wryly. "Siegmund Loge would have found all of this very amusing, wouldn't he? He'd have laughed and said, 'I told you so.'"

The words momentarily stunned and disoriented me. "*Jesus,* Garth," I finally managed to say. "You *understand* that?"

"Of course Garth understands that. Loge may have been mad as a hatter—like you think I am—but he understood exactly what he was doing when he manipulated all those people."

"Aren't you manipulating people?"

"Garth is manipulating no one. All of the people who work with Garth are volunteers. They came here of their own accord, and they can leave any time they like. It makes no difference to Garth what they do. These people aren't anything like the Children of Father."

"Aren't they? One of the things Loge was demonstrating was how easy it is to manipulate people who want or need something supernatural, occult, to believe in. They're always looking for humans to set up as gods to replace the heavenly gods who are never around when you really need them. Loge maintained that this flaw existed on a very deep, genetic level, and he predicted that it would be the ultimate cause of our extinction. How *nice* your followers are isn't the point; they're *exactly* like the Children of Father."

"Garth does not set himself up as a god."

"But others are—just as Loge predicted would always happen."

"Garth can only be responsible for his own actions. Do you disagree?"

"No, Garth; you know I don't disagree with that."

"Then where do you find fault with me?"

"I'm not finding fault with *you*. I'm just worried that you've become a part of something that can eventually prove very dangerous and destructive. I can't tell you *how* it's going to become dangerous and destructive, because it's just a feeling I have. But history is on my side."

"Garth will never be a part of anything that is dangerous and destructive."

"I'm talking about the whole movement that has grown up around you."

"Garth is not part of any movement. Garth goes where he must go, and does what he must do. He will not allow what others think or believe to stop him from doing the things that must be done."

"Garth, what do you *say* to all those people out on the streets?"

"Why don't you come out with Garth sometime and find out for yourself?"

"Maybe I will," I said, knowing I wouldn't. I wanted nothing to do with Garth's People.

"Garth tells them that their confusion is his; their pain is his pain, as is their cold and hunger. Garth tells them about his experiences with Siegmund Loge, and Valhalla. Garth asks them to help ease his pain; he says that the way they can help him is to allow themselves to be helped, and then perhaps go out and help others. To a woman who keeps all her belongings in a bag, Garth says that he knows what it is like to have virtually nothing, and not have anyone to share even that with. Garth tells them how he hurts, and then begs them to come with him to seek food, clothing, shelter, and comfort. Some do. They know Garth is telling the truth."

"That's nice, Garth," I said quietly, meaning it.

Garth shrugged, smiled thinly. "Garth also cries a lot when he's on the streets. That seems to mean a lot to the people Garth must help. Garth can't help crying, because he has been broken. He really *does* feel their cold, hunger, and loneliness. It's what . . . Garth feels most of the time."

"I know."

"All this pain is in the place where Garth's *I* used to be."

"I know."

"And so what Garth does now is really very selfish; he's simply trying to ease his *own* suffering. That suffering doesn't allow him much time to think of anything else. Now can you understand, Mongo?"

"I'm not sure."

"Is Garth wrong to try to stop his own hurt by stopping the hurt of others?"

"No."

"Forgive Garth, Mongo, for the hurt he's caused you, Mom, and Dad. Garth didn't mean to be hurtful. All of the suffering that he sees and feels is much more . . . immediate."

Now the tears in my eyes spilled over my lids and rolled

down my cheeks. "I don't want you to hurt, Garth. That's why I want you to stop all this, come back to the clinic and let the people there help you to get better."

"Can the people at the clinic make Garth's pain go away, Mongo?"

"I . . . don't know. I don't think anybody can promise that."

"Then Garth must continue to do what he can to help himself."

"There are dangerous people around you, Garth. They could bring harm to you, or to others."

"Who?"

"Marl Braxton, for one."

Garth shook his head. 'Marl isn't dangerous any longer. If you knew what he'd been through, if you'd met his maid of constant sorrows, you'd understand why he behaved the way he did in the past. All he needed was for someone to understand, and truly *feel*, all that he felt."

"Have you met Marl's maid of constant sorrows, Garth?" I asked in what I hoped was a neutral tone of voice.

Garth did not reply, and I pressed.

"Who is she, Garth? *What* is she?"

"Garth can't tell you," my brother replied simply. "He doesn't have the right."

One last try.

"Garth, you haven't done anything wrong or hurtful. But, in the end, I believe that great harm can come from this thing that's growing up around you. This is definitely a religious movement, whether you want it to be or not, and it's centered on *you*. Religious movements, whether they're centuries old or only months, always end up at some time or another with blood and destruction as fertilizer as the people in them try to make them grow even more, and faster. People are nailed to crosses, wars are launched in the name of holiness, bodies are broken, women's breasts are cut off and their babies' brains bashed out, kids are pushed down elevator shafts, rattlesnakes end up in dissenters' mailboxes. The souls of whole nations can be swallowed up. The religious impulse is an insane one, Garth, and it's probably at the core of all the rest of humankind's insanities—a lesson driven home to our hearts by Siegmund Loge.''

"Garth agrees with everything you say, Mongo. Siegmund Loge taught us both the same lesson."

"Then come home with me, Garth. First, we'll have ourselves a good, stiff drink, and then I'll drive you back up to the clinic."

"Garth isn't a part of any religious movement. He doesn't lead, and he doesn't ask anyone to follow. He wants only to help people who need it."

"The movement exists, Garth. If it ends up smelling of death and mental slavery, I don't want any of that smell rubbing off on you."

Suddenly, Garth's eyes filled with tears. "Have you smelled what's out on the streets, Mongo? That's where the death, destruction, and mental slavery exists, and that's where my battle must be fought."

I sighed heavily, bowed my head. I tried to think of something else to say, but couldn't think of anything. It was time for me to leave. Again, I wanted to hug my brother— but that gesture was still beyond the wall, beyond me. I stepped forward and held out my hand; Garth gripped it.

"Good luck to you, Garth."

"And to you, Mongo. Thank you for all the years . . . Thank you for *truly* being Garth's brother, in spirit as well as in flesh."

"Good-bye, Garth."

"Good-bye, Mongo."

My eyes were still wet when I walked out of the office— into a hall filled with a couple of hundred people, all staring at me. I pushed and shouldered my way toward the main entrance, tensed when I felt somebody's hand grip my shoulder.

"What will you do, Mongo?" Tommy Carling asked in an anxious voice.

"About this? Nothing. I'm gone. Thanks again, Tommy, for what you did for Garth. Good-bye, and good luck to you."

When I emerged on the street, the strange odor I'd noticed inside the bathhouse was gone. And I still didn't know what it had been. I remembered words from *Ulysses*, something about the "cold smell of sacred stone," and I wondered if what I'd smelled inside had been what Joyce was referring to.

16.

It was at the beginning of the second week in December when my parents unexpectedly appeared at the door of the apartment I had once shared with Garth. Their visit surprised me, since we'd already made plans for me to visit them in Nebraska at Christmas; it also embarrassed me, since—although it was only four o'clock in the afternoon—I was half lit. I'd been very much out of sorts for the past two months—drinking too much, not eating right, and generally not taking care of business. I'd been turning down P.I. work, and a book on urban patterns of juvenile crime I'd been planning to finish in my newly acquired spare time still sat on my desk in piles of uncollated sheets, pages of statistics, and notes on half-formed ideas. I found it impossible to concentrate for extended periods of time. I felt defeated, frustrated; I also thought I knew how Dr. Frankenstein must have felt after his creation had gone lumbering out the door to terrorize the villagers. Garth wasn't terrorizing anyone; quite the contrary. Still, I desperately wished I had never brought *Der Ring des Nibelungen* to the clinic to play for my brother, and couldn't help but wonder how things might have worked out if I hadn't "imprinted" him with the music of Richard Wagner. Whatever might have happened, at least I wouldn't be sitting around feeling guilty and responsible for creating an entirely new personality for Garth.

"You don't look well, Robby," my mother said as she shifted slightly on the living room sofa, where she sat next to my father. I sat across from them in an overstuffed easy chair.

My mother, dressed in her Sunday best for her visit to the big city, still looked the embodiment of what I thought of as country simplicity and virtue. Her white hair had been neatly coiffed, and she looked beautiful to me in her simple print dress. She sat somewhat tensely, with her hands folded in her lap; her blue eyes were fixed on me with a gaze that was both loving and anxious. My father's gaze was a bit more stern; he knew Scotch when he smelled it.

"I'm all right, Mom—just a bit tired. I assume the two of you came to New York to see Garth. Have you been to his place downtown?"

"We've been down there," my father said in a slightly curt tone, "but we didn't see Garth."

"Yeah, well, I guess it's hard to know when he's going to be around. Maybe later the three of us can go—"

"We went to the place where we were told your brother lives and works now," my mother interrupted in a soft but strong voice. She clasped, then unclasped, her hands. "We spoke with a man who looks and sounds like your brother, but it wasn't him. That was definitely not my son."

"That's him, Mom. Like I've told you over the telephone, he takes some getting used to."

My father, who was the embodiment of what Garth would look like in twenty years, with twenty less pounds, cleared his throat; it seemed an ominous sound. "Robby, what are you doing about it?"

"Doing about what, Dad?"

"Your mother and I assumed you were still watching over your brother, doing all you could to help him get well. This man who looks like Garth says that he hasn't seen you in over seven weeks."

"Garth and I don't have much to talk about anymore, Dad."

"In the beginning, after his collapse, you were by his side constantly. In fact, you told us you thought he was getting better—until all of these very strange events began to occur."

"I told you what happened."

"You told us about the traitor, and about the killings at the clinic; you told how Garth was taken away by this Tommy Carling, who's with him now and who seems to think that Garth is some kind of god. All of this you explained to us. What your mother and I are asking is why you've left him alone in that situation."

I choked off a bitter, slightly drunken laugh which my parents would never have understood. "I wouldn't exactly describe Garth as 'alone' down there, Dad. Right now, I'd say he's the most famous Frederickson there ever was, or ever will be. He's supported by a cast of tens of thousands of people all over the country, and more believers are coming out of the woodwork every day."

"Don't joke about this, Robby, please," my mother said, her voice quavering slightly. "You know exactly what your father means. Garth *is* alone, because none of the people who surround him really know him, or love him the way we do. Garth is in terrible trouble, and we don't understand why you're not doing anything about it."

"There's nothing I can do about it, Mom," I said, swallowing the sour taste of afternoon Scotch which lingered at the back of my throat. "There's nothing anybody can do. Even if we tried to have him committed, which I think would be virtually impossible at this point, I don't think it would be right. If you've talked to him, then you know he's perfectly rational. He's doing exactly what he wants to do, and he's doing an enormous amount of good. Anyone who watches television or reads the newspapers knows that."

"People are saying he's the Messiah," my father said, scorn and disbelief in his voice. "They say he performs miracles."

"Where's the harm?" I asked, a shrug in my voice. "Besides, in a way he *is* performing miracles—just like all those TV preachers do, except with more grace, style, and wit, and denying all the time that he's doing anything. The blind man Garth supposedly cured has to be a phony, but I'd say that most of the others aren't. There are people who claim to have been cured of everything from warts to paralysis just by seeing his picture, or watching him speak on television. And they probably *have* been cured—because whatever they were suffering from was psychosomatic to begin with. *All* miracle cures are psychosomatic, but that doesn't mean they're not cures; just because pain is in the mind doesn't mean that it doesn't hurt. People have faith in Garth; they believe he can make them well, and so a lot of them get well. Flip the TV dial any Sunday morning, and you'll see a host of guys with toupees and capped teeth doing the same thing—and then asking for money. I prefer Garth's style."

"There are groups of these so-called Garth's People springing up around the world," my father said in a flat voice.

"Dad, a lot of people respond to the things he says, because what he says usually makes a lot of sense."

"But he speaks *against* religion."

"All religions are intrinsically against religion—other people's. Garth's People listen to what he says, interpret it the way they want, and then put their own spin on things."

"It's blasphemous for people to compare Garth with our Lord."

"But it's not Garth committing the blasphemy, Dad. What's happened is ironic, I grant you, but it's not exactly unprecedented. People hear what they want to hear, believe what they want to believe—a lot of people, at any rate. Some of the things Garth says are very powerful; what he *does* is very powerful. Even though Garth speaks against religion, a lot of people can only absorb his message in a religious sense.''

"President Shannon even called to *congratulate* us on our son's 'divine mission'—his words. You've met him. Is the man a fool?''

Now I permitted myself a small laugh. "Kevin Shannon is a lot of things, Dad, but he's no fool. He's nothing if not a very canny politician—and not the first who's going to be pestering you. They've been waiting in the wings, seeing which way this thing with Garth was going to go, and now a lot of them are going to be jumping on what they perceive to be the bandwagon of an important international religious leader.''

"But Garth doesn't claim to be a religious leader,'' my father said in a distant voice. It was the first time in my life I had seen him apparently bewildered, spiritually bruised by seemingly contradictory situations and events that were beyond his comprehension. "Quite the contrary.''

"It doesn't make any difference, Dad. I told you; people now insist on believing about Garth what they want to believe. Garth's goodness just brings out the craziness in a lot of people—and they're going to grow in numbers, and get even crazier now, after the deaths of Bartholomew Lash and Timmy Owens. Now the messianic movement around Garth is going to grow even stronger, with people claiming not only that Garth has God on his side, but that God is bumping off the opposition. You might as well prepare yourselves, because that's what you're going to be hearing.''

"Terrible, terrible,'' my mother said, dropping her gaze and speaking in a small voice.

I wasn't sure whether she was talking about the deaths, or the fact that thousands—maybe millions—of people believed, or at least strongly suspected, that God might have intervened to strike down Garth's two most vocal opponents, so I said nothing.

Bartholomew Lash and Timmy Owens, two prominent television evangelists who had seen their ratings plummet and their coffers empty in inverse proportion to the growing popularity of Garth and his little homilies, had each had the unbelievably bad taste to die of a stroke within twenty-four hours after a televised vicious verbal attack on Garth and Garth's People. Lash had called Garth the "spawn of the Devil," and Owens had actually called for God to strike my brother dead. Tacky. It had been even tackier when each had proceeded to kick off, thus giving Garth and the movement growing around him millions of dollars' worth of free publicity. The word "messiah" in conjunction with my brother was heard more and more frequently—including on television and radio newscasts. This had served to aggravate what I tended to think of as Millennium Madness, with Garth looked upon as the long-awaited Messiah who would usher in said millennium. Even the chiliasts had adopted Garth; they believed that Garth was going to kill everybody in a very short time—except, of course, for Garth's People, who would begin to glow with golden light once the mass killing had begun. The bathhouse, a massive glass dome now finished and in place, was now used primarily for ceremonial occasions—meaning press conferences, or just when Garth felt like telling one of his little "parables"; "caring houses," various facilities where the homeless and hungry were cared for by Garth's People, had sprung up all over the city, the state, the nation. The world.

And my mother and father wanted to know what Robert Frederickson planned to do about it.

"You and your brother were always so close," my father said at last, pain and disappointment clearly evident in his voice.

"Dad," I said wearily, "you seem to think that there's something I should—could—be doing about what's happened to Garth. There isn't. I'm beginning to think there never was."

Except not to play *Der Ring des Nibelungen* into his blank mind. But I hadn't told my parents about what I had done and the implications of that act, and I didn't plan to now; not when I was half-drunk.

"People are using Garth as an excuse to repudiate our Lord, Robby," my mother said, shaking her head. "It's blasphemous."

"Mom, Jesus Christ has been taking care of Himself for two thousand years, and I have to assume He'll survive Garth."

"Don't *you* be blasphemous, Robert!"

"I'm sorry, Mom," I said quietly. "It's just that Garth isn't claiming to be any messiah, and he's not hurting anyone. On the contrary, he's been directly or indirectly responsible for helping untold numbers of people."

"He's denied God, Robby," my father said sternly. "And he's denied our Lord."

"What difference does it make?"

"What kind of a question is that?!"

"Dad, he hasn't burned anyone at the stake in the name of God, and he hasn't tortured anyone in the name of our Lord. What people believe about Garth may be patently ridiculous—but then, what a lot of people in other religious movements believe is patently ridiculous. As far as religious leaders—or even messiahs—go, I'll take Garth any time. Everything he says *is* common sense, and it's not his fault if a lot of people get crazy when they hear his common sense. Don't you understand, Dad? Mom? Gods and messiahs and angels and demons of one kind or another have been with us since we dropped out of the trees and crawled into caves, and they'll probably always be with us—until the end of the world. Nobody—or very few—want to face the fact that these hings don't exist, that we have only ourselves to help ourselves. As far as gods and messiahs go, I say Garth is the best of the bunch. So if people want to believe that he's some kind of divine Western Union operator, there's no—"

Abruptly, but much too late, I stopped my whiskey-talk when I noticed the expressions of hurt and astonishment on my parents' faces. I lowered my head, stared at the floor. Filled with too much afternoon booze, my mouth had slipped its moorings and uttered things deeply hurtful to the two lifelong devout Christians who were my parents. My words were beyond apology, and I would have done almost anything to be able to take them back.

My mother said very softly, "You speak like that, Robby, because, in your own way, you grieve for Garth as much as we do. But this thinking among so many people that he's somehow like our Lord must be stopped."

"It can't be stopped, Mom," I said quietly, looking up into this beautiful woman's eyes. "At this pont, you might as well try to stop the tides." I paused, smiled tentatively. "Besides, looking at the bright side of things, you could argue that he's the world's ultimate ecumenicist. He's got *everybody*—Christians, Jews, Muslims, Buddhists, what-have-you—together in his camp, because each person sees him through the prism of his or her particular religious bias. Did you see the papers last week? The Israeli Knesset had an emergency session to debate whether or not the Jews of Garth's People in Israel pose a security risk—it seems loads of them have taken to picnicking and talking with loads of Arabs out on the desert. A growing number of Jews think Garth is their promised Savior, and a lot of Arabs are convinced they've got their Hidden Imam back. So everybody's happy—except, of course, for their political leaders. As long as Garth never chooses one over another—which he never will, since he tells them all that everything they believe about him is nonsense—Garth's People is one big happy family. Anyone who can get Jews and Arabs to wallow around together in the sand can't be all bad. I'm terribly sorry for what I said before, but where's the harm in what Garth is doing? I may miss him a lot, but I happen to be darn proud of him."

"The harm, Robby," my mother said in a low, ultrapatient tone which I remembered well from my childhood, "is that all the good he may be doing is nonetheless based on lies—many of them."

"Garth hasn't lied to anyone, Mom."

"The foundation of the movement which has grown up around him is a lie. Garth himself has become a lie; that man living in the bathhouse is not my son. In the long run, anything built on lies will bring only evil and destruction—despite what you see, or think you see, in the short run. This business can destroy your brother and untold numbers of the people around him, because what is a lie is evil. You, of all people, should know that after what Siegmund Loge did to you. It's terribly hard for your father and me to understand how you could have abandoned your brother at a time when he may need you more than he ever has in his life. Once, you would have given your life for him; now, with him trapped in a kind of living death which is his madness, you do nothing."

"Mom," I said in a quavering voice, my eyes filling with tears, "what would you have me *do*?"

"Rescue him, Robby," my mother replied in a firm, even tone. "Bring Garth back to himself and his family, where he belongs."

"Mom, Dad, there's nothing to rescue him *from*. I tried, and all I can tell you is that playing Devil's advocate, if you will, with Garth and the people around him gets you nowhere. There's nothing *wrong* with him."

"He was poisoned, Robby."

"Yes—and the poisoning changed him. He's *different* now, yes; radically changed. But he's not psychotic, and probably never was. In fact, there's probably a very good chance that he'd suffer a breakdown if he was somehow forced to *stop* what he's doing. Helping people has become the way he keeps his sanity now; it keeps him in touch with reality."

"Garth has always helped people," my mother said in the same strong voice as she tilted her chin up slightly and gazed hard at me. "Nobody is suggesting that he stop helping people, whether as a policeman or something else. But he must be rescued from this *monstrous* thing which has grown up around him."

"He'd still be who he is, Mom. I'm convinced of that. The Garth we knew just doesn't exist anymore."

I'd replaced him with a messiah.

My mother leaned forward on the sofa and thrust her hands out toward me in a gesture of supplication that I felt like a stab wound in my heart. "I've prayed, Robby. I know, because God has told me, that my son and your brother is still there in that man in the bathhouse. Destroy the lies."

"I don't believe that's possible, Mom."

"You must try; you must find a way to make all those people see that Garth is not what they think he is, and then maybe they'll all go away."

"Then Garth will be alone, Mom."

"Garth will never be alone, as long as he has us to love him. But you've lost faith, and your will has weakened. Garth was sick, and he's still sick. If you can destroy the lies around him, maybe he'll finally heal."

"I'm not sure he hasn't healed all he's going to, Mom."

My mother shook her head adamantly. "At the least, you must destroy the lies about his being the Messiah and performing miracles. My son must not be even an unwitting ally to such blasphemy. The Lord will guide and help you."

"Please, Mom . . . try to understand something. Even if I could do what you ask, and I don't see how, I'm not sure I have the *right* to interfere in his life like that. Even if I thought I did have the right, what you're asking me to try and do is impossible." I paused, touched the scar on my forehead. "I've already had a sneak preview of what the response to any action I might take would be; the Messiah's dwarf brother has been marked, like Cain, by God in order to warn Garth's People to disregard anything he does or says. It wouldn't work, Mom. All I would manage to do is make more of a mess and get us all a lot of bad publicity—and publicity, good or bad, just wins Garth's People more converts. My orchestrating an attempt to discredit my own brother would have about the same effect that Bartholomew Lash and Timmy Owens had when they picked such lousy times to die."

Having said my piece, I sat with my parents in uncomfortable silence for long minutes; I was very conscious of the rapid beating of my heart, and I felt short of breath. Very slowly, as if shouldering a weight almost too heavy for him to bear, my father finally rose to his feet. He did not look at me as he removed his wallet from his back pocket, took out some bills, and dropped them on the coffee table in front of the sofa. He still would not look at me as he spoke; his voice, filled with hurt, rumbled like distant thunder.

"When your mother and I came to this city, Robert, we feared we had lost one son; but we believed that our other son was doing everything in his power to bring his brother home, or to some place where he could be cared for and healed. Now it appears that we've lost both our sons. We can't do much for you, because you're in your right mind and are capable of making your own choices. But your mother and I must still do whatever we can to help our sick son. Over the years, we came to understand that you're a pretty fine private investigator—or you used to be, before you started drinking in the afternoon. We'd like to hire you to investigate and disprove the lies surrounding your brother. You've made it very clear that you don't want to do this thing, but I'd appreciate it if you'd think of it as a mission of mercy—if not for Garth, then for your mother and me. How much do you charge, Robert?"

I'd uttered probably what were the most hurtful things I could have said to my parents, and so it seemed only fitting that my father should say the most hurtful thing he could to me. I promptly burst into tears. Then it was my mother's turn to start crying. Only my father stood stony-faced and unsmiling—but he, too, softened when, blubbering, I asked them both to forgive me.

After a lot of moist hugging and kissing, my father finally put his money away and we all went out to dinner. Then we came back to the apartment and, after fixing up the guest room for my parents, I went right to bed. I wanted to be well rested; the next day, after taking my parents to the airport, I was going to have to start blasting away, like somebody hunting a whale from a blimp with a peashooter, at my brother's divinity.

17.

Heigh ho, heigh ho, it's off to work we go . . .

I was well aware that miracle bashing would be a most difficult task, and a thankless one at that. I could waste months speaking to the legions of ex-stutterers, ex-asthma sufferers, and people who now walked without the aid of their wheelchairs and crutches as a result of Garth's messiahship, and I would get nowhere. Garth's words and presence generated a kind of holy hysteria in all sorts of people, and it counteracted the not-so-holy hysteria that had afflicted these people in the first place. Consequently, there was no doubt in my mind that a lot of these "miracle cures" had actually occurred, and there was no way I was going to "disprove" them—even if I wanted to, which I didn't. However, it seemed to me that there was one glaringly weak link in the chain of events that had launched Garth on his new career as miracle worker, and that was the link I would attack.

Fortunately, Sergeant Alexander McIntyre was still feeling sufficiently guilty and embarrassed over the fact that *The*

National Eye had scooped the NYPD on Garth's whereabouts to enable me to prompt him to make good on his initial offer to let me review the file I wanted to see. I looked it over, made a lot of notes, thanked him, and walked out into a bleak, cold winter day to see what might fall out if I managed to shake Harry August's tree.

The middle-aged woman who opened the door of the modest frame house on a quiet residential street in Bayside, Queens, peered at me suspiciously.

"Yes? What is it?"

"My name is Robert Frederickson, Mrs. Daplinger. I wonder if I could—"

The woman gasped, put a hand to her mouth, and took a step backward onto the enclosed porch. "Oh, Lord."

"No, Mrs. Daplinger," I said dryly, reaching out quickly to prevent the door from closing on me. It was obvious that she knew who I was, and she was not at all pleased to find me on her doorstep. "Just Robert Frederickson."

"You're Garth's brother—the one who's been marked," the woman said in a hushed, small voice.

"I'm the only brother my brother's got, Mrs. Daplinger," I said, and flashed my warmest smile. It seemed the woman had become one of the faithful—which meant that I was going to have to choose all my words very carefully, or I'd find out nothing. "Would you be kind enough to answer a few questions for me? I'll only take a few minutes of your time."

"What do you want?" Mrs. Daplinger asked in the same breathless voice. She was obviously afraid of me—and I found that disturbing.

"You were one of the witnesses to the miracle Garth performed when he cured Harry August's blindness. That's what I'd like to talk to you about."

"How did you get my name and address?"

"I must have seen them in a newspaper article."

"That happened months ago."

"Yes, but I've only recently developed a strong interest in what my brother is doing. I think I've had a bad attitude toward him, and I'm trying to set that right by finding out all I can about his mission. May I come in?"

The woman thought about it, finally nodded. "Just on the porch, though. I'm not sure it would be . . . right . . . to invite you into the house."

"Thank you," I said, stepping onto the enclosed porch and shutting the door behind me.

"Garth *did* restore Mr. August's sight. I was there, and I saw it happen."

"I understand that someone tried to snatch your purse while Garth was healing Harry August. Is that right?"

"Yes. But the thief was caught almost immediately. I identified him to a policeman; he was arrested, and I got my purse back. But that wasn't important at all. Why do you even ask about it?"

"I'd like to hear from you exactly what happened."

"I just told you what happened. I was watching Garth restore Mr. August's sight, and a young man tried to snatch my purse. Everybody knows that. Do you want to cause trouble for Garth?"

"No, Mrs. Daplinger. I'd just like to hear from you in more detail what happened. I'd like to know the exact sequence of events. According to the newspaper accounts, there were quite a few people standing on the sidewalk watching Garth and August, so whatever was happening was already attracting a lot of attention—enough so that an amateur photographer even started snapping pictures. It was during all this excitement that the kid tried to snatch your purse, right? The thief figured that everyone would be distracted by whatever was going on between Garth and Harry August."

"What was 'going on,' Mr. Frederickson, was Garth restoring Mr. August's sight. I think you do mean to cause trouble. I saw what I saw with my own eyes, and nothing you can say will change that fact."

"Mrs. Daplinger, has Garth ever said to you or anyone else that I mean to cause trouble? Has he ever said anything bad about me?"

The woman hesitated a few moments, then shook her head. "Garth never says anything bad about anyone."

"If Garth hasn't said anything bad about me, why should you worry?"

The woman tentatively touched her gray-streaked brown hair, averted her gaze. "There are stories whispered about. Some people say that you're jealous of Garth's favor in God's eyes, and that you'd destroy him if you could."

"That's a very old tale, Mrs. Daplinger, and it certainly didn't start with Garth's People." I was beginning to feel like I had a starring role in Paradise Lost.

"Excuse me?"

"Who says these things? Marl Braxton and Tommy Carling?"

"No; I heard them from other people. Many believe it. It's said that you stole sacred relics from Garth, and have hidden them away."

A new wrinkle. "Sacred relics? What sacred relics?"

"For one, the Great Knife God gave Garth during Garth's Great Quest to battle Satan."

Whisper. Already strange and powerful religious myths were being formed as Garth's stories were absorbed into people's minds, smelted in the fires of imagination, then recast in unrecognizable shapes. I'd assumed that Marl Braxton and Tommy Carling had started the slander campaign against me, but I now realized that this wasn't necessarily the case. People caught up in religious fervor didn't need any prompting to form myths; the thought struck me that perhaps all religions, at least in their formative stages, need a Betrayer. This time around, I had the part.

"Mrs. Daplinger," I said quietly, "doesn't Garth teach that you should always speak the truth?"

"Yes," the woman replied, and her dark brown eyes flashed. "And I won't listen to any of your lies about Garth.

You stole the Great Knife, and God marked you for it.''

"I didn't come here to say anything at all about Garth, Mrs. Daplinger. I just want to know more about him. I'd like to hear the complete story of how he restored Harry August's sight—what happened on that day. Since it's the truth, I can't see how any harm can come from repeating your story to me."

"It was a lovely, sunny day," the woman said, smiling at the memory. "I'd gone into Manhattan to shop. I was walking down Eighth Avenue, and I remember how crowded it was—I guess a lot of people had decided to go shopping that day. I stopped walking when I saw a crowd gathered on the sidewalk; they were watching Garth talking to Mr. August. I remember . . . Garth was crying; his cheeks were wet with tears, and every once in a while he'd sob. He'd taken out his wallet and was shoving bills into Mr. August's cup. He was talking to Mr. August, begging him to come to a place where he would be taken care of so that he wouldn't have to stand on the street and beg. People were laughing at Garth, shouting insults and asking him to give them money. A couple of men even scooped up bills that had fallen out of Mr. August's cup.''

"It's getting chilly out here, Mrs. Daplinger, and I don't want you to catch cold. Don't you think you should get a coat or sweater?"

She shook her head, said distantly, "I'm all right."

"You weren't laughing at Garth, were you?"

"No. I thought it was a sad spectacle. I felt sorry for both men, and a little embarrassed. Mr. August seemed very uncomfortable, and he kept trying to push Garth away from him. Garth just kept shoving money into Mr. August's cup while he tugged at Mr. August's sleeve and begged him to come along with him. Mr. August kept trying to push him away.

"Then I felt somebody grab my purse, and I started screaming for help. I turned around and saw this young man tugging at my purse, and cursing at me. People started crowding around us. The young man kept tugging at my purse, and I tugged back. Then he pulled a knife, and everybody backed away. I let go of the purse. The young man put it under his arm, then went to get the money from Mr. August's cup. By this time, Mr. August had already been healed—but I'm not sure he even realized it. But he must have *seen* what was happening, because he snatched his cup away and started beating the young man over the head with his cane. The boy must have been startled and hurt, because he suddenly dropped his knife and tried to run away. Some men grabbed him and held him down on the sidewalk until a policeman came.

"By then, a number of people were staring at Mr. August, because they'd seen him strike out at the young man just as if he wasn't blind at all. His dark glasses had fallen off, and he seemed to be in a kind of state of shock. He was staring back at the people around him, and his right eye was in focus and seemed perfectly all right. People were starting to say ugly things, claiming that Mr. August might have terrible scars on his face but that he wasn't blind. They were shouting at Mr. August to give Garth back his money, and urging the policeman to arrest Mr. August along with the purse snatcher. Then, all of a sudden, Mr. August started shouting things I didn't understand—now I know he was speaking in tongues. Then he dropped down on his knees and started kissing Garth's feet. He was shouting that Garth had cured his blindness and made him see again. He begged Garth to take him along to whatever place Garth had been talking about. Garth pulled him to his feet, and they walked off together—with Mr. August shouting all the time that Garth had given him back his sight."

"The policeman wasn't interested in arresting Harry August?"

"I guess not; he was busy handcuffing the purse snatcher. Also, there was a lot of confusion; someone was snapping pictures, and people were just milling around. Some people were following Garth and Mr. August."

"What did you do, Mrs. Daplinger?"

"Then? I was . . . upset. I just went home. Then, after the stories started appearing in the newspapers, I began to realize that I had actually been present when a miracle had been performed. I searched for Garth, and I became a member of Garth's People. I guess a lot of people who were there on the sidewalk that day came to feel the same way, because I often see them at the caring houses where I go to help." She paused, cocked her head, and smiled at me. "I feel very blessed, Mr. Frederickson."

"Thank you for the time you've given me, Mrs. Daplinger," I said quietly. "I appreciate it."

The woman looked at my forehead, then into my eyes. "You don't seem like a bad man."

"I try not to be."

"It's strange how God works."

"It certainly is, Mrs. Daplinger."

"God chose Harry August to have his sight restored through the power of the Messiah; yet, I'm sure there are thousands of other blind men, women, and children who are so much more deserving. I know it's uncharitable of me to say this, but Harry August is such an *unpleasant* man."

Unfortunately, Sergeant McIntyre's guilt and embarrassment weren't sufficient to impel him to call a number of city, state, and federal agencies on my behalf, under the auspices of the NYPD. I had my own contacts, but milking them—and gaining access to certain confidential information—took time, as did checking out hunches and setting up a vigil outside the bathhouse for a couple of days in order to tail Harry August whenever he came out alone. However, three days before Christmas I felt I had gathered more than enough information to give Harry August an early Christmas present he definitely was not going to like.

Lawrence Harold D'Agostino was more than a little surprised to find me waiting for him outside his small, nondescript house on a nondescript street in Brooklyn, leaning against the Ford station wagon he'd owned—and driven—for eleven years. He spotted me when he was halfway up the block; his face went white, his jaw dropped open, and he turned and started to run away. I caught up with him three blocks later, in a small shopping center, when he tried to duck down a narrow alley between two shops. Gasping for breath, he wheeled around and threw a garbage can lid at me. I sidestepped the flying lid, then hit him in the stomach with sufficient force to knock the rest of the wind out of him and sit him down hard on a stack of old newspapers.

"You and I have a lot to talk about, Mr. D'Agostino," I said as I took a sheaf of papers out of my jacket pocket and waved them in his face. "For a blind man, you've led quite an active life for the past few years."

Harry August was starting to get his breath back—and with it, a semblance of calm and his usual cunning. "Fuck you, dwarf," he said, rising to his feet and brushing off his pants. "I've got nothing to say to you, and nobody's going to believe anything you say about me."

"No? How about the driver's license you've had since you were sixteen years old, and which has been renewed like clockwork every five years? You even got a speeding ticket two years ago—which is understandable, I suppose, since it would be hard for a blind man to see a speed limit sign or know how fast he was driving."

"Nobody's going to pay any attention to you, Fredrickson."

"Certainly Garth's People won't, but I don't intend to try to deal with them. Actually, I was thinking of going to the authorities with proof that you've been defrauding the city and state of New York, not to mention a couple of insurance companies, for years."

Harry August ran a hand back through his long, greasy hair, studied me with his one good eye, swallowed hard. "What are you talking about?"

"You know exactly what I'm talking about, Harry. You

were injured in an industrial accident fifteen years ago, when a battery you were handling exploded and acid splashed over your face. You got a lot of money from insurance companies for that accident, including a lump sum in cash which you were supposed to use for plastic surgery. I don't know what you did with that money, but you obviously didn't use it for plastic surgery. My guess is that you decided to use it for something else—the horses, maybe, or a stock market flyer. You pissed it away.''

"It's none of your business, Frederickson. Besides, Garth's People will protect me; those fools think you've been marked by God.''

"Pretty soon, everybody—fools and others—will know all about you, Harry. You've been collecting disability, which you're entitled to, since the accident, but somewhere along the line, early in the game, an examining physician made a mistake, or put the wrong entry in your file. The accident left you legally blind—20/200—in your left eye, but the right is perfectly all right; that's in the original medical report. But New York State and the insurance companies have you listed as *totally* blind, in both eyes, and they've been paying you accordingly.''

"The disability payments are nothing, Frederickson. Nobody could live on them.''

"Seven years ago you applied for welfare assistance. Not only did you declare yourself legally blind in both eyes, but you neglected to mention the disability payments—which you were legally required to do. About three years ago you set up shop on that street corner to bring in a little extra income.''

"People owed me, Frederickson,'' the other man said tightly, looking away.

"Ah. Bitterness. It seems to me that you were being pretty well taken care of. Why did people owe you?''

"You think you know the whole story, but you don't. That money I got at the beginning wasn't nearly enough to get me the kind of plastic surgery I needed—but I didn't find that out until the insurance company had pressured me into signing a settlement for a lump-sum payment. At the time I thought it was a lot of money, but then I found out it wouldn't fix my face. They screwed me good.''

"Why did your lawyer let you sign a settlement like that?''

"Ask him,'' Harry August said, and spat. "He did a lot of work for the insurance company—something my own company didn't tell me when they recommended him to me.'' He paused, suddenly thrust his face at me as if it were a weapon. His one good eye flashed black fire. "How'd *you* like to go through life looking like *this*, Frederickson? I couldn't get any kind of a decent job with a mug like this, and I knew it. What the hell good is money if you have to keep looking like something cats have been chewing on? So this guy who'd read about the accident and the settlement in the papers comes around and says he's got this really great deal for me in real estate, where I can triple my money—and don't laugh, Frederickson.''

"I wasn't even thinking of laughing, Harry,'' I said quietly. "You haven't said anything that's even remotely funny.''

"Sure, I was stupid—but I was desperate for money for the operations I needed, and I didn't know then the things I know now about people. I believed him, Frederickson; he was a real smooth-talking guy. I ended up losing everything, including every penny I had in savings. After that . . . it's like you said. But disability and welfare don't go far in this city. That's why I started begging. I'd certainly been fucked over enough, so I figured I'd fuck over other people for a change.'' He paused, licked his lips. "What are you going to do, Frederickson? What do you want?''

"The answer to both questions is that I'm not sure yet. It sounds like you've had—have—enough miseries without my adding to them. That's assuming any of the agencies involved would want to press charges.''

"Are you going to report me?''

"Let's just say that I'd prefer not to.''

"Which means that you want something from me."

"The first thing I want from you, Harry, is a videotaped repudiation of the notion that my brother restored your sight. We'll tape it at a time and place of my choosing."

"Why are you doing this, Frederickson? Your brother hasn't done anything to hurt you, and neither have I. I haven't hurt anybody. You really are jealous of Garth, aren't you? And you want to use me to dump on him."

"Harry, the motives for my strange behavior will have to remain a mystery to you. I will say that I'm not sure yet how I want to handle this; if possible, I'd like to minimize any damage to the people Garth has helped. But that's for me to worry about. For the time being, you just go on about your business with Garth's People as though this conversation had never taken place; that's important. I'll contact you about the videotaping after I've decided what I plan to do with you."

"This is blackmail."

"Yeah; something like that."

"When the authorities see that tape, they'll want to prosecute me anyway."

"Not necessarily. The whole world knows you as Harry August; knowing the way a lot of governmental agencies operate, nobody may even make the connection between Harry August and Lawrence Harold D'Agostino."

"Unless you spell it out for them."

"Right—but I doubt that I'd feel compelled to do their work for them if you cooperate with me."

"What the hell am I supposed to tell people?!"

"Your problem. No matter what you say, there's no way you're going to come out of this looking like Albert Schweitzer. All I'm concerned with is that you make it very clear that you could see perfectly well—at least with one eye—before you ever bumped into Garth. *That* part had better be convincing."

"Okay." Harry August mumbled. "I guess I knew this whole business was going to catch up with me one day."

"You reacted instinctively when that kid tried to take your money, right?"

"Yeah," the other man said, shaking his head in disgust. "Your brother was driving me out of my gourd, and I just wasn't thinking."

"Then your glasses got knocked off. Suddenly you found yourself staring back at all those people who were staring at you. It was an ugly, possibly dangerous, situation, and you grabbed hold of the only life preserver at hand—my brother. He got you out of there. What I don't understand is why you stuck around. Why didn't you just split when the danger had passed? For that matter, why are you hanging around now?"

Harry August mumbled something I didn't quite catch, and I asked him to repeat it.

"Money," he said. "Even the way his operation was back then, I could see that money was starting to come in. And I could smell more—a lot more. I had this feeling that I'd stumbled into something that could become very big." He paused, laughed bitterly. "I figured that one right, didn't I? A lot of good it's done me. The story of my life."

"You also figured it would be a good opportunity for a con man like you to get your hands on some of that money, right?"

"I'm cooperating with you, Frederickson. I just hope you're not going to give me any more grief."

"Did you plan to skim?"

"Yeah, I planned to skim."

"How'd you make out?"

Harry August shook his head. "I got food and clothing, but I never did get my hands on any money. Sure, there was a lot of money and goods coming in, but Tommy Carling already had that damn nun working with him, and she had eyes everywhere. That broad makes sure every penny is accounted for in her books, just in case anyone ever asks."

"And to protect against people like you."

"Yeah, I suppose so. Now there are dozens of volunteers—accountants, lawyers, money counters—to look after all the money and goods that come in. To tell you the truth, I haven't even been thinking much about stealing the past few weeks; the deaths of those two TV preachers kind of spooked me."

"Afraid God is looking over your shoulder, Harry?"

"Come on, Frederickson; I'm not like those other fools. I just figure it's best not to take too many chances. After the Christmas Eve thing, even more money is going to be coming in. Something real big is going to happen; I can feel it."

I frowned. "What 'Christmas Eve thing'?"

"That's right; you don't know about it. Carling's going to issue a press release tonight."

"What will the press release say?"

"Garth's going to make some kind of special announcement at midnight on Christmas Eve. Those fools think he's going to pronounce himself the Messiah." August paused, shrugged. "Maybe they're right. Hell, maybe Garth *is* the Messiah. I have to admit he'd make a good one."

I felt a chill pass through me that had nothing to do with the weather. "Garth told you this?"

"Hell, no. Nobody's even seen Garth for days. He's supposed to have gone into retreat to prepare for the big announcement. He'll hold a press conference inside the bathhouse, with the public invited to attend. It's going to be something; Carling plans to make some kind of satellite hookup so the whole world can hear what Garth has to say, when he says it."

"Who told you all this?"

"Tommy Carling. He actually runs the whole operation, you know. Garth doesn't care about anything but doing his own thing, so somebody has to take care of business. Maybe that will all change after Christmas Eve."

"And you don't have any idea where Garth could be?"

"No."

"Who does?"

"Carling may know, but if he does he isn't telling. He says Garth doesn't want to be disturbed."

"What about Marl Braxton? Does he know where Garth is?"

"I don't know . . . I don't think so. He's been just kind of moping around the place, looking lost, since Garth disappeared. Braxton's a tough man, but he spooks me. I think he's crazy, and Garth is the only thing holding him together." August paused, took a deep breath, then tentatively touched me on the shoulder. "Look, Frederickson, you're picking on me—but I'm not the only phony hanging around there."

"Harry, that wouldn't surprise me at all. You're not the only con man, I'm sure, who smelled money in the thing growing up around Garth."

"You don't understand what I'm saying. I may have made Garth famous, but I'm just a little guy in that organization; nobody pays any attention to me, and I don't have any say in what goes on. I'm talking about a big shot."

"Which big shot is a phony?"

"The nun."

"Sister Kate?"

"Yeah. She's good at keeping track of money, and I'd probably be a rich man now if she wasn't; but if she's a nun, then I'm Mickey Mouse."

"How do you know she's not a nun?"

"Because I *am* a con artist, and it takes one to know one— or even two. She and Tommy Carling are thick with each other, and I don't believe they met for the first time at the bathhouse; I think they knew each other before. I keep my dark glasses on for effect, and I guess maybe people tend to forget that I really can see. Well, I do see things, and I say there's something going on between Carling and that broad. They're always *schmoozing* with each other, if you know what I mean. I think *they're* planning to steal all the money eventually."

                              *   *   *

"Frederickson!"

"Hello, Dane," I said to the big teenager I'd found by himself, looking rather forlorn, staring out a thick Plexiglas window of the hospital's recreation room. His eyes had lit up when he'd seen me.

"What are you doing here, man?"

"I came to say hello, Dane. Christmas can be a lonely time when you're locked up someplace and you have nobody to share it with. I figured a lot of the other kids would be on home leave, and you might like some company."

The boy swallowed, looked down at his feet. "Yeah. The kids here miss you, Frederickson; *I* miss you. You're a good teacher."

"Thank you. I'll make it a point to visit more often. For now, how would you like to come out with me for the day?"

The boy quickly looked at me, then averted his gaze as sadness moved in his eyes. "I'd love to, Frederickson, but I can't. I'm DFY. I can't go home, and I can't go out with volunteers."

I still had my master key from the clinic, and I'd been pleased, if not surprised, to find that it opened the doors in the children's hospital as well. I'd been prepared to spring Dane Potter illegally, if necessary, but I'd found a better way. "A special dispensation from the director here, Dane. It seems you've been displaying some very positive changes in behavior and attitude, and your therapist thinks it may have something to do with the relationship between you and me; she thinks I'm a good role model—which you and I know is nonsense, Dane, but we won't tell her. I have permission to take you into the city for a few hours to check out all the decorations and lights. If it works out, they may let me take you out again."

"I'd like that very much, Frederickson," the boy said quietly. "I won't cause any trouble."

"Oh, I know you won't—because I'll kick the shit out of you if you try."

Dane Potter laughed. "Yeah, I know."

"It looks like you could use some clothes. Maybe we'll do a little shopping after we check out Rockefeller Center."

"You don't have to buy me anything, Frederickson. It's enough that you'll take me out of here for a couple of hours."

"Buying you slacks, sneakers, and maybe a sweater would be my pleasure. Dane. It would be a Christmas present, but it would also be a little payment for something I'd like you to do for me."

"What do you want me to do, Frederickson?"

"I'll let you know. You ready to roll?"

Dane Potter grinned. "Yeah, man."

Traffic was heavy with last-minute Christmas shoppers, and it took almost two hours to get into the city and down to the Bowery. I left the car in a garage, and walked with Dane Potter the three blocks to the bathhouse. I steered him around the traffic circle, took up a position across the street. There was a crush of people around the bathhouse, but most of them looked like tourists—with the needy now being cared for in various caring houses around the city. Police barricades had been set up, and the lines of people were being greeted by green-jacketed members of Garth's People, who were also handing out free coffee, doughnuts, and cookies. Above the bathhouse, the new glass dome gleamed like a diamond in this coal-mine neighborhood.

"What is it you want me to do, Frederickson?"

"Just be patient, Dane. Any time we spend here, I'll make up to you later, or on another visit."

"What are all those people doing over there?"

I said something about Christmas shoppers as I kept scanning the crowds in front of the bathhouse. There was no sign of Garth, but after about half an hour Tommy Carling and Sister Kate, both wearing green jackets, emerged from inside the bathhouse to talk with the people. My hands trembled slightly as I removed the binoculars I was carrying from around my neck and handed them to Potter.

"Dane," I said, "I want you to scan the people over on the sidewalk and let me know if there's anyone you recognize."

Dane Potter put the binoculars to his eyes, slowly moved his head back and forth. Suddenly he stiffened, reached out with his right hand and clutched at the sleeve of my parka.

"That's Marilyn—the woman I was telling you about! What the hell is she doing in a nun's outfit?!"

"Are you sure that's her?" I asked tightly. "You told me that the woman who helped you escape from the hospital and took you home with her had blond hair. That woman's hair is red."

"Then she must have been wearing a wig," the boy said breathlessly as he continued to stare at Sister Kate through the binoculars, "or she's wearing one now. That's *her*, Frederickson! I'm sure of it. I'm not about to forget the face of the best piece of ass I've ever had just because she turns out to be a nun." He lowered the binoculars, looked at me. His eyes were wide. "She *wasn't* all in my mind, Frederickson, was she?! Marilyn's real!"

18.

"NINE-six-seven-forty."

"This is Robert Frederickson. I must speak with Mr. Lippitt immediately. This is Valhalla priority."

There was a whir, a click, another whir, and then Mr. Lippitt came on the line.

"What is it, Mongo?"

"Tommy Carling is a K.G.B. officer, Lippitt. He was Slycke's controller, and maybe the man who entrapped the good doctor in the first place. The man's a virtuoso spy, and he's been playing me like I was the entire Guarneri Quartet.''

There was a pause of a beat or two. ''You're certain of this, Mongo?''

''I'm certain there's a woman posing as a nun in this operation who's been working with a most unholy devotion at having me killed from the moment Garth began to respond to stimuli. I say that makes her K.G.B., just like the two operatives who'd been planted at Prolix. She had to be plugged into everything that was happening up in the clinic— but she wasn't actually there. Someone else was.''

''Slycke.''

''Sure, Slycke; but he'd been set up from the beginning to be the fall guy in order to mask the *real* spider up there. I hear from someone whose opinion in these matters I trust that Carling and this woman are close buddies, and have been for some time. I say that makes Carling K.G.B. too. When you start to noodle that possibility, a lot of very scary things begin to fall into place.

''From the very first time Garth began to show any signs of awareness, Carling planned to cut me out so that he'd have Garth all to himself, without any interference from me. He certainly knew about Mama Baker's pathological hatred of dwarfs, and on the very first day I walked in there he set up the situation where Baker would know who—and what—I was, and kill me if he ever got the chance. But first Carling tried to kill me by having his girl friend manipulate a psychotic kid from the children's hospital. When that failed, and when I countered his move to have me barred from the clinic by filing a seventy-two-hour notice for Garth's release, he set up the trap in the clinic, with Slycke as the sacrificial bait. He'd removed Garth the night before, along with Marl Braxton— probably for the reason he gave me: Garth wouldn't leave without Braxton. It was Carling who doped up the patients before forcing Slycke to call me. Then he let everybody loose, ambushed me, and left me up in the clinic to die. The way he figured it, he'd be able to observe Garth's behavior at his leisure—and maybe run a few drug experiments of his own—without any interference from anyone. He fooled me good, Lippitt.''

''Us, too—if you're right.''

''I'm right. He knew you'd get the goods on Slycke, and assume that was the end of the matter. Incidentally, the phony nun I mentioned—''

''I assume you're talking about Sister Kate,'' Lippitt interrupted in a somewhat distant tone.

Stunned, it took me a few seconds to react. ''How the *hell* do you know she calls herself Sister Kate?!''

Again, there was a pause. I'd known the answer to my question almost as soon as I'd asked it. Lippitt was thinking about something else—probably the same thing I was thinking about. When he finally spoke, I could hear the tension—and a trace of fear, for Garth—in his voice.

''We began monitoring the situation as soon as we found out where Garth, Braxton, and Carling were, Mongo.''

''You've got a man in there.''

''Yes. The circumstances of Garth's illness and behavior have always had national security implications, as you're well aware.''

''Sure. But you might have told me you had somebody keeping an eye on him.''

''Perhaps you're right—although I'm not sure what difference it would have made. The two of you were obviously estranged from each other. I care a great deal for Garth personally, but he didn't appear to be in any danger. The D.I.A.'s concern was professional.''

''Yeah, okay.'' I paused, shook my had as I recalled Tommy Carling's words when I had asked him about financing for the reconstruction of the bathhouse. ''God provides, bullshit,'' I continued tightly. ''It's the K.G.B. which has been providing. I love it; Russian taxpayers have been paying to help feed New York City's hungry and homeless. We'll probably never know for certain how much of this business that's grown up around Garth was spontaneous, and how much was engineered by the Russians. Do you think the K.G.B. knocked off those two TV preachers, just to get the ball rolling a little faster?''

''It's quite possible, maybe even probable. We both know there are assassination techniques that will mimic strokes, or cause them. I don't see that it makes any difference, or why they bothered—if they did. Even before those sanctimonious cretins kicked off, the K.G.B. had everything going for them. At the beginning, they were able to monitor firsthand the effects of a new and potentially very powerful mind-control agent. Tommy Carling observed this closely, and then improvised brilliantly—I wish he worked for me. Now he and this woman have virtually complete control of a worldwide messianic religious movement which has its roots in the United States.''

''Carling also picked up on a few very sensitive secrets along the way.''

''Indeed,'' Lippitt said distantly. He was thinking again.

''How tightly wrapped is the cover story about Orville Madison dying in a hunting accident?''

''Pretty tight. What they've learned about Madison or the Valhalla Project isn't important right now.''

''Agreed.''

''Do you know about Garth's disappearance, and the announcement he's supposed to make tomorrow night?''

''Yes. I had a lengthy chat with Harry August—which is how I got on to Carling and the woman.''

''Could Harry August be K.G.B.?''

''No.''

''Are you sure?''

''I'm sure. I'm aware that August's claim that Garth healed him really kicked off the whole thing, but he had his own reasons. He's just a very sad human being, not a K.G.B. plant.''

"Mongo," Lippitt said tersely, "you must make every effort to find Garth and take him out. Before tomorrow night."

"My thoughts exactly. You agree that he's in danger?"

"Most definitely."

"This business about Garth going into retreat to prepare himself for some announcement that he really is the Messiah is bullshit; it's contrary to everything Garth has said and done up to this point."

"Precisely."

"It's why I called; I was hoping you could help me. Does your man have any idea where Carling could be keeping Garth?"

"No—and he's not in a position to find out, even if it were a good idea for him to risk exposure by pressing for information. He started off as just another guy on an air mattress, and now he wears a green jacket."

"Who is he?"

"Mongo, because of who you are and what we've been through, I'll tell you—but only if you insist."

"You don't want to?"

"No. The information won't help you. He's doing everything *he* can do right now to find out where Garth is being kept, and for him to be seen talking to you might totally destroy his effectiveness. It might even be a death warrant for him. I also think it could be extremely dangerous for you even to go there. Whatever the K.G.B. is planning, it's very close to the witching hour; Carling and the woman will be extremely watchful to make sure their plans aren't upset at the last moment. He's already tried to kill you twice before; this time, if you show up out of the blue after so many weeks and he even begins to suspect that you're on to him, he might decide to kill you out of hand. What excuse could you give for going there?"

"For Christ's sake, Lippitt," I said, feeling my frustration and fear winding up like a mainspring, "Carling and the woman are probably the only people who know where Garth is! How the hell am I supposed to find my brother if I don't confront them?!''

This time there was a very long pause, and I could hear the Director of the Defense Intelligence Agency breathing heavily on the other end of the line. He was thinking again . . . to no avail. "I don't have an answer for you, Mongo," he said at last in a very low voice. "Your death would upset me."

"I appreciate your thinking about me, Lippitt, but that still isn't an answer. I was thinking of walking in there and sticking a gun in Carling's ear."

"It wouldn't work, Mongo—and after you've given it some thought, you'll know it won't work. Both Carling and the woman are K.G.B., which means they're as tough as they come. Neither one will tell you what you want to know—and that's assuming you could get one or both alone, which may be a false assumption at this point."

"I'll get them alone—and I'll blow their brains out if they don't tell me where they've got my brother."

"In which case, you'd almost certainly end up blowing their brains out—and that wouldn't get Garth out of danger. You don't know how many K.G.B. soldiers Carling and the woman may have around them in there, and you don't know what contingency plans they may have. At the very least, you'd tip your hand. I've told you I don't know what way you should go, but I'm sure that isn't it—not yet. We still have a little over twenty-four hours to try other ways."

I screwed my eyes shut, sucked in a deep breath, slowly let it out. "You think they plan to kill him, don't you, Lippitt?"

"After hearing what you've told me . . . yes."

"But, damn it, *why* would they want to kill him *now*? Like you said, they have control of a global religious movement. Talk about . . . killing . . . the Golden Goose!''

"But they've never had control of *Garth*, Mongo. Also, if I read my history correctly, the death of the central figure in any messianic movement always solidifies that movement. Even after Jesus' crucifixion, it was a whole lot of years before Paul produced the writings that would form the basis of Christianity. I don't see the Russians being that patient. The K.G.B. may be thinking of solidifying their gains right now, taking over the whole operation by removing their one potential threat—Garth himself. I wouldn't be surprised if Harry August was also on their hit list. I think a more interesting question is why they felt Garth had to disappear days before this supposed announcement.''

I thought about it, suddenly felt short of breath. ''You think the drug could have finally worn off, Lippitt? You think Garth could be *Garth*?''

''It would explain what seems to be a lot of hurried action, and also the disappearance.'' Lippitt paused, continued quietly, ''There's something else you should know, Mongo.''

''What's that?''

''Two Mossad agents who'd been seeded into Garth's People are also missing.''

''The *Mossad*?! What the hell . . . ?''

''The United States is not the only country for which the phenomena surrounding Garth have presented difficulties, Mongo.''

''Right,'' I said, and sighed bitterly. ''Having a live, loose Messiah traipsing around the countryside is a real pain in the ass from a national security viewpoint, isn't it?''

''For every country in which the movement exists and is strong, yes. Because of the very nature of its existence, there's been a tremendous amount of turmoil in Israel over Garth and Garth's People. Although I'm certain that many other countries have intelligence operatives planted, it was the Mossad operatives who were recognized by my man. They disappeared the same time as Garth. In effect, all the intelligence agencies have been sort of war-gaming against God, predicting and taking steps to prevent political problems caused by a Messiah who might say the wrong things or motivate people to behave in a way that was not in a particular country's political, social, or economic best interests. The Russians, in their war-gaming, would have realized early on that they were in a unique position to *create* political problems, perhaps on a massive scale. And that could explain why the Mossad agents disappeared—the Russians recognized them too."

"Oh shit, Lippitt. You think *that's* what Carling plans to do?!"

"I think it's not beyond the realm of possibility."

"That's insane."

"Not if you're war-gaming this thing for the Russians. The Soviets always fish in troubled waters. Garth is perceived by many people as a Messiah—by many Christians, as the Second Coming of Christ. If Jews, specifically the Israelis, can be blamed for the death of *this* Messiah, it will have a disastrous impact not only on Israel's relations with the rest of the world, but with our relations as well. The entire western alliance could be sent into disarray, with Israel ending up even more isolated and condemned. Those are the benefits the Russians could reap if they kill Garth, and somehow manage to pin it on those two Mossad agents."

"Lippitt, what the hell am I going to *do*?!"

"I really don't know, Mongo," the old man said, real pain in his voice. "I just wanted you to be aware of all the dimensions of the danger to Garth, as I see them. We'll be doing all we can, and we'll have our people there tomorrow night when Garth is scheduled to make his announcement. But I'm afraid that if we can't find Garth before then, it may be too late."

"I've got to go, Lippitt," I said tightly. "I've got some heavy thinking to do; I've got to think of some valid excuse for walking into that bathhouse."

"Yes. Mongo?"

"What?"

"Go with God."

19.

I was at my bank in the morning when it opened. I gained access to my safe deposit box, took out the black leather attaché case inside, opened it and studied the magnificent knife and scabbard nestled in a bed of red velvet. I had not looked for years at Whisper, with her jeweled handle and blade made of Damascus steel by a process lost for centuries, and now memories cascaded through my mind. I had stolen it from a murderous commune which had intended it as an "offering" to a man they considered the Messiah—Siegmund Loge; now I needed the blade to try to save another man many people considered the Messiah. I closed the case, walked out into the morning. It had begun to snow.

It was after ten by the time I got to the converted bathhouse. The street in the front of the building was clogged with television equipment trucks; all three networks were to televise the Christmas Eve proceedings, and the broadcast would be relayed around the world by satellite. Whatever was going to happen, Tommy Carling had gone to great pains, on relatively short notice, to make certain a global audience would be watching.

I hoped it meant that Garth wasn't already dead.

In view of the fact that scores of sports figures, movie stars, and politicians had indicated their desire to attend the event, it didn't surprise me that the two green-jacketed men flanking the entrance to the bathhouse carried metal detectors. I'd anticipated some kind of security check; I unstrapped the shoulder holster holding my Beretta and slung it over my shoulder, then ducked under a police barricade, skipped over a treacherous sea of thick electrical cables, and went up to the entrance.

"Here," I said, holding out the gun to the burly, sandy-haired guard standing to the left of the door. "I assume you'll want to take this off my hands before you let me in there."

"What is it you want, Dr. Frederickson?" the thinner guard on the right said in a voice that was polite but cold. Both men ignored the gun I was holding out.

"I want to see my brother."

"You can see him tonight, sir. You're much too early. Nobody is allowed in the building now but our people and the television technicians."

"Garth's People used to be more hospitable."

"I apologize, sir, for the inconvenience. We feel these measures are necessary for the security of some of the people who will be celebrating here with us tonight."

"Check with Garth; he'll want to see me."

"He's not to be disturbed," the sandy-haired man said.

"Do you know where he is?" I asked the bigger man.

"He's not to be disturbed. We'll reserve a place for you in the reserved section if you'd like, Dr. Frederickson, but we can't let you in now."

"I have something to give him; it's very important to him, and to Garth's People."

"What?"

I slung the Beretta in its holster back over my shoulder, hefted the attaché case. "This."

"What's in it, sir?"

"It's for Garth. If you're not authorized to put me in touch with my brother, at least let me inside to talk to Tommy Carling."

The thinner man on the right switched on his metal detector, passed its steel wand back and forth over the surface of the case to an accompaniment of harsh, insistent buzzing. He shut off the detector, shook his head. "There's no way you can go in there with that, Dr. Frederickson; not unless you show us what's inside."

"Very well," I said with an exaggerated sigh as I rested the case on my left forearm, unsnapped the clasps, lifted the lid, and shoved Whisper toward the two men. "This is my gift to my brother and Garth's People."

My little theatrical flourish had the desired effect; the eyes of both men opened wider and they took a step backward as they stared at Whisper.

The thinner man licked his lips, then looked at me. "Is that . . . ?"

"Yes. It's the Great Knife. I want Garth to have it with him when he makes his announcement tonight." I closed the case, took my gun and holster off my shoulder, and once again offered it to the two men. "Now will you let me in to see Carling?"

The sandy-haired guard took my gun, set it down behind him, just inside the entrance to the bathhouse. "I don't know where Tommy is at the moment, Dr. Frederickson," the man said with just the slightest touch of awe in his voice. "He's been all over the place supervising things all morning. But you go on in, and we'll send somebody to scare him up for you."

I'd like to scare him up, I thought as I walked between the two guards, and I couldn't. But I was inside the bathhouse. And I was armed. As I'd hoped, the men with their metal detectors had been so distracted by all the hardware I was carrying upstairs, that they'd neglected to check downstairs; I still had my Seecamp in its holster strapped to my ankle. And I had Whisper.

Inside the cavernous bathhouse, hordes of workers and members of Garth's People were milling about, attending to their various tasks as they threaded their way up and down, back and forth across the hall through a polished wood sea of folding chairs tightly packed together in narrow rows. Speakers, klieg lights, and television cameras were mounted on the stone balcony ringing the hall, and at the far end, erected in front of the entrance to the showers, was a huge stage. At the lip of the stage was a lectern, and at the rear a huge bank of electronic equipment. Above the stage a massive green banner with the rings-and-knife logo of Garth's People hung suspended by wires strung from one of the four curved steel girders supporting the vaulted glass dome, which now glowed with milky light. I didn't like the light from that glass sky, which suffused the entire hall like a shroud.

Everything seemed to indicate that Carling planned to use Garth in whatever production he was planning, and logic dictated that Carling would have Garth locked up somewhere inside the bathhouse, ready to be marched out—drugged, or with a gun at his back—at the appropriate moment, if only to step through the curtains at the rear of the stage into bright television lights before being gunned down. At least that was the logic I had to operate on. If Garth was somewhere inside the building—and, if he wasn't, all of my machinations were going to be largely irrelevant—I had to find him. But first I had to run the gauntlet of Tommy Carling and Sister Kate, who sooner or later would learn that I was inside the bathhouse.

Wanting to get as far away from the main entrance as possible, I started walking casually down the side of the hall toward the massive stage. Carling intercepted me just as I passed a row of pea-green Port-O-Johns.

"Hello, Mongo," the ponytailed male nurse and K.G.B. officer said as he stepped down out of a staircase. His voice was flat, his eyes cold, as he studied me, and he did not extend his hand.

"Hello, Tommy," I replied, and forced a smile. The other man was not even bothering to play his usual role of good-natured, slightly effeminate healer, and I wondered why; it most certainly disturbed me. I heard a faint rustle in the darkness of the staircase behind him, but nobody emerged.

That, I thought, could very well be Sister Kate, riding shotgun. Something had happened to convince Tommy Carling that it was no longer necessary—or possible—to accommodate me with his fun and games, and I didn't like that one bit. "How are you?"

"I'm just fine, Mongo," Carling replied in the same flat voice. "How are you?"

"About half."

"What do you want here, Mongo?"

"Didn't you get the message?" I asked as I hefted the black leather case.

"I was told you'd brought the knife you call Whisper."

"And which Garth's People call the Great Knife. I'd understood that it had become an important religious symbol for a lot of you, but you don't seem all that impressed—or even curious. Wouldn't you like to see it?"

"Why bring it now?"

"Because I thought it might be nice for Garth to have it with him tonight when he makes his announcement—I assume he's going to tell the world that he is, indeed, the Messiah. I thought his followers might enjoy the experience of actually seeing the Great Knife. Don't you?"

"Why didn't you bring it to him before? Why now?"

"Why *not* now?" I replied with a shrug. "Better late than never. I want to make peace with my brother, Tommy. I still can't say that I believe he's the son of God, but there's no question that he's become a world-class religious leader, and will remain so for the rest of his life. I love him, I'm proud of him, and I just want him to have the knife; it means more to him and the rest of you than it does to me."

"I'll give it to him."

"No. This is a very personal thing for me, Tommy, and it will be for Garth too. I want to give it to him myself."

"Then you'll have to give it to him tonight. I have express orders not to disturb him for anything, no matter how important it may seem to me."

"When can I see him? I'd think he'd want to be carrying the Great Knife when he appears on stage."

"I won't know when he's emerged from retreat before he actually appears here. You're welcome to stay around and wait if you'd like. There's plenty of work left to do, and I'll assign you to one of our setup crews. Then you'll know the minute he arrives."

And Carling would be able to keep a close eye on me. "I'd love to, Tommy, but I've got a luncheon date, and then a whole load of last-minute Christmas shopping to do. I figure I can't be back here before seven or eight. One of the guards said he'd be able to save a seat for me in the reserved section."

"No problem," Carling said evenly. "I'll put you in the front row."

"See you tonight, Tommy," I said, and started back up the hall.

"Mongo?"

I stopped, turned back. "What?"

"Did this sudden change of heart you've experienced come before or after all the work you've been doing and the conversations you've been having during the past week? Did Harry make you a believer?"

Oh-oh. "How do you know what I've been doing in the past week, Tommy?" I asked in as mild a tone as I could muster.

"You're marked, Mongo, remember?" Tommy Carling said with what I thought was just the faintest trace of a humorless smile. "It's not only the scar on your forehead that marks you, but your stature. Garth's People are everywhere; they know who you are, and they very much fear that you mean to cause Garth harm. They repeat things."

It could very well be that Mrs. Daplinger had told Carling about my visit to her, but it was also possible that the K.G.B. had been tailing me. Or Harry August. Or both of us. It would explain Carling's attitude, and sudden lack of pretense. Game time had been over before I'd ever walked in the bathhouse door, and I hadn't even known it. The only question that remained was how much Tommy Carling knew I knew—or had guessed. Staying around to explore that question didn't seem like a good idea.

"What I did last week, or last year, is none of your business, Tommy," I said evenly. "I'll see you tonight."

"Good-bye, Mongo."

Exit stage right, very quickly. I'd feared that Carling would try to escort me to the door, but he seemed content to remain where he was as I turned and walked back up the hall. It was only after I had made my way through a knot of TV technicians that I abruptly turned left and ducked into the first stairwell I could find. It led down, which was fine with me; I had no idea of the dimensions of those sections of the bathhouse I hadn't seen, and in my search for Garth one direction seemed as good as another.

I emerged from the stairwell into a narrow, musty corridor that went both left and right. I went to the right, and passed through the first door I came to; it was a huge boiler room, complete with a tangled network of pipes and ducts, two enormous furnaces, and what sounded like a battalion of rats that scurried away as I found and turned on the light switch. I rummaged around inside the grime-encrusted room, but found nothing but more doors opening on to more corridors. All had to be checked out.

Lugging around the attaché case, I felt like a stockbroker on his way to work. I opened the case, took out the set of lock picks I had hidden under the red felt padding. Then I put Whisper into her scabbard, slipped it into the waistband of my jeans, behind my back, before going back out into the main corridor.

Working my way through the bowels of the bathhouse was dirty work; more important, it was maddeningly time consuming. There were a number of corridors, and in each a number of locked doors. I knocked at each locked door and called Garth's name, but the lack of a response didn't mean that I could go on; Garth could be bound and gagged, or drugged into unconsciousness. Each lock had to be picked, the room searched. Most were storerooms.

Sweaty and grimy, I was into my second hour, my fourth corridor, and inside my ninth room when Marl Braxton's voice came from the doorway behind me, chilling me.

"Stop right there, Mongo."

I wheeled around, found Braxton standing behind me just inside the door. His head and shoulders were cloaked in the shadow of a duct pipe, but I could see that his face looked drawn, his dark eyes haunted. He'd lost weight, and there was a marked tremor in both hands.

"Hello, Marl," I said quietly.

"What are you doing here, Mongo?"

"I'm looking for Garth. What are *you* doing down here?"

"Looking for you," the man with the haunted eyes said in a curiously halting voice. Marl Braxton, I thought, was in bad shape.

"Tommy Carling sent you, didn't he?"

Braxton nodded. "You didn't pick up your gun. Didn't you think Tommy would check to make sure you'd left?"

"I thought he might, fervently hoped he wouldn't. Do you know where Garth is, Marl?"

"Yes."

My heart began to beat faster. "Where, Marl?"

"He's in retreat, preparing himself for the moment when he will announce to the world that he is the Messiah, sent by God to save humankind."

"Wrong, Marl. Tommy Carling has him locked up someplace, and if I can't find him, he's going to die. I could use your help."

"You're a liar. You're the one who wants to harm him."

"Tommy Carling is a K.G.B. officer, Marl. So is Sister Kate."

"You lie."

"It's the truth. What the hell *do* you think I'm doing down here, if not searching for Garth? Did Carling explain that to you when he sent you after me?"

"You're hiding, waiting until Garth appears upstairs so that you can kill him."

"Marl, look at me; I'm covered with about fifty pounds of grease and spider webs. If I wanted to hide down here, don't you think I've have hunkered down before this?"

"You could be planting explosives."

"If you were going to explode anything down here and be assured of killing anyone, much less a particular individual, it would have to be an atomic bomb. Does it appear to you that I'm carrying an atomic bomb? You have to believe me, Marl—and you have to help me. You can move around through this building a hell of a lot easier than I can."

"Garth is the Messiah," Braxton said distantly.

"Help me find the Messiah before Tommy Carling kills him."

But Marl Braxton, deprived of Garth and his medication and removed from the psychiatric support system that had nurtured him for decades, had drifted beyond the meaning of anything I was going to say to him. Words could not pierce the gathering darkness of his madness.

"I will not let you kill him, Mongo," Braxton said in a low, barely audible voice. "I must stop you."

"How, Marl?" I said quickly as I watched him reach with his right hand across his body for the button on his left sleeve. "Will you kill me in the same way you killed Bartholomew Lash and Timmy Owens?"

That got his attention, and his hand froze with his fingers on the button. He stepped forward into the light, and I could see by the astonished expression on his face that my something less than totally wild guess had hit the target dead center. "How did you know?" Marl Braxton whispered hoarsely.

"I suspected for a while, but I wasn't sure until now," I said, speaking rapidly, playing for time as I searched for something I could say that might break through the roiling, murderous clouds in Marl Braxton's mind. I *did* need his help; and I didn't want to kill him.

"Having both of those TV preachers die of the same thing, both within twenty-four hours after attacking Garth and calling down God's wrath on him, was just a bit too much of a coincidence for the deaths to be natural," I continued in a flat, matter-of-fact tone which I hoped might be mildly hypnotic. "God certainly didn't kill them, which meant that someone else did. K.G.B.? Why not? Except that the more I thought about it, the more that seemed like a move which might be just a bit too cute for them. Both of those preachers were big-time celebrities, which meant that the mansions they lived in were at least moderately guarded. There is no question that the K.G.B. has the personnel needed to pass through that kind of security and carry out an assassination, but why should they bother? Why take the risk? So, who else did I know who had the sort of special training that would be needed, and who could kill a man and make the death look natural? Who else did I know who might want those men dead, who might think that the men posed some kind of real threat to Garth and *deserved* to die? You, Marl. You see yourself as Garth's avatar on earth, his protector. If I wanted to ask around here, or if I wanted to take the bother of checking airline records, I'll bet I could tie you to those deaths."

Braxton started to unbutton his sleeve.

"Leave your maid of constant sorrows where she is, Marl!" I snapped.

"Satan speaks to you!" Braxton shouted as he pulled up his shirt sleeve to reveal a thick, three-inch wire embedded in a stubby wooden handle wrapped in black tape and strapped to the inside of his forearm.

"Satan and I may be drinking buddies, Marl," I said evenly, keeping my eyes on the shiv strapped to the other man's forearm, "but he never tells me a damn thing. Once I figured that you were a likely suspect, I had to ponder the question of how you—or anyone else—would have done it. There are drugs that can cause, or mimic, stroke and brain hemorrhage, but they're fairly esoteric and I didn't see how you could have gained access to them. Wielded by an expert, a needle shoved up a nostril and threaded through the occipital orb into the brain will also do the trick quite nicely. That was it. Having figured that out, the rest fell into place. I remembered that you'd threatened Mama Baker with a visit from your maid of constant sorrows; you specifically said that she'd 'stick it to him.' At the time I took it as the obvious sexual metaphor, and it was, but it was also more than that." I paused, pointed to the sharpened wire he was absently, nervously, stroking with his fingertips. "My guess is that's a straightened spring from your bed. The Koreans literally tortured you right out of your mind with needles, and— "

"How do you know that?!"

"I know it. A lot of that torture was probably genital, and they made you impotent—except, perhaps, for pain-oriented sex. That shiv is your 'maid of constant sorrows' because you use her at night to hurt yourself for sexual pleasure. But you were also prepared to kill with your 'maid,' if the need ever arose—as it did, in your mind, when those two tube boobs threatened Garth. None of this is important, Marl; I'm telling you things we both know to be true so that you'll believe the other things."

Tears streamed from Marl Braxton's eyes, rolled down his cheeks, and dripped off his chin as he slowly withdrew the shiv from its sheath. "Garth gave me back my mind and my life," he sobbed. "He'll be here tonight. You mustn't hurt him."

I reached behind my back, gripped Whisper's handle, and drew her from her scabbard.

Shhhh.

"The Great Knife," Braxton whispered, stepping back into the doorway and staring wide-eyed at Whisper as I held her, like a talisman, before me.

I sent the "Great Knife" flying through the air, and Whisper landed with a solid *thunk* in the wood frame of the doorway, two inches from Braxton's right ear.

"If I'd wanted to, Marl, I could have stuck the Great Knife right between your eyes," I said evenly. "But the Great Knife is not meant to kill you, but to help clear your mind. Take it; feel it."

Marl Braxton slowly reached up, gripped Whisper's handle, worked it back and forth until the blade slipped free of the wood. Then he held it in the palms of both hands, at arm's length, staring at it. I sat down on the floor and brought my knees up to my chin, resting my right hand on my right ankle, over my Seecamp. My somewhat unorthodox therapy session with the other man was just about at an end; if the sight of Whisper couldn't clear the fog in his mind, I was going to have to cure him of his psychosis permanently, with a bullet in the brain.

"Heft the Great Knife, Marl," I continued softly, watching him carefully. "She's yours if you want her, to give to Garth. But know by the power that you feel in that blade and the fact that I've made myself defenseless before you that Garth, and maybe a lot of other innocent people, are going to die this night unless you help me find him. *Think*, Marl. You know this building. Where could Carling have him locked up? For that matter, *how* might Carling be planning to kill him for the benefit of a worldwide television audience? You mentioned explosives. Could he have rigged the stage to blow up without anyone seeing him do it? Could he have rigged the entire *hall* to blow up? Think, Marl; help me."

But I'd overloaded his circuits, and he couldn't think. Suddenly Marl Braxton's mouth dropped open to form a great, round O, and he began to moan; the moan grew in volume and went up the scale. His hands began to tremble violently, and Whisper slipped from his grasp and clattered on the floor. But he maintained his grip on the shiv, and for one horrifying moment I thought he was going to drive the point of his maid of constant sorrows into his eye; instead, he gripped his head in his hands and began to scream. Then he turned and ran from the room.

"Marl!" I shouted, springing to my feet and running to the doorway. "Marl, wait!"

But Marl Braxton had already disappeared from sight, and all I could hear was the receding, ghostly echo of his footsteps as he ran through the basement of the bathhouse, perhaps to be swallowed up forever by the night in his mind.

I picked up Whisper, put her back in the scabbard in my waistband. Then I leaned against the doorjamb, wiped sweat and grime from my face, glanced at my watch. It was two o'clock. I had ten hours—perhaps considerably less time if Tommy Carling found out that the Marl Braxton card he'd played against me had become wild.

20.

I spent another ninety minutes in the catacomb of corridors in the basement, found nothing.

The good news was that nobody had found me. I'd worried that Marl Braxton could very well have gone running amok up in the main meeting hall, which could have triggered an intensive search for me by K.G.B. soldiers. But either Tommy Carling had not heard about what had happened, or he was short of help; the only sounds I'd heard in the basement since Braxton had run away had been my own eavy, anxious breathing, the scuffle of my feet on the dusty loors, my knocking on locked doors, the scratching of my picks.

There was a freight elevator at the end of one corridor. Not vanting to risk being seen or intercepted on a stairway, I got nto the elevator, drew my Seecamp, and pushed the Two utton. The elevator lurched upward, the doors jerked open nto the relative darkness of the stone balcony ringing the all. I stepped out, pressed back against a wall, and glanced ack and forth. There was nobody in sight.

But something was wrong. Music was playing from the sus-ended loudspeakers—*Das Rheingold*. I darted across the alcony to one of the flat steel braces that was part of he support system for the great glass dome, looked down over he railing, and felt my heart begin to beat more rapidly.

The hall was already half filled with people, and more vere being admitted through the entrance far down the hall to ny right. Hundreds of men, women, and children sat in the vooden folding chairs; some were quietly chatting with their eighbors, while others had their heads bowed in silent prayer r meditation.

I tried to convince myself that the fact Tommy Carling was illing the hall hours before the scheduled announcement was ot necessarily ominous; it was cold, windy, and snowing utside, and Carling might simply have decided to provide he people with shelter.

Or the K.G.B. operative could have found out what had appened between Marl Braxton and me; rather than hunt for ne and risk an embarrassing shootout that could have un-nown consequences, he had simply decided to alter his imetable and move up the schedule.

If that were the case, I might have only minutes left, not ours.

There were four corridors branching off from the balcony, nd one of them was right behind me, to the left of the levator. I headed down it. There were doors on both sides, nd the first one I tried was locked. Reasoning that Carling

would have imprisoned Garth as far away from the centers of
activity as possible, I immediately went to the far end of the
corridor. I picked the lock on the door to my right, stepped
into the room.

The room was really no more than a cubicle, probably
formerly used for either dressing or sex. I had counted twenty
doors on my way down the corridor; assuming there were as
many rooms off the other three corridors, it meant I could
have seventy-nine more locks to pick—with no guarantee that
Garth was in any of the rooms. It was too many.

There was a radiator in one corner of the room. I went to
it, used the butt of my Seecamp to tap out an SOS in Morse
code. I did it three times, then paused and listened.

The signal, clear and strong, came back. Three times.

Now we were getting someplace, I thought, barely manag-
ing to stifle a raucous cheer that probably would have been
heard all the way down in the meeting hall. Garth was not
only in one of the rooms, but—judging from the strength of
the return signal—almost certainly in that corridor.

I hurried to the door, then abruptly stopped when I heard a
sound that caused the hairs on the back of my neck to rise.

The sound of my brother's voice was muffled, but unmistakable; he was singing not Wagner, but a Mozart tune.

"Twinkle, twinkle, little star . . ."

Welcome back, Garth, I thought, wanting both to laugh
and to cry and knowing I didn't have time for either.

"I certainly am wondering where the hell you are . . ."

I was too close to the meeting hall to run up and down the
corridor shouting, and so there was nothing else to do but try
to home in on the singing. I picked the lock and went in the
room across the corridor, immediately came back out when I
could no longer hear the singing. In the corridor I could hear
it again.

"Twinkle, twinkle, little star . . ."

I entered the room next to the first one I'd tried. Garth
wasn't in it, but something else was that caused a chill to run

up my spine. There were a number of small, oblong cardboard cartons strewn about the room, and in the bottom of one I found a piece of gray, gummy, claylike material that I immediately recognized as C-5 plastic explosive.

If placed properly, there would have been enough plastic explosive in the empty cartons to blow up ten stages—if that was what Carling was planning to blow up.

". . . *how I wonder where you are. High above*—"

Garth and two men in green jackets were in the next room, handcuffed to pipes. On a small table in the center of the room was a black case with three hypodermic needles, each filled with a pinkish fluid.

"It's about fucking time you got here, brother," Garth said with a grim smile.

"Pick, pick, pick. You know how busy everybody gets during the holidays."

"Well, I suppose it doesn't make any difference. You wouldn't have found us here before last night; we were kept someplace else."

"Are you all right, Garth?"

My brother nodded, swallowed hard, grimaced. "Yeah. But for a week I've had what feels like a hangover you wouldn't believe."

"I believe," I said, walking over to him and examining the pipe to which he was handcuffed; it, like the ones the other two men were cuffed to, was solid, with no chance of breaking it at the seam. The cuffs themselves were of high quality steel, and I knew I was going to have a difficult time unlocking them.

"Remind me not to eat any more of that spy dust shit."

"I'll remind you," I said as I began sorting through my picks, looking for the smallest.

"There's no time for that, Mongo," Garth said in a low, tense voice. "Incidentally, this is Aaron Lake and Samuel—"

"Mossad," I said, nodding to the two men. "I know."

The man cuffed to the pipe on the wall behind me said,

"Carling has one of the support girders under the dome laced with *plastique*. If that dome goes, it could kill everyone in the hall."

"Mongo, get the hell out of here and warn those people," Garth said tersely. "I know something about handcuffs, and I'm telling you you're not going to get these suckers open with those toothpicks you're using. Carling knows you're on the loose, and he'd have put a guard outside the door if he hadn't been afraid it would attract attention from the TV people. He was here forty-five minutes ago, and he'll be back. He's going to blow the place when the hall is filled, so you haven't got a hell of a lot of time. You've got to go warn those people."

The pick I'd been using was no good; I selected the next larger one, inserted it in the narrow keyhole and began twisting. Nothing was happening. "Which girder, Aaron?"

"I don't know," the man on the wall behind me said.

"How does he plan to set it off?"

"We think he's set a number of charges along the girder, and they'll all go off if an electrical current runs through them."

"He told you this?"

"No, but there were plans. Samuel and I found them; the Russian found us. Each charge has a primer embedded in it which is radio controlled. Carling is carrying a transmitter; the charges will go off fifteen minutes after he activates the primers. Samuel and I will be found in the rubble, with documents linking us to Mossad, and the transmitter on one of us. It will look like we accidentally blew ourselves up in an explosion we set off."

"Mongo, *go*, damn it!" Garth snapped. "You don't have time to screw around with these cuffs; he's going to be back here any minute."

"I'm not going to leave the three of you cuffed to these pipes," I said curtly. "It will take me longer to lock all the doors I left open around here than it took me to unlock them. If Carling even suspects I've been here, he'll just cancel the preliminary parts of his pageant, shoot the three of you, and blow the dome.''

"Now that won't be necessary, Mongo," Tommy Carling said from behind me. "The show will go on as scheduled."

I wheeled around, grabbed for my Seecamp, froze when I saw Tommy Carling standing just inside the room with a 9mm pistol aimed at my head. The woman, still dressed in her nun's habit, was standing beside him.

"Drop your gun, Mongo. Do it!"

I did it. "Tommy—"

"Colonel Vladimir Kreisky," the K.G.B. officer with the ponytail and earring said easily. "You may as well know me by my real name, Mongo."

"Tommy," I repeated. "You have all the information you could possibly want on the effects of NPPD poisoning. Why do you have to kill us and all of those people out there? It doesn't make any sense."

"I'm truly sorry, Mongo," the man said as he nodded to his companion. "You have a point, but I have my orders."

I watched as Sister Kate picked up one of the hypodermic needles, pressed the plunger slightly, and shot a thin stream of pinkish fluid into the air. "Cut new orders. For Christ's sake, Tommy, take what you know and go home. All of this killing isn't necessary!"

"You're wasting your breath," the Israeli chained to a pipe against the far wall said.

"What you're planning won't work, Tommy."

"Really, Mongo? Why not?"

"For one thing, Mr. Lippitt knows all about you, and he knows about your plan to pin all these murders on the Mossad. He'll get the truth out."

"Will he? Somehow, I don't think the word of the Director of the D.I.A. will be believed when it's weighed against the evidence that will be found here.'' He paused, took a small gray box with a black button out of his pocket, held it up for me to see. ''I'm sorry none of you will be around to see how the debate is finally resolved.''

At another nod from Colonel Vladimir Kreisky, the woman went over to Garth and pulled up his left sleeve. The man I had known as Tommy Carling was watching her . . .

Shhhh.

I hurled Whisper and flung myself to one side as the gun exploded. A bullet slammed into my right thigh, spinning me in the air—but not before I had seen Whisper bury herself to the hilt in Tommy Carling's chest. Blood spurted from the man's mouth and nostrils, and he slumped to the floor.

Lying on my side and clutching at my bleeding thigh, I glanced over at the woman. The hypodermic needle had fallen from her hand, and she was staring in shock at Tommy Carling's corpse. The Seecamp was ten feet away, closer to me than to her, and I started crawling for it.

But Sister Kate was closer to the door. She recovered, saw that I almost had the gun, then snatched the gray control box from her companion's lifeless hand and darted from the room.

Fifteen minutes.

''Mongo, you've got to get her!'' Garth shouted. ''If you can get the control box back, you may be able to deactivate the timing mechanism before the charges go off!''

I struggled to my feet as pain knifed through my right leg. Holding my thigh with both hands, I staggered across the room to Tommy Carling's body, began fumbling in his pockets.

''Mongo!''

''I can barely walk, Garth,'' I said through clenched teeth. ''There's no way I can catch her. When those charges go off, this whole building could collapse. I'm not going to leave the three of you here. Carling may have keys on him.''

''Then drag the prick over here! I can search through his pockets as well as you can! Get out there and at least try to warn those people! Even if they panic and rush for the exits, at least some will survive; if this place collapses on their heads, nobody is going to get out. You just make sure you get *yourself* out before it blows. *Go*, Mongo! Do what you have to do! If the keys to the cuffs are in his pocket, I'll free us; if they're not, there's nothing you can do for us anyway.''

My brother had a point. I yanked off Carling's belt, used it as a tourniquet around my leg. I withdrew Whisper from Carling's chest and replaced the knife in the scabbard in my waistband, then dragged the corpse over to where Garth could reach it.

"Garth . . . ?"

"Damn you, Mongo, *go*! And keep an eye on your watch! If we get out and you get blown up, I'm going to be really pissed at you!''

Clutching the loose end of the belt tied around my thigh, I hobbled as fast as I could out of the room and down the corridor toward the stone balcony. Already I was feeling faint from shock and loss of blood, and the fiery pain in my leg had become a dull ache—not a good sign. I desperately hoped Garth would be able to free himself and the two Israelis, and that they would survive.

My situation was different. I had limited strength and mobility, and very little time—no time at all to do what I had to do, and still get out. I didn't much care for it, but I was resigned to the fact that if and when the building collapsed, I was going to be at the bottom of the rubble.

21.

THE hall was full. *Die Götterdämmerung* was playing through the loudspeaker hanging on the balcony just below me. I leaned over the railing, ripped the speaker loose, and dropped it in the aisle just below me. It landed with a resounding crash, causing those people in the immediate vicinity to jump out of their seats. In the rest of the packed hall heads turned as people looked in that direction, and then up at me.

"Listen to me, everybody!" I shouted through cupped hands, struggling to be heard over the music playing through the remaining loudspeakers. "Please listen to me! You are in great danger, but if you do what I say and don't panic everybody will be all right! In a few minutes this ceiling is going to collapse on you! You must all start leaving now, quickly but in an orderly fashion! As you leave the building make sure you keep going across the street so as to leave plenty of room for those coming out behind you! Please start leaving now!"

Somebody yelled, "*Judas!*"

"Damn it, this place is going to blow up! You have to get out!"

And then the music abruptly stopped.

"*Please be still, everybody. This is Sister Kate. Everything is all right.*"

I glanced to my left at the stage, but it was empty except for the lectern and a standing microphone which were now bathed in a spotlight. The woman was patched into the public address system—undoubtedly a safe distance away from the main hall. I wondered if she had pushed the button on the control box, knew I must assume that she had.

"You have to get out of here! This place is going to blow up!"

"Garth will join us as soon as the marked intruder is driven from our midst. We can do that by calling him by his real name. Judas!"

"Get out!"

The crowd began to chant: *"Judas! Judas! Judas!"*

"You're all going to be crushed or slashed to bits!"

"Judas! Judas! Judas!"

So much for good intentions, I thought as I quickly loosened the tourniquet to let some blood flow, then tightened it again. There was nothing more the "marked intruder" could do where he was except keep shouting, to no avail, until he went down with the balcony, and that seemed a rather futile gesture. In whatever time I had left, I intended to go back to see if my brother and the Israelis had managed to escape—and live or die with them, as the case might be, if they hadn't.

I was starting to turn away from the balcony when suddenly a forearm with a leather sheath strapped to it dropped out of the shadow darkness of a girder twenty yards or so out over the hall. Blood, black-purple in the gleam of a klieg light that illuminated the forearm, flowed freely down the arm, then dripped off the fingertips onto the upturned faces of the people below. Then the arm began slowly to swing back and forth.

Marl Braxton was beckoning me.

I pulled the belt tourniquet on my leg even tighter, then clambered up on the railing of the balcony. I gripped the edges of the girder's support footing and hauled myself up into the darkness overhead.

I had hauled myself less than five yards when my right hand touched a gummy mound that could only be *plastique*;

there was a hole in the center where a primer had been torn out.

Something I had said—or the sight and touch of Whisper—had gotten through to the insane D.I.A. operative. Marl Braxton, still the consummate professional, had anticipated what his K.G.B. opponents might be planning, and he had set out to stop it. Now it was up to me to finish the job.

Marl Braxton was still alive when I got to him—but he wouldn't be for very long. In his effort to attract my attention, he had draped himself across the width of the girder, and the upper part of his body now hung precipitously over the edge; I could clearly see the large exit wound of a bullet in his back, and I wondered how he had managed to stay alive as long as he had.

"The woman," Braxton rasped, coughing blood. "Crack sharpshooter . . . rifle with silencer . . . watch out."

I loosened the tourniquet. Blood from the bullet wound in my thigh mingled with Marl Braxton's, dripped onto the people below. The music suddenly began to play again—full blast; it would be more than enough to cover the sound of rifle fire, silenced or not. I gripped the far edge of the girder with one hand while I reached down with the other, grabbed the back of Marl Braxton's shirt, and tried to pull him back up on the girder.

"Too late . . . for me," Braxton said in a voice I was just barely able to hear over the cascading roar of the music. He coughed more blood. "Defuse . . . charges. But don't expose yourself. She . . . got me from . . . wherever she is. She'll get . . . you."

"Don't talk, Marl," I said, pulling on the back of his shirt. "Save your strength. You're not dead yet."

"Soon will . . . be. Charges all along . . . this girder."

"I know, Marl. Don't talk."

"No matter what you . . . say . . . Garth is the Messiah. I was right. I'll be . . . with him in paradise."

"Yes, Marl," I said with a sudden surge of emotion that

was probably the closest I had come to experiencing a genuine religious feeling in my life, "you'll be with Garth in paradise."

I never heard the rifle shot, but suddenly Marl Braxton's lowered head snapped to one side and a hole opened in his right temple. I released my hold on his shirt, and his corpse slipped off the girder to tumble down into the sea of people below. There was a shocked silence after Marl's body landed, which lasted two or three seconds, and then the people below began to scream and scramble blindly in a sharp crescendo of panic. I ducked back, pulled the tourniquet tight.

If Sister Kate was in firing range, as she obviously was, it had to mean that I still had a few minutes left. That was encouraging; what was not encouraging was the fact that she was winging shots at me.

A bullet ricocheted off the steel an inch from my head, passed up through the glass dome. Snow trickled onto the back of my neck. I flattened myself on the girder, pulled myself upward.

I found the next slab of C-5 ten yards farther on. Using Whisper, I dug the primer out and let it fall into the milling crowd below me. The frenzied screaming of the people filling the hall rose above the music that thundered in my ears and *thrummed* through the girder I was moving on. Glancing over the edge of the steel, I watched in horror as men, women, and children were trampled, limbs caught in folding chairs and snapped. People were dying. Sickened, I looked away and pulled myself along the girder.

I didn't bother looking at my watch; I had lost track of time, but it didn't seem to matter. The shooting had stopped, and I took that as a decidedly bad omen. I wondered how long the woman had given herself to get clear of the building. Five minutes? One minute? Thirty seconds?

Suddenly the music was cut off, and my brother's voice—in the sharp, commanding tones of a veteran police officer—came over the public address system, cutting through the cacophony of screams and splintering wood.

"Stop! Stop it! Everyone stop moving and listen to me!"

Garth's sudden appearance in the spotlight on the stage, and his voice over the P.A. system, had the desired effect. Suddenly it was still in the hall, except for the moans of the injured. I kept crawling, found another slab, cut out the primer.

"Everyone remain calm and do as I say! Right now, wherever you're standing, look around you. If you're close to an exit, walk out of it. Those of you in the middle of the hall, lie down right now and curl into a ball. If you're near a chair that's in one piece, try to get at least your head under it. Cover the injured. Do it now!"

Out of the corner of my eye I watched as the two Mossad agents hurried across the stage to Garth, flanking him and wrapping their arms around his body, forming a protective shield of their flesh between Garth and any more bullets that might be fired.

But there were no more shots. The woman was gone—which meant that the remaining charges might go off at any moment, raining broken glass and steel down on the helpless people below.

I had lost all feeling in my wounded leg, and I knew that I could lose it to gangrene even if I survived. But there was no time to loosen the tourniquet; I kept crawling.

After disarming two more charges, I reached the apogee of the curved girder. From there it was literally all downhill. I pulled myself down the girder at a pretty good clip, carving away the primers on the last three remaining charges. I reached the end of the girder, fell off the top of the support footing and landed hard on my side. I immediately reached down to the belt on my leg, loosened it. More blood rushed out over my already soaked pants leg.

"You meddling little son-of-a-bitch," a woman's voice rasped.

I looked up as Sister Kate stepped out of the shadows in one of the corridors that radiated off the balcony. The rifle she was holding was aimed at my chest. Her finger on the trigger was just beginning to tighten when a brawny arm reached out of the same shadows. A hand cupped her chin, jerked her head to one side, snapping her neck. Her shot whistled over my head, the rifle fell from her hands, and she slumped to the cold stone of the balcony as a familiar figure stepped over the body, reached down, helped me to my feet.

All along, I'd been looking for help from Mr. Lippitt's man inside the organization. Only now did I realize what I should have realized before; Lippitt's man was undoubtedly dead—discovered and executed earlier. But the guardian angel who'd shown up was more than an adequate substitute.

"Mr. Lippitt sends his regards, Mongo," Veil said evenly.

"Jesus Christ," I managed to say when I recovered from my initial shock at finding myself still alive. "Where the hell did you come from?"

"Oh, I've been around all along doing the best I could to keep an eye on you. Lippitt asked me to ride shotgun, remember? But I had to stay way in the background, or they'd have made me. I lost you when you came in here, and I couldn't get in until they started letting everybody in." He paused, removed his false beard, nodded at Sister Kate's corpse. "Sorry I couldn't manage to put that bitch out of commission sooner. I got caught in traffic down on the floor."

"Believe me, you're forgiven," I said, shaking my head, leaning on the balcony railing for support. In the distance I could hear the wail of many sirens, approaching from all directions. I waved to Garth to signal that I was all right, then picked up the fallen rifle, leaned on it.

"You'd better lie down right there, Mongo," Veil said. "From the looks of that leg, you've lost a lot of blood. Ambulances will be here soon."

"There are people down there in a lot worse shape than I am," I said as I shook off Veil's hand and began hobbling across the balcony. "I want to help—and I want to be with Garth."

I'd gone a few steps when I felt Veil's hand clutch the back of my shirt, helping to hold me up as I struggled toward the stairs.

22.

USING Sister Kate's rifle as a crutch, and with Veil holding me up from behind, I made it down the stairs, hobbled into the meeting hall from a stairwell just below and to the right of the stage. I stopped, lowered my head, and groaned inwardly at the legacy of pandemonium, the sight of dead and broken bodies.

"You've done your job, Mongo," Veil said quietly but firmly. "Now you've got to get off that leg, or you're going to lose it."

"I have to help," I said in a hollow voice, looking around me in horror.

"There's nothing more you can do, except wait with the rest of the injured for the ambulances."

The people still standing on their feet seemed to be slowly milling about in separate knots of varying sizes, and all seemed to be suffering from various degrees of shock—including Harry August, whom I glimpsed wandering through the chaos as if in a daze. I sensed clearly that the initial calming influence of Garth's appearance and words was wearing off, and there was a sick, moist smell and feel of renewed mass hysteria in the air. A man in the back began to scream mindlessly, and after a few moments a woman off to my left joined him in an eerie, chilling duet of terror and horror.

Unable to go on any farther, I simply released my grip on the rifle barrel and slumped to the floor. Veil removed the belt tourniquet from my thigh, then used Whisper to cut away my pants leg, which he rolled up into a ball and applied to

my wound as a pressure bandage. A lost, whimpering, terri-
fied small child crawled close by; I picked her up in my
arms, held her to my chest.

"You must stay calm," Garth said into the microphone
from his place at the front of the stage, above me. *"The
police and ambulances will be here to help everybody very
soon. For now, stay still—or try to help anybody nearby
who's injured. The greatest danger has passed, and now we
have to try and make certain that no more people are hurt."*

From somewhere in the middle of the hall, a woman
shouted: "What's happened, Garth?!"

*"This isn't the time for explanations, ma'am. Just try to
remain calm until help arrives."*

A man shouted: "What have you done to us, Master?!
How could you have let this happen?!"

Garth didn't answer. Feeling a growing sense of unease, I
glanced up at the stage. The Mossad agents had jumped off
the stage into the audience to help the injured, and now Garth
stood alone in the spotlight. I wished the Israelis had stayed
where they were.

"Master?! Tell us what's happened! What have you done?!"

"My name is Garth," my brother said in a low, even tone
which nonetheless echoed throughout the hall as it was am-
plified through the loudspeakers, *"and it always has been.
I'm not anybody's master, and I never was. I've been very
sick as a result of being poisoned. Certain people took
advantage of me—and you—for their own purposes. They
used me to manipulate you."*

That was not exactly what his audience had come to hear
from Garth, and angry shouts erupted all over the hall.

"You were supposed to announce that you were the son of
God! The Messiah!"

*"That's not true; I've told you from the beginning that it
was nonsense to think I was some sort of messiah, and I
never planned any announcement. I've been held a prisoner
for the past week by the same people who've been manipulating*

you and me. All of us were brought here so that we could be killed. Now, thanks to my brother, that isn't going to happen. Try to understand that I'm very proud to be my parents' son, not God's. I am what I am; just Garth Frederickson.''

More shouts of anger and confusion arose from around the hall.

"Blasphemer! You've brought the wrath of God down on us! We've been tricked and this is God's punishment!"

It was clearly beginning to look like an argument my brother couldn't possibly win, and I motioned rather urgently for him to get down off the stage. He ignored me.

"Stay calm! You deserve to be told the truth, and that's what I'm telling you. During the months we've worked together, you've shown to yourselves and to the world how good you are—how good people can be. It's you people who've done the work that needs to be done, not God. God doesn't feed hungry people; other people do. You don't need gods, or the sons or daughters of gods, to show you what's right. Your reward has been the good feeling you've had in your hearts about yourselves, and about other people. Continue to do what you've been doing, and you'll continue to feel good about yourselves. Do it with or without God, as you please, but you have to do it now without me. You don't need either of us.''

"Garth!" I shouted. "Stop your Goddamn preaching and get off that stage! They don't want to hear it!"

"You betrayed us!" a woman screamed from somewhere right behind me. "You tricked us! You took our money, wasted our time, and now you've killed a lot of us! Satan!"

"I felt I owed you the truth!''

A jagged chair leg sailed through the air, bounced off the lectern less than a foot from Garth's head. It ricocheted into the darkness at the back of the stage, impaled itself in a huge piece of equipment in a bank of electronic gear. Sparks flew, and there was the chilling crackle of unleashed electricity.

Suddenly it seemed that everyone was shouting in either

rage or panic. Fistfights broke out, and more pieces of chairs flew through the air. Garth stayed where he was, pleading for calm, shouting into a microphone that had gone dead. Still holding the child with my left arm, I reached up for Veil's with my right hand, and he hauled me to my feet.

"Garth!" I screamed. "Get the hell off that stage! Get out of there!"

It seemed that chairs were flying everywhere, bouncing off the lectern and stage all around Garth. I cringed, clutched the little girl close to me, and watched in horror as electrical power cables that had been strung along the underside of the balcony were torn away and broken; more sparks flew. A fire had begun to blaze around the electrical equipment at the back of the stage; blue-white electrical fire flickered over the wires, dancing on bare metal. Two loudspeakers suspended from the balcony suddenly exploded.

"*Garth, come on!! This place is going to blow!!*"

He couldn't have heard me in the din, and I was being rapidly swept away from the stage by an inexorable tide of milling, churning bodies—but Garth's eyes suddenly met mine. Desperately, I motioned with my free hand toward the sparking wires, then up at the glass dome and the girders. He nodded, again tried to shout into the dead microphone just as a man emerged from the flame-streaked darkness behind him and smashed a chair across his back, driving him to his knees. The microphone flew through the air with its sudden feedback sounding like an electrical scream of protest.

"*Garth!*"

Now people had begun to surge onto the stage from all directions. Garth shook his head to clear it, took a series of deep breaths, then abruptly stood up. Almost absently picking a thick, bloody, wood sliver out of his shoulder, he leaped down off the stage and walked straight toward me. Most people parted as he strode forward, and the others he pushed aside. I was trying to scream warnings to the people around me, but no one would listen. I looked up, saw translucent blue fire dancing along the support girder at the farthest end of the hall.

And then Garth was beside me. He scooped both the child and me up in his arms, and then both he and Veil began to push toward the closest exit, fifteen years to our left. We were only a few feet away when the electricity reached the slabs of C-5. There was a deafening explosion, and it felt like a steel fist struck me from behind, knocking me from Garth's arms, throwing us all to the ground. Chunks of steel, slivers of glass and wood whistled through the air over our heads. I struggled to drape my body over the little girl's, and then something struck me in the head and I passed out.

I couldn't have been out for more than a few minutes, because I was suddenly aware of hands clutching at the child and me, pulling us from the rubble, placing us on stretchers. Desperately, I looked around for Garth—and found him lying on a stretcher next to me; he was conscious, staring back at me. We reached out, touched each other's hand. Then our stretchers were raised and we were carried away through a nether world filled with the scream of sirens and swirling smoke.

Somebody shoved a television camera in my face, and I swiped at it and turned away in disgust. As I did so, I caught sight of something that filled me with renewed horror and tore a strangled cry from my throat.

Harry August was lying on a stretcher on the ground, cluthing at his face as attendants struggled to strap him in. Blood oozed through his fingers.

Mercifully, I passed out again.

EPILOGUE

THE memories associated with the Christmas Eve carnage, like the memories of Valhalla, remained—as they would always remain. But, with the passage of time, the nightmares ceased, and we were whole again, in mind and spirit as well as in body.

There had been no way to prove that the K.G.B. had been responsible for the bathhouse explosion that had killed dozens of people, and injured hundreds of others. Even if there had been proof, it was doubtful that it would have been presented; as Mr. Lippitt had correctly predicted, the government of the United States had not shown any great urgency to get out the truth about what had happened, for fear that the resulting publicity would damage relations between the two countries. The Soviet premier had delivered a personal, oral apology to President Kevin Shannon for the "deplorable, unauthorized acts of an insane Soviet citizen," and as far as

Kevin Shannon was concerned that was the end of the matter. That was fine with Garth and me—and with Veil, who'd had a tad more than passing experience with government debacles and hastily arranged cover-ups. What the leaders of these two great powers of the twentieth century did to, or with, each other was of little interest to the three of us; in the short run, it at least seemed to mean that the Soviets owed us one. Despite the savage lessons of Siegmund Loge and the Valhalla Project, Garth and I had refused to give up hope—and one of our hopes was that humankind had a future; we also hoped that whatever new, dominating nation-states arose in that future would show considerably more wisdom, and considerably less insanity, in their stewardship of our planet and its peoples.

Garth's People would end up a little less than a chapter, a little more than a footnote, in the history of bizarre religious cults spawned in the United States of America.

In the stories that had surfaced in the press and on television, I'd somehow come out a hero, Garth something less than that. I'd feared that Garth would be bitter, but that hadn't been the case at all. In the preceding months he had been keeping a decidedly low profile, but he had kept busy reading a great deal, thinking a great deal, and performing all sorts of volunteer charitable work in situations where he could be reasonably assured of anonymity. For some ridiculous reason I had always considered myself the "softer" of the two Frederickson brothers, and I'd been wrong. It was Garth, not me, who had inherited the largest part of our mother's transcendent tenderness and mercy. For the first time in years, since the funeral in Peru County, Nebraska, for our nephew which had sucked us into the maelstrom of the Valhalla Project, my brother seemed completely at peace with himself, totally unperturbed by the opprobrium heaped upon him in some religious and political quarters ever since his Christmas Eve "recantation" and the storm of death and destruction that had followed.

"I've been thinking of asking my brother for a job," Garth said evenly as he pulled off the Haverstraw exit of the Palisades Parkway. We were back in Rockland County, but this time we were heading for the Helen Hayes Hospital.

I looked over at my brother to see if he might be joking, but he apparently wasn't. I thought he looked good in his beard, and with the dark glasses which he now habitually wore. "Which brother is that?" I asked with some surprise.

"The only one I've got—the short guy."

"You'd have to give up your disability payments."

"I'm not disabled anymore."

"I thought you were considering going back to the force."

"I've been giving that as much consideration as you've been giving to going back to teaching. Hell, they wanted to make you chairman of the department."

"It's true that I could teach again if I wanted to; I don't. I've still got a bitter taste in my mouth after the number they did on me during the Archangel business. Maybe one day; not now."

"You've got more P.I. business now than you can handle, and I thought you could use a partner. Are you turning me down?"

"Shit, Garth," I said with mock seriousness, "I was really hoping you'd go back to work as a cop. If you go to work with me as a P.I., who am I going to have in the NYPD to pump for information when I need it?"

"It'll be good for your character not to have me to run to every time you need sensitive information from the police. Besides, you don't seem to be hurting in that department; half the cops in the city would probably prefer to talk to you than to me." He paused, and his thin smile faded. "I'm not that person anymore, Mongo; I'm not a cop. I'm not sure what—who—I am now, and I'm hoping I may be able to find out with you. How about it? Are you going to let me come to work with you?"

"It sounds good to me," I replied with a grin.

Garth grunted. "My name comes first, since I'm the oldest and biggest brother. We'll call the agency *Frederickson and Frederickson*."

"No way," I said with a firm shake of my head. "I'm not only the founder, but I'm the smartest and best-looking brother. We'll call the agency *Frederickson* and Frederickson."

"You drive a hard bargain, Mongo," Garth said with a sigh. "Incidentally, you don't have any idea what this woman we're going to see wants?"

"Nope. Dora's an occupational therapist at Helen Hayes, and a friend. I met her a thousand years ago, when I was with the circus and we used to do benefits for the children's division."

"But she doesn't know me. Why would she ask you to bring me along?"

"You can ask her when we get there. Turn left at the intersection."

Ten minutes later we pulled into the parking lot of the Helen Hayes Hospital. We went up to the second floor, where Dr. Dora Freed had her offices. The sprightly, gray-haired occupational therapist greeted us both warmly, then asked us to wait in a large, empty recreation room down the corridor.

The man who came through the door five minutes later was clean-shaven, well dressed in blue slacks, highly polished black loafers, a blue wool sleeveless pullover worn over a white shirt. The man's face was still scarred, but plastic surgeons had obviously been working on him, for he didn't look nearly as disfigured as he once had. There was a broad, almost dreamlike smile on his face.

"Harry!"

"Hello, Mongo," Harry August said, turning in the direction of my voice and tapping his way toward us across the hardwood floor with his white cane. I shook his extended hand. "Thank you so much for coming—I was so excited when I found out that Dora and you know each other. Is Garth with you?''

"I'm here, Harry," Garth said, putting a broad hand on the other man's shoulder. "I'm sorry about what happened to you. Mongo and I didn't know."

"Please, please, don't be sorry!" Harry August said quickly.

"If we'd known you were a patient here—"

"But I'm not a patient—not any longer. Now I work here."

My brother and I exchanged glances. Garth started to say something, but Harry August cut him off.

"Garth, there are two reasons why I asked Dora to call Mongo and have him bring you here. First, I want you to know how grateful I am to you."

Garth frowned slightly. "Harry," he said quietly, "if you hadn't become involved with me, you wouldn't be blind now. What are you thanking me for?"

Harry August shook his head vehemently. "If I hadn't become involved with you, I wouldn't have been blessed with the only sight that matters." He paused, tilted his head toward the ceiling, and once again his face was wreathed with a dreamlike smile. He looked years younger. "I *was* blind before I met you; my whole life was filled with bitterness and hatred, clouding my vision. *Then* I was crippled. After I lost my eyes in the explosion . . . I've had a lot of time to think in this new darkness, which for me isn't nearly as dark as the darkness I used to live in. It was only after I lost my eyesight that I could remember and fully appreciate the peace and happiness you brought to so many people. I didn't realize it at the time, but I was *happy* when I was with you—probably the happiest I'd ever been in all the years since my face had been splashed with acid. But there was so much bitterness and hatred for people in me, I was so crippled in my heart that I didn't even *know* I was happy. And so I was constantly trying to think of ways to cheat you and Garth's People."

"Harry," Garth said in a low voice, "that isn't important now, and there's no need for you to talk about it."

"But I *want* to talk about it. It's why I wanted you to come here, so that I could tell you how you changed my life and made me whole again. I believe with all my heart that God sent you to me on the sidewalk that day; God sent you to save me, to help erase the bitterness in my heart. Now I've been reborn, and I'm a baby in the living heart of Jesus Christ, our Lord and Savior. I feel as if I have—I *do* have—a whole new life to begin living, and it's one that's filled with unspeakable joy. I thank God for sending you to me, and I thank you for helping to show me the way. There are many people who hate you now; they blame you for all those deaths, for what happened. But they're wrong. I love you, Garth, and I want you to know that I'll never, ever, forget what God and Jesus Christ, through you, have done for me."

I looked at Garth, who was staring intently at Harry August. There was a strange expression on my brother's face which I couldn't read at all, and I wondered what he was feeling and thinking.

Finally, Garth asked softly: "What was the second thing you wanted to say to me, Harry?"

"All of these months, after God and Jesus had entered my heart, I thought about the stories you'd told of the Valhalla Project, and of how Siegmund Loge had come up with this mathematical formula called the Triage Parabola that predicted humans would soon be extinct. The stories were true, weren't they?"

"Yes, Harry," Garth answered, his tone flat. "The stories were true."

"But Loge's conclusion wasn't; that's the second thing I wanted to tell you. He may have been a genius, but there's no way any mathematical formula can predict the impact one man, such as yourself, can have on the lives of others—like me. The Triage Parabola is flawed because God, and His miracles, cannot be computed. We will not become extinct, because that is not God's plan. We will survive until that day when Jesus Christ returns to rule us and bring paradise to earth. I thought you should know.''

Now there was a prolonged silence. I had nothing to say, and I was almost afraid of what Garth might say. But then Garth simply wrapped his arms around the other man, gently hugged him. My brother's expression was still unreadable.

"I'm glad you're happy, Harry," Garth said evenly.

"Listen!" Harry August said brightly. "There's a bar just around the corner. Will the two of you let me take you there and buy you a drink?"

"I'll drink to that!" I said quickly—and too loudly; my voice echoed in the large, empty room.

Garth looked at me and laughed, and then we followed the blind man out of the room and down a corridor toward the elevators.